THE
COMMISSION

THE COMMISSION

Sergei Pavlovich Zalygin

Translated by

David Gordon Wilson

Northern

Illinois

University

Press

DeKalb

1993

© 1993 by Northern Illinois University Press
Published by Northern Illinois University Press,
DeKalb, Illinois 60115
Manufactured in the United States using acid-free
paper ⊗
Design by Julia Fauci

Library of Congress Cataloging-in-Publication
Data
Zalygin, Sergei, 1913– [Komissiia. English]
The commission / by Sergei Pavlovich Zalygin :
translated from the
Russian by David Gordon Wilson.
p.   cm.
ISBN 0-87580-177-3
ISBN 0-87580-558-2 (pbk.)
I. Title.
PG3476.Z33K613 1993
891.73'42—dc20   93-7009
CIP

CONTENTS

INTRODUCTION

David Gordon Wilson

Sergei Pavlovich Zalygin was born in 1913, in what later became the Bashkir Autonomous Republic of the USSR. His family moved to Barnaul, north of the Altai Mountains in Western Siberia, in 1920. Though he developed literary interests early in life, Zalygin pursued a technical education and career. At the age of fifteen he entered the Agricultural Technical Institute in Barnaul and worked as an agronomist after graduation before continuing his studies in hydrology and land improvement at the Omsk Agricultural Institute. While living in the Omsk in the 1930s, Zalygin began writing short stories set in Western Siberia's collective farms; his first collection of stories appeared in 1941. He was drafted in 1942 and spent the war years working as a hydrologist in the far north of Western Siberia. After the war he defended his dissertation and served for some ten years as chair of the department in which he had studied at the Omsk institute. His second volume of stories, published in 1947, attracted the attention of the literary establishment in Moscow, and in 1949 he was invited to the capital for a discussion of his work. He was admitted into the Writers' Union shortly thereafter.

In the 1950s Zalygin published several pieces of satirical fiction and a series of literary sketches inspired by his own experiences on the collective farms of Western Siberia. The collection of sketches, "In the Spring of This Year" (*Vesnoi nyneshnego goda*), in the literary journal *Novyi mir* in 1954 marks the beginning of Zalygin's national reputation as a writer. These pieces were part of the journalistic treatment of the contemporary Soviet countryside championed by writer Valentin Ovechkin, spiritual father of what would blossom in the 1970s into Village Prose, a Russian literary movement that lamented the disappearance of the traditional culture and moral values of a preindustrial age. Although Zalygin's development as a writer carried him away from the mainstream of Village Prose, his works still show an affinity to their themes, and he has frequently promoted other writers more closely associated with the school.

By the late 1960s Zalygin had moved to Moscow and had become established as a major Soviet writer. His first novel, *Altai Paths* (*Tropy Altaia*, 1962), is the story of a scientific expedition in the mountains south of his native Barnaul. The novella "On the Irtysh" (*Na Irtyshe*, 1964) marks the beginning of Zalygin's exploration of watershed events of Soviet history, the direction that became the cornerstone of his literary reputation. "On the Irtysh" raises questions about the justice and wisdom of Stalin's collectivization of agriculture. The work was later praised by dissident voices such as Alexander Solzhenitsyn, whose anti-Stalinist "A Day in the Life of Ivan Denisovich" had been published in *Novyi mir* by the same editor, Alexander Tvardovsky (to whom Zalygin dedicates *The Commission*). *Salt Valley* (*Solenaia Pad'*, 1967), the story of a short-lived autonomous government in Western Siberia during the Russian Civil War, illustrates Zalygin's mastery of the longer form of the novel, continued his penetration into Soviet history, and won its author the State Prize for Literature in 1968.

A series of literary articles, less pieces of formal scholarship than personal reflections and philosophical musings, followed *Salt Valley*. When Zalygin turned again to fiction in the 1970s, he at first abandoned the historical backgrounds and themes that had gained him so much praise in the past, and set his new works in contemporary Soviet reality. The novella "Oska, the Funny Little Boy" (*Os'ka, smeshnoi mal'chik*, 1973) is a complex and difficult, symbol-saturated fantasy with an ecological message. *The South American Variant* (*Iuzhnoamerikanskii variant*, 1973), set in modern Moscow, is the story of a woman's search for love and happiness in the modern urban environment. Though it pales in comparison, the novel can easily be seen as a parody of Lev Tolstoi's nineteenth-century classic *Anna Karenina*. It is also the only one of Zalygin's novels to be published in the West in English before the present volume.

Zalygin's departure from the historical themes and purely realistic technique for which he became known in the 1960s pleased neither his readers nor, in particular, the official literary critics. "Oska" and *The South American Variant* were greeted with an almost complete lack of understanding and an expression of disbelief that they could have been written by the Zalygin of the past. The critics found neither the content nor the style of these works acceptable—the novella was ignored, and the novel was attacked as an insult to Soviet women. These reactions can be explained to some extent by conservative Soviet literary politics and practice, which preferred that its writers stay comfortably within the bounds of established and assigned categories. Another part of the negative reaction is due to the extensive use in both the novella and the novel, though predominantly in "Oska," of elements of fantasy in the form of dreams and hallucinations. Though Zalygin's use of fantasy is mild in comparison with the imaginative leaps of such Russian writers of the 1920s as Mikhail Bulgakov and Evgenii Zamiatin, the use of fantasy as a literary technique was still suspect in the climate of highly refined censorship in the Soviet literary world of the 1970s. At the time there was an ongoing polemic in the critical press over the propriety of fantasy as a technique for Soviet writers, who were still theoretically guided by the now amorphous and meaningless precepts of "socialist realism." Fantasy is also a frequent feature of Zalygin's short stories of the 1970s, ranging from the lyrical "Angel's Night" (*Angelskaia noch'*, 1970) to the science-fiction satire of "My Papa in Suspended Animation and I" (*Moi letargirovannyi papa i ia sam*, 1979), which for the most part were met with the same lack of understanding. It must be noted that Zalygin was not only employing fantasy in his fiction but also defending its use in his literary essays and interviews.

Given the poor reception of Zalygin's two previous major works, it is easy to understand why the publication of *The Commission* (*Komissiia*) in the fall of 1975 was hailed by Soviet critics as the return of a writer who had strayed from the straight and narrow. The previously disappointed Soviet critics greeted the new novel with loud praise and an expression of relief that the author had at last returned to the theme of early Soviet history and the method of traditional realism which he seemed to have abandoned. Leaving aside official Soviet opinions, the novel is without argument the most successful piece of fiction Zalygin had written since "On the Irtysh," and is unequalled by any of his subsequent works.

The writer then labored for ten years on the lengthy novel *After the Storm* (*Posle buri*), published in two volumes from 1980 to 1985. It is set in the time of the New Economic Policy, the period of controlled capitalism that Lenin's government instituted in the 1920s in order to rebuild an economy shattered by revolution and civil war. This massive novel continues Zalygin's exploration of early Soviet history, but with less artistic success than in his previous historical works. The diffuse narration is episodic, confusing, and heavy in comparison with "On the Irtysh" or *The Commission*. Social and political ideas expressed in the novel were reflected in subsequent discussions of the NEP period in the Soviet press.

A new phase of Zalygin's career began when he was appointed chief editor of the prestigious flagship literary journal *Novyi mir* in August of 1986, the first non-party editor to achieve this influential post. In the first years of his tenure, Zalygin presided over the publication of a series of long-forbidden literary masterpieces, including Boris Pasternak's *Doctor Zhivago* and works by Alexander Solzhenitsyn and Vladimir Nabokov. Zalygin continues to write and publish short stories in *Novyi mir* and elsewhere. Political and social commentary and satire dominate in these stories, in which his tone becomes sharper and more acrid. The humor that marked earlier pieces has hardened as Zalygin explores a darker and more dismal side of Soviet reality. The political themes in the more recent stories reflect Zalygin's own increased involvement in politics. A secretary of the Russian Writers' Union since 1969, he became a member of the *buro* of the secretariat in 1986 and was elected from the Soviet Writers' Union to the Congress of People's Deputies of the USSR in 1989. The early 1990s found Zalygin increasingly preoccupied with the struggle to save *Novyi mir* from extinction amidst the financial and economic chaos of post-Gorbachev Russia.

▲▲▲

It is not difficult to understand which features of *The Commission* most calmed Zalygin's critics. At first it might seem to the reader that the novel is a politically oriented and rather ordinary Soviet product. There are indeed elements of Soviet convention in Zalygin's novel, such as the negative portrayal of the *kulak* ("fist" in Russian), the rich farmer, particularly one who hired labor, reviled by Soviet ideologists as an exploiter of his own class, and the obligatory evil of the White officers who so cruelly intervene in Lebyazhka's affairs at the end of the novel. However, a complexity typical of Zalygin's work always undercuts these stereotypical elements of simplistic literary-political dogma. There are no party-line heroes in Zalygin's prose, and the characters whose views are closest to the Bolshevik cause are portrayed as extremists who are as far from the true path of peace and justice as are the most antisocial, or anti-socialist, characters.

The protagonist, Ustinov, is a reluctant hero. He is a talented and successful farmer who strongly recalls Chauzov, the hero of "On the Irtysh," who was exiled as a *kulak* sympathizer. Ustinov is an introverted reader of books whose internal meditations on human life, God, and nature are the philosophical focus of the novel. As Ustinov is caught in the push and pull of opposing forces, extreme positions are criticized, be they politically Red or White, and the hero searches for a middle path between them, a theme typical of Zalygin's works—the multiplicity of possible variants in life and the search for an harmonious Golden Mean.

The fictional village of Lebyazhka is located somewhere in the general vicinity of Zalygin's own Barnaul—in the southeast corner of Western Siberia, northwest of the Altai Mountains and northeast of the vast Central Asian steppe of Kazakhstan and Khirgizia, whose Turkic peoples provide an occasional exotic detail in the background of the novel. Since the sixteenth century, the enormous territory of Siberia has served Russia both as a place of harshest exile and a land of milk and honey. In the Russian imagination, Siberia represents all aspects of a New World—it has been both America's Wild West and Australia's Botany Bay. The Russians who settled this frontier have traditionally been considered, both by themselves and their European countrymen, as a breed apart, fiercely independent, elemental and rugged. Far from the center of power in Moscow or St. Petersburg, frontier Siberia experienced both the excesses of self-serving provincial governors and the freedom afforded by distance from authority. The institution of serfdom did not develop there as it did in European Russia, and the land was a place of refuge for dissidents and adventurers of all kinds. The ancient founders of Lebyazhka were a mix of two groups of such settlers—the "Poluvyatsky" folk from near Vyatka in the north of Russia, who sought fertile new land, and a group of religious dissenters known in Siberia as

Kerzhaks, who were escaping persecution. Siberia continued to attract new settlers, such as those Lebyazhka has turned away condescendingly—except, of course, for Zinaida Pankratov, one of the strong and handsome heroines of Zalygin's novel. With the laying of the Trans-Siberian railway at the turn of the twentieth century, the number of new settlers increased dramatically. After Russia's war with Japan in 1904–1905 and the social unrest of 1905–1906, the tsarist government encouraged internal immigration to Siberia, and several million European Russians moved east between 1907 and 1911.

Lebyazhka is a traditional Russian village in terms of organization and government. The state would allot land to the village, and each household would then be assigned a plot of land by the village council, which was controlled by the village elders. Peasants worked their own fields but only while they were assigned to them: the land held by the village would be redistributed every few years. The permanent home, barnyard, and outbuildings of the family would be in the village. Privately owned livestock would join those of other villagers in a common pasture, and certain agricultural activities, such as hay mowing, would be communal responsibilities. The agrarian reforms instituted in 1906 and 1910–1911 by Interior Minister Pyotr Stolypin (1862–1911) were intended to weaken the revolutionary movement among the peasantry by granting individual farmers property rights and encouraging them to leave their village communes. Grisha Sukhikh, Ustinov's counterpart, is a Stolypin freeholder.

The action of the novel unfolds amid the political chaos and uncertainty in the lull before the violent storm of all out civil war. Ustinov is one among the masses of Russian soldiers in the First World War who left the front without official orders after the abdication of Tsar Nicholas II in 1917. The Provisional Government then established in Petrograd (the Russianized name of St. Petersburg used 1914–1924) with Alexander Kerensky as President would rule in a state of continuing disintegration until the Bolsheviks took power in October. The novel opens in the the autumn of 1918. Lenin's revolutionary government has established itself in the heart of Russia. Ukraine and Finland have broken away from the former empire. The Bolsheviks have ended their participation in the Great War by signing a separate peace with the Germans at Brest-Litovsk, ceding vast territories and agreeing to heavy reparations. The civil war has begun in European Russia, and to the east of the Urals there is a shifting patchwork of provisional governments and independent local administrations and an absence of stable central authority. The peacetime economy is shattered, and lines of supply are disrupted. The civil war has penetrated into Siberia with the Czech Legion, an army corps of former prisoners of war organized and financed by the Allies. In May the Czech Legion had revolted against the Bolsheviks and begun to fight its way to the Far Eastern port of Vladivostok, from whence it hoped to be evacuated and repatriated. As the civil war starts in earnest in Siberia, the fate of the Czechs is quickly intertwined with that of the Whites, the collective forces fighting against the new Bolshevik government. The Allies, including the United States, have landed forces on Russian soil in Archangel, Murmansk, and Vladivostok, and foreign advisers and materiel are being provided to the Whites. Foreigners, former Allies of Russia, are aiding the Whites, who are fighting the Reds, and independent partisans, the Greens, are fighting both sides. In Western Siberia, a regional government elected during Kerensky's tenure was suppressed by the Bolsheviks, whose Soviet regime was routed in turn with the help of the Czech Legion, at which time the Western Siberian Commissariat assumed charge of the area until the Siberian Provisional Government with P. V. Vologodsky as Prime Minister took over in June 1918. In November Admiral Kolchak, formerly an officer of the Black Sea Fleet, is installed as Supreme Ruler of Russia after a coup d'etat in Omsk. The Czech forces, by now no longer an organized army, fall under Kolchak's command as he faces the advance of the Red Armies.

Against this chaotic background Zalygin develops a polemic concerning the rightful sources and applications of political power and the causes of harmony and disharmony in the human world. The novel uses the historical setting for the discussion of broad philosophical questions rather than offering a unified political interpretation or justification of historical events. The political and historical aspects of the novel will seem much more topical to the contemporary readers of this edition than they did to Zalygin's original audience in 1975. The unpredictable and volatile political climate in which the action of the novel unfolds produces a strong resonance with the unsettled conditions which prevail in Russia and the other republics of the former Soviet Union at the time of this writing. Now in Moscow as then in the Western Siberian village of Lebyazhka, all manner of goods are in short supply, currency is practically worthless, and civil violence is a palpable potential.

All Zalygin's favorite themes and major directions as a creative writer are successfully combined in *The Commission*. The historical explorations that had become his trademark in the 1960s, his ongoing ecological concerns, the use of fantasy as a literary technique, and his personal meditations on the human condition find expression in the novel. These various elements do not merely coexist in the narration but are skillfully woven into its fabric. The novel represents a harmony of its component parts, organically united in an artistic whole.

Zalygin's use of fantasy in "Oska" and *The South American Variant* provoked a particularly negative response in his critics, but in *The Commission*, fantasy takes the more tame and acceptable form of folk tales and legends. The tales that relate the founding of Lebyazhka perform several functions. They contribute significantly to the creation of the fictional setting, the village of Lebyazhka. At times they provide simple comic relief; at other times they seem to be enigmatic allegories about the novel's protagonists and general parables applicable to human life. As the novel progresses, the tales take on increasingly greater meaning and become more and more prominent, rising to the surface slowly until their mythic reality coincides with the narrative reality in the last lines of the novel. The tales and legends also form a major organizational structure that connects the political, ecological, and philosophical planes of the novel.

The philosophical plane is particularly visible in the thread of religious thought and imagery that runs through *The Commission*. Though Lebyazhka's little church and docile priest are seen only in the far background, Kalashnikov talks warmly of his earlier love of church ritual, and after Ustinov's death, the body is to be taken to the church after the secular service held by the commission. More importantly, the history of Lebyazhka is a chapter taken from the history of the Russian Orthodox Church—the Kerzhak settlers are religious dissidents, members of one of the many groups of "Old Believers" descended from the schismatics who rejected the church reforms advocated by the Moscow Metropolitan Nikon in the mid-seventeenth century, which were intended to close the gap that had developed between Russian Orthodox practices and liturgical texts and those of the Greek mother church. Many aspects of Old Believer culture and experience are to be seen in the Lebyazhka tales, such as the use of two rather than three fingers to make the sign of the cross and abstinence from alcohol, tobacco, and tea.

Ustinov's meditations on the nature of God are at the center of the religious imagery of the novel. In his personal cosmology, the building blocks of reality are circles and lines, and the source of any motion is the principle that "every line tries to become a circle and to turn back on itself, that is, to close" (Chapter 12). God is the largest circle—

> The one that everything else fits into. The one that is so big, so huge that it seems like a straight line to everything else on earth, so that everything else moves and repeats itself endlessly within that greatest of circles, in the birth of children from their parents, summer from spring, winter from fall, in the winds and waters and all manner of things. . . . (Chapter 12)

Ustinov's internal meditations reveal a second, anthropomorphic and deistic concept of the Supreme Being—God, Ustinov decides, must be a peasant like himself.

In opposition to Ustinov's great circle of God is the linear path of human sin on earth, the extremist Christian vision that sees the history of mankind as a straight line with the Fall at its beginning and the Apocalypse at its end.

Apocalyptic imagery is plentiful in the novel, and many characters make reference to the end of the world, most often in reference to the fratricide of civil war that threatens Lebyazhka. Ustinov ponders that the approaching civil war might make possible the ultimate fratricide of humankind against nature, a spector far more real in our time than in the historical setting of the novel. The character Kudeyar is the main representative of an apocalyptic vision and represents the most radical aspects of the Old Believer heritage. Kudeyar is also a representative of a long tradition in Russian folklore, art, and literature—a "holy fool" (*iurodovyi*). Historically a mix of ascetics practicing self-humiliation and genuinely mentally disturbed individuals, holy fools, also known as "God's folk" and "fools for Christ," were wandering religious eccentrics, both men and women, who behaved irrationally, often without concern for their own well-being. Believing that they were facing the end of the world and the corruptions of the anti-Christ, many congregations of seventeenth century schismatics burned themselves along with their churches rather than accept Nikon's reforms; and in the following century Old Believers would see the anti-Christ in Peter the Great's westernizing reforms. Kudeyar interprets the events of his own time as the attack of the City on the Country, the violation of Mother Earth by Fallen Man. For Kudeyar, the circle has been broken, and there is no hope for life—the end has come from which there will be no new beginning. This is a despair that Ustinov cannot share. When the civil war finally breaks upon Lebyazhka, it is expressed with the culminating apocalyptic image that closes the novel.

The apocalyptic imagery in *The Commission* serves as a second major organizing principle and contributes greatly to the artistic success of the novel. It unifies the various thematic and narrative planes of the work. An apocalyptic perception of historical events permeated the world view of the religious schismatics who were the founding fathers of the village of Lebyazhka. It flows out of the legends of Lebyazhka, which form a story within a story, into the main narration and provides the artistic resolution of the novel, resonating with a Russian literary tradition of apocalyptic visions of revolution and civil war, which is by definition apocalyptic, an unraveling of the fabric of a nation, a society, a culture.

▲▲▲

In a recent address, Zalygin repeated the use of the Christian concept of Apocalypse as a metaphor for ecological catastrophe and again intertwined the ecological and religious meditations we find in *The Commission*. Such statements emphasize the importance of noting the ecological message woven into Zalygin's historical novel when striving for a thorough understanding of the work. Soviet critics focused their initial attention on the political aspects of the novel, which seem at first to be dominant; the English language reader may also feel that the historical setting and the political themes carry the main weight of the work. But despite page after page of political discussion and angry argument between characters who represent different political and economic points of view, the unifying message of the novel is as much one of ecology as of politics, as much about the relationship between humankind and the natural world as about relationships between human beings. Eventually Soviet critics acknowledged this aspect of *The Commission,* and one went so far as to call the novel "a passionate attempt to avert the fatal threat which now hangs over our planet."[1]

Zalygin's biography gives the reader ample cause to see an ecological message in *The Commission.* His professional career and extensive field work brought him into intimate contact with the villages and collective farms of Western Siberia and with the natural environment of the vast region from the arctic north to the Altai Mountains in the south. These experiences provided material for his early stories, and later, the philosophical side of his scientific education also found expression. Among the themes of Zalygin's essay "The Writer and Siberia" (*Pisatel' i Sibir',* 1961) is that of the changing human–nature relationship as it is expressed in literature. Zalygin calls for the perception of humankind as a part of nature, powerful but not independent. The essay includes a direct call for writers to deal with ecological concepts and problems in their creative work. His first novel, *Altai Paths,* features positive characters who experience a lyrical and metaphysical oneness with nature and strive for unity between science and nature. The negative characters, on the other hand, are interested in nature only for advancing their personal careers. The natural world of the Altai Mountains, with its stunning beauty and physical power, is the true hero of the novel. In the 1960s Zalygin had engaged in a one-man struggle against the construction of a massive hydroelectric dam on the lower Ob River in Western Siberia that would have flooded an enormous area and produced unknown ecological and climactic changes. His independent efforts may have slowed the juggernaut, but the project was cancelled only after the discovery of gas and oil in the threatened territories. An ecological theme can be identified in almost all of Zalygin's fiction of the 1970s. The fantasy "Oska, the Funny Little Boy," which preceded *The Commission* is overwhelmingly devoted to this theme.

Ecological concerns were not a taboo subject in the 1970s, but neither were they the most comfortable topic to pursue. Facing ecological problems at home eventually meant questioning the wisdom of government attitudes and policies that involved the unbridled exploitation of natural resources

---

1. Vsevolod Surganov, "Voskhozhdenie. Proza Sergeia Zalygina i sovremennaia literatura" (The Ascent: The Prose of Sergei Zalygin and Contemporary Literature), *Nash Sovremennik* 11 (1983): 184.

and an industrial complex that ignored the rampant ecological damage it was inflicting. Zalygin's long-standing ecological activism increased in the decade of the 1980s as glasnost made it possible to discuss openly issues that challenged government policy. His was an important voice in the organized opposition to the vast engineering project to reverse the course of Siberian rivers to deliver water to the cotton monoculture in the Central Asian republics of the former Soviet Union. The government announced the cancellation of this grandiose scheme in the same month that Zalygin became editor of *Novyi mir,* and since then he has not hesitated to use the podium provided by his editorial position to warn the public of the potential ecological disaster threatened by such feats of engineering, to rail against the general abuses of industry and misuses of technology, and even to call for the criminal prosecution of responsible parties in government ministries. Zalygin has served as a member of the Committee of the Supreme Soviet of the USSR on Questions of Ecology and the Rational Use of Natural Resources, and is currently Chairman of the Board of the organization Ecology and Peace. Zalygin's ecological views and activities have recently brought him more recognition in the United States than did his literary activities, and in 1991 he was presented with the Conde Nast Traveler Environmental Award. It is quite likely that more of the small number of Americans who have heard of Sergei Zalygin know him as an ecologist rather than as a novelist.

On the social and political level, the relationships between individuals in society are most important; on the ecological level, the relationship between humankind and nature is primary. For Zalygin, these two sets of relationships may not be separated from one another. The character of a human society is determined by the relationship its members have with the natural world. In his essay "Literature and Nature" (*Literatura i priroda, Novyi mir,* January, 1991) Zalygin stated that "people's attitude toward one another is also their attitude toward nature, to the world as a whole, perceived as a unity."

The Lebyazhka Forest Commission in Zalygin's novel takes on additional civil duties and authority as the story progresses, but its original "commission" was that of a caretaker of nature. The village's concern for the proper management of its forest resources reflects Zalygin's concept of the proper relationship between humankind and nature. When the Commission composes its appeal to the people for unity in the face of the increasing disorder and danger brought by the approaching civil war, it bases its political mission on ecological principles, declaring the natural world as the proper model for the human world. The characters in Zalygin's novel constantly look to nature as an illustration of order and as a source of supportive arguments in their polemics with one another. Nature is as much a source of their world outlook as the forest is the source of economic life for Lebyazhka.

Zalygin's lyrical introduction does not focus on the village, the characters, or the historical framework of the novel, but on its unique natural setting—the ribbon forests of Western Siberia. The setting is one in which the human and natural world interpenetrate, where human life is made unique by the uniqueness of the natural world. The protagonist, Ustinov, is a focal point for the interpenetration of the animal world and the human world. These two worlds are interconnected, and what threatens one threatens the other. Ustinov is spiritual heir to Syoma Prutovskikh, the old forest warden, whose name derives from the Russian word for twig, a protector of the forest with seemingly supernatural powers. Syoma had lived off the forest, at peace with its nonhuman inhabitants, and appeared as if out of thin air at the first sound of an axe touching a tree without his permission.

Zalygin's vision is ultimately not one of destruction, but of hope in the struggle for physical and spiritual renewal. The straight line of Apocalypse must bend upon itself in its striving to become a circle. The opposition of the imagery of straight line and circle found in *The Commission,* as in "Oska" before it, will be familiar to the readers of *The Closing Circle* (1970), the influential work of the American ecologist Barry Commoner.

▲▲▲

The Commission, the novel Zalygin values as his most successful work, is the centerpiece of a long and varied literary career. It is exemplary of themes the author has explored throughout his creative life and which continue to absorb his attention—the relationship between humankind and nature; the multiplicity of perspectives within the Russian historical experience; the nature of the male and female human essences; the dualistic power of imagination; and in combination with all of these, the search for balance, harmony, and order. The novel is the story of one man's struggle with the responsibility forced upon him by the historical developments of his time. Ustinov is constantly torn between his overpowering urge to live and work as he feels God intends, and the social and political duty to which he is called. Faced with historical events that would seem to lead in a straight line into the nothingness of social and ecological destruction, Ustinov, and Zalygin's readers, must close the circle, a task that is nothing less than a human moral duty, a "commission" which may not be resigned.

A NOTE ON THE TRANSLATION

The translator freely acknowledges and accepts responsibility for any loss of flavor and texture in his English rendering of *The Commission*. Although far from an ethnographic transcription of native Siberian Russian dialect, the language that Zalygin's characters speak is heavily marked by the cadences and vocabulary of an authentic folk idiom with which the author is personally familiar. Zalygin has a natural talent for capturing the essence of this idiom. The complexities of dialect present the translator of prose with his or her greatest challenge, and, as is the case with the rhyme and rhythm of poetry, much is unavoidably left behind. I hope that the present translation will give the English reader at least some small measure of the linguistic feel of the original. In this same spirit, I have retained the pre-revolutionary Russian system of weights and measures used in the original—verst (roughly .66 miles); sazhen (roughly 7 feet; there are 500 sazhens in a verst); arshin (roughly 28 inches; there are 3 arshins in a sazhen); vershok (roughly 1.75 inches; there are 16 vershoks in an arshin); desyatina (2.7 acres); and pood (roughly 36 pounds). Russian names for pre-revolutionary political-territorial divisions have also been retained—(in decreasing size) the gubernia, or central imperial province (oblast on the periphery of empire); the uyezd; and the volost, the rough equivalent of a midwestern American county. As to the transliteration of Russian proper nouns, I have violated ideal practice by choosing to borrow from several systems, sacrificing scientific accuracy and consistency for the sake of spellings that, in my opinion, are most likely to produce an approximation of the Russian name in the mouth of the native speaker of standard American English unfamiliar with Russian phonetics. I have also resorted to occasional Anglicization of historical names. Those readers unfamiliar with Russian names should note that in the Russian tradition both men and women have—in addition to a first name and a last name—a middle name, or patronymic, formed by adding a suffix to the name of one's father's first name (-ovich or -evich for men, -ovna or -evna for women). The patronymic is used together with the first name in polite address, and in familiar country style, a patronymic is frequently used in place of a first name. Most Russian first names also produce a number of diminuative, endearing, and pejorative variants. Thus the protagonist of the novel, Nikolai Levontyevich Ustinov, is refered to variously as Nikolai Levontyevich, Nikola, Kolya, or Levontyevich.

This translation of *Komissiia* used the text of the novel found in volume 4 of Sergei Zalygin, *Sobranie sochinenii v chetyrekh tomakh* (Moscow: Molodaia gvardiia, 1980).

LIST OF CHARACTERS

The Lebyazhka Forest Commission

Nikolai Levontyevich Ustinov
Lebyazhka's most educated and generally respected citizen.

Vasily Deryabin
The most political Commission member, a Marxist.

Pyotr Kalashnikov
The "Co-op man," Chairman of the Commission.

Mikhail Polovinkin
The peasant's peasant, uneducated and apolitical.

Ignashka Ignatov
A man of questionable ethics and character, the Commission's messenger and spy.

Other Lebyazhkans

Domna Ustinov
Nikolai's wife, the first lady of Lebyazhka, known for her beauty and her skill as a storyteller.

Zinaida Pavlovna Pankratov
Domna Ustinov's rival, the strong and independent wife of the woodcarver Kirill.

Ivan Ivanovich Samorukov
Lebyazhka's village elder and "Finest Man," the highest authority in the eyes of the citizenry.

Grigory Dormidontovich Sukhikh
A wealthy farmer, known for his physical power and unsociable behavior.

Rodion Gavrilovich Smirnovsky
A retired officer from a long line of military men, Ustinov's wartime commander.

Kudeyar
Lebyazhka's "holy fool," who proclaims the coming of the apocalypse.

Characters from the Lebyazhka Tales

The Elder Lavrenty
A holy man who in the distant past lead a group of Old Believers into the Siberian wilderness.

The Elder Samsony Krivoi
The leader of the group of dissenters that splits with Lavrenty and settles on the future site of Lebyazhka.

The Poluvyatsky Maidens—Ksenia, Domna,
Natalya, Yelena, Anna, and Yelizaveta
The young women who marry the young men of Samsony's following and become the founding mothers of Lebyazhka.

THE
COMMISSION

THE FORESTS THROUGHOUT VAST SIBERIA are varied in nature. Some are transparently green and light, others bluish and dark. Some are bright island-groves pierced by the sun, scattered through the steppe along slopes and river valleys; others stretch in unbroken waves over thousands of versts. Some climb into the mountains to the snowline at the edge of the eternal ice. Others fall to the north toward cold and almost lifeless oceans. Some tenderly cultivate a lush undergrowth in their forest litter and foster new shrubbery. In other places the forest soil is made only of brown conifer needles, gray mosses, and the remains of fallen trees.

But then there are the ribbon forests. These uncoil from south to north or north to south in narrow strips along small rivers in grassland or lakeland, having sprung up no one knows how or why. Invariably a ribbon forest accompanies the flow of waters with ancient Tatar names—Karasuk, Burla, Kulunda, Kasmala, Barnaulka, Alei, Charysh—which are now merry and boisterous, now barely touched by motion.

It is not these little rivers but the forests that accompany them everywhere that transform the earth and essence of the steppe, blending their scent with its scent, their color and light with its color and light, their silence with its quiet whispering, their rustle and roar with its blizzards and storms. They change the entire world that surrounds them.

Since ancient times human life has also changed wherever it touched the ribbon forests of conifers. It was not the forsaken life of the steppe nor the isolated life of the backwoods. It was a life spacious with cultivated fields and rich with the forest and its gifts. It was not a life removed from the rest of the world, nor was it covetous. It did not cling only to the wealthy and the waterways and highways of commerce. It was a life in itself, with its own style and customs, with its own roots deep in the soils of the forest-steppe . . .

The Founding Session

What an event had taken place in the village of Lebyazhka—a Forest Commission had been elected! Certainly this could have happened only in Lebyazhka, not in any other village or settlement.

The autumn of 1918 had begun, and with every day life became more confusing—there was less and less order and more and more fear, the war came closer and closer, and just who was in power became more and more of a mystery. The old men wanted to judge by the money: whoever's currency was in circulation must be in power. But even this made little sense. Tsarist money was in circulation, and so were the Kerensky rubles of the All-Russian Provisional Government. Huge paper notes with someone's red and black seals on them were also in circulation, and even Soviet money was seen from time to time. But no one had faith in any of them. Indeed, what kind of faith could there be?

Until now Decree No. 3 of the Siberian Provisional Government of 26 July 1918, "On the Regulation of the Grain Trade," had hung above the desk of the Lebyazhka clerk. This decree concerned free market prices and at the same time indicated what these prices should be: 690 kopecks for a pood of wheat and 573 kopecks for oats. This was a mockery and an insult to the peasant, his labor, and his whole life. Who could say what such a price was worth? You could sell your wheat for so many kopecks, but what could you then buy with them and where could you buy it? This insult was signed by P. Vologodsky, the Chairman of the Soviet of Ministers and Minister of Foreign Affairs, and the Ministers of Internal Affairs, National Affairs, and Justice, and was countersigned by Director N. Zefirov.

The peasants would have long since used up this edict of the Provisional Government for rolling cigarettes, but the village clerk had smeared it too thickly with flour paste when he stuck it up on the wall and had thoroughly ruined the paper. Much more faith was put in secondhand goods—a peasant's cloth jacket, a soldier's overcoat, a woman's skirt, a child's cap, needles and thread, matches—these had value, and no small value at that. The co-op tried as hard as it could to do business, but there were always problems—someone would embezzle its funds, or the authorities would close it down, or the peasants themselves didn't trust it.

The dealers in secondhand goods turned out to be more reliable, and it was they who brought news to Lebyazhka about Siberia, Russia, and the rest of the world. They didn't all report accurately, but they were no worse than the newspapers that made their way to Lebyazhka from Omsk, Tomsk, Ufa, Samara, Chelyabinsk, Semipalatinsk, Novonikolayevsk, Barnaul, and from various governments and authorities. There were so many of them, all temporary, that it seemed that life itself would become temporary as well. Yet one thing was known for certain: a civil war was going on in Russia, and neither Siberia nor Lebyazhka could escape it.

The village of Lebyazhka knew how to stand up for itself before the rest of the world, and most important it knew how to live in accordance with its own customs. It didn't allow others to meddle in its affairs, and it didn't stick its nose into the affairs of others. It knew how to satisfy the authorities, but in such a way as to keep its distance from them. When at one time the rumor was going around that Lebyazhka might be made the volost seat, a market and church town, the citizens of Lebyazhka passed up all these honors, preferring instead to go to market in Krushikha. They hung on to their own humble priest in his little wooden church because he was obedient to the community, and the priest was satisfied because the community generously compensated his cooperation.

For many years everyone around knew you'd best not insult a Lebyazhka peasant, drunk or sober. All the shopkeepers in the volost and even in the uyezd took careful note—God help anyone who cheated a Lebyazhka man when measuring goods or giving change. Such offenses would be long remembered, and even a year later the shop window might get broken or its sign vandalized, or the shopkeeper himself might simply turn up all black and blue. A Lebyazhka drunk might be lying somewhere on the road, and some peasant might drive by and pretend he hadn't noticed anything. Later the Lebyazhka boys would find him and ask, "So, you lazy louse, your little peepers don't see so good, eh? Then we'll fix 'em for you!" And fix them they would. Nothing need be said about horse thieves—they didn't come within thirty versts of Lebyazhka.

But what were things like now among the Lebyazhka folk? In the past few years, during the war, the Lebyazhka community had become quite different than what it had been before. Before the war anyone could stand wherever he wanted at the village assembly. Now, however, the front-line veterans crowded to the front of the room. These people were used to having political meetings and arguing with one another, and indeed, had they not won the right to stand in front of the others? But it didn't mean much when they stood in a clump, shouting more loudly and making more demands than anyone else. That was only for show. Since the overthrow of Soviet power, even they had calmed down and stopped making noise in public, more often whispering among themselves far from prying eyes. It was the solid peasants, the Kruglov brothers, submissive, quiet, standing somewhere in the back, who would turn the assembly in whatever direction they wanted. What can you get from a veteran? You can't get anything. But the Kruglov brothers might make you a loan when you were in need. If they wanted to.

The war divided people into separate groups again and again. It made some into cripples and others into widows. The widows stood silently at the village assemblies, not where their husbands would have stood, but off to the side, forgotten. The war brought benefits to a few older peasants or those with a limp or a bad eye who were still able to work. The slightly disabled were not taken into the army, and during the war years they managed to improve their households, acquire machinery, and dress their women and children in proper clothing. But there was more need for charity in Lebyazhka than ever before. The village was overflowing with widows and orphans and cripples, and who would help them and how? There was no commerce at all except for the dealers in secondhand goods. The cow pasture needed at least fifteen versts of new fence. And then there was the forest.

There was need of order in the Lebyazhka woodland, or else the local people, including Lebyazhka's own peasants, would take advantage of the absence of authority to chop down the forest completely. In such times people needed a strong and harmonious community more than anything else. But where can you find solidarity and friendship when what little there may be is already falling apart before your very eyes? Even so, the Lebyazhka assembly had convened and elected the Forest Commission.

The election took a long time. Each neighborhood in the village put forth its own candidates and shouted and argued loudly in every possible kind of Russian. Suddenly some were even shouting in German! These, it turned out, were Lebyazhka men who had been German prisoners of war and the few Austrian prisoners still living in Lebyazhka who were explaining how the forest was protected in Austria. That was fine, but how about the distribution of timber for firewood and lumber? Was there any sense in talking about the affairs of the forest or the affairs of one's own neighbor in a foreign language? And what about the peasants who had returned from the war with weapons, or with books and newspapers about the Revolution, or with nothing at all but ideas?

But no matter how things stood, no matter who was thinking what, it was still clear to everyone that the forest must be protected and that standards must be set for its use. A price for firewood and construction timber had to be established, and all the neighboring villages had to be shown that the Lebyazhka forest was Lebyazhka's, not common property. At the assembly the old men said if the village could not do this by itself, then the reason for chasing away the Tsar had lost its meaning. The Tsar knew how to protect the forest—you couldn't get near a single tree without a real fight with the forester. You had to pay good money for a permit, or else fight. But nowadays everyone harnesses up his team and drives off to cut to his heart's content.

At this point in the debate Ivan Ivanovich Samorukov, whom twenty-five years ago the Council of Village Elders had given the title of Finest Man in Lebyazhka, lost his temper and said, "It's true my eyesight ain't as sharp as it used to be, but I'll still go into the forest and shoot the first wood thief I come across!"

It made no difference that everyone knew that Ivan Ivanovich had not fallen behind the others and had managed with his kinfolk to fell three full-grown trees and six smaller ones. It would be too late to argue the point if he went out and fired a handful of buckshot into someone's hide. What would you do with Ivan Ivanovich then? He was already so decrepit that his whole right side was higher than his left, his head almost lay on one shoulder, and except for a few pitiful remains, all his whiskers had fallen out. But he meant what he said: it was time to put an end to personal piracy in the woodland. For those who lived in the vast forests three hundred versts to the north, the forest had little value. If a fire started they could afford to let it burn until it put itself out. But in the prairie regions, next door to the desert steppes of Kirghizia, the slender ribbon of woodland was an inestimable treasure.

And so the Lebyazhka Forest Commission, abbreviated LFC, was elected. It consisted of five men, with Pyotr Kalashnikov as Chairman, and a forest guard of twenty-four men, one from each group of ten households. From these candidates the Commission itself was to select ten men of the first rank. It was understood that these ten had to be handpicked. They were to be the very best, honest and incorruptible, devoted to the community rather than their own personal interests, expeditious and courageous. Who could say what situations might develop, not just with wood thieves from their own area, but, more important, with those from the distant villages on the steppe? Those villages had always envied Lebyazhka because it had taken up the best land for itself right at the edge of the forest. Now they very well might make a real incursion into the woodland. During the course of any dispute, these ten men would have to hold the line and stand firm until the entire population of men physically able to defend Lebyazhka could respond to the alarm. If the slightest hint was given that the Lebyazhka folk could not defend the Tsar's former property, which they had publicly declared to be socialized for the benefit of their own community, there would be no lack of enthusiasts hungry for the property of others.

And so the Forest Commission met at the Pankratovs' house and set to work. Kalashnikov opened the proceedings with a speech.

"Citizens and Comrades! Members of the Commission and other guests! Master and mistress of this house, where we have gathered today to do our best to fulfill the mandate and mission given to us by the people! Three years ago, perhaps less, it seemed strange to us that we peasants should ourselves make laws about the forest, or any other kind of laws. But now after all these fires of revolution, just the opposite seems strange to us—how was it that we, the peasantry, could have been brought up to feed and clothe all of mankind through our labor and service as beasts of burden, while we ourselves got by as best we could? The laws that governed our lives were considered none of our business, and we were not allowed to approach those who made them! But if you think about it seriously, as I have for more than a year, how can there be any justice if the law which governs my life in no way belongs to me, if my life is one thing and the law entirely another thing? From the day I was born I was placed on the same footing as a criminal, since no one would ask a criminal if he likes the law or finds it human or inhuman. This means that the criminal in me was nurtured since childhood, so it should come as no surprise that when the opportunity came to take to the forest and cut down the community's timber, I, paying no attention to my own thoughts, which, as I said, I have been thinking for more than a year, harnessed up and went, and cut a bit of wood, altogether five full-sized logs and as many smaller ones. In so doing I forgot that the Revolution that we the people made ourselves took this forest from the hands of the Tsar and put it into our own.

"Now we need to understand the circumstances under which we or anyone else would refrain from such theft and not allow anyone else to commit it either. This restraint would be possible only if the law that I obey, even if it's only a law about the forest, was made by me, or at the very least if someone had asked for my consent. And so if we want to stop our own disgraceful thievery once and for all, we have to make a legal expert out of every Lebyazhka man of legal age, and maybe of every woman, too. That is, we must give all citizens a free say in our future forest legislation in Lebyazhka, and then on this common basis make laws truly binding for young and old

alike. We, the Commission, are called on to deprive every citizen of the freedom to violate the common rules of life and in its place to instill a higher
awareness and social conscience.

"Comrades and citizens! Members of the Commission and other visitors!
And especially the master and mistress of this house, which has been
scrubbed for our coming till it is shinier than for the most gala holiday!
Why do I mention this fact? So we will begin this very minute to fulfill the
solemn mandate of the people with the same purity and bright spirit that
went into the cleaning of this house. Let us proceed to our necessary and
noble task without further speeches and conclude it successfully. All those
present who are not members of the Commission may stay with us in this
bright home for a moment longer, ponder all I have said, thank our hosts,
Kirill Yemelyanovich and Zinaida Pavlovna, and then quietly withdraw so
that the Commission can face its appointed task."

▲▲▲

Kirill and Zinaida Pankratov had scrubbed their house with lye and pol-
ished it to a shine. The curtains in the room were so clean that the windows
seemed half-covered with snow, and the panes of glass seemed to be clear,
frozen air. While the Chairman of the Commission was giving his speech,
Kirill stood motionless by the tiled stove, only bowing his head from time to
time as if in precise and leisurely greeting. His wife, Zinaida, had found a
place closer to the table where the Commission was sitting. Although not a
big woman, she was strong, and with her hands folded on her breast as if
praying, she looked around with unusual interest, especially at Commission
member Nikolai Ustinov, Lebyazhka's scholar and book lover.

Ignashka Ignatov sat next to Ustinov at the table covered with glistening
oilcloth. He was a complete good-for-nothing who had attached himself to
Lebyazhka years ago, no one knew exactly how. He had been elected to the
Forest Commission precisely because of his worthlessness. He would be useful if it became necessary to run and fetch someone, dispatch someone to a
neighboring village to sniff out information, start a rumor, or perform
some delicate task for which the other men could not be spared or that they
would be ashamed to do themselves. Ignashka, however, was oblivious of
these reasons. He was terribly proud of his position as a member of the
Commission and sat stroking his streaky, scraggly mustache. Thinking that
Zinaida Pankratov was looking at him, he began to fidget and to stroke his
mustache with both hands, but she shot him such a look and tapped
her foot so hard that he froze and fixed his eyes on the ceiling. He used
to be called Methodius, but this serious name with its hint of saintliness did
not suit him. Ignashka, however, fit just as comfortably as a first name
or a last name. Most likely someone had once made a slip of the tongue
and called Methodius Ignaty, and the mistake fit the man so well that the

name stuck to him for life.

After Kalashnikov's speech there was a period of silence during which everyone wished the whole world could be as tidy as the Pankratovs' simple home. Having stood for a while in this quiet purity, the guests, about fifteen men, women, and children, thanked their hosts and left. Only then did Kalashnikov sit down on his chair, heave a sigh, and look at the host and hostess. They bowed and left the main room for the kitchen.

"Well then, comrades," Kalashnikov said, "let us begin! We will start with the confirmation of candidates for the forest guard. While we are writing the common law for the forest, the guard must assume its duties on Friday, Monday at the latest. As you know, a candidate has been nominated from each group of ten households, twenty-four men altogether. From this number we must select the ten most deserving and honorable men. I will read the list. First comes Innokenty Stepanovich Glazkov. All those in favor—"

"Don't be in such a hurry, Petro!" Ustinov interrupted him. "Whether we accept a candidate or reject him, we can't just vote. We must give everyone a reasonable explanation of our decision. It's our obligation to show the community as well as each candidate the reasons behind any positive or negative opinion!"

"That's true," agreed Commission Member Mikhail Polovinkin. "It's not like we're in the army and can give the order 'ten men, three steps forward!' Public service, now that's a horse of a different color!"

"But with as many of 'em as there are, twenty-four men, and with all there is to say about each one of 'em, we could be here till morning!" Ignashka burst out.

"And so we will sit!" Kalashnikov answered him. "You were right to bring it up—I thank the members of the Commission for their correction—we have to discuss all the reasons behind our decisions and enter them in the minutes. Who has something to say about Innokenty Stepanovich Glazkov?"

Just as Ignashka had feared, the Commission finished its work well after midnight. In the course of the evening Zinaida Pankratov fed them twice with golden, fragrant wheat kasha* made with milk and eggs. The minutes of the meeting of the Commission on the evening of 7 September 1918 were duly recorded.

1. Comrade Innokenty Stepanovich Glazkov. Health good. Fit for service in mounted forest patrol, can shoot with either hand if he has to. Accepted into the guard unanimously.

---

*A porridge made from grain, a traditional Russian staple.

2. Comrade Yevstignei Nikolayevich Anikanov. Self-interested. Every day he'll make demands, even if just a little, on his own behalf and complain that he's bad off. Decline.

3. Comrade Andrei Petrovich Kulikov. Manages his household well and is fit for any job. But besides all that, in his own home he teaches reading, writing, and arithmetic to the kids from the outskirts of the village. Let him keep on teaching, and exempt from the guard because of personal duties.

4. Comrade Semyon Petrovich Kulikov. In 1909 at the market in Krushikha was caught appropriating 7 rubles, 28 kopecks not belonging to him. Decline.

5. Nikolai Nikolayevich Semyonov. Fully suited, and no one has any objections. Accept.

6. Aleksei Artemovich Ubyogov. Had a fire at his house three times, in 1901, 1912, and even in the current year of 1918 when he was already at the front. So if he were in the guard, he would set the forest on fire without fail. Decline.

7. Comrade Gavril Alexandrovich Glazkov. Accept, but pay particular attention to his extreme pride and inclination to start arguments, which is not suitable for service in the forest guard.

8. Comrade Prokopy Semyonovich Kruglov. Not a politically trustworthy peasant. Last month at his own daughter Yelizaveta's wedding he started singing "God Save the Tsar" and incited the whole wedding party to sing such songs. Decline.

9. Comrade Serafim Mikhailovich Gulyayev. Fully fit for the guard, but so exceedingly meek and obliging that he never refuses a request. Accept, but caution him that while serving the public he must not neglect his own household and kids.

10. Comrade Vladimir Ivanovich Mikhailov. Fully fit for the guard, but unfortunately has a long-standing feud with the peasants from Barsukova, so upon meeting them in the forest he could have at them with any weapon at hand. Decline.

11. Comrade Ivan Ivanovich Kuznetsov. You should absolutely never put a weapon in his hands, he'll sell it for sure. Decline.

12. Comrade Fyodor Alekseyevich Glazkov. Accept for now, but when the assembly nominated F. A. Glazkov, he expressed his indifference to the whole business. So he should be warned that the community has little need for such carefree types and can do without him at any time.

13. Kirill Yemelyanovich Pankratov. Accept, but caution him to be a little livelier.

14. Comrade Afanasy Kupryanovich Mitrokhin. In the absence of any objections, accept.

15. Comrade Alexander Alexandrovich Kuropatin. Too old (born 1849). Decline.

16. Matvey Kupriyanov. Too young, though in good physical shape. Decline.

17. Com. Vasily Nikol. Ubyogov. There is no consensus of opinion in the Commission concerning this comrade. Accept and see later which members of

the Commission were right and which were wrong in the discussion of this candidate.

18. Com. Boris Leonidovich Mitrokhin. Already spends a lot of time who knows where. If accepted he would never be at home or with his family. Decline.

19. Com. Georgy Alexandrovich Kuropatin. Not suited for leadership in the guard, but in the ranks he would put on airs as if he were. Decline.

20. Gr. Yevseyev. It was ridiculous to even nominate such a candidate. Decl.

21. Com. Terenty Mikh. Lebedev. Let him keep playing the accordion. Decline.

22. Com. Dm. Guskov. What sort of guardsman would someone be who in 1911 lost his own horse and cart along with six hundred pounds of the finest wheat flour? Decline.

23. Leonty Afanasyevich Yevseyev. This man is completely at home in the forest. Accept as an exemplary simple guardsman, then later consider for promotion to the leadership of the guard.

24. L. M. Grigoryev. Has never displayed any interest in serving the community and has no aptitude for it. Accept so he can acquire some practical experience.

Deryabin wrote the minutes. Back in 1915, he had come home from the war with a concussion, but now he sat in the Pankratovs' house as if he had just arrived from the trenches. He was wearing a soldier's tunic and overcoat and had not found the time to shave, let alone get a haircut. He wrote intently, using up half of a brand-new pencil, wetting it with saliva and smearing his mouth thoroughly in the process and also messing up the minutes—the letters were very neat and distinct in places but hard to see where the pencil had gone dry.

Ustinov paid close attention only at the beginning, and was soon caught up in his own thoughts. His bright face seemed ready to smile or laugh at any moment, but then he neither smiled nor laughed, only looked thoughtful and mocking.

The lamp on the oilcloth-covered table in the main room shone brightly and the wick crackled. Amazing though it was, the lamp was filled with real kerosene. For more than a year you could search in vain for kerosene in Lebyazhka, but in this matter, too, Zinaida Pankratov had done her best. As soon as it had begun to get dark, she had filled and lighted the lamp, and it was still burning brightly. Commission Member Polovinkin huddled on his chair, looked at the cheerful little flame, and sighed. A hard-working peasant, thrifty and conscientious, he could not help thinking about the expense with which the Forest Commission was burdening its hosts. Feeling guilty, he strained to hear if perhaps out in the kitchen Kirill might already be cussing out his wife for such a waste. But it was quiet in the kitchen, the spinning wheel humming steadily, and it was impossible to say what Kirill was doing. Most likely he was sitting and waiting to see what the

Commission would decide about him—after all, he was a candidate for the guard.

"Thank God they took Kirill into the guard," Polovinkin thought, "even with the warning to be more lively. That's even better. What if we had tramped around his clean house in our boots and burned up his kerosene and then turned him down? That would have been real bad for Kirill, completely out of line! This guard is nothing but trouble and bother, but if you're nominated for something and then they turn you down, it's awkward." Polovinkin didn't vote against anyone except Semyon Kulikov, who had been caught with someone else's money at the Krushikha market in 1909. He really was opposed to that one.

After all the members of the Commission had signed the minutes, Kalashnikov said, "First thing tomorrow we will gather the candidates, all twenty-four of them, and read them these minutes. Then, in consultation with the confirmed candidates, we will appoint a captain of the guard. I think that Leonty Yevseyev will be our captain. You won't find a better man. We will also see to it that each man finds himself a weapon. That's not much of a task these days with all the equipment that's been dragged home from the front!"

"And what will we, the Forest Commission, do after that?" Ignashka wanted to know. "What questions will we consider, what minutes will we write then?"

"Then, Comrades of the Commission, the most important work will begin!" Kalashnikov began to explain. "Don't we need to write instructions for the forest guard? Yes! Do we need regulations about penalties for unauthorized woodcutting? Yes! And a price list for timber? And regulations for allowable use of the forest? A common law that includes everything, reforestation, regulations for grazing, haymaking, and hunting, the keeping of forestry documents and plans, a policy on taxation—there's enough to make your head spin! To tell the truth, I'm counting a lot on Ustinov. Ustinov, you're an educated man and know the forest, too. You've even worked with the Tsar's forest inspectors."

"It was a long time ago," Ustinov sighed. "I was still a lad. Still single. But I haven't forgotten anything. I remember it all—"

"But why so many different laws?!" Ignashka interrupted. "I don't understand it at all! We should make one general law, to let each man cut and steal as much as he can as best he knows how! Then there wouldn't even be a word for thievery. And we wouldn't need any judges or papers or any Commission. You could pile up all these pieces of paper as high as a mountain, and all the same someone will crawl across it and pinch whatever he needs!"

"Ignaty!" Kalashnikov shouted, almost straining his voice. "Are you a counterrevolutionary or some other enemy of the working people?! Or are you a member of our Commission? Answer me!"

"I didn't mean nothin' by it," Ignashka protested, tugging in fear at his mustache. "I didn't mean nothin', honest to God! I agree with everything! Let there be a whole heap of laws, just not so many stiff ones. They won't do no good. Did the people knock over the Tsar so that afterwards they wouldn't be allowed to touch nothin'? So again this would belong to someone else, and that would belong to someone else, and another thing, and a third and a fifth and a tenth, and, since I didn't have nothin' before, I ain't got nothin' now? Well, I don't agree! Something should be mine somewhere! It's got to be!"

Red-faced, Pyotr Kalashnikov was about to lose his temper completely and shout something, but Deryabin interrupted him and said severely, "It will be just the opposite of what you are saying, Ignaty! Is that really how you figure it? That there isn't any kind of authority around these days? Or that if there is, it's far away in the city or on the railroad? So it can't touch you? You haven't understood that the forest guard we are creating now is the only armed force and real power in Lebyazhka and for a good distance around it. That being the case, it could take into its hands at any moment not only the laws concerning the forest but any other law as well. And if it has to, it can simply grab you or anyone else by the hair and break him in two. Get it?"

Ignashka began to blink.

Ustinov, changing the subject, said, "The forest is even more important than the fields in our parts." He was really thinking out loud. "In the fields every few acres have their own master who uses them as he sees fit, and it never comes into his head to cross the boundary into someone else's field. But the forest is different. The forest doesn't have a master now. It is no longer the Tsar's, but the people's. The people have to show if they are masters or only brigands who can take things away from you or punch you in the face but can't manage their land wisely. Can the people see to it that all stolen timber becomes a disgrace? That a person would be ashamed to live in a house built of such timber? That they wouldn't give a young bride away in such a house?"

"What else can you expect?!" Polovinkin exclaimed. "When life all around is nothing but thievery and speculation! It's not a life at all, but an empty cloud—it makes thunder, but not a drop of rain."

"Enough about clouds and the sky," said Deryabin. "What do you really want, Polovinkin?"

"I want good laws, Deryabin. Laws for living. So that you can harness them like a pair of good horses and go where you need to go!"

After thinking for a moment, Pyotr Kalashnikov sighed, "Well, then, till tomorrow, Comrades!"

The members of the Commission scraped their feet under the table, ready to stand up and go home, but then there was the sound of the kitchen door opening. Someone had come in from the street.

"Are the master and mistress already asleep?" No one answered. Their hosts, Kirill and his wife, had surely gotten tired and gone to sleep, but this didn't trouble the visitor. "Well, of course, they should be asleep at this hour!"

"That, Comrade Members of the Commission, is Ivan Ivanovich!" Ignashka guessed. "It's Samorukov himself!"

The door from the kitchen opened and Ivan Ivanovich appeared. Holding his right shoulder higher than his left, he took off his cap, crossed himself, blinked at the bright light, came into the room, and asked in surprise, "You're burning kerosene? Will you tell me that isn't real kerosene?"

"We won't lie to you, Ivan Ivanovich," Ignashka assured him. "That's genuine kerosene burning in the lamp. Would you be so kind as to have a seat?" Offering his own stool, he took a seat on the windowsill.

Ivan Ivanovich sat down, yawned, and smoothed the sparse and motley fuzz of his whiskers. He took a pinch of tobacco out of his pocket, but, changing his mind about the snuff, he put it back and asked, "Well, how are you doing, Comrade Members of the Forest Commission? You are comrades, aren't you? Or are you gentlemen?"

"We are comrades," Ignashka replied. "Without a doubt, that's what we are!"

"In other words, authorities and bosses?"

"What do you mean, 'bosses'?" huffed Ignashka, not without regret.

"Well, so what, Ignaty? Without authority or government, you can't get near a thing, not even your own wife. But tell me, what are your most important reasons for being in this here Commission?"

"Me?"

"You . . . "

"Well, different reasons, Ivan Ivanovich! So as not to be left behind! So's I might get my hands on some good timber, too! In a word, no one wants to be a fool!"

"There it is, the greatest misfortune of all mankind!" Pyotr Kalashnikov sighed loudly and sorrowfully. "There are so many Ignaty Ignatovs in the world! And these days there is a little bit of Ignashka in almost everyone, more in some than in others. He sits and waits for his chance. When it comes, he gets his way and muddies clear water: if something has been done wisely, he's sure to do it stupidly. Why? It is not because you, Ignaty, are so stupid by nature, though, of course, that could be true. It is because a man will live in whatever way is easiest and most comfortable. He will live like a pig, and avoid anything that is difficult to accomplish like a human being. Sometimes a person is too lazy to be a human being, and sometimes, too busy. For many people it's too much work to be a human being."

"There you are!" agreed Ivan Ivanovich. "Wherever you go, everything is temporary: the money is temporary, the authorities are temporary, the law—temporary. Watch out that life itself doesn't become temporary, 'cause then Ignaty will have lots of moves to make! That'll be the life for him!"

"But in the Commission we have to cultivate social consciousness, no matter what! In everyone! Even in Ignaty!" Kalashnikov insisted.

"I understand," Ivan Ivanovich nodded. "But that's like trying to walk on water. It worked for the saints, but not for all of them, as I recall."

Clearing his throat, Deryabin asked Samorukov without any formalities, "And why have you come to us, Ivan Ivanovich?"

Ivan Ivanovich put his hand into his pocket again, and this time he put the pinch of tobacco neatly into his nostril and sneezed. Then he replied, "Another day has passed . . . It's already late at night, and it's like the day never was."

"Well, so what?" Deryabin shrugged.

"I wonder how the day vanished . . . Well, for instance, how did it vanish in this Commission of yours? To what purpose?"

"We haven't been wasting time here, Ivan Ivanovich," answered Kalashnikov. "Not in the least! We opened the Commission with a solemn speech and appointed ten men to the forest guard. The first of these is Comrade Innokenty Stepanovich Glazkov, the second, Comrade N. N. Semyonov, and the third . . . "

But at this point Kalashnikov stopped talking. What had happened here? he silently asked himself. Ivan Ivanovich just had to drop by upon seeing the Forest Commission's light, and the Chairman immediately made him a full report? That is exactly what would have happened two or three years ago. It would have been impossible to imagine any community business being conducted without Ivan Ivanovich. But wasn't the old regime gone now? There were no more masters, not even old men! So maybe now Ivan Ivanovich was the most old-fashioned of men, and the least politically aware?

Commission Member Deryabin cleared his throat angrily and gestured with his hand as if to ask, "What is this, Mr. Chairman? Are you really allowing this?" Polovinkin, on the other hand, stared at Kalashnikov silently and motionlessly. Then Kalashnikov looked at Ustinov—what was he thinking?

Breaking his long silence, Ivan Ivanovich turned to Ustinov to ask, "Tell us, Nikolai Levontyevich, what are you thinking, eh?"

"What?" asked Ustinov, startled out of his meditation.

"I know, Nikola, that every time you start to think, it's like you've silently climbed to the top of a hill. Well, what heights have your thoughts taken you to?"

"I'm thinking about different things . . . I'm thinking about how much harm men can do themselves. They can wage a war that kills millions, drop bombs from airplanes, and attack each other with gas. One nation can completely destroy another nation, and all with a delighted 'hurrah!' Heroically. But a man doesn't know how to do even the slightest bit of good for himself. Here we are trying to organize a guard and to decide on the rational use of the forest, and at the same time we don't know if we will be able to do it. Is our attempt useless? Maybe there's no sense in it at all?"

"You're right, Ustinov." Ivan Ivanovich pulled his nose and heaved a sigh. "I've often thought about it myself. Why weren't cannons invented for doing good? So we could load one up with good words, aim and fire, and there would be a good deed done! From a well-aimed shot! Have they made that kind of cannon yet, Nikola?"

"No, Ivan Ivanovich, not yet . . . "

"Too bad, really too bad! We sure need that kind of cannon these days."

"There was a time when I wanted to become a deacon." Shaking his head, Kalashnikov had begun to reminisce thoughtfully. "I was strongly attracted to religion, and especially to church ceremonies. I learned the *Instruction on the Church, the Liturgy, and All Divine Services and Utensils* by heart. Like the ABCs. The priest used to forget why, at the evening service, he was to enter with hands lowered and empty. But I remembered: 'thereby to show that Christ, being in essence God, for our sake took on human flesh and appeared to us in that humble form.' Or Father Konstantin, a good man, but forgetful, would whisper to me, 'Petka! What was written there about confession?' And I would remember in a flash: 'If a Christian sins after the cleansing of sins in the baptismal font and his entrance through it into the covenant of grace, then there is but one means and sacrament for redemption—confession!' And therefore confession is a second baptism. It gives you the sensation of being born again, as if the confession were for your whole life before that moment! Isn't this why so many people support various new ventures? Doesn't everyone want to be born again and wash off his former life in the font of new deeds as if it had never been?"

As Deryabin began to laugh, Kalashnikov nodded in agreement. "True, it's funny! But I still haven't explained why I took such a liking to church rituals back then. I'll tell you why—I liked the word made flesh in human actions. It was said: 'the mind's Sun of Truth, Christ, appeared from the East,' and in reality people pray to the East! Every movement in the entire service has some meaning behind it. Maybe our life could also be without thoughtless and meaningless actions, and we could join word with deed."

"You should give up all this priest talk, Kalashnikov!" Deryabin advised. "There is no place for it here in the Commission!"

"I'll give it up!" agreed Kalashnikov. "Why not? Everyone knows I soon gave up on religion, took up working for the co-op, and got carried away with it. But once something happens to you, you can't just forget it."

"It's all right for you, Petro. You can indulge yourself!" Polovinkin sighed. "First your older brothers did your work for you, then later your grown-up sons, while you, strong as you are, fiddle around with hobbies!"

As all the members of the Commission looked at Kalashnikov with envy, he was momentarily embarrassed.

Ivan Ivanovich snorted knowingly through his tobacco-filled nose and asked, "Aren't you afraid now, my dear Forest Commission? Aren't you just a little bit afraid, with all that is going on here?"

"Just what have we got to be afraid of, Ivan Ivanovich?" asked Ustinov, rubbing his curious blond cowlick.

"Well, everything! Everything there is! In such bad times as these, any public service is a very risky business! The first person the Commission treats differently than he expects to be treated won't just take offense but will attack. It's the same everywhere in the country. No matter what authority or order there might be, even a co-op, some other one will come along that's more powerful and banish the first, not to just any old place, but straight into jail. And jail would be a good thing because the firing squad is just as possible!"

"If you say so, Ivan Ivanovich!" Ustinov smoothed his cowlick with both hands. "But the Forest Commission won't pursue its business to the point of fighting. Why should we? We aren't interested in government or politics, only in the forest, in nature, nothing more than that."

"Fine, if that's the way it is!" Ivan Ivanovich nodded in agreement. "But night has long since fallen, Comrade Peasants! And you've been burning someone else's kerosene all this time!"

"And I adjourned our founding session a long time ago!" Kalashnikov said happily. "It's time for all of us to part till tomorrow, before dinner! Let's go now."

The Pankratovs, Husband and Wife

The Pankratovs did not sleep that night. He was on the sleeping bench against the wall, she on the one above the stove, but neither was sleeping. They heard Ivan Ivanovich when he came in and the sounds made by the Forest Commission when they extinguished the kerosene lamp and at last went home. When it was completely quiet and dark in the house, Kirill recalled the decision made by the Forest Commission. Under the unlucky number thirteen in the list of forest guardsmen was written: "Kirill Yemelyanovich Pankratov. Accept, but caution him to be a little livelier." That had been written in vain because Kirill Pankratov had never been lively and never would be. They had accepted him only to avoid offending the master of the house where the Commission had met that day and where they would continue to meet. Kirill was surprised. What kind of game was this? The day before he had been thinking he had to hang on to the same kind of life as everyone else. But now he wondered, could he turn away from the rest of the world? Finally he had it figured out: you don't have to be shy or afraid of people if you don't want anything from them and the only thing you need is to be left alone! Taken as an overwhelming majority or as individuals, they made you weary with their lack of honesty. When he understood this, he felt lightness and simplicity everywhere, most of all within himself. Now he didn't care if he was to blame or if other people were to blame. It was too late to figure it all out, and it didn't matter anymore. What had happened in those cruel war years had happened; there was no turning back.

A lot had happened . . . Kirill had fought, been wounded, fought again, and then had wound up in an escort unit. There he was once ordered to shoot two German prisoners. Night, fog, rain, darkness. He had no idea just why the prisoners were being dealt with that way nor of how he would be able to come home to Lebyazhka and his wife, Zinaida, after such a thing. For many generations the Pankratovs' Old-Believer forefathers had avoided military service. They had hidden their lads in the forest and sat in prison for refusing to serve. Kirill and his cousin Veniyamin were the first to accept the three-fingered cross and to go into the army. And then right away he got into such a mess. Kirill had constantly preached to his wife against war and killing, and then what did he end up doing himself?!

The same sort of terrible life had now taken shape in his own home. There he was, a man, but dependent on his woman in every way, and people were laughing at him. Let them laugh. Zinaida had invited the Commission into the house. Kirill had wanted to object, but he just waved his hand in resignation—let her invite them. Maybe she would dominate one of the other men in this Commission, or maybe she would turn and twist the whole thing to her own liking. Let her! Kirill felt uncomfortable with other men in his house—all right! Now he couldn't sleep—fine! He didn't understand right away what had happened, why he felt so calm and collected, but then he understood and wanted to lean over the edge of his bunk and tell his wife about it because he knew she was not asleep either.

"Zinaida," he wanted to tell her, "you and I argue so much about this Commission. I didn't want it in my house, but you did . . . Well, you've got your way again: the Commission met in our house till midnight, and I can see how pleased you are! Well, fine. May your pleasure continue! I don't care. I don't care about anything in the whole world except my woodcarving. When I carve I feel I am creating something from the fragrant wood, turning by turning, pattern by pattern. Only in this do I sense myself, and nowhere else. Everything is in the wood for me—the earth and the sky and you, Zinaida, but most of all myself, Kirill Pankratov. I am always ready to carve. The only other thing I need is a little bread and, of course, my tools. If I have all that, I won't say a single sharp word to you. Live the way you want, with one or even two Commissions! What do I care about the Commission? They won't do anything anyway. They won't create a single thing on God's green earth, not one thing of true beauty that you can look at, touch, and think: 'Ah, you pretty thing, you were made with these hands! They will return to the earth as dust, but you will remain—so remember them! Tell people about them, amaze people. Forgive people their sins, their blood and murder!' "

Thoughts of the life beyond and a distant unknown something made Kirill dizzy. Was there anything left? Or had it all fallen into savagery? The bloodshed in the war had been terrifying. All right! There would be more blood. Kirill Pankratov would still live his life and do his work, and if not, still his soul would not perish! But Kirill said nothing to his wife, not a single word.

▲▲▲

As a matter of fact, Zinaida's life in Lebyazhka had actually begun with her getting her way with the menfolk. It had happened long ago, in the summer of 1894, but everyone who lived in Lebyazhka still remembered.

Siberian through and through, the village of Lebyazhka held on tightly to its own way of doing things. No matter how much the wandering immigrants from European Russia begged to be let into the community, none were successful—the Lebyazhka folk wouldn't allow it. So as not to offend God completely, they would toss a good armful of hay and some oats on an immigrant's wagon and stick a loaf of bread in his hand. If there were children with him, they would tell the first woman who came along to give the kids as much milk as they could drink, but then they said, "Christ be with you, don't think badly of us, friend! This road goes to Krushikha, that one to Barsukova. We hear the Barsukova folk take in immigrants!" These Lebyazhka ways were known in all the neighboring regions, and the Lebyazhka folk loved to talk about them and repeat, "That's just the way we do things . . . "

And then a young girl, about fifteen years old, had stood before the village assembly and explained that she had come with her sick father and aged mother all the way from Tambov Gubernia, that her older brother had died during their journey, and that she was asking to join the Lebyazhka community, especially since she had managed to arrive while the assembly was in session. She was a barefoot little girl in a tattered jacket, dirty and dusty from the road, her hair dangling in two disheveled braids—in short, she was a beggar. But she stood tall and straight and spoke boldly with the men, though with the mild little voice of a child. In the village square, in front of the homely building that housed the Lebyazhka village assembly, stood an emaciated little mare, harnessed to something that could not be called a wagon or a cart—except for its wheels, God only knows what it was. A twisted-up little peasant was lying on this conveyance and moaning under a coarse sackcloth blanket, while an old woman, also just skin and bones, sat next to him, nodding her head in agreement.

"That's how it is, God's truth, that's how it is . . . "

"Even if it is the truth, not even able-bodied immigrants are accepted into our community," the Lebyazhka folk told the girl. "We don't have much faith that they will become good householders and stand on their own two feet, and you want us to take you? To provide food and drink for the three of you as long as you live?"

"But what else?" the girl asked in surprise. "Of course you would feed us—we're not asking to come starve to death with you! We're asking to live with you!"

"Just look at this girl, men! What is she thinking?"

"You look at yourselves, too, people of Lebyazhka! What kind of men are you if you're so afraid—as many of you as there are, to feed three Orthodox Christians for a time? It's shameful even just to ask you for it!"

"And just how many years would we have to feed you?"

"Three years, maybe four."

"And then?"

"Then, God willing, I'll get married and raise some real men, the like of which you've never seen in your village before! And if you take me and my parents in, I will never forget it, and you will have my eternal thanks! Isn't such thanks worth anything to you?"

At this point Ivan Ivanovich Samorukov, already the most senior old man, the village's Finest Man, stood up, spat loudly at his feet, and said, "She's just like the plague, men—you can't chase her away and there's nowhere to hide from her. We'll have to take them! She'll be a lot of trouble, but take her we must!"

Little Zinka had touched Ivan Ivanovich's soul. But Ivan Ivanovich also had in mind that for some time the authorities had been threatening him for continually turning immigrants away. As it was, the Lebyazhka community had an excellent land allotment based on a rate of fifteen desyatinas per person as counted by the census, three desyatinas for the growth of the population, and another three for the relocation of exiles and other people.

When they decided to accept Zinka and her parents, they unanimously resolved to give the refugees some sort of dwelling, to issue grain from the communal store for food and for next year's sowing, and to provide them with livestock and fowl. They also warned the girl to behave herself as she should. "Or else," they said, "we'll drive you out by the same road you just came in on! We'll take no excuses—we'll rid ourselves of a pestilence!"

That's how Zinaida was accepted in Lebyazhka and how the Lebyazhka men gave in to her. But their prediction had been fulfilled—their troubles did increase with this girl's arrival, and noticeably so. The girl grew up and became attractive. Her parents were still with her, but it was almost as if they didn't exist. They were little more than mouths to feed, and there she was in the fields, alone, and going into the forest for firewood, again alone, and even driving to Krushikha on market days to buy or sell something, always alone. It was not just that it was sad to see how she had to do every difficult chore by herself and that if you took pity on her you would wind up helping her. That couldn't cause any problems. But what if someone took a hankering to her when she was all alone? That would surely be a shame and a disgrace for the whole community! And what if it wasn't a stranger, but one of their own Lebyazhka lads that took a hankering? Then it would be Lebyazhka's shame before the whole region, a disgrace before the whole uyezd! It wouldn't be such a problem if she were squint-eyed or limped, but in fact it was just the opposite.

At first the old men told her neighbors to keep a better eye on her. They forbade Zinaida to go into the forest alone under any circumstances whatsoever or to spend the night alone in the fields, and they told her to join the camp of her neighbors, the kind and pious Pankratov family.

After a while Ivan Ivanovich Samorukov himself summoned her and said sternly, "Enough is enough! I want you to be married before the Feast of the Intercession,* Zinka!"

"No," said Zinaida, contrary again. "I'll get married all right, but there won't be enough time before Intercession. I won't manage to find a suitor by then."

"Who do you think you're talking to?!" Samorukov asked with heartfelt exasperation. "Do you think I haven't seen how the boys stare at you from dawn to dusk? And especially after sundown! You have until Intercession, and there'll be no more talk about it. Tomorrow you give someone a nod, and that's all there is to it. Tomorrow is Sunday, so the young people will be getting together for the holiday. You give someone a nod then. If you pick a rich boy who hesitates because you are poor, you just come and tell me about it. If it comes to that, the village will put together some kind of dowry. So not another word from you! By Intercession!"

But that Intercession passed, and yet another one, and Zinaida was still a maiden. Many in Lebyazhka began to get angry at her. The women at the well would pretend not to notice her. When she said, "Hello!" they would answer, "Hmph!" But why were they so angry? The boys made fun of her in their own way. "Look out, Zinka! If you keep being snooty, all that will be left of you will be skin and bones! Maybe you're already skin and bones. Can we take a look?" The girls stared at her, silently wondering, "Where does she get the gall?!"

Ivan Ivanovich Samorukov summoned Zinaida's parents, who might be sick and useless, but they were still her parents, after all. When Zinaida's father understood that Samorukov himself was asking for his cooperation, he spoke out proudly, "But it's true, Ivan Ivanovich, our little girl needs a very special kind of suitor!"

Ivan Ivanovich almost lost his temper, but later he thought better of it and secretly gave the old man a bottle of vodka and a pair of worn but serviceable boots. Zinaida's father accepted the gifts, but a week later he spread his hands in resignation and said, "It's beyond my power, Ivan

---

*Festival of the Protection of the Virgin, a holiday celebrated on October 1.

Ivanovich. But don't take it wrong. Since that's the way it is, I'd be glad to return the boots!"

And Zinka herself almost went down on her knees before Ivan Ivanovich to protest, "Do you think I like it? I don't, it's terrible! How many times I've been plowing and stopped my horse and sobbed out loud! I'm sorry for myself! I feel like my youth is dying! I cry and tell myself, 'That boy there, I like him. By God, I like him a lot!' But that very day I meet him on the street, and I've gone all cold. 'No, no, he's not the one, I don't like him at all!' "

"Use your brains, Zinaida, and think what you are doing. You once promised the village that you would be grateful forever, and that means obeying us. Are you going back on your word?"

"No, I'm not."

And then finally it happened. Zinaida married Kirill Pankratov, the youngest brother in that kind family that Ivan Ivanovich had entrusted with looking after Zinaida. Ivan Ivanovich gave her a downy Orenburg shawl as a wedding gift, and his wife, an ancient woman who could not be there herself, sent a pair of yellow shoes with laces and heels. The wedding was a grand one, but there were many who could not understand how it had happened. Kirill was a very quiet and delicate lad, more of a fair maiden himself than a boy. It would be more fitting for him to be looking for a husband himself than for a bride. He might do as a best man, but not at all as a groom. But it wasn't the old men and women who had second thoughts, for they had succeeded in getting rid of the girl, and it wasn't the other boys, who could only blink their eyes. It was the grown men who were troubled in spite of themselves. What if Zinaida started to send her dear husband, Kirill, running off on errands and kept him busy with this, that, and the other? That would be an embarrassment to every male in Lebyazhka! How would they stand the ridicule from the neighboring villages and settlements or even from their own Lebyazhka women?

But a year passed, then two, then three, and nothing in particular happened. It was a family like any other, a typical household, properly prosperous, and two little boys were born to the Pankratovs. Everything was as it should be. No man would come to grief with such a hard-working wife, and neither did Kirill, though he turned out to be mediocre as the master of the house. You couldn't say that he had a talent for it. And then war was declared with Germany, and Kirill went off to the front.

Life was turned upside down, and with half the men away from home, the village of Lebyazhka was not itself. At first the old men and the old women, too, watched after things, kept them in order, and never let the soldiers' wives out of their sight. But later when able hands were in short supply, Lebyazhka asked for Austrian prisoners of war as workers. Groups of these Austrians began arriving, dozens of them. It was said that in all of Siberia there were half a million such prisoners and that they were in all the settlements, and Lebyazhka got its share. When the prisoners began to learn some Russian and were settled in those houses that were missing a master, even the strictest of the old men gave up in resignation. Under such conditions you couldn't keep a proper eye on the soldiers' wives, no matter how you tried! The only thing the old men could do was to reproach the wives and continually hold Zinaida up to them as a good example. She didn't invite any of the laborers into her house or even allow them to cross the threshold, and she did all her own work herself, both in the vegetable garden and in the fields. But her example had no effect on the other wives.

"Zinaida has the strength of any two men!" they said. "It makes no difference that she's not so tall—she's done a man's work since she was a girl. She's used to it. Not everyone is that kind of woman!"

At the end of the winter in 1918, the soldiers began coming home. Some found that things at home were fine, but many returned to ruined households. Kirill Pankratov returned, took a look around, and was amazed—it was as if he had never gone to war, or as if he'd gone only to the market for a week. Everything in the household was in good order, even improved. But Kirill was surely quite troubled by this. Everyone had gotten along fine without him, or they had gotten along no worse than if he had been there, and maybe even better. Instead of resting and taking it easy for a while before diving head first into the work of the farm, he took a notion to build a porch onto his house.

He decided to build a marvelous porch with balusters, decorated with woodcarving, with a little tower on the top and a granite foundation. In the countryside around Lebyazhka there wasn't a rock the size of a chicken egg, so he harnessed his team and drove for more than a hundred versts to get his building stones. Many of the Lebyazhka men would visit Kirill, have a smoke, and take a look at the work he was doing.

"Are you in your right mind, Kirill?" they would ask.

"I'm not crazy," he would reply.

And he would tell them how when he was fighting in some village in Galicia he had seen a house with just such a marvelous porch. Then and there he had promised himself that if he survived and returned to Lebyazhka he would add a porch to his house that was every bit as good, and with five steps in front of it.

"But how will you have five steps? Your house is built low, and the doors are set low."

"I'll raise the house later. I'll make it as high as it needs to be!"

"Kirill, you're crazy. There's no doubt about it!"

"Maybe . . . ," Kirill agreed quietly, smiling, looking into the distance with his blue, almost childlike eyes, and stroking his light-colored beard. "Maybe it's true that I am crazy to everyone else. But to myself, I'm as sane as can be."

"Then at least have pity on your wife, Kirill! All the real work has fallen on her shoulders!"

"That's the way it has to be," replied Kirill, heaving a great sigh and taking up his carpenter's tools again.

And when, after one or two alterations, this unusual porch was almost finished, a military column marched through Lebyazhka. The men with experience estimated there were about two battalions of infantry, an incomplete artillery battery, and a machine-gun detachment. It was not clear whose uniform these infantrymen, artillery men, and machine gunners were wearing. They were of a darker color than those of the former Tsar's army, but lighter than German ones, and the cut of their overcoats was unfamiliar. But the villagers knew better than to stop one of the soldiers to ask for a bit of tobacco and to find out who they were. Let sleeping dogs lie. So they hid in their houses and barns, closing their shutters and their garden gates as best they could. The column moved quickly, the officers on horseback, the soldiers pounding along, some in boots, some in thick-soled shoes. The two artillery pieces, rocking slightly as they went along, were aimed at the sky, and the wheels of the gun carriages creaked.

"Well," surmised the Lebyazhka men, peeking through their shutters and gates, "something has happened over there where the column is headed. Most likely some peasants have rebelled against some power or other. If so, our turn is sure to come . . . "

The column kept marching quickly, maintaining a tight formation, and only when they were across from Kirill's porch did the soldiers slow their pace.

"What handiwork!" they marveled.

"How'd you like to spend the night in that house?"

"Some oddball built that, for sure!"

"Maybe it'll be a church or something."

"Some scummy bastard must have had it made. How much you think it cost?"

"Maybe he did it himself, for nothing."

"He needs to plow his field, not build a palace like that!"

"Let's torch it! We haven't burnt nothing for a long time!"

Immediately not one but two soldiers jumped out of the column, grabbed an armful of hay from the machine-gun cart, tossed it onto Kirill's porch, and struck a match. It all happened in the blink of an eye, faster than a seasoned soldier could present arms. At that moment Zinaida came running through the gate with a bucket and splashed water on the match and on the coat of the arsonist. He tried to take a swing at her. She shoved him in the chest with both hands. Staggering a bit, he fell spread-eagled on the ground. The other soldier threw himself at Zinaida, but again she stood her ground.

Then Kirill came rushing through the fence, but not in defense of his wife. Throwing his arms out to his sides and shouting madly, he shielded the porch with his body. "I won't let you! Kill me, cut me down, but I won't let you!"

Zinaida, as quick as she had been before, grabbed him around the waist and began to push him back into the yard. The soldiers in the column hesitated, some finding it so funny that they laughed till they were ready to drop, others shouting that they ought to go ahead and burn both the porch and the whole house. An officer of unknown rank, wearing a strange cloak, rode up at a trot and ordered, "Break it up! Back in formation! Step lively!"

Bunched together more tightly than before, the column marched away at a quicker pace, and some soldiers rushed off to catch up with their units. But Kirill Pankratov, the submissive and quiet peasant, didn't go back into his house. He grabbed a heavy iron bar and waited, hidden by the garden gate. He knew that at the end of every column there was always that one soldier who was the most pitiful of the lot, always bringing up the rear, sick and clumsy, trudging along with bloody feet. And sure enough, that soldier soon appeared, almost completely lost in his greatcoat, big enough for two beanpoles like him, and shuffling along like a child with two left feet. When Kirill went out the gate to meet this soldier, once again Zinaida threw herself at her husband and began to cry out more wildly than before, "What kind of people are you men? What sort of animals? God forgive the lot of you! Get out of my sight, Kirill! Git!"

▲▲▲

Why do men, even the most passive men, go off to war? Zinaida wondered. Didn't even Kirill fight and kill? Didn't he want to smash a nameless, limping, straggling soldier with an iron bar because another soldier had almost burned down his porch? Did even Kirill need to commit murder? Oh Lord, it was horrible! Zinaida wouldn't have gone to war. Let them kill her for disobeying orders! So what? At least she would know why she was being killed, and that was better than to kill or be killed for some unknown reason in a war. She wouldn't have gone, and no power on earth could have made her!

When she had seen her eldest son off to war in 1917, she had whispered to him, "Vasily, don't aim your gun at a living person. Shoot somewhere off to the side of him!"

"I can't do that, Mama!" her son had grinned.

"Why?"

"Because the enemy would take aim at me first thing and kill me!"

Her own son, who had never been to war, already knew everything about it! Vasily had been lucky—they sent him to Kazan to guard the supply depot. Because he was diligent, they made him a noncommissioned officer, so he served on in Kazan and wrote letters to his mother. There had been no letters in the last six months, but during that time no one in Leb-yazhka got any letters, and Zinaida believed that nothing bad had happened to her son. But when her younger son, Volodka, was coming of age, she could no longer simply accept fate. She understood that she had to take a hand in it. So she began to take milk, eggs, and homespun cloth to the schoolteacher, though the teacher already loved Volodka without all that and was giving him private lessons. Volodka, who was very talented, went to the city where he was accepted into a school run by the railroad company and became a telegraph operator at the station at Ozyorki. When he came home once to see his mother, he was dressed head to toe in state-issued clothes, but, more important, he was alive. The draft couldn't touch him because he was already doing service.

"Why should you be afraid of the war?" the women asked Zinaida. "It's only your husband who is fighting. That's not so bad!"

But she was even more afraid than those fearful women who envied her. She could hear the terrible thunder of war, unjust, man-made but inhuman, and listening to it, Zinaida imagined that all the soldiers were wounded, weak, unhappy, and impoverished, all praying to God for life as if begging for alms. The brave ones were the same as the others, for their bravery was also God's grace, and nothing else. She felt herself weak and disgustingly powerless because she could just barely hear that distant rumbling.

In Lebyazhka she was known as a courageous person. Everyone remembered how as a young girl she had persuaded the men to take her into the village, but what was the truth? When a featherless baby bird cheeps in its nest, no matter who comes near, a person, or a cat that has crept up to eat it, it still opens its beak wide. "I'm so glad you've come! Now give me a little bug or a worm or a crumb—I'm hungry, I want to live!" That's how it had once been with her. She had wanted to live, and her old parents had wanted to stay alive. So before the whole Lebyazhka village assembly, she had opened her mouth wide and loudly demanded her own little worm, her own crumb of bread. If she were dying, even more if her children were dying, she would go to the most notorious brigand and demand at the top of her voice, "Save us!"

But she had also discovered something else—that the strong go after the weak. As a girl, she had kept a sharp knife hidden in the top of her boot for times she had to spend the night in the fields or go into the forest. Because the handle of a boy's knife would stick out of the top of his boot, everyone could see that he was a tough guy, but her boots were covered down to the heel by her skirt, so no one could tell what was hidden there. Once or twice she had had to threaten someone with that knife, to pull it from her boot, and though she had never struck anyone with it, she knew how it was done. Because she had carried a sharp knife in her boot for more than a year, she suspected what war and blood might be like.

At first she believed that all this evil had come from the Tsar, that it was he who couldn't get by without murder. He wore a saber and a uniform with epaulets and a military cap. Then they had kicked out the Tsar, but everything remained as it had been: the taxes, the draft, the Tsar's guard in the Lebyazhka forest, the government offices in the county seat of Krushikha, and the clerks in these offices, but most of all—the war. It still hung over their lives as before. Zinaida waited more anxiously than ever, day after day, hour after hour. What would happen now? And then that Provisional Government that had driven out the Tsar was itself driven out of St. Petersburg, and it was proclaimed: "Land to the peasants, factories to the workers, peace to all peoples!" Maybe the peasants in Siberia didn't have all the land they could want, but there was enough to go around, and factories didn't concern them at all, but peace—that was something they could all understand, and Zinaida understood it, too. "Well now," she rejoiced, "I have lived to see this day, so I wasn't born into the world without a good reason. Life has not cheated me!" She looked up at the sky and studied it. What had happened way up there?

At first it seemed that nothing had changed, but then, hurrying home for the planting season, the soldiers really did begin to return to Lebyazhka. And once they were home they were also quick to do what they had never done before: they refused to pay taxes. At last they disbanded the Tsar's forest guard and dealt with the government agents in Krushikha and in the other larger settlements and cities. They collected grain from the rich farmers for the hungry people in Petrograd and for their own cripples and widows.

Life became strange and unfamiliar, as if observed from another village, from a distant place. It gave Zinaida hope and put her in a constant state of expectation, but it did not explain exactly what there was to expect. Try and figure it out for yourself! How often during this time did she let the soup boil over, oversalt the food or not salt it enough, or forget to feed the livestock on time? Why wasn't the woman herself? Why did she have these mysterious expectations, brood about these unanswered riddles?

Kirill came home. His face hadn't changed—he still had the same light brown beard and blue eyes. He was still a handsome and affectionate man, and he seemed to have brought home some word, some answer. But it turned out that there was more of the boy in him than the man. Zinaida had waited for him, feeling guilty that she hadn't thought about him and loved him the way she should have during his absence. She had waited in the hope that he would return with a new wisdom and maturity and understand her hardships. But he was more of a boy than before. As soon as he came into the house, he took his tools out of their box, laid them out on the table, and explained to his wife what kind of woodcarving he was going to do now. Here was another way that war, playing its tricks, could cripple a man. And since it could, it did, and a front-line soldier sat under an icon, sober, but not talking about himself, nor asking his wife about her health or the household affairs or about his sons, whether they were alive somewhere in the world. Instead, he tenderly stroked chisels, planes, drills, and files. Kirill didn't see the sky with his sky-blue eyes or recognize any objects on the earth. For him the earth was empty. Even the war he couldn't see. He saw only the carving of wood, and nothing else.

Again Zinaida persuaded herself, "I can live for a while even without words. For a while I will live alone, but I won't just get used to it! The war is over, after all!" But the war had not ended. The Provisional Government drafted the young men in the village of Chorny Dol. They took the lads in August, during the harvest, when the peasants were at their busiest. So the peasants from Chorny Dol left the harvest, took up arms, went to the town of Slavgorod, freed the young men who had been drafted, and killed Fuchs, who was the mayor and the miller. They say this Fuchs—or maybe it was Foks—had been imprisoned by the Tsarist government for selling rotten grain to the army, but during the Revolution he had been freed and had become the mayor of Slavgorod. A few days passed, and then Annenkov's punishment brigade* appeared in Chorny Dol, set the village afire, and killed many of its people. Since that time there had been no peace in their part of the world because either the Provisional Government was killing peasants, or the peasants contrived to kill members of the militia or even regular soldiers. They were waging war against the war, to save their sons from the draft, but it was still a war. It was then that the military column that had almost burned Kirill's porch and his whole house had marched through Lebyazhka.

Once more Zinaida began asking someone for an occasional newspaper, and at night, after Kirill had planed wood till his bones ached and was sleeping a deep and righteous sleep, she would light a lamp and read, following the words with her finger and moving her lips, to see what was being written about the war. She read about the world war between the Germans and the French and other nations, about the civil war that was closing in on them, raging in the Urals, in the Semirechye region, in the East, and in so many cities that were unknown to her and whose names became confused in her mind. She read about the war the partisans were fighting already close by in the next uyezd.

The newspapers were gray and yellow, or some other poisonous color, and if they had been printed on thinner paper, they would have been torn up to roll cigarettes and would never have come into her hands.

---

*Annenkov, commander of Cossack units in support of the Whites, was particularly cruel to his opponents.

Lady's black STOCKINGS are on sale at the establishment of E. Mortensen, 30 Gogolevskaya Street.

The world class motion picture *Salambo,* a story from the epoch of Rome's war with Carthage. A cast of more than 50,000! A thrilling plot! A magnificent production!

The State Land Board announces the formation of the following departments: 1) Secretariat, 2) Instruction, 3) Accounting, 4) Taxes, 5) Education, 6) Agronomy, 7) Insurance, 8) Charity, 9) Medical, 10) Veterinary, 11) Economics, 12) Land, 13) Statistics, 14) Road Construction, 15) Libraries.

Reading without understanding, Zinaida was frightened. How did people remember all these endless services and offices? How could they remember the war with their heads stuffed full of all this? She had been in the provincial center once, when she had taken her younger son to the school for telegraph operators and had gone around to various offices. At first she remembered an abundance of different offices, but after a year had passed all she remembered were doors. Everywhere she had turned there had been a door leading to someone's office, but now all the people had disappeared from her memory, and there was only a blank space where they had been. And what kind of women's black stockings, what departments of the State Land Board, what long-ago wars could be interesting and necessary to people during the murder now going on all over the world? It was a crime and a great sin to live in such a time as if nothing were happening, not to cry out or weep, not to take the weapons away from the soldiers, but to hand them weapons and incite them against one another. Fifteen different departments in the State Land Board, but not a single one against the war? Maybe the Library Department was the one against the war?

LOST: 600 rubles, at the secondhand goods market. I ask the finder to please return it. I know who it is, but I don't have his address or last name. I will prosecute in case of concealment.

Who Is That Under the Bed?
A Comedy in 3 Acts
A sea of laughter!

Of course, one should take into account
That there's a great host of office workers everywhere,
And more friends and relatives than one can count:
This one needs a full-length fur, this one just a jacket,
This one a muff, that one a stole,
This one, as a present for his sweetheart,
Is aiming at a piece of Astrakhan fur.

The paper went on to explain how someone had stolen various furs from a store to give to his friends and acquaintances. None of it made any sense!

Truly the only righteous life these days was the life of the peasant! He who plows and sows has the obligation and the right to live, for, as long as breath remains in a body, it needs bread. Zinaida hoped to meet with truth, with an answer to this inconceivable life, among the peasants, and so she sat, lost in thought over her newspapers, but with the hope of such a meeting warming her heart. If it weren't for this impending encounter, what reason would there be to live? If it weren't for this hope, it would be time to enter a convent. She did not consider herself a sinner. Perhaps she had sinned, but she had atoned with the overwhelming, almost unthinkable labor she had performed all her life for her parents, her sons, and her husband. But the sins of mankind would not let her go and were attributed to her. She didn't have much faith in monks and nuns. Because their words were confusing, so were their thoughts and their lives. And then right in the middle of all these doubts, the village of Lebyazhka elected its Forest Commission.

Zinaida had always loved the forest and been attracted to it. It seemed to her that only good and wise people could be concerned about the fate of the forest, especially the Lebyazhka forest, which was so beautiful and unique amid the endless steppe. It stretched for three hundred versts, and the part of it that crossed over from one low, wide knoll to another consisted of pine trees and was called the White Wood. It was named long ago by two people who were not married but loved each other. They had left the world and the company of other people and had gone into this forest, and there they had bid farewell to life forever. The name of the White Wood was often remembered in Lebyazhka.

Zinaida had invited the Forest Commission into her house. "Have your meetings, gentlemen, write your papers, talk about all your business—it's interesting to hear!" Even if she understood nothing, it would make her happy just to listen to other people talking in her almost completely silent house. She didn't need much, just a little joy, not even joy itself, but simply the hope of it, and she would feel like a real person, a woman, and she could receive guests, give them food and drink, sing for them, and entertain them.

And so that night she didn't sleep, but she remembered how the Commission had sat around the table, who had spoken, and what they had said. And she also remembered who had said nothing. It was Nikolai Ustinov, their scholar, who had said the least, and she wondered why.

▲▲▲

Early the next day Kirill called to his wife from outside the house. "Come out here! I want to talk to you."

Zinaida went out, full of hope.

Kirill was sitting on his porch, on the top step. Slapping the place next to him, he said, "Sit down, right here."

The autumn morning was just beginning, without even a touch of sun. When the dim sun presently appeared, the day came meekly, still uncertain of what it was approaching—was it late summer or early fall, late fall or early winter?

Kirill and Zinaida Pankratov sat silently under the intricately decorated little roof of the wondrous porch. Above their heads the patterns played such tricks and made such turns, hiding in one another and then emerging again, that it was hard to believe that they were made of hard wood and couldn't bend and move freely or at least stir on the sly. The carvings spread down from the roof onto the bannisters and balusters, and in the midst of this splendor sat the Pankratovs.

Zinaida waited for Kirill to tell her something. She thought he would thank her for saving the porch from the soldiers and for saving him, too. He would explain why he had become nothing more than a crazy woodcarver. He would ask her forgiveness for his madness. At last he would ask her how she had lived without him for three years, how she had waited for him. He would reproach her for something, cuss her out. He would talk her out of bringing the Commission into their house, and without a second thought she would say, "Thank you, gentlemen, for opening your Commission in my and Kirill Yemelyanovich's house and making your speeches here! We respectfully thank you for this honor!"

But Kirill didn't say a word or ask a thing. He sat silently for a while, then stood up. "Well then . . . ," he said, and went off to the workshop he had made in a small shed.

Didn't he understand that he was obliged to tell her his opinion to stop her from seeking the opinions of others?

The Kupriyanov Wood Thieves,
Father and Son

The Forest Commission, all except Deryabin, who was giving instructions to the elected officers of the forest guard, met at the Pankratovs' house the following day around noon. Before they could determine the available reserves of newly matured and long-standing timber, they had to become thoroughly familiar with the forest survey conducted in 1914 and the record of woodfelling and natural growth in subsequent years—technical matters, one might say. It was a good thing that the papers of the former forest authority were now in the hands of the Commission. When the government changed, these documents had been requisitioned by the people, or more precisely, by Pyotr Kalashnikov. It was also a good thing that they had a real expert who understood all these materials—Nikolai Ustinov. He understood the affairs of the forest and many other things as well.

Ustinov was a man who was curious about everything, hard-working, and sharp-witted. When he was still a young man newly independent of his father, he could have improved his farm and made a lot of money, but he had pursued other interests. For a month or two every year, he would always take on some outside work with the land-use team, in highway or bridge construction, or with a well-digging co-op. More often than not, he worked with the forest management teams, and now, leafing through the charts, reports, and other papers of the former forest authority, he was not at all confused. Now and then he paused in thought, chewing on his pencil and working the beads of an abacus, then explained to the other members of the Commission what each report meant and how it should be understood. Polovinkin and Kalashnikov listened to him attentively and followed what he was saying, but it was all wasted on Ignashka Ignatov, who yawned, gazing out first one window and then the other.

"The only reason a man is given a brain is so's he can use it to help himself," he said. "Just look at the brains some people have, but what good does it do them? Hardly any! Not enough to notice!"

Kalashnikov looked up from some piece of paper and asked, "Just who are you talking about, Ignaty?"

"I'm just talking," Ignashka replied, but he had broken everyone's concentration.

After a moment of hesitation, Kalashnikov, trying to reestablish the tempo of their work, explained, "Everyone knows how much we need the forest ourselves, but we also need to leave the forest for our children, and our children's children, and so on into the future, so that our descendants won't curse us for our stupid behavior and shameless greed after we, their fathers, are gone. Nature is for all people and all times, and whoever robs it or wrongs it today will be the enemy of humankind forever! But let's get back to the question at hand: why do we come up with such a small allotment of timber for each person? It's true, you can live with it as long as you don't think about it too much and make comparisons, but as soon as you begin to think even the least little bit about real life, right away it seems completely insignificant!"

"Exactly!" Ignashka was again quick to answer. "You shouldn't think about it! It's stupid! Children? By God, let me take care of my own life, and not worry about anyone else's! Why should I think about me having one little mare and an old gelding with a sore on its right hind leg, and those who will live after me having maybe five or more good horses standing in the yard, and not a sore on any of 'em? So what if they have to go to the northern forests or to the Altai for timber? It's all the same to me. Am I supposed to suffer for their sake now? Ain't that stupid?" Once again, Ignashka was managing to bring the work of the other Commission members to a halt, one man against three.

Heaving a sigh, Kalashnikov remarked, "You know, it's just like it was in the trenches. As soon as you start to think about it, death comes after you, and you can't escape it. But if you don't think, you live on peacefully. Lots of times, of course, you do get wounded. That's the way it is—just about any human thought always brings you around to thinking about death if you don't watch yourself!"

Beginning to examine the map of the Lebyazhka forest tract attentively,

Polovinkin asked, "Where did you get this, Nikolai Levontyevich? And on such thin paper?"

"When I was working for the forest assessors," Ustinov was happy to explain, "I noticed that they would transfer the original map onto transparent paper, that is, copy it, work with it for a day or two, then throw it away, and then copy it over again. I just collected what they threw away. I just had a feeling that it might come in handy."

"Really?" Kalashnikov asked with animation. "You may very well have been right! Once again, this is just like it was in the trenches. Whenever the generals showed up at our positions, we used to cheer them. But when the time came for battle, they all left us far behind, and we began to tell ourselves that our generals really weren't so great! Instead of cheering them, we should have given it to them in the neck and ripped the epaulets off the lot of them! We had a feeling for the future then, too . . . "

So, having talked about one thing and another, the members of the LFC bowed their heads over the wax-paper tracings of the map of the Lebyazhka forest tract. The map was unusually beautiful, drawn on colored tracing paper. Everything on it, though in miniature, was just as it was in real life: the green forest divided into sections by white clear-cuts, the little circles of corner posts and benchmarks with their assigned numbers, the black curves of roads, the dark-blue stripe of the river, and the sky-blue edge of Lake Lebyazhka. Farther on, in a surprisingly thin but nonetheless distinct line, here and there broken by little crosses, or rather little x's like multiplication signs, were the fields and meadows and the Lebyazhka pasture that adjoined the forest and lake. At the western edge of the map were the buildings of Lebyazhka, not all of them by far, only those in the part of the village called "the forest side." A dozen or so houses and their plots of land were shown in detail and colored in shades of dark and light yellow.

It was an organized and precise land. A thin black line with one thing on this side of it and something else on the other makes it perfectly clear that here the meadow ends and the fields begin, or the fields end and the pasture begins, or the pasture ends and the lake begins. Everything on earth has a beginning and an end, its own order and name. Each part of the land itself knows, and so does each body of water, what it is and what it is meant for. The forest exists to supply wood to build houses and to keep the houses warm; to allow human children, instead of suffering from the cold like other offspring, to crawl around the house bare-tummied and to clamber happily on the benches without catching a chill. The fields exist to provide daily bread and thus to make it possible to keep all kinds of other necessities, for young and old, in the house. The wet and dry meadowlands exist to provide haycocks for brown cows, black cows, white cows, cows of whatever color you like, to graze upon; to feed horses, too, in payment for their heroic labor; and to let every hungry four-legged creature nibble some fresh grass. The village lots exist to prevent houses, barns, bathhouses, and vegetable gardens from crowding too closely together along the streets or spreading out so ridiculously that, deafened by isolation, you might see a house without ever hearing your neighbor's voice in it; they exist to arrange the streets of the peasant community according to its own sense of harmony and order. The curly brown head of Pyotr Kalashnikov, Chairman of the LFC; Polovinkin's, tinged with red; Ustinov's, blond as a child's; Ignashka Ignatov's, with its sparse, colorless hair—all these heads, now and then bumping against one another, bent over that beautiful map, the work of a master craftsman.

"Look, here's Petrukha Nogayev's house!" Ignashka suddenly discovered, jabbing a finger at a little black square.

"Is your finger clean, Ignashka?" Ustinov asked sternly.

After this question it grew completely quiet in the house, as if a holy icon had been brought in and it had been announced, "You may look, but don't speak out loud"; or as if a book of Holy Writ had been opened and it had been promised, "Read a page in silence, and the mystery of mysteries will be revealed to you . . . " It was a joy to recognize your own life on this map, your own house, your own field, or even just your neighbor's, all that land that you had long since known to the finest detail with your own eyes and measured thoroughly with your own footsteps.

"The road to Barsukova! What circles it makes!" Once again Ignashka could not restrain himself from breaking the silence, but this time the others also began to speak all at once.

"That's where it goes around the Cranberry Wetlands!"

"Which clearing in the forest is this here? I can't figure it out."

"What do you mean? That's where Ilyukha Kondakov came across that stray bear one time on Candlemas Day!"

"That wasn't just any old time, it was in 1911. That was a hungry year, dry and lean. The half-starved bears couldn't sleep in their dens and would wander over here. Boy, did Ilyukha get a scare that time!"

"It didn't bother him. He doesn't get scared. He had a skittish horse, and it smashed his sled to pieces against the trees!"

"Right here on the lake there's a little spit of land where I've gone swimming lots of times, but you can't even see it on the map."

"The scale is too small. If the scale were bigger, you could even see yourself!"

"Well, boys, we're getting some real practical experience here! We'll become experts! Lawmakers!"

"Look, the grazing land is laid out here all in one piece, but really there hasn't been any by the forest for a long time. It needs to be fenced off."

"That's what a map is for—it shows order, not disorder . . . The map has no concern for what we've messed up ourselves. If we cut the forest down, the map would still show these green sections for a lo-ong time to come."

"Everything is there all right," sighed Kalashnikov, "but what is missing here, boys, eh?"

"Well, what?"

"There's no sky here . . . No sky."

"When I worked with the surveyors, with the master surveyor Pyotr Nesterovich Kazantsev," Ustinov began to reminisce, "whenever Pyotr Nesterovich Kazantsev ran into someone, he would say, 'Here's a map of your area, take a look at it, and show me where the field I'm looking for is. It's around here somewhere, but it's not shown on the map.' " Ustinov raised his head above the other three, looked around attentively from above, then lowered it again and continued his story. "And do you know, the peasant would always point out that very place. If not at the first try, then always at the second. And the master surveyor would exclaim in amazement, 'An illiterate peasant, but he can read a map?' When I explained to him that a peasant can understand a map better than the alphabet, he didn't agree. 'I didn't learn to read a map very well myself until my second year of surveyor's school! No, Ustinov, there's something else here—instinct!' 'What's that?' I asked him. He explained, but you could just barely figure out what he meant. This 'instinct' is like the way a dog senses things. It's like just knowing what the truth is without thinking."

And so, pressed close together, head to head, the sounds of their breathing mingling, the men went on studying the map. Life in a land that wonderful could surely be arranged and apportioned with harmony and propriety. That which was good could be placed ahead of them, and that which was bad, somewhere behind them. That's what human wisdom and skills were for. Yes, it was true! If they could just once attain true wisdom, try hard, study, understand, and work, then life would return to its true furrow, from which it had been knocked long ago and from which it had wandered aimlessly ever since. The time had come to put life in its proper place, before it fell apart completely, before its unity with the earth was broken, and the earth became one thing and life on it entirely another! They needed to get on with the job. They had to! Wasn't that the task of the Forest Commission? Yes, it was! Hadn't the most important hour come?! The most important year, though bleakly unbefitting, the year 1918?!

And the members of the Commission thus began to calculate the useful reserves of the Lebyazhka forest tract, the timber fit for firewood, construction, and poles, how much of it there should be and in what sectors. Ustinov recalled that somewhere near the city of Omsk they had even planted a forest from seed, like wheat in a field. Lebyazhka could do the same! They began to make notes of the results of their counting and calculations.

"But don't we have too many numbers here?" asked Polovinkin.

"There's no end to these figures!" Ustinov laughed. "Beget as many as you like, you don't have to worry about feeding them! For the time being," he added after a pause.

The work was progressing nicely. One person would write, though sluggishly; someone else would ponder a question and then express his thoughts; another would make calculations. True, there was a hitch in the last task—the abacus was in bad shape. Its frame was cracked, and it was missing some beads. One person could hold the abacus with both hands so it didn't fall apart, and another could move what beads there were, but there just weren't enough beads to add up some of the sums. For some reason their inability to solve this problem irritated Polovinkin more than anyone else. His face kept reddening and he cursed through his teeth in the name of all the saints, sometimes right out loud.

"Watch out, Polovinkin," Kalashnikov finally warned. "The missus will hear you and take offense!"

"Then I'll take this abacus and smash it on the floor and see how it likes that!"

But a few minutes later the door suddenly swung open, and Zinaida came into the room with an abacus so huge it could have been rough-hewn with an ax. Setting it on the table, she laughed, "Here you are, gentlemen of the Commission!"

Polovinkin clasped his hands and reddened again. "What, you had such a thing all along, and we didn't know it? And . . . sinned?"

"It's from the neighbors! I borrowed it from the Kruglovs! From Fedot Kruglov."

"But their old man is so stingy! Did he give you the abacus himself, or wasn't he at home?"

"He was home all right, but I took it myself! I know what nail it always hangs on, and I just went in and took it. 'They need it,' I said!"

"You're right! We were sweating blood! But the Kruglov brothers and their cousins and second cousins, they're all so stingy!"

"Would you all like to have some kasha now?" Zinaida asked.

"Hardly, we've got a full head of steam on."

They were all so flushed with excitement, working so hard, that no one wanted to take time off. But Zinaida loved the feverish activity.

"Well, how about when you cool down?" she asked cheerfully. "Perhaps you won't refuse then? You will cool down sometime, won't you?"

"We won't refuse!" Ignashka replied for all of them. "We will honor your wishes, Zinaida Pal'na!" As Zinaida went off to the kitchen, he added, "Look at her go, what a stride! She's a healthy one, spry as a nanny goat. Look at her kick up her heels! Just like a young maiden, only a little wide in the hips, and everywhere else!"

"Ignaty!" Ustinov said indignantly, "how can you flap your mouth like that, and you a guest in someone's home?! Wouldn't you be ashamed if the mistress heard you?!"

"But what is there to be ashamed of, Nikolai Levontyevich? It ain't nothing at all!" Ignaty protested. "If you say that a woman past forty looks like a maiden, she'll hear that through two log walls and feel nothing but satisfaction! And you think you're smart, Ustinov?"

"Nevertheless, Comrades, this is not a fitting conversation for the members of our Commission!" Kalashnikov insisted sternly.

Everyone resumed his work with the same enthusiasm as before, everyone except Ignashka. He went out into the kitchen, sniffed at the cooking kasha to see if it was left over from yesterday or made fresh today, sneaked a sly peek at Zinaida, and then darted outside. "I'll be back in a bit, Zinaida Pal'na! You can count on it!"

Deryabin arrived shortly thereafter and reported that the forest guard would in fact begin its duties Monday morning and would meet again tomorrow evening to practice drilling and to familiarize themselves with the duty roster. Then he asked, "Well, boys, are you attacking someone? It's like you're carrying out a military action, eh?"

Without waiting for a reply, he began to add up some figures himself. He and Kalashnikov were trying to determine the number of forest consumers. Kalashnikov for some reason called them "those desirous of the forest." They began to go through the long, detailed census lists. Everything possible was recorded in them: the number, sex, and age of every living soul in every household, personal property and real estate for each of the last ten years, tax assessments at the end of 1917, and many other details.

"Those desirous of the forest," Kalashnikov was saying, "need to be counted down to the very last one! If we can find out how many babies will be born these next few years, we should count them, too!"

"Not at all," argued Deryabin. "If we count every single soul, we'll come up with an individual allotment the size of a toothpick, or even less, and the people who elected us will not be pleased. We should consider only the heads of households as consumers and divide them into categories according to the number of their dependents and their social significance. Then the allotment will be clear and understandable to everyone. Or maybe let's divide the timber supply only among males and widows. After all, if a woman lives with a man, she keeps warm by his fire, too."

"But Comrade Deryabin," protested Kalashnikov, his indignation aroused again, "why did the Revolution take place if more than half of the human race still remains under oppression? The Revolution is being made, not for the sake of the minority but for the sake of the great majority! I would rather die of shame than support such a revolution!"

"Well, don't support it! The Revolution doesn't need small fry like you! And it won't be asking you what to do!"

"Who will it ask?"

"No one but itself!"

"No! No one makes a revolution just for its own sake! They make it for the sake of justice and the good of the people! And nothing but!"

"And you are the Chairman of our Commission! Can you still call yourself a politically mature comrade? What is needed for the good of the people? The victory of the Revolution! And when will victory come? When the Revolution first and foremost takes care of itself by any and all means and isn't hindered by the question of anyone's happiness, not even by the people's. First it should be victorious, and then later it can establish justice!"

Kalashnikov and Deryabin argued passionately with one another while Ustinov and Polovinkin calculated the timber reserves almost in silence, but still the work took its proper course with all of them until Ignashka came back into the house and hurriedly began to look for something under the table.

"Ignaty, what are you fumbling for under the table? Ah, your hat. Why?"

"So, boys, the forest guard will get to work on Monday! And in the meantime? Right now practically the whole of Lebyazhka is off in the woods cutting and hauling while we, the Commission, are sitting here as if nothing was happening! Like a bunch of lop-eared puppies! Even the forest guard is out there chopping!"

"Stop wagging your tongue, Ignaty, and just tell us the facts," said Kalashnikov. But Ignashka had found his hat, snatched it from under the table by a torn ear flap, slapped it on his head, and was about to rush away with his hat on back to front when Kalashnikov grabbed him firmly by the arm and ordered, "Stop, Ignaty, do you hear me? Don't move a muscle, you snake!"

All the other members of the Commission also stood up, pushing away the census lists, maps, reports, and their still unfinished calculations.

"So, Comrade Commission Members," said Ustinov with a deep sigh, "so now . . . "

"Well, go ahead now, Chairman Kalashnikov! Give us all our orders!" said Deryabin, swallowing hard. "Well?"

Shuddering and running his hand through his curly hair, Kalashnikov ordered loudly, "We'll meet here at Kirill's porch in half an hour, all on horseback and armed with rifles or whatever you have. We'll meet here and go into the forest to stop this outrage, this swinish thievery!"

Jostling each other at the doorway, the members of the Commission left the house. Zinaida followed them with her eyes. She had just turned to the oven to pull out the kettle of kasha and was left standing with the oven fork in her hands.

▲▲▲

It was a magical time of year in the White Wood. Summer was late in leaving, and autumn in arriving. Or perhaps summer and autumn were there together, meeting as lovers. Perhaps they could not bear parting with one another and had hidden in the depths of the forest to wait for their inevitable separation. This shared, unseen waiting made it quiet. No longer did the horseflies buzz in the forest, the mosquitoes whine, the gnats hum, or the birds sing. All the forest sounds were still. If a bird flew over the wood, you could hear its wings cut through the still, blue air, and when a hawk cried, the forest was deafened. The forest had grown unaccustomed to sound.

It was cool in the forest, but it was a friendly and comfortable coolness. It was as if a huge Russian stove had been stoked up a few days before, and now the trees, the withered grasses, the brown pine needles that covered the forest floor, and the very earth of the forest were all slowly cooling.

Mushrooms had already begun to appear throughout the forest, milk-agarics and saffron milk-caps. The maslyata didn't count—the Lebyazhka folk never gathered them. The milk-agarics and saffron milk-caps were early, the first swallows of the mushroom season, but their real time had not yet come. Once the cold became sharper, the milk-agarics would appear. Covered by gray drops of water, a large one would stick up out of the earth, with little hills around it. If you opened the hills and brushed away the pine needles, in each hill you would see a milk-white marble funnel, crisp and fragrant and cool, as if chilled in a root cellar. You would have the urge to pop this tiny, delicate funnel right into your mouth instead of your basket. But only worms and snails have a taste for raw mushrooms—people like them pickled. With sour cream and hot, crumbly potatoes, they're wonderful. The saffron milk-cap is almost the same, but a little more delicately flavored and tastier with a little vodka. There were still very few milk-agarics and saffron milk-caps to be seen in the forest, but you knew they were there, for the carpet of needles already smelled of them, and with every hour their scent grew stronger while the smell of resin grew weaker.

The sun pierced the forest, not directly from above, but from the side, from the steppe, from the distant wilderness. The tall, slender pine trees, many of them bare of foliage right up to their crowns, were illuminated, not from the top down, but along the whole length of their trunks, their light-gray bark gleaming and sparkling and melting in the sidelong slant of the sun. The pines, always so stern, had now grown numb, and although they didn't show it, they were resting from their summer growth, from their almost incessant sunward striving. Already they could feel the the coming of winter and their own hibernation, with snow-covered branches and roots frozen hard.

The White Wood was not completely wild, though various beasts inhabited it, mushrooms and berries grew there, and it was not hard to get lost in it. It had been made habitable, almost tamed, well tended, and settled. Almost a hundred years before, the forest managers had divided it into sectors and placed numbered corner posts and benchmarks along the boundaries. Later they had built immense observation towers here and there. You would climb for half an hour on a shaky ladder, breathing hard, your heart racing from a trot to a full gallop, but once you had reached the observation platform with its little table for surveying instruments, you would cool down and be able to see, for twenty versts all around, the dark-blue forest and the green, yellow, and black fields under the light-blue or gray sky. It would seem close enough to touch. You would look around—was there any smoke? Was a fire consuming the forest? If not, you would take it easy, breathe deeply, and feast your eyes.

This forest was a model for many other Siberian forests and for people, too. It was depicted not only on maps but in illustrated books. One or even two of these books could be found in every house in the village—the foresters had distributed free copies in Lebyazhka and the other forest settlements. In the pictures the villagers could recognize their own men carrying surveying instruments, setting corner posts, lifting beams during the construction of the watchtowers, or sitting in a circle, shoulder to shoulder, listening to a forester's lecture. The foresters wore uniform caps and suit coats with bright buttons.

It must be said that the Lebyazhka folk—a willful people, obstinate, stubbornly independent, crafty, and suspicious of anything the least bit unfamiliar—treated the forest with respect. When they got a chance, there was no question about stealing a good piece of timber or roughing up a forest warden, especially if he was from somewhere other than Lebyazhka. Anyone could do that if he had the strength, the wits, and the opportunity, but it was considered a shame and a sin to be a vandal, to cut a pole and then toss it aside because a better one came into view, or to crush a sapling with your wagon, let alone to start a fire in the forest. Boys who did this sort of thing got their hides tanned, and not lightly, and an adult offender would find that the time had come to board up his house and move to a village on the steppe.

The forest was respected and loved for its kindness and generosity, for the fact that, though it belonged to His Imperial Highness, the Tsar, it never forgot the peasants. It had more concern for a simple man than for the Emperor himself—the one lived close by, but the other was far away. If a peasant man or woman visited the forest, he or she would never return empty-handed but always with a gift—with berries, mushrooms, medicinal herbs,

or with a rabbit, a gray-hen, a wood grouse, a hazel-hen, or a partridge, or
with a sack of pine cones for kindling, an armful of long and pliable pine
tree roots that the old men used to weave baskets and entire wicker chests,
with a jar of resin that the children chewed to make their teeth grow strong,
with a bundle of birch branches for the bathhouse, and many other things,
too many to count! There is not much of that sort of kindness in the world.
Whoever does not understand what it is worth is worthless himself. The
Lebyazhka folk understood.

But when the Tsar in St. Petersburg was overthrown, and the forest tract
ceased to be the Tsar's, when it seemed as though the previous order in the
forest had never even existed but a new one had not yet been established,
the Lebyazhka folk began to feel uncertainty. Now it seemed possible to
take from the forest, not just from the edge and in little pieces, but right
from the middle: to go into any sector and fell any pine, for there was no
one there to stop you, fine you, take you to court, or say, "It is forbidden!"
This possibility frightened them. It is easy to take something, but nothing
on earth is taken without a price. You can take it and walk away today, but
tomorrow the time for payment will come, the time for questions: "How
much did you take? Well, well, how about an answer, foolish, greedy, and
grasping man? You have a weakness for wanting something for nothing! At
public expense!"

The Lebyazhka folk waited for a month, and then another. Who would
be the first to begin? Ignaty Ignatov began first—he cut three trees and sold
them on the steppe. The men judged Ignashka among themselves: it's not
good that he sold it, not good at all. If it's for yourself, well, that's another
matter. But at the same time the men also expressed gratitude to Ignashka,
jokingly naming him the new forest manager, and they, too, went off into
different sections of the forest. Those with hale and hearty horses went in
the farthest, while those with broken-down nags set to work almost at the
edge of the wood. It was an amicable woodfelling, and no one lagged behind anyone else. When the widows tearfully complained that the assembly
had ordered people to help them out, a good number of people willing to
help them appeared. Were these well-wishers atoning for their own sins in
the forest and elsewhere?

At this time, when all the villagers already had some timber lying in their
yards, the Forest Commission had been elected. The people elected them,
but they did not have much faith that anything would come of it. The Commission was not a real authority, and the management of nature required a
serious authority. However, although the Commission had not yet seriously
begun its duties, the first, albeit weak, sign of order had already hatched
from it. The men began to keep their eyes on one another and to reproach
one another: "You're cutting down a tree? But didn't I see you raising your
right hand in favor of the Commission at the assembly?"

But even though they had voted for the Commission, today they were also chopping trees. They cut in a feverish hurry. The clatter of chopping filled the forest tract, and the metallic ring of axes was heard near and far.

▲▲▲

Right from the start that day, the Commission had bad luck. The first timber thieves they came across turned out to be Sevka Kupriyanov and his son Matveyka, a lad of about sixteen. Sevka Kupriyanov was a quiet and sober-minded man, polite and kind to everybody, except Ignashka Ignatov. The two were neighbors on Nagornaya Street. Not only had there never been peace between them, there was not even the slightest dream of a chance for it. If one of them shouted, "Yes!" at the assembly, the other would howl, "No and no!" right in his face. If the Kupriyanovs' cow, Whitey, came home from grazing and gave no milk, it meant that the Ignatov's Blacky had ruined her appetite in the meadow. If one year Ignashka's oats fared poorly—and his oats, like everything else with him, often fared poorly—then the Kupriyanovs' oats would leap up two arshins tall. If some matter concerned Ignashka Ignatov even the least little bit, the normally staid and judicious Sevka Kupriyanov would go mad, begin to shout, make threats, spit, and curse in the name of all the saints. No matter how amazed the other men were at his behavior, and no matter how they tried to persuade him to spit a good thick gob at Ignashka and forget about him, they were unable to convince him. It was just the opposite with Ignashka. The only time he behaved wisely, cleverly, and even with a little dignity was in his encounters with Kupriyanov. How did he ever manage it? On the surface it almost always seemed that Ignashka was in the right and that *he* wasn't picking a quarrel, but Sevka Kupriyanov was, and that *he* wasn't shouting without reason, but once again Kupriyanov.

When the Commission came riding up to Sevka, he and Matveyka, a young lad strong for his age, had already felled a pine tree and, straddling its yellow trunk, were trimming it, moving toward one another, Sevka from the butt-end toward the crown, Matveyka from the crown toward the butt-end. Two identical bay horses, one of them particularly well-groomed and well behaved, but both with a torn left ear and sleepily blinking eyes, stood harnessed to a long wagon. Over the sound of their axes, the Kupriyanovs did not hear the approach of the Commission. When they did notice, the men were quite close, and the Kupriyanovs froze in confusion. Throwing his axe on the ground and burying his hands in his already graying hair, the father emitted a heavy, drawn-out sound, "E-e-kh!"

"So, Seva! You seem to be doing well for yourself, eh?" said Kalashnikov as he rode up and was about to say something more.

But Ignashka suddenly began to shriek like an old woman. "A-a-a!" he howled. "Those Kupriyanovs always need more than anyone else! They're such greedy gluttons it's a horror to think about it! Little Kupriyanov is still a snot-nosed brat with milk on his lips, but already his father is teaching him piracy, robbery, thievery, more thievery, and every kind of lowdown trickery! They'll both wind up in prison for sure! I'm really sorry for this little Kupriyanov pup!"

Sitting on his gray mare with his arms raised, Ignashka would have continued his crying and wailing, but just then Matveyka Kupriyanov grabbed Ignashka's left leg, and, before anyone could blink, Ignashka was on the ground, and Matveyka was hammering him with his fists wherever he could. When Deryabin rushed to pull Matveyka away, Kupriyanov Senior went after Deryabin, and Kalashnikov and Polovinkin after Kupriyanov Senior. Blinking frequently and quietly repeating, "Here now, Comrade Commissioners," Ustinov alone stayed in the saddle.

The first to break free of the pile was Deryabin. Brushing the wood chips, bark, and needles from his clothes and wiping his scratched cheek with his sleeve, he looked around, then rushed right back into the scuffle. He had not been at the front very long—he had come home in '15—but he had learned to give orders. Thrashing around in the pile of bodies, he shouted orders now: "Knock 'em down! There! Hold 'em! That's it! We'll tie them up, this way! Got 'em? Got 'em? We'll lift the log together: one, two, heave! Ignaty, back the wagon under the log! Come on, don't stand there with your mouth hanging open! One, two, heave! That's it! Aargh, it's heavy! Once more, one, two! Good, that's it . . ." Then, still rubbing the scratch on his cheek with his sleeve, he raised his arm. "There, that's right! That's everything! Let's go, push it! Ignaty, do you hear?!"

The Kupriyanovs' bays pulled the wagon, to which the fallen tree was lashed with its untrimmed branches sticking out at the center of the trunk. The Kupriyanovs, father and son, were tied flat on their backs to the tree, the father to the front, the son closer to the top of the tree, just behind the wagon's rear wheels. Deryabin followed on horseback, leading Ignashka Ignatov's gray mare with its lopsided Kirghizian saddle, hemp-fiber stuffing protruding from its ragged pad. The other three members of the Commission—Polovinkin, Ustinov, and Chairman Pyotr Kalashnikov—followed behind Deryabin. Polovinkin and Kalashnikov rode silently, but Ustinov still repeated from time to time, "Here now, Comrade Commissioners."

After they had ridden well away, Kalashnikov spoke out. "This has all happened because we, the Forest Commission, who are only legislators, have now taken on executive powers!" All were silent, and then Ignashka unexpectedly supported Kalashnikov.

In the meantime Sevka Kupriyanov, tied to the timber, protested, "Men! Even if you are the Commission, you still don't have the right to treat me this way!"

"There aren't enough rights to suit him!" Dumbfounded, Ignashka urged the horses onward. Then he asked Kupriyanov, "If you try to attack the Commission, to mock it and destroy it, just how many rights do you want?"

Looking up at the tops of the pines and blinking and squinting as if some kind of dust were falling into his eyes, Sevka breathed heavily. Two or three strands of gray kept appearing and disappearing in his thick brown beard whenever he shook his head. "Men!" he groaned. "If I get the chance I'll do the same to you as you are doing to me now! Even the Tsar's agents never treated a wood thief the way you're treating me and my son! You're making it bad for yourselves! Bad!"

"Well," said Polovinkin with embarrassment, "if it happened to me, if I, let's say, cut down a tree, and there ain't no law now against cutting one down, so I cut one down, and here come five men riding up on horseback and blather at me and splatter me with insults from head to toe . . . What would I do? Maybe I wouldn't have thrown my axe on the ground. Maybe I would have held on to it and made straight for those blatherers, by God!"

"You wouldn't have gone for them, Polovinkin, let alone with an axe, no, you wouldn't! But I would have!" Deryabin said. "And I would have cut down all, well, not all, but anyway a couple of us! But still, a fact is a fact. The Kupriyanovs not only felled a tree illegally but also made an attempt on the integrity of the members of the Forest Commission. We won't review the facts again, but we'll take the prisoners before the assembly. Let the whole of Lebyazhka see that no one has the right to treat the Forest Commission any way he wants!"

"All the same," sighed Kalashnikov, "we ourselves have violated the people's democracy. First of all, we should have recorded in the minutes our right to arrest and even tie up wood thieves, especially if they resisted, but we don't have such a resolution written down yet. This is the resolution we need to make: 'The forest guard, as well as the Forest Commission itself, will arrest forest poachers, especially if they resist, and will take them by force to the village assembly for further proceedings against them.' Who is in favor? Let's have a vote right away, and we can enter the result in the record later. Who is in favor?!"

Three members of the Commission stopped their horses and raised their hands. Ignashka raised the hand holding his horsewhip. Ustinov abstained.

"Ustinov, why didn't you raise your hand?" Kalashnikov asked.

"The law has no retroactive force. That's why."

"Fine," Kalashnikov agreed, "four 'ayes' and one abstention. That'll look even better in the minutes. That means that there are different opinions on the question. But cooperation is necessary! It helps the poor and checks the rich and so makes for general equality. And if there is real equality, then there is not much need for authority, only enough for parades and public appearances. On the other hand, the more inequality there is between people, the more need they have for authority, for big and little lords! For those like us, the members of the Commission!"

No one was surprised by Kalashnikov's reasoning. Before the war he had worked for many years as the chairman of the creamery association and the retailers' commission and was the head of all of Lebyazhka's cooperatives. And even though they had laughed at Kalashnikov and called him "the Co-op Man," they always listened to him with interest. Despite the nickname, stuck on him by a visiting instructor from the creamery union, he was still their own Lebyazhka man.

Meanwhile, Ignashka was skillfully driving the Kupriyanovs' bays, maneuvering the long wagon between the trees without getting caught up anywhere. Probably this was not the first time that Ignashka had had to haul a long log out of the forest without using the road. He often stopped the horses and ran ahead to look for the best way to pass through. He would have long since been on the road, but he was taking his time and kept veering to the left because he wanted to enter Lebyazhka, not by some back alley, but by the main street. He wanted to show the trussed-up Kupriyanovs to everyone. And probably that is why they came across yet another wood thief—Grishka Sukhikh.

Sukhikh was the richest homesteader. He wasn't drafted during the war because of a slight limp in his left leg, but he was amazingly strong and powerful. Grishka could work hard day and night, to the point of frenzy, filling up with blood and malice. For instance, if he had to load several carts with grain or flour all by himself, he would first walk around them in a circle, muttering something and shaking his fist threateningly. Then he would shed any unwanted clothing and sometimes even his boots, light up a cigarette, and whisper something to himself over and over without taking his eyes off the carts. Then he would suddenly pitch the cigarette butt far away, spit, and fling himself at the bags, sometimes managing to grab up two at the same time. It had been rumored many times already that Grishka Sukhikh had ruptured himself and would soon die, but through the years he only got stronger and more powerful.

Grishka did not live in Lebyazhka itself but in an isolated field about four versts from the outermost houses of the village, at the edge of the forest. He had moved there almost the very day he heard about the Stolypin Reforms granting privileges to freeholders. In just one year, even less, he set himself up on his plot of land with a house, a barn, a bathhouse, and cattle sheds, all surrounded by a high fence behind which there were two watchdogs. It was not a residence but a fortress. Grishka had hired a carpenters' artel* for the construction but not a local one—he had traveled to the

---

*A workers' cooperative in which members share income from their labor.

railroad line for it. He stood the artel members a round of drinks for their speedy and excellent work, and then, carrying their tools, the artel left by the Krushikha road, one of them, who had overstrained himself, riding on a cart. Then Grishka Sukhikh hung a lock on his new gate, and since that time no stranger had ever been in his house, and no one even knew for sure what was in it or how it had been built. Of course, managing a farm that used ten workhorses was beyond even Grishka's strength, and some gloomy-looking hired hands, not local men either, lived with him. It was said they were escaped convicts and prisoners.

During the Revolution Grishka was the first one to be called a kulak, a bourgeois, an exploiter, a bloodsucker, and many other names, but he simply announced that he had given his hired hands their own plots of land, implements, and horses, and that there were three farms on the freehold, one of the middle class and two of the poorer class. He said that the Lebyazhka community was obligated to help these poor farmers. Was Grishka Sukhikh supposed to take care of the poor all by himself? The community sent Deryabin to meet with Grishka's hired hands to find out what help they were getting from their master. The hired hands stubbornly insisted, "The community is obligated to give us grain and so forth as members of the poorest class." Grishka Sukhikh himself patted Deryabin on the back and said, "Go ahead and find out everything from them, they'll tell you just how it is!"

And now, as the Commission unexpectedly emerged into the little clearing where Grishka and two of these hired hands had already stripped the branches off three pines and were sawing a fourth, Deryabin attracted Grishka's attention first of all.

Straightening up over the saw, Grishka pulled at his wide shirt to cool his hairy chest and asked, "You aren't coming back to see me again, are you, Citizen?" It was as if the other men weren't there at all, and Grishka didn't take any notice of them.

Deryabin answered that Citizen Grigory Dormidontovich Sukhikh was exactly whom he had come to see.

But Grishka ignored Deryabin and went up to Ustinov to ask, "Do you have something to smoke, Nikola Levontyevich? I have my own, but I remembered that you always have Turkish tobacco. Treat me to some Turkish stuff!"

Ustinov began to pull out his tobacco pouch as Grishka held on to Ustinov's stirrup and nodded to the hired hands to continue sawing. As they started up again with a jerk, the saw began to sing out in a thin voice. A minute passed. Before Grishka had finished rolling his cigarette, something in the tall pine, straight as an arrow or a ship's mast, tore loose. It shuddered, seemed to rise a bit on its stump, then fell quietly and neatly. It thudded once on the ground and was still. It was as if it wanted to fall, as if it no longer had the strength to stand straight and tall through the centuries.

Taking a drag of Turkish tobacco and turning around to look at the pine, Grishka asked Ustinov, "It's a nice one, eh? Not a bad choice!"

"Citizen Sukhikh," said Kalashnikov, "we five are the Forest Commission. And these two here are our prisoners. And we also have a question for you: what right do you have to be cutting down trees?"

"What do you mean?" Grishka asked in surprise, taking his cigarette out of his mouth. "What has the Commission got to do with me? Are you crazy? Do you ride around in the forest, armed, badgering free citizens like this? What right do you have?"

"We have the right of society behind us!" Kalashnikov explained. "The community has called on us to guard the forest and bring order to it. And just who are you? Are you part of the community? Or are you just yourself?"

"I'm just myself!" Sukhikh replied.

"Then it'll be even easier with you!" Deryabin said. "It's real simple to take action in the name of the people against those who are separated from the people!"

Sukhikh shrugged. "Well, take action then! Go on, I'd like to see if your action will be against me! Well?"

"Then tell us, why you are cutting down trees?"

"All right, I'll tell you: to build a new life for the poorer class. My two former workers are now free citizens again. I'm helping them out as much as I can!"

"We will arrest you, Citizen Sukhikh! For starters! And then we'll see what the community will decide to do with you!"

"And just how are free citizens being arrested these days?" asked Grishka. "I'd like to know. Maybe like these two here, whoever they are. Could it be the Kupriyanovs?"

"Yes," confirmed Deryabin, "it's them. And you will see that citizens are not arrested without a good reason. They're arrested for resisting the Forest Commission!"

"And who tied up the Kupriyanovs? Was it you, Ignashka, who dared to do that?"

"What do you mean, Grigory Dormidontovich?" asked Ignashka, bending over as he sat on the log. "Could I have managed to do that on my own?"

Walking up first to Matveyka, then to Kupriyanov Senior, Grishka asked, "Is it really you, Sevka Kupriyanov? I've been hearing rumors that you raised a ruckus against me at the assembly and said, 'Grigory Sukhikh is a bourgeois,' and so on. No matter how much you blabbered, I'd still untie you and let you go free. But no, I won't let you go. Just see what you

get for blabbering against people and calling them names. Just see . . ."
Then Grishka—huge, shaggy, limping with his left leg—slowly went up to
Deryabin's horse and pushed its croup. The horse began to mince forward.

"Ride on, Commission, ride on! Don't get into a mess for nothing. Don't
interfere with people." As Grishka gave Ustinov's light-bay horse a push in
the same way, Ignashka waved his whip, shouted at Kupriyanov's horses,
and made haste to leave himself.

"You're not alone in the forest today, Grigory," Ustinov said. "You have
your hirelings with you. Even if you were alone, I don't know if the five of
us could overpower you or not. Maybe yes, maybe no. But you can't protect
yourself from us, from the people, for long. The people will tie you hand
and foot. Never forget that!"

Sukhikh stood silently, heard Ustinov out, and, using both hands,
flapped his shirt on his huge, slightly twisted body to cool himself off. Then
he asked loudly, "Well, so what? That doesn't mean much. Today I squeeze
someone, and tomorrow someone squeezes me. But you know what I'm
against, Nikolai Levontyevich? I'm against being squeezed by someone
weaker than me! That would be the shameful thing. I'll never in my life allow that! Never and no-how! But whoever is stronger, let him squeeze me!
I won't be offended!"

Slowly and quietly, the Commission went on with the wagon. Even Ignashka had fallen silent. No longer going to the left with the intention of
coming out on the main street of Lebyazhka, he steered between the tree
trunks to reach the forest road as soon as possible. They could still hear
axes ringing, not far away and from more than one direction, but the Commission was no longer listening to these sounds.

As soon as they reached the sandy road, sprinkled with pine needles
down the middle and broken by wheel ruts on the sides, Polovinkin jumped
off his horse and began to shout, "Stop, stop, stop! I'm talking to you, Ignaty!" He shouted as if Ignashka and his wagon were galloping past him.

Frightened, Ignashka also began to shout at the bays, "Whoa! Whoa,
damn it! Where do you think you're going?!"

Polovinkin ran up to the wagon, pulled a knife from the top of his boot,
and in a flash had cut the ropes binding Sevka Kupriyanov to the log. Then
he ran to Matveyka and freed him in the same way.

As Ignashka was about to protest, Deryabin yelled, "Shut up now,
Ignaty!"

Sevka, staggering, stood up and heaved a deep sigh, still holding on to
the log with one hand and not looking at Matveyka, who sat hanging his
head at the other end of the wagon.

"So now, Savely," Deryabin said, "the Commission has released you voluntarily, hasn't it? Now that's it! Go your own way. Get on your mare, Ignaty, and let Savely have his seat back!"

Ignashka reluctantly climbed down from the driver's seat, angrily threw down the reins, and got up in his saddle.

Sevka Kupriyanov still stood silent and motionless. Then turning to Pyotr Kalashnikov, his voice quavering like an old man's, he said, "You, cooperator, you talk about equality everywhere, but one of your own, a citizen equal to yourself, you tie spread-eagled to a log? Like a sheep? You let Ignashka insult somebody that's equal to you? Take this timber! Choke on it! Choke on it once and forever! Choke on it together with your bosom buddy Ignashka Ignatov, your trusted ally and mate. You're as alike as a pair of boots! O-o-oh, you bastards!"

Sevka ran to the rear axle of the wagon, lifted the top of the log with a jerk and threw it to the ground, and then whipped up the bays. As the horses pulled forward sharply, the other end of the log also fell to the ground. Matveyka jumped up onto the empty wagon, which squeaked and rattled as they drove the horses down the sandy, uneven road. Whipping the horses, Sevka Kupriyanov began to accompany this squeaking with a howl of despair. Seen from the side, he seemed to be whipping himself and howling in pain, "Cooperators! Equalizers! The Commission be damned! Just wait, you'll get yours!"

The members of the Commission sat on their horses beside the absurd log discarded on the road. The branches had been trimmed from its top and bottom, but in the middle they stuck out in various directions. One branch, thick and gnarled, stuck out farther than the others. Why had Sevka Kupriyanov, a sensible man, cut down such an absurd tree? Cutting in haste and agitation, he hadn't even chosen a decent tree. They would have to leave it on the road. What could they do with it? How could they haul it away, and what use would it be if they did?

School Day

After the incident in the forest, the Commission worked out penalties for the unauthorized cutting of wood. For a large tree, the wood thief would lose the right to drive his cow out with the village herd. For a small tree, he would lose the right to drive his sheep out with the village herd. For offering resistance to the guard, a wood thief would be forcefully brought before the assembly for public trial. In the case of repeat offenders, the court might impose any penalty up to and including expulsion from Lebyazhka. Many more such rules and regulations were established that gradually made up the Lebyazhka Forest Code.

All these rules and regulations were announced to each representative of ten households. If there were any disagreements with the Commission's decisions, a representative could convene the village assembly, which had the right to change or replace any regulation in the code, elect a new Commission, or simply dissolve it. However, no one protested or demanded a meeting of the assembly. That Saturday and Sunday almost the whole village of Lebyazhka was out in the forest cutting trees, but then on Monday the guard appeared, and the wood became quiet and calm.

Despite all this quiet and calm, the Commission felt that something was still missing, something without which the Commission could not command the recognition, respect, and attention of the citizenry. It was then that the Commission recalled—Kalashnikov remembered it—that at the time of the first change in the government, in the spring of '17, the village assembly had decided to build a new school. They found the resolution of that past assembly in the papers of the village clerk and expanded it into a new document.

> Record No. 7 of the Lebyazhka Forest Commission
> Concerning a New School
>
> Our village school in no way meets requirements; more precisely, it is falling into ruin and is cold and crowded. Whereas the property of the former Tsarist Government has passed into the hands of the people, and whereas now, more than ever before, there is a demand for literacy and the education of the younger generation, the Lebyazhka Forest Commission turns to its community with a call to build a new school, to which purpose it:
>
> 1. Calls on the citizenry to participate in the construction this coming Sunday, which will be proclaimed as "School Day."
>
> 2. Calls on any citizen who has in his yard seasoned timber fit for construction to voluntarily contribute it to help meet the above-mentioned community need for the education of the people.
>
> Note: In return for seasoned timber, the Commission pledges to issue to the citizenry twice the amount in official cutting permits or permits for timber cut in the past few days.

The Commission had their reasons for making this last point: they hoped that seasoned timber would be brought in and permits issued for the timber that had been cut on Saturday and Sunday. The members of the Commission imagined that any citizen who had not completely lost his conscience would at least partially legitimize his recent thievery.

School Day began like a holiday. A red flag was raised on a tall pole, and Kalashnikov and the aging schoolteacher, whose hair was cut mannishly short, made speeches about the benefits of education. It drizzled in the morning, and the soaked flag drooped down the pole. The people were also soaked, but there was not the slightest bit of despondency among the adults, and especially not among the children.

The men in Lebyazhka were skilled carpenters who loved their work, and, as expected, there were more than a few willing volunteers. They rolled the logs from the pile of timber to a cleared space and marked them with charcoal, and two men with axes began to dress the ends of each log. The most skillful men cut tenon joints or even dovetails. Then they assembled sawhorses, lifted the beams onto them, and began to cut planks with a pit saw. The joiners in turn cut these planks, still warm from the saw, into lumber with which they began to fashion windowsashes and ledges. Kirill Pankratov was already carving out some sort of figure for the roof, perhaps a rooster—no one could tell just yet.

The members of the Forest Commission had loudly encouraged all the villagers to help with whatever materials they had, and in an hour's time the wagons were making their way to the building site. One brought bricks, another nails and staples that, though mostly the products of the local smithy, were reliable and strong, and others brought two or three panes of glass or a couple of baskets of tow. Those who all their lives had begrudged their neighbors a single nail now ran home to their yards and searched in their barns, pantries, and attics and brought back something or other, sometimes even something from a pre-war supply. The people were answering the call! All it took was one person to put on a cheerful face and shout out, "I have some of that, I'll donate it!" and things just took care of themselves.

Nor were the women left behind, the bold Lebyazhka women known far and wide. Despite the cold they hiked up their skirts, each one higher than the next, and began to mix clay in the mortar trough. While their legs grew as red as those of geese, they struck up such a song about love—"Fly, Cossack, Fly Like an Arrow," about a Cossack hurrying home to his sweetheart—that the carpenters' axes could not be heard above their singing. The drizzle stopped then, the sun peeked out at their song, the work went on at full swing, and the red flag stirred in the breeze. When the women were out of breath, Ignashka came running up from somewhere and began to play "The Hills of Manchuria" on a borrowed accordion. Because Terenty Lebedev, who with his Austrian accordion was Lebyazhka's main musician, had gone to take his horse to the veterinary in Krushikha that day, Ignashka was standing in for him. He didn't play well, but he played loud.

The members of the Forest Commission acted as foremen. One directed the carpenters; others saw to the men digging the foundation or hauling materials. Once again it turned out that Nikolai Levontyevich Ustinov was chief among them. The day before, he and Kalashnikov had laid out the construction plan so that four of the school's windows looked out onto the lake and the two doors opened out onto the playground where the children would run about during recess. They had begun work at first light, sorting the logs and deciding which would be best for walls or rafters or for cutting into lumber. Now they were occupied with all kinds of tasks. They supervised the measuring of the windows, sashes, and sills to prevent the carpenters and joiners from coming into conflict with each other, and the marking of the doorways and the numbering of the beams to prevent misfitting or confusion later when they began to set up the frame of the building, and they also made sure all the materials were used wisely and without waste. They even troubled themselves a bit about the dinner that had been planned, checking that none of those who had a strong taste for hooch brought any with them. It was fall, the grain had been harvested, and moonshine season had arrived. The smell of moonshine hung thickly over many houses in Lebyazhka where stills were working at full capacity. It was profitable to distill moonshine those days. You couldn't find buyers for bread, but there were all you could want for moonshine in your own village or any other. They almost missed the old state monopoly on liquor that everyone had used to cuss about. When it disappeared they began to miss it and to curse that invention of the war years, the moonshine still.

Everything was calm on the building site as far as liquor was concerned. Since no mischief was foreseen from anyone, Ustinov bustled about supervising, running here and there, arguing with some, demonstrating something to others. He enjoyed all of it. "Now this is a Commission!" he rejoiced. "Really a serious Commission!" Under his cap, set at an angle, his childishly fine blond hair was damp, and his excited, freckled face was shining with sweat. He had changed little since he was a lad.

Sitting in a bunch on the same log like roosting hens, the old men of Lebyazhka watched Ustinov and praised him. They liked his way of doing things. Not on the log but next to it sat Ivan Ivanovich Samorukov, examining his team of old men. Someone had brought two stools to the building site, one for the accordionist and the other for Ivan Ivanovich, and there he presided as he always had in the village until quite recently. Before then it would not have occurred to anyone in Lebyazhka to believe that Samorukov was just an old man like any other, instead of their Finest Man.

The old men were convincing one another that Lebyazhka was a special village, peaceful and friendly, that would move a mountain to help the community. There weren't any villages like that anymore, none at all! But when Ivan Ivanovich said nothing, the old men also fell silent, thinking that their conversation offended him. Perhaps he was asking himself, "How can it be a friendly village if it doesn't honor its Finest Man?" Conjecturing about the thoughts in Ivan Ivanovich's ashen gray head, they turned their conversation to Ustinov. They knew that Ivan Ivanovich loved Ustinov very much and remembered that there had even been a time before the war when Ivan Ivanovich, squabbling with the lot of them, had said angrily, "I'll up and die, but before I die I won't name any of you fools as Finest Man! I'll name Nikola Ustinov!"

None of the old men were offended that Ivan Ivanovich had called them all fools. When he got mad he would say even worse things, despite his Old-Believer ancestry. But his extolling Nikola Ustinov over them, a man not yet forty at that time—now that was an insult. They had sent a delegation of two men to find out if he had spoken seriously or simply in anger. After Ivan Ivanovich had served the delegation tea with jam and a bit of something else, it returned in a cheerful mood, but without having discovered a thing.

Now, ten years later, the old men thought to settle their quarrel and praised Ustinov, especially because at the present time the title of Finest

Man was not forthcoming for any of them. But Ivan Ivanovich just sat on his stool without saying a word. Then he suddenly said, "Soon this here civil war is going to start up in our parts, and then we'll see what kind of friendship we'll have between us Lebyazhka folk. Today they build a school, and maybe tomorrow it will go up in flames."

"But why would the war have to start up in our village?" one of the old men asked Ivan Ivanovich. "It doesn't have anything to do with us here in Lebyazhka!"

"And how is this war to avoid us and our Lebyazhka? It has nowhere else to go. It will grab hold of us, too, without a doubt."

"Sometimes, Ivan Ivanovich, it's possible for a whole village to burn down, but to leave a single house standing untouched in the middle of it."

"It can happen!" Ivan Ivanovich agreed. "But never for anyone who counts on such a happy ending in advance. It never happens for them!"

"Well then, have you read the Order of the Siberian Government, Ivan Ivanovich? Have you read it or not? The one about reconciliation of opinions?"

This was Order No. 24, signed by the Provincial Commissar and the representative of the Commander of the 1st Central Siberian Corps, the order which for some time had been pasted on the door of the Lebyazhka village assembly and in which it was written:

> On the basis of Article 9 of the Resolution of the Siberian Provisional Government of 15 July 1918, the following are FORBIDDEN:
> 1. The arousal or incitement of one segment of the population against another.
> 2. The dissemination of false reports about the activities of government institutions, officials, troops, or military units that might incite antipathy toward them.
> 3. The dissemination of false rumors that might arouse public alarm.
> Those found guilty of violating this order will be subject to imprisonment for up to three months or a fine of up to 3,000 rubles.

Ivan Ivanovich, of course, remembered the order. Taking a pinch of snuff, he inquired, "Which one of you old gentlemen is asking me this stupid question? About the reconciliation of opinions? I didn't hear because of the snuff. Who was asking?"

No one answered him. Once again Ivan Ivanovich sat silently with his hands on his knees, chewing his lips and sighing, and all the other old men watched him in silence. It was exactly as it had always been when they had looked to him in the Council of the Finest Men. When there was a difficult problem to solve and no one knew how to decide the issue, there was nothing to do but wait for the word of Ivan Ivanovich.

Meanwhile the women—the wives, the widows, and the eligible maidens—sang with all their might:

> Fly, Cossack, fly like an arrow
> Through mountains and forests.
> My love is already with you,
> And I will always wait for you . . .

They had already set up planks and boards as tables for the common dinner and were now mixing clay with their bare feet. They were cooking mutton in copper kettles, tossing fresh wood chips into the fires, and arguing with the men who were using the same fires to scorch posts before setting them in the ground. There were heaps of dry kindling for the fires, fragrant and painted with resin patterns, for the men were cutting lumber without a break. When one man had cut, sawed, and chopped to the point of sweaty exhaustion, he would yield his place to another. The beams buzzed and turned at a steady pace, forming rafters, lath, foundation beams, planks, and slabs. Timbers were shortened or lengthened and joined together with tenons and dovetails.

Polovinkin had worked himself to exhaustion, but unwilling to let anyone relieve him, he trimmed one log after another. "Polovinkin," someone said, "you're surely going to break in two and fall on both sides of that log! Let another cutter take your place." But he ignored the comment and without looking up kept swinging and swinging his axe just a bit higher than his head, cutting large wedges of wood from the log, first on one side and then on the other. The men worked hard, and no one was idle. Those who had cut more in the forest than the others now worked especially hard to atone for their sins.

"That Zinka Pankratov sure sings more lively than the others," one of the old men said. Listening silently to the chopping of the men's axes and the women's singing, they were letting their thoughts wander. "And she can hit them high notes better than the others. Do you remember, gentlemen, how we took her in? She was a snot-nosed refugee, but we took her in anyway, along with her parents. Do remember, Ivan Ivanovich?"

Ivan Ivanovich nodded.

"So why is Zinka hanging around the Forest Commission now? Isn't there something going on here, gentlemen? Is there something going on here, Ivan Ivanovich?"

Without replying, Ivan Ivanovich gave a slight wave of his hand as if to say, "It's none of our business!"

Indeed, Zinaida Pankratov was singing her heart out like a bird in the sky, and always repeating the same song. One of the women would start up with "Ah, they have forgotten me, a young man in a foreign land," or "The pretty maid went to her sweetheart through the dewy green valley," or "Do you remember, do you remember, my dear?" But at the same time, "Fly, Cossack" would be heard again and again, and the voices of the women would split in two. Those who were following the Cossack would gain the upper hand, taunting the others, whose voices would gradually fall silent or trail off. The first group steadily summoned the Cossack "through mountains and forests" and other obstacles. You couldn't make out just where Zinaida Pankratov was among the crowd of women, whether she was mixing clay with her bare feet or cooking broth over the fire, her face flushed. But you could certainly hear her voice above the others.

Dinner was eaten in two shifts. Knives, forks, spoons, and bowls had been collected from houses near and far, along with all the salt and pepper that could be found. The next day many housewives would have to go searching through the village to find a pinch of salt or pepper. But everyone was too busy to think about that today.

Ivan Ivanovich Samorukov and Nikolai Levontyevich Ustinov were seated side by side in the place of honor at the end of the long table put together from planks and boards. Opposite them at the other end sat the second honored pair, the teacher and the "Co-op Man," Kalashnikov. The pre-war rules of etiquette were observed: the Finest Man was recognized, then Ustinov, as the chief foreman of the construction, then Kalashnikov, who in the past had chaired the cooperative and now headed the Forest Commission, and then the teacher, because, after all, the day was meant for her and was her personal holiday. She had crossed the unattractive and never quite clean threshold of the Lebyazhka school as a young woman. She had given her youth to it, and by now, since she was an old maid, her whole life. If the teacher could recoup some of her losses today, they needed to give her that opportunity. And so they seated her beside Kalashnikov at the foot of the table, all the more appropriate since she had at one time helped him in the cooperative by doing correspondence and keeping the books until he learned to do so himself. Looking at her now with her short gray bangs, her stern but innocent eyes behind spectacles, and her cheeks flushed with excitement, you might believe that this day really might compensate for half a lifetime, and maybe even more. Kalashnikov wanted everything to be pleasant for the teacher, so when he took out the piece of newspaper that he used to roll cigarettes, before tearing a piece of it off, he handed it to her to let her read something.

More than twenty thousand educated refugees and political émigrés have been sent from Samara to Novonikolayevsk. Among them are doctors, lawyers, and members of other professions who served in departments of the provincial and city governments, agents of public organizations, etc. Public institutions, departments of urban and rural government, and public organizations that desire to make use of this human resource are invited to inform the Provincial Commissariat about the number of individuals in each area of specialization that may find employment with them.

V. Malakhov
Provincial Commissar
V. Kondratenko
Director of the Provincial Commissariat

"Look at this," Kalashnikov said. "Here in Lebyazhka, though, we don't need anyone from outside! If they sent twenty thousand, a hundred thousand, or even a million teachers to us here in Siberia, we wouldn't trade you, our dear mentor, for any of them!"

As the teacher thanked him gratefully and blushed, Kalashnikov tore off a piece of the newspaper and passed the remainder to the others to use in the same way. Nowadays not many newspapers were printed on paper thin enough for cigarettes, and most of them used such leathery stuff that it wouldn't even ignite.

As they spooned up their food and conversed loudly with each other, all the villagers were happy. But at the same time, though their mood was merry, the topic of conversation was often far from lighthearted. Some people were joking, but others were not.

"And just how will this year of 1918 end?"

"I tell you, everything is all confused about the left and the right; about where things are done by command and where by free will; about where there is honor and where deception! Everyone understands things in the way that brings them the most good!"

"Well, so what?"

"Is that all you can say?"

"And just what is freedom exactly? I don't need to get it for free! I've had my fill of looking at it through three changes of government! Everyone does whatever strikes their fancy—they kill, rob, and spout a lot of slogans that beat on your ears like a fist! A peasant don't care about any of that. Give him the land and the forest and a few rights, and that's all he needs. It's only all those different lords who need more freedom than that. They're the only ones who're thinking up all that stuff! All in all, a man who is completely free is nothing but a wild animal!"

"All right, then try this—we'll stuff something in one of your ears, put a patch over one of your eyes, and tie up one of your arms so you can't make a free move! How would you like that?"

"Ah, boys, but what about the desire for justice?" Kalashnikov sighed loudly but gently. "There is nothing as patient as that desire. How the people have hungered for it and dreamt about it!"

"Tell us, Kalashnikov, just what is justice?"

"Justice, first and foremost, is equality! Just like there is between us right now!"

"Petro!" Fyodor Obechkin, a former sailor in the Amur fleet, began to laugh loudly and to shout over the voices of several people. "There's no sense in your talk of equality! It doesn't exist and never will! Everyone who is below the waterline hollers about it in envy of those above! If you manage to climb up onto the bridge, you won't have any more reason to shout, and you'll forget all about equality! It all comes down to one person wanting to trade places with another!"

"That's not true, not true, Comrade Obechkin!" shouted Kalashnikov just as loudly. "Man was given a brain and his senses, and if he doesn't have the strength to use them for equality, then what good are they? Only for oppressing other people?"

"I'll tell you what they're good for—all the easier to topple each other from above to below! Because nothing can be above unless something is below, just like there can't be a ship without a waterline!"

"So, Obechkin, you're saying that equality never existed, is that right? And in your opinion it never can?"

"There's only one way you can reach it—by a change in command! Let whoever was on top go down below, whether he wants to or not! Let him wait for his chance to use his wits to come out on top again!"

"It's thanks to people like you that a revolution dies, Obechkin! Some make it, others destroy it!"

"You're right! Someone will pinch the Revolution, maybe they've pinched it already. If not the capitalists, then our own side will think up something."

"Is that what you have to say about higher justice?"

"Yes! Will justice remain untouched when it's human nature to swipe even a copper five-kopeck piece? Never! It's a tasty little morsel! You think people will walk around it licking their lips and not touch it? Ha! They'll swipe it in the middle of the night or even in broad daylight! If things were any different, then life would have found justice a long time ago! They'll steal it or pay too much for it. The other day I read in the Kadet newspaper* that 'the Revolution means working less but receiving more!' "

"On the contrary, Obechkin, the Revolution is a great uprising of the spirit and the spontaneous action of the people! Just like it is with us this very minute in Lebyazhka! Are you a Kadet then?"

"What has that got to do with me? I'm a farmer without any political party and nothing more! I don't want war—what kind of a Kadet would I be?"

---

*Organ of the "People's Freedom" party, known also as the Constitutional Democrats ("Kadets," from the Russian initials KD), who advocated a constitutional monarchy for Russia.

"You don't want war, but you also expect some benefit from a civil war in Russia. If the Russian peasants and Soviet power stand their ground and don't give the land back to the landowners, then we in Siberia will get rent relief on our land, and we will put the squeeze on these little Cossacks with their allotments of hundreds of desyatinas. You surely understand this much about Soviet power and the Bolsheviks!"

"As everyone else understands, so do I, a farmer without any political party! When some power is on top, why shouldn't I, a farmer without a party, support it?"

"Eh-h-h . . . ," Samorukov said quietly, leaning toward Ustinov. "Everyone talks about life! They've learned to talk about it with a passion! Two years ago there had never been such talk among the men! But now everyone talks about life endlessly, day and night, drunk or sober. But all the same, no one knows how to live . . . No one knows how to live, Nikola. No one wants to live the way it was before, but no one knows how it will be in the future! And why isn't Sevka Kupriyanov here with us on a day like today?"

"No, he isn't here, Ivan Ivanovich. I noticed that. He feels insulted . . . "

"And Grishka Sukhikh is not here either!"

"Him neither."

"There are many who are not here. Kudeyar, for example . . . "

"That's all right. All he knows how to do is to proclaim the end of the world."

"Smirnovsky isn't here, Rodion Gavrilovich Smirnovsky."

"It is a pity he isn't here, even if he is too much of a military man. He never seems to have the time for any sort of public business. Well, so what if they aren't here, Ivan Ivanovich? It means they don't want to be here. If only the work weren't here either!"

"It also means that there is never a time when everyone is completely together even in one little thing, Ustinov. If only just once it could be like it is in a fairy tale, all for one and one for all. No, people don't know how to live with each other! Fight with each other—now that they know how to do! All of us sitting here at this long table making speeches are maybe closer to civil war and murdering each other than we are to the equality and brotherhood we are talking about all the time! It's real bad, Nikola, that so many didn't want to come here. That's not the way it was before. Before, if it was said, 'let's all come together as one,' then all would have come, and those too sick to walk would have crawled on all fours."

Ustinov said nothing.

Deryabin, however, who was sitting nearby and had heard Ivan Ivanovich, said, "But we will get by, Citizen Samorukov, without those who aren't here now and who always turned away from the people. And even without those who make a show of being for the people but really do everything against them and pull the wool over their eyes!"

"Just how do you think you will get by without them?" Ivan Ivanovich asked Deryabin. "If there weren't any of them at all in our Lebyazhka, then I could understand. But what if there are, what if they do exist?"

"That's what war is for, to decide once and for all any questions or disagreements between people!"

"You, Citizen Deryabin, always did know what to do and how to do it. Others would think it over, rack their brains, but with you it's 'one, two,' and you're ready, you've got it all figured out!"

"A man is a man and not some kind of animal exactly because he should know what needs to be done and how to do it, how to bend life to his own liking!"

"I understand," Ivan Ivanovich agreed, "but, Citizen Deryabin, I haven't noticed the kind of order there should be in your garden, house, and field if you always know the right way to do things."

"That's so," Deryabin agreed. "But there is order in Grishka Sukhikh's garden, and so in your opinion Grishka Sukhikh does everything correctly, right? He's an expert, right? That exploiter and bourgeois?"

"You're both against society," Ivan Ivanovich sighed, "only from different directions!"

In the middle of the table where many of the women were sitting, they had begun to tell stories. The folktales of Lebyazhka were unique. They were told in different ways, both with laughter and sadness. They had their own authentic history that began back in the time when two groups of immigrants, the Kerzhak Old Believers and some other people from near Vyatka who were then called the Poluvyatsky folk, that is, "half-Vyatsky," clashed with one another on the knoll between the lake and the forest where Lebyazhka now stood.

The Kerzhaks had the greater right to the land because they had camped on the knoll and had planted and harvested a crop, but that was only a temporary halt in their journey. It was not to that place that the Elder Lavrenty was leading them away from the German Empress,* but into the far and distant land beyond the Baikal Sea. And so after they had brought in the harvest there, they continued eastward. But in the East, beyond the Baikal Sea, something happened: they disagreed and broke up into two groups. Some remained in that empty wilderness beyond Baikal, but another Elder, Samsony Krivoi, led a smaller group back to the place from which they had come. He brought them to that place where they had once sown their crop, that place that had been imprinted in the minds of many of them like a picture: the knoll of green grass, the deep lake, the blue forest, and beyond that, the endless stretch of rich and

---

*Catherine II, Empress of Russia 1762–1796, was born a minor German princess.

virgin fields. Although this picture was not an icon, it was like an image of Christ.

It took Samsony Krivoi almost a year to lead his flock of more than twenty families back to this holy image. The whole way he was devoutly atoning with prayer for the sin he had taken upon his soul, for his schism with the great Elder Lavrenty. Because of this sin and despair, the road back was even more difficult than the eastward road had been. The settlers walked from dawn to dusk, but sleep eluded them in the darkness, and, following Samsony's example, they whispered prayers of repentance. All those who were weak in body or spirit died, but those who survived reached that promised land, that green knoll between the lake and the forest. The cold weather was just beginning, but they didn't even have a proper supply of food for the winter. And when they got there, they couldn't believe their eyes: smoke from the chimneys of houses was already drifting into the sky above the green knoll, and the houses were not poor and ramshackle but solidly built. On one house there was even a merry carved rooster, showing off so much that it all but crowed. These were the homes of the Poluvyatsky folk, also about twenty families.

"Get out of here!" the Kerzhaks demanded. "This land is ours! We turned the first furrow here, we sowed the first seed. Get out, or we'll burn you out! We'll kill you!" To show that they meant business, they burned the two nearest houses. "That's what we'll do to your whole village!"

But the Poluvyatsky folk could not abandon their new households and go off into the winter either. That would have meant death for them, too. "It's true that you are stronger than we are," they told the Kerzhak camp. "You have more men than we do. But we have six maidens, six brides—why don't we intermarry? We'll join our families. Kinfolk will not feel crowded—there is always more than enough room for relatives!"

"Oh, you blasphemers!" the Kerzhaks shouted from their camp. "You want our lads to take on your three-fingered whores? Would you have us sow the seeds of the anti-Christ, of shame and dishonor in the human soul, and insult the true faith again and again? Would you have our lads suffer the curse of all true believers? We'll kill you! We'll burn you all like we've already burned the two houses of the anti-Christ! This is Siberia; the authorities are far away, and there is no one for you to complain to!"

"Well then, burn us!" the Poluvyatsky folk answered. "Kill us! Then you can live on without women or maidens, without families or descendants! Reduce us to ashes and yourselves with us! How will you live without maidens, how will you multiply? When can you expect any other new people to arrive?" Then and there on the knoll, they brought out their six maidens to show the Kerzhaks and to boast, "Just try and find maidens such as these in the whole wide world! But even if you don't want to be our relatives, you can still stay for the winter—we'll feed you!"

The Kerzhaks had nowhere else to go, so they dug sod houses into the other side of the knoll and stayed for the winter, but they never ceased cursing and threatening. "You can burn your maidens alive, burn your whores, burn them in flames of fire!"

But in spite of these violent protests, that winter and spring the Poluvyatsky maidens accomplished more among the Old Believers than the German Empress herself could have. They married the Kerzhak lads and mixed the two-fingered cross with the three-fingered cross. The days of the Kerzhak-Poluvyatsky village of Lebyazhka were counted from that winter, as were the laws and traditions that ruled its existence on that green knoll between the lake and the forest.

The first tradition was that all the newborn females of the village were named only after those celebrated and almost saintly maidens: Ksenia, Domna, Natalya, Yelena, Anna, and Yelizaveta. There were also six tales about how these maidens had tempted and married the Kerzhak lads. The tales were told in various versions—one might be only for men, while others were reverent, merry, or mournful. Because people told them as they knew how or as the spirit moved them, there was no end to the tales, and no one in Lebyazhka ever grew tired of telling them or hearing them.

The tale about the maiden Lizaveta was being told now at the table. There had been a lot of noisy arguing about who was to tell the tale. If a woman told it, the tale would be intelligible to everyone and fit for everyone's ears, but if a man were to tell it, there would be no guarantee of that. As the women won out, the tale would be told "with the eye," that is, in this way . . .

▲▲▲

The maiden Lizaveta did not have to be the first one to wed a Kerzhak. Three of her girlfriends had already run across to the Kerzhak side—a path had been trampled out there and back again—or had found their husbands in their own parents' homes. But although Ilyukha, the Kerzhak lad who had been found for Lizaveta, was handsome enough, he had only one eye.

"I won't marry him!" Lizaveta kicked up a fuss. "I won't marry that one-eye even if you torture me and kill me! I'm just as good as the other maidens!"

And she really was every bit as good as the other maidens. If you thought about it, she was even better. Such stubbornness benefited those on the Kerzhak side still hiding their lads from the Poluvyatsky maidens, but this time it seemed the Kerzhaks' pride got the better of them.

"So, that's how it is, is it? If one of your six takes a liking to one of our lads, then you want him here and now, but if one of ours wants to have one of yours, she won't even look at him? We will never agree!"

"But your groom is one-eyed," the Poluvyatsky folk answered. "No matter how you look at it, she's fit as a fiddle, with everything in its proper place, but your lad has only one eye! So don't tell us he's such a good catch!"

"Well, so what? Our finest man, our Elder, with whom we returned to this our former rightful land, is also one-eyed! That's his name—Samsony Krivoi, Samsony the One-eyed! He's fallen ill now."

"A maiden could marry a one-eyed Elder, but a one-eyed youth won't do. A young man will live for a long time!"

"Oh, you mischief-makers, oh, you blasphemers, you tribe of anti-Christs! Stay away from us!"

"You're wasting your time. A holy Elder could be completely blind, it would even be fitting. But then Elders don't go out as grooms to court the maidens!"

Hearing this discussion, the maiden Lizaveta stood fast and threatened, "If you give me away to the one-eye, I'll take a rolling pin and knock out the one eye he's got left! Then let them kill me, I'm not the least bit afraid!" That's the sort of maiden she was.

But Ilyukha also stood his ground and insisted, "This is the maiden who is dear to me, and no other! I wouldn't look at another even if I had three eyes!"

At this point someone—from the Poluvyatsky side, it seems—gave him some advice: "Don't dawdle, Ilya—run off to the Altai Mountains. A master craftsman lives there, Yerokha they call him, who goes around in a red hat and a green sash even on workdays. He makes jewelry from precious stones for the neck and hands of the Queen Empress herself. And when the queens of different kingdoms get together for a name-day party, they brag to each other. 'Look here, sister,' says one to the other, 'see what a sparkling necklace I am wearing, and what a gem I have on my right hand!' 'No,' replies the other one, 'you take a look at what a belt buckle I have here on my belly, and then I'll take a look at your pretty things!' The queens keep on bragging and squabbling so much they'll probably be enemies all their lives and on into their graves. But that doesn't have anything to do with you, Ilyukha. You just run off by yourself to the Altai Mountains and ask Master Yerokha to make you an eye out of a stone!"

Fine, if that's the way it is. Ilyukha didn't dawdle and ran off to the Altai Mountains. After running for a week, and then a few days more, he came to two huge mountains. Between the mountains he saw with his one good eye a deep millpond, its foaming water rushing onto a mill wheel three sazhens wide, turning various grindstones in a factory where craftsmen were polishing stones of great value.

They wouldn't allow Ilyukha into the factory, but after they had let him peek through the window, he went into the factory town to ask where

Master Yerokha's house was. But he didn't even have to ask, because there it was, standing in the middle of town, with six windows and an iron roof. They wouldn't let him in there either. Flanking Yerokha's gate were two guardhouses with two soldiers armed with rifles and bayonets, and two other, smaller guardhouses with two sharp-toothed dogs. The soldiers were guarding Yerokha so he wouldn't accidentally run away, and the dogs were guarding the soldiers so they wouldn't desert their post. Fine, if that's the way it is.

Waiting for the Master to come out of the house to go to the factory, Ilyukha said to the soldiers, "It seems that the Master is not free then, if you're guarding him."

"What do you mean?" the soldiers asked. "He's free. We're here just in case. For the sake of order. And because it's our job."

Ilyukha waited and waited, and then he asked the soldiers, "When will the Master leave for the factory today?"

"It won't be soon today," they answered. "Today is Monday!"

"Well, so what if it is Monday?"

"That means that yesterday was Sunday!"

Ilyukha the Kerzhak, who neither smoked nor drank, of course didn't understand that the Master might be quite hung over on the morning after his only day off. He waited some more, and finally it happened: the two dogs marched back and forth from left to right, the two soldiers marched back and forth from right to left, and in the middle came Master Yerokha, a bit short and wearing a red hat and a green sash.

Without wasting any time thinking, Ilyukha plopped himself down at Yerokha's feet and begged, "Pity my bitter fate, Master Craftsman! I need an eye something fierce. Even a stone one would be fine, as long as it's skillfully made!"

"Get up and stand straight, lad," the Master answered, "and don't hide your one eye by looking at the ground. Look up at the sky with it!"

Ilyukha got up on his feet and looked at the sun without blinking.

"Now," the Master instructed him, "stand still and look at your right shoulder without turning your head.

Ilyukha looked.

"Now try your luck—look at your left shoulder!"

Ilyukha didn't have a left eye and had never seen his left shoulder, but all the same, he gave it a try.

"All right, now look straight at me!"

Ilyukha goggled at the Master and held his breath—his moment had come.

The Master heaved a sigh, chewed his lips, and stroked his mustache. Then forming a tube with his cupped palms, he took one last look at Ilyukha through it and said, "Well, I'll make your eye for you if you're of a mind to get married. There's a little brown stone in my cache that will do the job."

Dumbfounded, Ilyukha asked, "How do you know about me getting married, Master Craftsman?"

"I just know," he answered. "I forgot to ask, what's your name?"

"I'm Ilyukha, Ilyukha Prokopyevich, devoted to God, and your obedient servant! But how can I serve you, how can I show my thanks?"

"Here's how: in three days, a little after this hour, come to my house to try on your new acquisition. You'll bring me a good-sized bundle of boubliki,* a box of Chinese tea, and in both your pockets you'll have something a little stronger, in glass bottles. And then we'll fit you with your new eye. Do you understand?"

"I would be happy to," Ilyukha said to the Master. "I would be more than happy, but I have a problem: I cross myself with two fingers. I'm of the old faith and don't partake of liquor or even Chinese tea!"

"I have a problem, too," Yerokha the Master said sadly. "I can't do it either. My supply of stones, assigned to me through the generosity of Our Little Mother, the Tsarina, is committed for the next eight and a half years, so I really can't do anything for you. There's no way! But if you bring me something to sprinkle on the work, I'll know what to do with it, and, God willing, I'll take care of your share, too! I could manage it then!"

"You're not allowed to do that, Master!" the soldiers interrupted. "And since it's not allowed, we won't let any guests enter your house! It's against the rules!"

"In that case," said Yerokha the Master, "get the same provisions for my guards. Then would it be allowed, dear soldiers?"

"Then it would be possible!" they agreed. "But our dogs would bark too much!"

"Well then, Ilyukha, you'll bring each of the dogs about three pounds of meat," the Master suggested. "Will they bark then?"

"They won't bark then!" the soldiers assured him.

So settling his red hat on his head and his green sash on his belly, the Master set out for the factory to fill Ilyukha's order. And as for the new brooch for the Tsarina—he told his boss that it wasn't coming along too well, that it had been begun with the wrong kind of stone.

Fine, if that's the way it is. So some time later Ilyukha returned home, that is, to what is now the village of Lebyazhka. His father, who was sitting on the sleeping bench above the ramshackle stove, fell flat on the floor, crying, "Lord save and preserve me, am I dreaming?" He called out to his old woman, and, crossing themselves with two fingers for all they were worth,

---

*Doughnut shaped, slightly sweet bread rolls.

they asked, "Can it be that you can see through that second eye of yours, my son?"

"Maybe I can even see through it!" Ilyukha answered his parents. "I don't even know myself now which eye is blind and which sees everything! So, Mother and Father, there is no time to waste—let's all go to my bride's house, to my dear little Liza!"

"Wait a minute now, Ilya!" his parents said. "Maybe you're not used to having two eyes and aren't seeing straight, and that's why you're in such a hurry to take a wife of the new faith, a maiden you've come across by chance! Don't rejoice, don't be merry, don't try for more than the one true God has given you! Beware of anything in excess of that, for all excess is fornication and is against our God!"

"No," Ilyukha answered, "the great Master didn't make me my eye for me to shut it and not use it to see everything around me! Where is my little bride?"

And then there she was herself—dissolved in tears, she had come running to Ilyukha's house. "I was scared to death, my dear Ilyukha, when you ran off to the Altai Mountains after your eye! I was afraid you would perish in some faraway foreign land. I blamed myself. Things would have been fine the way they were—two people with three eyes between them can live as good as anyone else!"

The wedding was soon arranged. And at that wedding the Kerzhak Ilyukha drank Chinese tea. And the young husband had a sip not only of golden tea but of the other stuff as well. All the wedding guests saw that he and Master Yerokha had made a good job of fitting his new acquisition. Children resulted from the marriage—one, then another, then a third, and then more. And that's how the family name of Glazkov, from the word *glaz*, or "eye," came about in Lebyazhka.

Fine, if that's the way it is.

▲▲▲

That was how the tale went, and it sat well with the company at the table that day. The story was about a master craftsman, and more than half of those at the table were craftsmen—carpenters, joiners, stove-setters. They sat and listened, pleased and chuckling. It was also a good thing the tale had been told "with the eye." It was also well known in another variant, "with the bellybutton," in which it was told how the Master had made Ilyukha a bellybutton from a stone, and how this article had been of service to him in life, both at home in Lebyazhka and in his later travels. But that would have been a purely masculine narration. Perhaps this version, too, was true, for there was also a Pupkov family in Lebyazhka, from *pupok*, the word for "bellybutton." As they say, "Fine, if that's the way it is."

Many people were fond of the tale, Ivan Ivanovich most of all. It was

Domna, Nikolai Ustinov's wife, who had told the story this time. Although the women had banded together to shout down the men and had won their way, their unity had ended right there, for they had begun to disagree with each other. Some loudly insisted that Zinaida Pankratov should tell the story of the maiden Lizaveta, while others wanted Domna Ustinov. Zinaida had been the leader of the singing that had gone on endlessly all day, and the women wouldn't let her be the storyteller.

"Why is it always Zinka? Does the world begin and end with her that she is to sing and tell stories, too? Let Domna tell the tale!"

"Why me?" Domna had demurred at first. "No, Zinaida tells it better than I do!"

But then she took up the story after all. She had an ever so slightly husky voice, so when she had to speak the part of a man, Ilyukha or Master Yerokha, it was even more interesting than when she spoke the part of the maiden Lizaveta. Domna's high-cheekboned face had a slightly Kirghiz look, but at the same time she had the fairest complexion of all the Lebyazhka women. As she told the story, she looked attentively from one listener to another, so that each unwittingly waited for her glance.

Ustinov listened to his wife quietly and respectfully from his end of the table. What he couldn't quite hear from where he was sitting he guessed at, nodding slightly. Zinaida Pankratov, sitting just opposite Domna, was silent for the first time that day. She did not take her eyes off Domna the whole time, as if she were constantly surprised about something. The story came to an end, but she still looked at Domna in amazement.

After the storytelling, Ivan Ivanovich took heart, straightened up, smoothed his ashen gray hair, rapped on the table with his knuckles, and announced loudly, "Enough! We've sat and chatted for a bit, now that's enough! It's time to get back to work, now that we've made a start of it!"

The people got up and left the table noisily, jostling one another. After a few minutes those who had eaten had already taken up their axes and saws again, and those who had been chopping and sawing, the second shift, had sat down at the same table, hollering that it was about time that Ivan Ivanovich had chased those loafers away from the table and put things in proper order.

Ivan Ivanovich, who was close to ninety—some thought he was eighty-six, others eighty-eight—acted as if he were a young man again. He grabbed an axe and cut out a dovetail on a log six vershoks thick. It was a pleasure to see! True, after that bit of work he turned blue, and his hands began to shake, but all the same it made him happy: his eyes sparkled, and his voice came back to him, not exactly loud, but confident, and after dinner there were two men directing the others—Nikolai Ustinov and Ivan Ivanovich Samorukov.

The work continued, not exactly more quickly, but more noticeably because the support pillars were already set up underneath the school and the carpenters had begun to lay out row upon row of beams. A solid frame was growing before their eyes. There was a crowded commotion around the building.

"Whoever is not needed, clear away from here!" Ivan Ivanovich warned everyone and chased away those who were not working. "If someone gets crippled by a falling beam, it will ruin the community's day, and the new school will be jinxed, too!"

Thank God, the frame was now finished, and the carpenters and their assistants, huffing and puffing, were raising the last of the rafters onto it. But now at the height of the work, the early autumn twilight was coming. The men were still itching to lift and haul, to fit and put in place, and then to step back to see how it all had worked out and how the new structure looked. Everyone was sorry that the twilight had fallen upon them so quickly and so unexpectedly.

Terenty Lebedev got back from the veterinary at Krushikha. He came with empty hands, without his Austrian accordion. Going over to Ivan Ivanovich, he began to tell him something quietly. Ivan Ivanovich chewed his lips and told Terenty to speak up for everyone to hear. It was alarming news that Terenty brought from the postal station. It turned out that the column of White troops that had not long before passed through Lebyazhka had been pursuing a Red Army Workers' Brigade that had been retreating to the south after the fall of the Soviet government. The Whites had caught up with it and defeated it and had then punished those peasants who had let the Red Army soldiers spend the night or had given them supplies. The local kulaks had betrayed their fellow villagers . . . The Siberian government had also issued an edict on the exaction of taxes set under the Tsar. Lebyazhka was not in arrears, so it amounted to only a trifle, but still, if that was the case, then what had the Revolution been for? Or had it even taken place in Siberia? There was another bit of news: the authorities were attracting Cossack units to their side for service as punitive troops, and they were plundering the countryside of the steppe. What kind of government needs brigands? The citizens of Lebyazhka fell quiet as they listened to Terenty.

"It's as if we lived in an animal's lair and didn't know anything," Nikolai Ustinov sighed. "How long can we do without our own wisdom? Russia has Lenin, but whom do we have?"

"What does it say in your books about such difficult situations in life?" they asked him.

He often heard such questions nowadays, for indeed he was a book lover with a whole cabinet full of books in his bedroom. He always had to give the same answer: there was nothing about the current situation in his books.

For the first time that day, the men and women of Lebyazhka were quiet, as if waiting for something. Meanwhile, everything around them was changing according to the natural order of things. As the distant shore of the lake with the Krushikha bell tower disappeared, the colors began to fade from their side of the lake. Deep blue became blue-gray, the blue-gray lost its color and turned to gray, and the gray disappeared into the darkness. The lakeside meadow, long ago the pasture for the calves, gave off the strong smell of rotting hay, wood shavings, and the stew that the women had been cooking in their soot-stained kettles. The nearest trees in the forest had retreated into its depths. Darkness was flowing over the entire forest, and a noticeably warm breeze was blowing from it, redolent of pitch and mushrooms. The smells of the water, the forest, of all places near and far, of human food and life, which had been hiding away during the light of day, now thickened and began to wander about like shadows, crossing each other's paths.

The work came to a stop, but after their labor and the news they had heard from Terenty, no one wanted simply to go home. So, noisily breathing the damp, fragrant fall air, they all began to talk among themselves, some standing, others sitting on logs, on the freshly built porch of the school, and up on the last rafter of the new frame. Up there the faces of the carpenters were illuminated by the last light of day and by the expectation of what tomorrow would bring. The light played on the carpenters' axes stuck into the uppermost beam and sparkled on the hobnails in their boots.

At this expectant moment Ivan Ivanovich found it appropriate to clear his throat loudly and make a speech about the old days when the residents of Lebyazhka still remembered Samsony Krivoi's exhortation to live peacefully with each other like one family and not to sin grievously against each other.

"And just how did they manage it?" asked a woman's voice, most likely Zinaida Pankratov's.

"But it's really very simple," Ivan Ivanovich explained. "It was done the same way that we did it today, in the same spirit of cooperation. Only they gathered together for common labor on many days, not just on one day. Often they would lead the cattle away from the village together and watch them during the week. In the winter they would fish on the lake, cutting through the ice and pulling in their nets for three or four days, and then they would load the village wagons with fish for the merchants in Krushikha. Although they would sell cheap, they could manage a lot at one time and would get themselves a good supply of fish to last until spring. Petro Kalashnikov has already mentioned the tar-extraction business, and they really had one going in the early years! An artel of three or four men distilled tar and turpentine for the whole village and were well paid for it with grain. We've been talking about helping the widows and orphans as much as we can. They had that taken care of, too! In every season—winter, spring, summer and fall—there was a day for the widows, or even two or three, when the whole village worked for them. They chopped their wood, wove canvas for them, repaired their houses, and sometimes built new ones, like we did with the school today! If all that hadn't gone on, then where would our Lebyazhka of today have come from with its more than 240 households? It would have vanished forever! No one remembers how many different villages and settlements throughout Siberia have died out, burned down, or fallen into ruin and scattered in different directions. If Lebyazhka stood firm, then don't we need to remember how it used to be and how things were done?"

"Life will never again be the way it was," Deryabin interrupted Ivan Ivanovich's reminiscences. "That life has already aged to its foundations. But what will the future be like? That is the most basic and most important question! That's the question you should be trying to answer in your old age, Citizen Samorukov!"

"I'll tell you how it will be," answered Ivan Ivanovich. "Almost the whole village is gathered here now. It's already dark, but still no one is in the mood to go home. So let's stay a little longer and by agreement of the assembly gathered here decide on this: the village will finish the school down to the last nail. We'll establish a tar artel, set up a day of labor for the widows and orphans no later than a week from now, and send out men who don't drink with five or six carts of moonshine to trade for some kind of clothing for the children and sewing needles and the like for the women. And we'll keep doing the same, on and on! I don't see any other way out of our misfortunes than cooperative life! I see nothing else!"

"And who will do all this?" asked Deryabin, unconvinced. "The civil war is already right next door! It's time to concern ourselves with that, not with some widow's firewood!"

"Your Forest Commission will see to it all," said Ivan Ivanovich. "Let it justify the trust the people have put into it! And first of all, let it fight against war, Citizen Deryabin!"

"That, Citizens, is entirely beyond our powers," said Pyotr Kalashnikov from where he sat on a rafter joint. "It hasn't been many days since we were elected, but we've already made a string of mistakes that everyone knows about. Sevka Kupriyanov in particular should remember them. No, it's beyond the power of the Commission. We can't cope with it."

"What do you mean you can't cope with it? You have to! You have Nikola Ustinov in the Commission, and Petro Kalashnikov, the "Co-op Man," besides. And Polovinkin there . . . Can't you cope with it, Polovinkin?"

"But I . . . Ivan Ivanovich, I'm the least of the Commission members. My head spins from all the Commission's talk."

"You just try! Won't you?"

"How can I . . . ?"

The Lebyazhka public supported Ivan Ivanovich: "No one is asking you members of the Commission for anything beyond your strength. But do everything you can, and do it in the sweat of your brow and according to your conscience! The hopes of the community are resting on you!"

That's what the Forest Commission was told that evening. It was completely dark when the Lebyazhka folk went home, each bewildered in his own way. Some believed in the Commission, and others, not in the slightest.

Nikolai Ustinov's Speech

That night Ignashka Ignatov knocked on Ustinov's shutter and was answered by Ustinov himself, a light sleeper.

"Who's that?"

"It's me, Ignaty!"

"What do you want?"

"Come outside, Nikolai Levontyevich! Quickly!"

"Is it really necessary?"

"Yes, Nikolai Levontyevich! Is it ever!"

Ustinov pulled his boots on his bare feet, threw on a jacket, and went outside, shivering in the damp autumn cold.

"Well, is there a fire somewhere, or what?"

"It's happened, Ustinov, woodcutters are coming to the forest from the steppe. They're coming with some sort of document . . . There's a lot of them!"

"How many?"

"Maybe fifty carts, maybe eighty. Maybe a hundred, from Zhigulikha and Kalmykova Volosts!"

"Who have you already told about this, Ignaty? Who have you warned?"

"No one else . . . "

"What about the guard? Kalashnikov? Deryabin?"

Fidgeting, stamping his feet, and circling Ustinov, Ignashka explained,

"Well, Nikolai Levontyevich, I wanted to ask your advice. Should I maybe pretend that I don't know nothing either? That no one knows, and me less than anyone? You just tell me I don't know nothing, and that will be that!"

"You really are a fool, Ignaty! Is this a reliable rumor?"

"It's not a rumor at all, Nikolai Levontyevich. I know it as sure as we're standing here talking!" Ignashka stamped one foot and then the other.

"How do you know this?" Ustinov asked.

"I know, Nikola. Except for me, you and the rest of the Commission are like little children, you don't know nothing. I'm not happy about it myself, but I know everything. I have my friends, not only in Lebyazhka, but in all the other villages, too. I have friends, Nikolai Levontyevich, oh boy, a lot more than you do!"

"All right, Ignaty! Run and wake up Kalashnikov! And then go to Deryabin! And wake up any of the forest guard who live along the way. Tell them we'll meet on horseback by the new school! As soon as I get dressed and saddled up, I'll grab my rifle and be there, too."

Men from the steppe had come to the forest in previous years, not in eighty wagons, but in strings of small carts. This had in no way disturbed the Lebyazhka folk; on the contrary, it played right into their hands. While the Tsar's wardens were struggling with the steppe men, those from Lebyazhka would not waste any time. They would come in from the other end of the preserve and cut themselves a good-sized tree apiece at their leisure. The wardens could see no logic in opening action on two fronts at the same time. But those times were gone. Other times had come.

▲▲▲

The darkness of the forest was motionless and uniform, but in the darkness of the steppe, swayed here and there by the wind, something was always moving. Though the moon was not visible overhead, it illuminated the frost-covered wheat stubble and the wild grasses that had withered to their roots. Here and there the empty space of the steppe seemed to freeze into motionlessness and then to stir again. The Lebyazhka forest guard waited for some sort of sound from this movement. Finally there was the squeak of a wheel. For a long time after that, everything was quiet again, but everyone knew: they were coming!

Very soon the Lebyazhka men, bunched together at the edge of the forest, caught the fleeting sound again. Although not loud, it was distinct and clear—the rattling sound of many wheels. Rattling iron wagons freshly lubricated with tar burst into the darkness of the forest from the darkness of the steppe. Because the steppe men were coming after heavy cargo and because wooden wagons were not suitable for such a convoy, they had smeared their iron wagons with tar for all they were worth. Although they lived out on the steppe, the thrifty farmers had still managed to find enough tar to grease their wagons, though some had used up a year's supply or more. There was nothing else they could do because there were a lot of wagons that all had to travel together. That's what the Lebyazhka men figured.

After the rattle of wheels came the neighing of horses, then the stamping of hooves, and finally the sound of human voices. Deryabin rode out from the Lebyazhka side of the forest and shouted, "Sto-op!" And again: "Stop, stop! Whoa!"

In the resulting confusion, the lead horses in the invisible train of wagons stopped, but because those in the rear were still moving, they crowded up against those in front. A few men from the wagons came forward to find out what all the shouting was about.

"Who's hollering? One of our boys?"

"Did we come here to listen to some loudmouth? Go on, men, forward!"

"It's the forest guard of the people of Lebyazhka!" Deryabin announced loudly.

"Well, so what? And we're woodcutters from Zhigulikha and Kalmykova Volosts. Understand?"

"Why have you driven so far for nothing, woodcutters? And at night! Do you have a permit?"

A small fire was lit not far from the edge of the forest, and by its light an extremely tall steppe man, with a whip stuck in the top of his boot, removed his fur hat, took a document out of it, and began to read:

> This permit is hereby issued by the general assembly of the working peasantry of Zhigulikha and Kalmykova Volosts for the cutting of wood in the formerly private Lebyazhka forest, now under people's revolutionary control, in the amount of one to two large logs per two-horse wagon, depending on the size of the felled tree and the pulling strength of the horses.
>
> In order to avoid excessive cutting, three-horse teams are forbidden. Two-horse wagons in the number of eighty-seven have been considered and confirmed by the above-mentioned assembly only from working households in greatest need, and all applications and requests of those proven to be exploiters of the labor of others have been denied.
>
> The assembly therefore requests that no obstruction be presented to the owners of the indicated number of two-horse teams confirmed in the attached list of names, and that, on the contrary, all possible cooperation be accorded to them.
>
> A. P. Bodrov
> Chairman of the Assembly of
> Peasant-Workers of Zhigulikha
> and Kalmykova Volosts

While the man from the steppe read loudly and smoothly, his companions heaped more dry weeds on the fire so he could see better. After he had finished, the whole crowd from the convoy of wagons that had gathered around remained silent, expressing their respect for their reader and the document that he had made public.

No one fanned up the flames for Deryabin. He jumped down from his horse and had to crouch low by the fire. Smoothing out his own document on his knee, he began to read:

It is hereby certified that, on the legal basis of revolutionary order, the direction of the guard protecting the Lebyazhka forest, which has passed into the hands of the people, that is, the community of the village of Lebyazhka, is conferred on Lebyazhka Forest Commission Member V. S. Deryabin.

To this end the following rights are granted to him:

a) the inspection of the forest guard militia in all matters;

b) the imposition of fines and other penalties for unauthorized woodcutting;

c) the utilization of all armed personnel of the forest guard for the purpose of opposing the cutting of timber other than by permit issued by the Forest Commission;

d) the mobilization, with the approval of the Forest Commission, of the entire male population of the Lebyazhka community for the protection of the forest.

signed, P. Kalashnikov,
Chairman of the Lebyazhka Forest
. Commission

Having listened to Deryabin's rather quiet reading, several of the steppe men went into the forest to find out if the guard really was there or if the others were trying to frighten and trick them.

Deryabin guessed the purpose of the scouts and shouted out, as if giving a command, "Guardsmen! Given the current situation, you are to let no one into the forest, whether on horseback or even unarmed and on foot!"

At the edge of the forest, there was the clatter of the bolts of sawed-off shotguns, and men on horseback suddenly showed themselves. The steppe men stopped as if stumbling over their own shadows.

"What an outrage! Are the Lebyazhka men masters of the forest? First the Tsar was master, and now them? That's a fine thing! Now you understand who we made the Revolution for in '17!"

Other voices joined in.

"If they're the people and own the people's property, then who are we?"

"So the forest Siberians get the Tsar's property, but we from the steppe are to be treated like lice, to kill or let go as they like?!"

"Come on, boys! Let's force our way into the forest right now! Let the Lebyazhka men take a shot, just let them try!"

"And we *will* try!" they shouted back from the forest. "We've tied our own hands and won't allow each other to cut a single tree. We've been taking care of this forest all our lives, then you come along and see what happens!"

"Men of Zhigulikha and Kalmykova! Can the Lebyazhka people scare away two whole volosts? Are we to leave empty-handed just as we came?"

"Everyone can do what they want, but I'm going into the forest, and that's all there is to it! Just let the Lebyazhka men fire at peasant-workers. We'll see what all the other villages will do to them! Who's bold enough? Who's with me?"

Leading his horse by the reins, Deryabin approached the forest and also commanded, "Shoot at the people only as a last resort! Shoot at the horses first!"

The steppe men, now already quite close to the dark band of the forest, stopped again, and again everything was quiet on both sides. But this was the last moment of silence, and it did not last long. Someone from the steppe side shouted out, "G'yup, Ryzhka! G'yup, now! Let these Lebyazhka bourgeoisie shoot you or me! We'll die for justice! Or have I driven you for a hundred versts for nothing?" And yet another person drove his horse from the already brightening steppe into the still-dark forest.

"We have our leaders, too!" the Lebyazhka men shouted back. "How many times have we saved this forest from fire—where were you then? Now we take care of it day and night, and once again our troubles don't concern you! You're more than ready to grab! Well then, boys, you just wait and see, you'll have yourselves to blame! We have grenades! Maybe not many, but we've found a few nice little lemons!"

"Men of Kalmykova! We're just as good as the men of Zhigulikha! Forward!"

"Think it over, lads! If you do cut wood, do you think we'll let you haul it away? When you're loaded down, those of us on horseback will tear you to shreds!"

"We threw out the Tsar, and we'll put Lebyazhka on its back! We'll burn Lebyazhka, and that's that! We didn't come unarmed either. We knew where we were going and who we might meet!"

"We Lebyazhkans aren't the first to use force. But as for everything else, you know us well!"

The wheels rattled once again, and the rumble of cursing voices had already begun.

At this moment Nikola Ustinov rode out to meet the men of the steppe. He rode up to the dying fire and raised his hand:

"Men! People! I ask all of you, from Lebyazhka and from Kalmykova and Zhigulikha Volosts: what's going on here? In a minute or two we really will begin to shoot each other with shotguns and rifles, and those who have brought grenades home from the front really will begin to throw them. We'll manage even in the darkness. That won't stop the veterans on both sides who fired at Germans and Austrians and Rumanians and Turks. Some of them did that for four years, but they survived and came home to Siberia to gladden the hearts of their fathers and mothers and wives and children. And for what? To be killed now by a shotgun blast in the gut or the heart at ten paces? By their own countrymen, by a man who has fought and been wounded just like he has? Whoever was at the front after the first change in government, even more so after the second change last October, will remember how the hearts of all the soldiers burned when the orators explained how that inhuman international war got started! They explained about the German Kaiser Wilhelm, how he ordered the Austrian Franz Josef to give an ultimatum to Serbia, after which there was no way to avoid war. Maybe you have forgotten that already? Well, then you will remember how our Tsar Nicholas II, a grown-up child, started a war with the Japanese and led whole ships full of sailors to their deaths in the Far East. And how many more regiments of Siberians and others did he send into the hills of Manchuria, simply ignoring the fact that the Japanese had offered peace negotiations how many times? But he did not profit from this experience at all, and ten years hadn't passed before he was again pushing us, the people, into a terrible slaughter!

"Do we really have no more brains and no less greed than that Tsar, whom we, the people, did away with once and for all because of his madness and endless greed?! If we have forgotten about it, is our memory then not worth a copper penny? Has our blood, poured out over the whole earth, been spilled for nothing? The Zhigulikha people live closest to us, and they know about Lebyazhka's holy fool Kudeyar, how he runs around the streets proclaiming, at the top of his voice, the end of the world and the end of the peasantry. So maybe our holy fool is right after all. Is it all of us who have laughed at him and said he was crazy who are really crazy ourselves?"

It was a dark and quiet autumn night. An owl hooted in the forest for a long time, and then other sounds were heard, the horses breathing and shifting their weight from foot to foot, the squeaking of their harnesses, the steppe men talking among themselves. There was no sound from the Lebyazhka men, hidden in their forest. At last an answer came from the steppe side, though not a very loud one.

"The Lebyazhka men are trying to fool us! We should attack! Did we come a hundred versts to hear about the Tsar one more time? It's an outrage!"

"Stop, boys! This Lebyazhka man is right. It's Nikola Ustinov, that's who! I recognize him!"

"And who's that yapping 'he's right'? There's no reason to stop. Hit the Lebyazhkans and cut the wood!"

"Stop, people!" Ustinov shouted again. "Stop! You don't believe me? Well, then I'll tell you something you will believe, by God!" After pausing a moment in the new silence, Ustinov shouted out loudly, precisely, and smoothly, exactly like a military commander, "Co-ompany, re-eady arms! Forward against the Lebyazhkans, charge! Forward, to victory against the Lebyazhka men, cha-arge!"

The men and the horses listened for what would come next, but nothing happened.

"Well, how long do I have to yell orders at you?" Ustinov demanded.

The steppe men hesitated. They couldn't throw themselves at the Lebyazhkans at the command of a Lebyazhkan! They had had their fill of this command to "charge!" in the war and had cursed it long since. It would have been altogether different if Ustinov had cried, "Shoot, boys! Don't just stand there, shoot! Don't be afraid, go to it!" But Ustinov had known what to do . . .

After a little while the wagons began to move slowly along the outer edge of the forest, searching for some other place where they could more easily turn into the wood without running into the Lebyazhkans and that damned peasant Nikolai Ustinov. But there was no such place and couldn't be, for the Lebyazhka patrol moved with them and never took its eyes off the string of wagons.

The eighty-seven wagons with their two-horse teams moved along the edge of the forest more and more calmly, singly and in clumps of two or three. The eighty-seventh team was pulling a large barrel of water. When the steppe men had prepared for their journey, they had figured that they might find themselves without water in the forest in the middle of the hurried and hot work of felling trees, so they had brought their own supply. Now this water barrel was being jounced around the steppe for nothing, and it was long since time to empty it. Before the train of wagons made its final turn back into the steppe, a horseman detached himself from the group and rode up close to the edge of the forest.

"Lebyazhkans! Siberian Kerzhak kulaks!" he shouted through his cupped hands. "You don't have much time left—the score will soon be settled with all the kulaks and bourgeoisie in the whole world. Just see what happens to you then! It won't be long!"

Deryabin's temper flared, and, wanting to fire into the air, he put his shotgun to his shoulder.

"What are you doing, Vasily?" Kalashnikov stopped him. "Why do you have to shoot, even if it's just into the air? Haven't we managed to get by without a single shot being fired?" Then, riding forward out of the forest, Kalashnikov shouted, "Citizens of the steppe, don't swear at us! Don't call us names! We are always ready to talk sense with you! You can be sure of that even now!"

The steppe man made a few more threats, then turned his saddleless horse around and galloped off with his legs stretched out wide on either side. The Lebyazhka forest guard felt somehow out of place and ill at ease. Whenever they were called kulaks the Lebyazhkans had always been angered, but nowadays they had even less use for this name. It made them uncomfortable. These days it was bad to have any enemies in the world, and for a kulak they were everywhere. Nowadays the word *kulak* had become the worst of all obscenities. The Lebyazhkans had driven off the steppe men, but they themselves had got the worst of the fight!

The break of day dissipated their dark thoughts and revealed the distant train of wagons one last time. They could see that the touch of the morning sun brought no joy to the men on the wagons, who sat as hunched and cold as they had before. Alternately sympathizing with the steppe men and making fun of them, the men of the Lebyazhka guard rode along the edge of the forest. The sun shone merrily for them, and they talked with each other about how they had prepared themselves for the battle in the night that had never taken place. Ignashka talked more than the others, about how he would have shot the woodcutters with his single-barreled shotgun and how he would have used its butt in hand-to-hand combat, and so on.

"You'd best drop behind a bit, Ignaty, by a verst at least, if you want to go on talking about yourself," Polovinkin finally said. "You're making my ears buzz!"

Paying no attention to Ignashka, Deryabin talked about how the forest guard should be strengthened and armed in case the woodcutters from the steppe made a new incursion. Kalashnikov, though not a very religious man, crossed himself and thanked God that they had managed to avoid bloodshed.

Ustinov rode a little to one side, deeper in the forest than the others, and wondered what would happen next. The steppe men would not give up on the forest. Sooner or later they would return, not with eighty-seven wagons, but with two hundred, and all armed. And then? There would be a real war, to say the least! War was now popping out from behind every corner. Was it time for some sort of government to appear? Maybe not a completely just one, not completely of the people, not the one for the sake of which the people had made the Revolution, but one at least capable of bringing some kind of order and protecting the forest and everything else in the Russian nation! Because it had so much more than other nations had, it required order, yes, order, lest everything be stolen and carried away. In place of great wealth there would be poverty, hauled around the empty steppe like the woodcutters' useless water barrel.

The next morning a delegation from the steppe dwellers appeared in Lebyazhka, two old men and two younger, both veterans. The old men wanted to meet with Ivan Ivanovich—the veterans, with Ustinov. It was explained to them that Lebyazhka had a Forest Commission and that they could negotiate with it, but the delegates insisted on having things their way. Kalashnikov came to Ustinov, told him about the delegation, and asked for his advice.

"This is how it should be," Ustinov said. "I'm going to keep myself away from this delegation altogether! Tell them I'm not in the village. I'm tired of all these words, Kalashnikov. I need to do something with my hands for a while now."

This was indeed the truth. When the village was still building the new school, Nikola Ustinov, aching to do some carpentry for himself, had been thinking, "If only I was working like this on my cabin out in the fields! My old cabin was built before the war and has fallen apart. There's no sense in trying to repair it, I need to build a new one! With a stove and glass windowpanes and a wood floor!" Now an opportunity had presented itself to do just that.

"That's just what I think, too!" Kalashnikov agreed. "Whenever the Kalmykova and Zhigulikha delegates pose too serious a question, we can say, 'We would be happy to give you an answer, but our Ustinov is not here to make it a unanimous decision!' "

There was yet another reason why Kalashnikov had agreed so willingly with Ustinov. Deryabin had already told the steppe men that Ustinov wasn't there, that he had gone off somewhere right after he had yelled, "Charge!"—either to Krushikha to see the veterinary or maybe to the Barsukova forest. Deryabin wanted the delegation to conduct its business with the entire Forest Commission, not just with Ustinov. Deryabin had also intended to stop the two older delegates from meeting with Ivan Ivanovich, but without asking his permission they went to Samorukov's. They were sitting with him at that moment, drinking carrot tea and Chinese tea reserved for special occasions. No one knew for sure just what they were talking about.

Ustinov was very pleased by all these circumstances. After accompanying Kalashnikov to the gate, he gathered some food and his carpentry tools, put his Danish-made plow on his wagon, and quietly rode through backyards out of the village and onto the road that led into the fields. Then he urged on his horses, stretched out more comfortably on the wagon, and began to sing, first "Oh You, My Falcons," and then the song about the Cossack who flies like an arrow through mountains and forests. When you are riding out to your field like this, that's the life!

▲▲▲

Ustinov's field cabin, homely and dilapidated, was everything to him— his house, his workshop, his church, and everything else that a man needs for life on earth. The little cabin had only one misfortune—Ustinov had spent too little time living there. Something had always gotten in the way. Before the war it had been affairs of the village community, even if only the creamery cooperative, which had elected him as inspector. And then the war with the Germans had called him away from the cabin to a foreign land, and now it was the Forest Commission! If it weren't for the cooperative and the war and the Commission, nothing could have tempted him away! He would have come home to the village once a week, on Sunday, to see his wife, Domna Alexeyevna, maybe to put things in order in the garden, and see after the livestock, the cows and sheep and other creatures, and then he would have returned again to the cabin to speak tenderly to his field. He was never really alone there, but always with his horses, and sometimes with his trusted friend Barin. That was his dog's name, Barin, or "Lord." Barin's fur coat looked exactly like a lord's—brown, with a rich white collar and white on the chest as if it were a shirt front. And from all around Ustinov's little cabin to the four corners of the earth, there were a million different things, difficult or easy, to be done—all obvious and clearcut, all requiring his skill, and all so interesting. But Ustinov had never come across any task as important as his work at the plow. What could be more important than bread?

When the surveyors had let Ustinov take a look through their instrument and through the little round lenses he had seen a little piece of the landscape, clear and sharp and turned upside down, he had been breathless with amazement, but all the same he felt just a little bit sorry for the surveyors. Though they saw the world in such a beautiful way, it was still upside down, while he saw it as it was in reality, saw it and felt it as none of them could see and feel it. That is most likely why the young stake-setters called him Nikola or even Nikolka, but the old and gray-haired engineers who had stamped around more than a few different lands in their time addressed him respectfully as Nikolai Levontyevich. Senior Surveyor Pyotr Nesterovich Kazantsev, for instance, never called him by any other name and always kept him at his side. If someone was to carry the theodolite for him, search for baseline stakes, or stretch out the surveyor's tape, it was always, "Nikolai Levontyevich, if you please, and carefully!" And Nikolai Levontyevich would take such care that his shirt would be soaked with sweat. He would not allow the least little error. Peasant and plowman, he measured again and again and as accurately as possible the land that stretched out before him.

Ustinov considered surveying just about the most learned and wondrous of all the arts. It had to be able to measure any piece of land and depict it on a map. But just the same, it was not the surveyors, but he, the peasant and plowman, who was always closer to the land, and the land was in turn closer to him than to them. Just think about how many different names and honored titles are given to the peasant: farmer, grain producer, breadwinner, tiller of the soil, steward of the land, sower and reaper. Not one of them is a name empty of meaning, simply for the sake of eloquence or useless invention. They are all accurate names, but there is yet another name for a farmer that Ustinov liked more than any—plowman! Plowing was the starting point not only for the peasantry, but for all humanity.

There are many different tasks in agricultural work. A farmer has to know how to sow, and reap, and thresh, and cut hay, and take care of the animals, and repair any number of different objects, and also cut timber. If there isn't already a proper Russian stove, then he has to know how to put together some sort of stove at least. In his lifetime he performs a multitude of labors on his land and in his farmyard. Ustinov had read in one scholarly book that the farmer performs 360 different tasks in his field and at home. But there is no more primal labor, no truer sweat and blood on the face of the earth, than the sweat and blood of the plowman, now or at any other time.

Plowing is the same for the Russian peasant as tending herds of horses on the endless steppe for the Kirghiz herdsman, the same as casting nets into the fathomless ocean for the Norwegian fisherman, the same as tracking sables for the Ostyak tribesman, the same as panning precious gold from common dirt for a prospector in any country in any part of the world. There is heavier farm work than plowing, and some that is easier but demands more skill. Plowing is right on the dividing-line between the one and the other. If it were just a little bit more difficult, many farmers would not be able to manage it; they wouldn't have the strength. If it called for just a little bit less skill, anyone who had the physical strength could plow with ease, and such a hotshot would not have to be a peasant, would not have to learn anything from the earth or know how to do anything with it.

If a young lad grew up in a peasant family and was taught from childhood to harrow and mow hay and work with horses, he would still be wet behind the ears until he could plow two or three desyatinas of land without a gap in his furrows. If you can plow, then you're a real peasant, and only then if you want can you take a wife or go to the bazaar and buy yourself a pair of shiny boots with a red lining. Then you have every right to do just that.

If you catch sight of a woman out in the fields walking behind a plow, shouting in her own woman's way at the horses, urging them on, while the horses, not understanding a thing, flick their ears, then her bitter fate will certainly put a lump in your throat and a tear in your eye. It means that she has been widowed, that her life has come to an end, that there is no help for her in the human world, that she is a woman left all alone except for the children clinging to her skirts, and that there is nothing and no one for her to lean on. If she dreams of some longed-for meeting, it can only be in the next world, for in this world she has no reason to hope.

The act of plowing is not only labor but also man's fate and lot in life. It is also nature's commandment to man, and so long as man obeys nature's commandment, he will know what human life is. But if the commandment is forgotten, man will know nothing about himself, who he is, what he is, how he came to be, or why he is here. In such uncertainty man will lose his way. Ustinov did not want to wander lost in the unknown, and surely that is why he was an excellent plowman. He didn't care that not everyone in Lebyazhka knew about his mastery and skill—*he* knew about it. Plowing came easily to him. The slab of upturned soil would lie down beautifully for him, and he made it look like simple work. Where another would lean on the plow with his whole body, it was enough for Ustinov to take this weight on one arm.

Back in 1905, the year of the disastrous war with Japan, the Lebyazhka men had begun to get rid of their old wooden plows and to buy new ones made in Denmark. But since then, because many had failed to choose an implement that was suited to their hands, their horses, and their own little piece of land, they had discarded the first of these plows that they had acquired. They weren't used to such a plow, so they couldn't use it. But Ustinov had not been in a hurry. He had spent a week at the agricultural machine and implement lot of Randrup the Dane, trying out different plows, listening to the instructor's explanations, making note of who among the peasants cut a test furrow not far from the implement lot and how they did it, and himself cutting several dozen such furrows. Only then did he announce, "This plow here will be mine!" And in fact, that was the one plow that was, by its very own, albeit metallic nature, meant for none other than Nikolai Ustinov.

Of course, the most important plowing is done in the spring. Lordy, who doesn't offer his eager help during the spring plowing, who doesn't have a special fondness for it, who doesn't hurry out to its furrows? The rook, the crow, the starling, and the field mouse hurry along the bottom of the furrow. When furry-nosed little creatures scurry around and a young hawk is already circling above a sun-maddened mouse, the plowman warns, "Look out! Don't be caught napping, little mouse!" All the livelong day the larks are intoxicated with their self-satiating song, and the wagtail sparrow first runs along behind the plowman, then flies around him and rushes ahead of his team, looking over its shoulder, fluttering its rump and tail, urging the plowman and his team on after him like a tiny little racehorse. The earthworms, bugs, and beetles fill the furrow in such swarms that you can't tell them apart from one another. There is only one kind then—the springtime kind. Only later will they all come to their senses and crawl off, each to its proper place, some deep in the earth, others near the surface of the soil. Later the plowman will also come to his senses, but at first he also feels the intoxication.

Nikolai Ustinov's grandfather, Yegory, had felt a compulsion to walk naked behind his plow, if just for an hour. Back then in that distant, still dark time, they had laughed at him, calling him Yegory the Pantless, but he didn't stop doing it.

"And what if body and soul demands it?" he would ask. "What if they don't give me no peace till I give in? What then?"

A plowman of great repute, he always took pity on the horses long before himself and told his grandson, "Ya got to work, Nikolko, same as ya sit at the table t'eat. It's the same thing, only differ'nce is when ya eat yer putting it in ya, an' when ya work yer putting it out of ya. One should be the same as t'other—work as much as ya eat! Keep eatin' as long as it goes down into yer belly, an' work so's ya got just enough strength left to pull off yer boots. Maybe not even both boots, maybe ya only have the strength to pull off one of 'em, that's even better. Then yer already a saint of a man, then ya've done as much as ya could, as much as God gave ya the strength to do, an' then there ain't a care in the world that can take a step in yer direction!"

Ustinov didn't always follow Yegory's words, but he remembered them. Plowing lends itself to remembering. What is there that you won't ponder or remember when you plow one, then another, then a hundredth, a thousandth, and, after many years, a ten-thousandth furrow? But when you make your turn you can't think with your head, only with your hands—so there won't be a gap in the rows; so you won't jerk the horses unnecessarily, but turn them smoothly, like you turn a boat with a scull; so the end of the furrow or the beginning of the next one won't be too shallow, or else instead of wheat, only gill weed will come up, rejoicing at your lack of skill; so you won't dig the plow in too deeply either and have to back it up to free it from the ground.

During the turns you see neither the nearby road nor the distant sky. You see nothing but the horses as they move to the left and to the right, pushing against each other's ribs, and you see the plow as it swings around behind the horses. You need to choose just the right moment to put it to work, so that the plowshare roots itself in the earth smoothly and quickly and to just the right depth. Every part of you is engaged during this moment of the turn. It's as if your liver and spleen, your heart in your chest, and your brain in your head also lean to one side, trying to help, showing their eagerness and ability. Use them! Look sharp!

The turn and the movement from one furrow to another are like any of life's little turnings, for it is really the same way in life—you keep plowing and plowing your furrow, and then the moment comes that calls you to turn, and it's inevitable that what was to the right of you suddenly appears on your left, and what was before you is now behind you. You make your turn, you begin a new furrow—and how the farmer loves a long furrow!— and your hands are calm now, and your heart is back in its proper place, and your head returns to normal. It's filled with thoughts, thoughts about what the harvest will be like, and what you'll get for a pood of wheat, and why the Germans were getting the best of the Russians in the war, whereas earlier it had been the other way around, or why a bird flaps its wings when it flies, but an airplane doesn't. One thought lies down right up against another like the furrows of your field. Like the soil, you are also laid bare and plowed up, turned toward the light, toward the sun, made ready to take the whole wide world into yourself.

It was fall now. There had been hoarfrost and a dusting of snow, but there had been no winter yet. It was in no hurry to come, and while the sun still warmed the ground nicely every noon, the worn-out plowed land recovered from the nighttime frost and caught its breath. Ustinov figured that in these hours he could double the summer fallow. It would be a good thing if he managed it. Tall weeds, spurge, and the ever-present goosefoot had begun to grow in the summer fallow. Now if he could cut them down and plow them under, the plowed land would be as clear for the coming year as if it had been scrubbed clean. Then it would be ready to be sown with high-quality wheat. He could do two or three strips of land now, two or three the next day, and two or three more the day after. And then he could build a new field cabin. That's what he wanted to do, what his hands and heart were aching for, and what he had been dreaming about.

Ustinov rode up to his old cabin. A windowpane was broken, and there was a rag stuffed into the hole. There were dark gaps between the log beams, and the door hung lopsided on one hinge. It was a crying shame! What kind of master did this cabin and this field have? He's a son of a bitch if he's alive, lazy and good-for-nothing, a shame to the whole peasant class, to all honest working men! Being dead could be his only excuse, or perhaps fighting far away, alongside other working men like himself, for they're the only ones who don't have the time to hang a door on a house the way it ought to be hung! But Ustinov, hale and hearty, with both arms and legs, and his head on his shoulders, had no excuse! It was a shame and a sin!

It was quiet all around. From somewhere far away, sounds drifted to Ustinov. They were audible when the breeze blew and silenced, as if forever, when the breeze died down. But nothing in this place could be hidden from Ustinov, and he immediately understood, not with his mind so much as with his ears, that somewhere to the south, far off, horses were walking in a circle, four of them most likely, driving a power train that was turning the rattling drum of a threshing machine. Women, probably two, turbaned with towels to keep the dust out of their faces and hair, were raking out the chaff and straw while the farmer, also wearing a towel, was feeding the disheveled sheaves from the platform into the drum. The main thing in threshing is to feed the sheaves in evenly so that the drum is neither overloaded nor running empty, to put the ears of wheat on the teeth, meanwhile being very careful not to thresh a finger or two together with the wheat. After the peasants began using threshing machines, there were noticeably more Siberians with fingers missing.

Well, thank God, Ustinov was finally alone! At last! At long last! Till then he had been surrounded by other people, and when there are other people around, something or other always has to be divided up with them, the forest or anything else. If two people do something together, they have to agree beforehand on how to share the task: "Look, I'll do this part here, and you do that there." Words have to be divided up—once someone has said something, the other person can't repeat the same thing—that wouldn't be right—but he can't remain silent either, so he just has to look for other words. The air has to be divided up—someone like Ignashka Ignatov will talk and breathe right into your face, and you'll have to share your space with him and take a step back. Shame of any kind also gets shared. One man lets his house go to hell until it's falling down. You would think that's his own business, that it doesn't have anything to do with anyone else, but it only seems that way. You are silently judging him, just as everyone judges you. When someone shows up, you can't help asking yourself what he is thinking about you and about what kind of farmer you are.

After Ustinov had unharnessed his horses and unloaded his plow from the wagon, he sat down for a while on a stump near his cabin to breathe in his solitude and savor it. But then—what could it be?—there was the rattle of a wagon on the same hidden field road that Ustinov had just ridden on. Who was it? Who would need to come here and why? It had to be somebody coming to fetch him. "They're calling me back to the Commission," Ustinov guessed. "Well, the damned Commission can go to the devil! I won't go back right now, come hell or high water!"

Zinaida Pankratov drove up. She stopped her piebald mare, took a look around, and mumbled a joyless greeting, "Hello, Nikolai Levontyevich!"

"Hello, Zinaida! What do you want?"

"Me? Nothing . . . "

"So why did you come?"

"No reason."

"What do you mean?"

"Nothing . . . "

"Well, be on your way then!"

"I'm not going anywhere . . . "

Her shoulders slightly slumped, her legs hanging over the edge of the seat, and her hands on her knees, Zinaida sat motionless on the wagon. She had nothing with her, neither a bag of something to eat nor a canteen of water, nothing but a riding whip. She was dressed in a homespun skirt, once dyed red but now faded, a green jacket, and a man's heavy cloth coat, unbuttoned. On her head she wore a clean, fresh, colorful flowered kerchief, not a holiday kerchief, but not an everyday one either. The face under this kerchief was also clean and fresh, almost without any wrinkles or flabbiness, neither thin nor plump, surprising for a woman of her age and the life she had led. Her labors and troubles should have put at least ten extra years on her face and covered it with wrinkles, but it was just the opposite, as if ten years had fled from her face, as if a woman in her thirties, though a pensive one with a lost expression, sat on the wagon.

"I'll tell you what, Zinka," Ustinov said. "Don't go wandering around the steppe for no good reason. Know where you're going! Or in the end your ever-so-quiet Kirill will take that whip and show you where you should go and where you shouldn't!"

"Where is he?" Zinaida asked with a sigh. "He isn't up to it!"

"Get going, Zinaida! Go on home if you have no business here!"

"I have some business . . . "

"What?"

"All of Lebyazhka is talking about nothing but Ustinov, how he made a speech to the woodcutters, how he avoided bloodshed. Everyone talks about Ustinov, but not one living soul is allowed to look at him?"

"Is that so?!" Ustinov exclaimed. "So now they're talking about my speech!"

"That's just what they're talking about."

Ustinov hurriedly hitched his horses to his plow and drove them to the part of the field that had been fallow for the summer. You wouldn't think you could even begin to plow the half-frozen soil of the stubble field, let alone with only two horses, but the Danish plow cut through the soil smartly, laying it over, crunching through the roots of gillweed, spurge, and goosefoot, and turning them under the earth. The plow worked so well in the fallow field! But somehow the pleasure and calm that Ustinov had expected when he hurried to his field were missing from this plowing. Looking in his direction and shading her eyes with her palm, Zinaida Pankratov sat for too long a time on her wagon by the cabin.

It was only just before dark, when it was time to stop working, that the wheels of her wagon rattled in the road as she left. Now the sun was setting with finality. It floated slowly along the dark slice of the horizon, sinking ever deeper, then disappeared completely, leaving a rosy effervescence in the dazzled sky.

"Sleep now, sun!" thought Ustinov. "We'll see each other again tomorrow, God willing!"

Ustinov wasn't a very strong believer in God, but you couldn't say that he didn't believe either. God had to exist, but He couldn't be as important as the priests said He was. The sun, for instance, always seemed more important to Ustinov—everything alive came from it, and maybe everything dead as well. Of course, at some time God could have set the sun ablaze, but that was such a long time ago that everyone had forgotten about it, including God Himself, and now He, like every other living soul, warmed Himself in the sun, rejoiced in it, and was thankful for its heat and light. It was another matter entirely that He rejoiced in His own way, as God does.

That's the way it was. But Ustinov had not the slightest desire to think of God as the biggest boss of all, let alone the strictest. More likely than not, God was a peasant. What else could He be? Not some factory worker amid the smoke and soot, not some high official with a cockaded hat, not some potbellied merchant, not a priest or a monk! More than anyone else, monks and priests were inclined to words and prayers, and not at all to deeds, whereas God had created the whole wide world! No one could be more involved with that turning of the first furrow, that first primal, human labor, than God. No matter how you figured it, He should look more like a peasant, like a plowman, than anything else. So Ustinov was happy to bless the sun with the sign of the cross on behalf of God as well as himself, as a favor to the sun as well as himself. It was always a pleasure to do someone a good turn! God had made today and tomorrow, then suggested, "Now you do something good for me!" It was a joy to think over and over again about how much had been created—the sun, the earth, and every sort of living thing. There wasn't much left to do, only to bring order and understanding to all this life. Was that so much, compared to what had been done already? It was nothing at all! If so, then it just had to be done, the millstone had to be repaired and any confusion ground into clarity, war into peace, lawlessness into strict but just law.

And so she wouldn't stir up trouble for herself or anyone else, someone had to stop Zinaida Pankratov from wandering about on the steppe on her piebald mare.

The Visit of Grishka Sukhikh

Ustinov had three horses, Grunya, Solovko, and Morkoshka. The mare Grunya was already getting on in years and worked in the fields only in the busiest parts of the spring and fall. As for all women, there was more work for her at home than in the fields. She fetched water from the lake, firewood from the forest, and hay from the meadow, and knew all about going to the market in Krushikha. You could leave her with the wagon in the market all day, and she wouldn't budge. She wouldn't go wandering off if her master went somewhere.

Solovko was the plow horse. He didn't know anything but work and wasn't interested in anything else. If you didn't work him for a couple of days and didn't give him a touch of the whip for good measure, he didn't know what to do with himself. He would just lie there and heave a tearful sigh or pace back and forth in the yard, languishing, or stamp his feet impatiently—he needed to be going somewhere and pulling some load. All he had to do was catch sight of his collar, and he would stick his head through it willingly, smacking his lips with pleasure. If you harnessed him up and hitched him to a well-loaded wagon, he would pull it steadily, neither too slowly nor too fast, at the same pace from beginning to end, even if it were for thirty versts, without turning his head. "He's not a horse," Ustinov's neighbors would say, "he's pure gold!" But it was not this horse that was dearer than gold to Ustinov, but another, the gelding he called Morkoshka.

Though a gelding, Morkoshka still pranced like a smart young stallion. His name came from the Russian word for "carrot"—his one great passion in life was to jump the fence of his master's or the neighbor's vegetable garden and pull up carrots. Of course, just about any horse loves that vegetable, but Morkoshka was ready to sell his soul for it. He was diligent and quick-witted, a good worker, but Ustinov kept thinking that maybe he should get rid of him. Surely sooner or later some Gypsy would steal him away—he would just show him a carrot, and Morkoshka would follow him like a puppy. Later the Gypsy would throw his hat on the ground and swear up and down that he was not to blame, that the horse just followed him, and he couldn't shake him off! That is, if they caught the Gypsy. But what if they didn't catch him? Wouldn't it be better just to let such a hopeless case go beforehand, just to be rid of it?

But then something peculiar happened. Ustinov had been plowing with Morkoshka and Solovko. Solovko, the golden horse, pulled the plow evenly and smoothly. Although the plowman sees his horse only from behind, Ustinov nevertheless knew what Solovko looked like as he pulled. His eyes would be closed, his lower lip hanging down, the muscles on his chest bunching and relaxing rhythmically, right-left, right-left, like a pendulum. Ustinov could only guess how Morkoshka was behaving with his teammate. Probably he was looking from side to side, sniffing at something like a dog, and while he was preoccupied with distractions, his traces would alternately be pulled taut as a string or sag till they nearly touched the ground. And if someone out on the steppe rode by within a verst of him, Morkoshka wouldn't miss it and would turn his noggin toward the sound to ask: "Who's there? My master won't let me go, so why don't you come on over here and say hello?" And then suddenly Morkoshka had stopped in his tracks as if all four legs were rooted in the earth. Ustinov had walked around the team and inspected the horses and the plow, but everything was in order. So it wasn't enough for Morkoshka to play around instead of working. Now he had decided to be stubborn too, the bastard! So Ustinov gave the loafer a good touch of the whip, first on the back, and then in the belly, too. Solovko lunged forward, his hide shivering as if he and not Morkoshka had been beaten, and Morkoshka shook his head and cried, but held his ground and wouldn't move. Ustinov gave it to him again, and again, and then even in the face. Morkoshka stood firm; he wouldn't move if you beat him to death.

Horsewhipping had not been much tolerated in Lebyazhka since the olden times—the maiden Ksenia wouldn't allow it. Ksenia was one of those half-holy "half-Vyatsky" maidens. A mute with a pockmarked face, she wasn't counted among the marriageable maidens, but she had the power to charm horses. When she moved her lips and looked at a horse with her blue eyes, that horse would not be able to move an inch. And so when three wagons full of Kerzhak schismatics decided to leave, to take their remaining eligible young men away from temptation and delusion, Ksenia charmed their horses. The horses stood still, and though the Kerzhaks began to beat them, they wouldn't take a step. The Kerzhaks beat their horses for two days and two nights, until they had beaten them to death, but the horses never moved. The Kerzhaks left the green hill between the lake and the forest on foot, leading their young men. But God punished them for killing their horses. They all became stutterers, and a sad fate befell Ksenia as well. Closing her mute blue eyes at the sight of the horses' slaughter, she died of horror. Since that time the Lebyazhka men had taken care not to beat their horses for fear of becoming stutterers, and if they did beat a horse, they would atone for the sin by lighting a candle to the sainted Ksenia in their humble little church.

Without the superstition of this fairy tale, Ustinov might have beaten Morkoshka even worse. But then he stopped to think: it couldn't be as simple as it looked! There must be a reason the horse was being so stubborn! Beginning to look for this reason, he saw something glint in the dirt just behind Morkoshka and just in front of the ploughshare. When Ustinov bent over and picked up the object, the iron tooth of a harrow, he recalled that he had lost a tooth off his own harrow some three years back. If Morkoshka hadn't stopped so stubbornly, the tooth might have fallen beneath the ploughshare and ruined it. Morkoshka had been pulling the plow along, and though his gaze was wandering, he had noticed that tooth. He hadn't understood right away what it was, but when he did—maybe he had stepped on it with a hind foot, or maybe he had just guessed—he realized that he just had to stop. Even though he had been beaten for it, he stood still.

From that day, Morkoshka was a friend, almost a brother, to Ustinov. Morkoshka was a glutton for affection and loved the caress of human hands. When you went to harness him in the morning, he would be lying mournful from head to hoof. He would open his eyes at you and heave a long sigh. "My life is over, Master . . . My soul is tormented. Where is my youth, where are the golden days of my life? Show some sympathy for me!" You would show him some sympathy, scratch him behind the ears, and he would stand on his feet. So you would harness him up and set out. After an hour or two, he would still seem to be slumbering, with no will of his own, and nothing on earth of interest to him. Then suddenly something would stir in his horse's soul, and he would give you a merry look, raise his head, his legs trembling, and begin to run excitedly down the road. And as for work, well, he would throw himself into it so much that you would have to hold him back a bit to settle the dust.

But there was one thing in which Morkoshka was consistent—his indifference toward Solovko, his eternal teammate. It wasn't any sort of enmity;

there was none of that. He would even yield his feed or his place in the sta- ble to Solovko, but while he was doing so it was as if he didn't even notice him. It was all the same to Morkoshka whether Solovko was there beside him or if he was gone for days at a time. He showed an interest in any other horse he might meet, but none at all in Solovko.

He paid more than enough attention to the dog Barin. If they were go- ing somewhere and Barin struck off to the left, Morkoshka would also bear to the left, curious to see where Barin was running off to. If Barin went galloping to the right, Morkoshka would always try to go clomping off in the same direction. If Barin started licking Morkoshka in the chops, Morkoshka would give his master a look of pure satisfaction: "See how an understanding and sincere creature treats me! Make a note of this, Ustinov!"

Ustinov did make note of it, and he pondered long and seriously about different animals, horses most of all. And sometimes when Morkoshka or Solovko would knock a leg on something or get a sore on his back, Usti- nov's own leg or back would get sore and hurt him. Now that he was back in his cabin, things felt all the more right and proper because he had missed being with his horses and working with them. Today the three of them— Ustinov, Morkoshka, and Solovko—had accomplished a lot. After all, they had doubled the size of the summer fallow!

Taking advantage of his active mood, Ustinov immediately went on to accomplish another task he hadn't thought of earlier—repairing the well. He cleaned it, deepened it, and added two rows of beams to the frame. In the morning, just as soon as it was light, he meant to begin the real car- pentry work—building a new cabin. Ustinov had prepared the lumber for this job that spring, and it was all neatly stacked, timber by timber, pro- tected on top by a cover of pine branches. From a distance or from the road it looked as if the farmer had laid in a supply of brushwood and intended to stay in his cabin till winter.

▲▲▲

The dawn was slow in coming. Since it was autumn, the sunsets came early and the dawns late. Ustinov woke and had a bite of breakfast and something hot to drink, but there still wasn't enough light to begin work- ing, so he curled up again in his bunk. Then he heard someone fumbling around by the door.

"Who's there?" he asked. Then he figured it out—who else could it be but Barin?

The door opened slightly, and there he was. All you had to do was think of him, and he appeared with ears, nose, and tail erect, but not exactly pleased. The door had stayed shut too long.

"What am I, a dog or something, to be left hanging around the door?

You could be a bit livelier, you could have gotten up and opened the door and greeted your guest!"

"All right, all right," Ustinov replied. "Why have you come to visit? Have you come to call me home?"

No, nothing had happened at home. Barin had simply come, for no particular reason.

"Well then, you're welcome to sit for a while, but don't stay too long!"

"Why are you upset with me, Master?" Barin asked. "That's a fine how-de-do! I treat you nicely, but you say bad things about me! If that's the way it is, I can go back to the village this very second!"

"Well, go then," Ustinov retorted. "You've gotten as lazy as can be. You don't keep your eye on the horses to see they don't wander too far, and it's the same with the cows!"

"Ai-ai-ai!" Barin looked at Ustinov reproachfully. "What an attitude the man has! The horses are here with you in the fields, and right now you couldn't chase the cows away from the garden with a stick. They've been given a whole pile of carrot stalks and such, and another one of cabbage leaves left over from the canning and pickling. What an attitude! Phooey! I can't even look at you!"

"But what will the two of us eat?" Ustinov asked. "There are only two loaves left in the breadbox. Am I supposed to give you one and then go home for more? Maybe you'll eat oats, Barin? Morkoshka will share his oats with you. He's a nice horse, and you two are friends anyway!"

"And he's a liar to boot!" Barin was completely insulted by now. "Isn't there mutton on ice in the root cellar? The door is blocked with a log so nobody can get at it! As if I didn't know! As if I haven't run around the cabin and taken a sniff to see what is going on here!"

"Mutton is not for you, even if you are a lord. It's for me."

"But what about the bones? You won't eat mutton bones yourself. Without me they'll go to waste, go into the ground and rot without doing anyone a bit of good. I'll find something to eat in any case, a gopher or a rabbit!" Barin took a look around the cabin and squinted. "Didn't you bring your gun, Master? That was stupid! You should have brought it so we could go after rabbits!"

"All right," Ustinov said. "I can't get the better of you in an argument. Stop it now!"

Barin went up to Ustinov, licked his hand, then licked himself, and grabbed himself at the root of his tail.

"You could at least do that somewhere else," Ustinov scolded, "not here in the middle of things."

"That's no longer any of your business," replied Barin with an annoyed look, continuing to chew on his tail. "I can do without your remarks. Build an entryway in your new cabin and hang a proper door, and then I'll know that I'm not supposed to come in any farther than that. It would be silly for me to be shy in this broken-down hut!"

Barin nipped the flea from his tail, stood up on all fours, stretched, examined his brown fur jacket with its white shirt, and shook his shoulders. To tell the truth, Ustinov had at times considered doing different things with Barin just as he had with Morkoshka. The thought had occurred to him that this brown coat with its collar and white shirtfront would do well for mittens and a hat. But he didn't think about it for long. They understood each other too well and had had too many good talks for one of them to entertain such a thought about the other for very long. But Ustinov couldn't assume the same thing about the other Lebyazhka men. It would be easy for any of them to do it, and when Barin was away from home for a day or two, Ustinov would sigh sadly and think, "Now when the cold weather comes, will I have to see who is wearing my Barin?" But Barin also knew the value of his own skin and kept a sharp eye out for it. It wasn't so easy to trick him and tempt him into a strange yard.

Ustinov had also had the idea of putting Barin on a chain and turning him into a watchdog. But because Barin had grown up to be a cheerful and, more important, a clever dog, he simply wasn't the right breed for a watchdog. What good is cleverness to a guard? He has to know only one thing, that no one is to be let in here or there, and that's all the wisdom he needs. Besides, it wasn't the custom in Lebyazhka to keep watchdogs. Grishka Sukhikh kept dogs on chains at his place, and so did the Kruglovs, but they were a particular kind of peasant. They had big operations, and because they hoped to have even bigger ones, they were protecting their future wealth in advance. But other folks didn't need it.

So Barin was as free as a bird, except that he lived on the earth rather than in the sky. For a good distance around Lebyazhka, there wasn't any place he hadn't been, sniffed around, and left his mark. That was probably the way it should be—someone unfettered and carefree had to live in close association with the peasant, the eternal laborer. But intelligence, a quick wit, and a good heart were also needed. God forbid that Barin should stupidly get in Ustinov's way. Barin, however, never caused him any problems whatsoever. For instance, Barin had never trampled the wheat in the fields while running madly after a quail and had never bothered Morkoshka while he was working. Barin didn't harvest wheat, but he knew its worth. He understood what was going on. Whenever Ustinov harnessed the horses to go to market at Krushikha, Barin would run around the yard like crazy, but when he harnessed them to go into the fields, Barin would sit quietly and seriously on the porch and keep a close eye on his master. "Did you take everything you need? Take a good look. Don't forget anything important!"

Now Barin fidgeted some more in the middle of the cabin, then lifted his head and barked in the autumn morning that, though late, had at last arrived. Sniffing the air, he barked again. This is why he had come—to warn his master that someone had been to Ustinov's house, had learned from Domna that the man of the house had gone into the fields, and had set out to find him. Barin had come, too, but much faster than the other. "The Commission?" Ustinov thought again. These days, no matter who summoned him, no matter who needed him, the first thing that came into his head was the Forest Commission. "I won't take a single step from this field till I've built my new cabin!" Ustinov repeated to himself firmly.

It was Grishka Sukhikh who had come, on horseback. He threw the reins over the frame of the well and stood for a moment, examining Ustinov's cabin attentively. Here was someone who understood its indecent appearance and the shame and dishonor of its owner!

And having understood everything, Grishka bent over, squeezed through the doorway into the cabin, and kicked Barin. "Ah, so you got here already, you spy!" He pushed Barin with his foot again and then Ustinov with his hand. That's how he greeted people. "Howdy, Nikola!"

There were days when Ustinov saw no one and talked to no one except animals. He would express his thoughts to Morkoshka and even Solovko. Solovko would listen to his master with half-closed eyes and with his lower lip hanging down, but he listened nonetheless. Though Ustinov's conversations with Barin were brief, they were still conversations, and the two of them had managed to talk about quite a bit. But now he had to speak with a human being, with Grishka Sukhikh. Barin was quiet; his eyes had become a wild beast's. He had bared his teeth when Grishka had kicked him, but without growling or barking, and laid down in the corner, with a fear in his eyes that he didn't hide. He didn't pretend that he wasn't afraid of anything, that he was just as happy as he had been before, that Grishka Sukhikh didn't have anything to do with him. Barin showed no sign of that, even though he was a past master at pretending one thing and another.

As Barin sat in his corner with his fur standing on end, Ustinov was fully aware that Barin was saying, "I'm afraid, Master, but don't imagine that I'll run away and leave you here alone! I won't! When the time comes, believe me, I'll forget my fear and everything else on earth and rush to help you! Pay no attention to the fear in my eyes. That makes me feel bad!"

"All right, all right," said Ustinov. He wanted to add, "What are you afraid of? It's just Grishka Sukhikh, wild and shaggy, but a man all the same!" But he didn't say it.

Grishka, huge, limping slightly, bending at the waist to avoid bumping his head on the beams of the ceiling, measured the cabin from corner to corner. In the tiny cabin, the huge Grishka seemed to be running around in a cage, as if he had entered not of his own free will but because he had been forced into captivity. It occurred to Ustinov that those ancient schismatics who had wandered in Siberia for so many years and who had hunted bears with spears had most likely been just as huge and shaggy. But they had been peaceful. They had defended themselves by burning themselves to death when others had persecuted them for their faith.

Grishka Sukhikh paced quickly around the cabin, stopped, and, jabbing Ustinov with a huge and hairy finger, asked, "Should I finish you off, Ustinov? In other words, Nikolai Levontyevich, should I strangle you?"

It didn't sound like much of a joke. Barin's fur stood on end even more than before as he growled in his corner.

"You be quiet," Ustinov told Barin, and then asked Grishka Sukhikh, "What for?"

"Just to be rid of you!"

"But tell me why!"

"I said, to be rid of you, Nikolai Levontyevich Ustinov, citizen of Lebyazhka!"

"I don't understand you, Grigory!"

"I'd feel better now if you weren't around, Ustinov!"

"Have I been bothering you for long?"

"Yes, for a long time now!"

"How long?"

"Twenty years! And more!"

"That's strange!"

"You can't understand, Nikola! Where you . . . No, you can't understand! And I thought that you were such a fine man! I reconciled myself to your existence. 'You just have to accept this one, this Ustinov,' I thought. 'He's not the same kind as the rest of 'em!' But what are you? You turned out to be a piss-ant! You had me fooled!"

"What am I?"

"A piss-ant!"

"And why do you see me like that, Grigory?"

"Anyone who takes a close look at you can see it! Who've you taken up with, Nikola Ustinov? Who is your friend and brother now, Nikola Ustinov? Vaska Deryabin? Ignashka Ignatov? And isn't Petya Kalashnikov, the 'Co-op Man,' even your boss now? Aren't you ashamed about any of this? It would be shameful for you even to use the same outhouse as they do!"

"I'll tell you who I feel bad about, Grigory—the kind of person who doesn't want to understand the other people around him, that's who! And besides, all of us were elected into the Commission by the whole village of Lebyazhka, and if you're against those elected by the people, then you're against everyone who elected them, too . . . "

"Of course I'm against them! How can anyone, even if it's the whole village or the whole world, decide who my comrades and friends will be? It's impossible! That's an insult! It's my own affair who I want to do business with or pass the time with, who I want to look at with my own eyes or listen to with my own ears. I'll be the one to choose them! Me, and no one else! If they shut me up in prison, they won't be asking me who I want to have there with me. But as long as I'm free, I'll choose my own friends and comrades! If I can't do that, then I'm already in that prison! If they can tie me to some piss-ant, then I'm a piss-ant myself already!"

"And just whom would you choose as your friend, Grigory Sukhikh?"

"I'd pick you, Nikola," he said quietly.

"Me?"

"You! And I'd be doing both of us a favor. I'd be freeing you from all those Ignashkas! And I'd forgive you once and for all for what you did to me. I swear it—I would forgive you!"

"I'm not guilty of anything, Grigory. I haven't committed the slightest sin against you."

"Yes, you have! And it's not a slight one, it's a big one!"

"I don't know anything about it."

"But I know. I haven't told anyone about it. I can't do that! But I know about it! And I'll forget about it only if one thing happens—if you become my friend and partner. As long as you stand apart from me, you are my enemy, and I'll blame you to the end of your days!"

"Don't look for a friend in me either—you won't find one!"

"I won't?"

"No! Our lives have gone separate ways, Grigory! You took a liking to having money and making a profit, to having your place out there by itself in the country, but I live heart and soul with the whole village. We were never friends before, but now we've parted company once and for all!"

While Ustinov sat on the edge of his bunk in the corner, Grigory paced the room, three steps forward, three steps back, then stopped and repeated his question, "I won't? And if that could mean your death?"

"Then all the more so . . . People can't be friends against their will or under the fear of death."

"It does happen, Nikola, yes, it does! You know nothing about how alliances and friendships are arranged between people. Nothing!"

"I know this much: there has never been a friendship of fear in Lebyazhka!"

"There are a lot of things that haven't happened yet in Lebyazhka, but they will! What were the olden days really like? It was a dark time, Nikola, because back then the Elders Lavrenty and Samsony Krivoi did the thinking for people. And now? Nowadays every man thinks for himself, about how to make things better for himself, how to gain more and make things easier for himself and no one else! This is the most important change! This is progress!"

"That's not so, Grigory! There has been one revolution, and then another, and for what? To stop those who have nothing on their minds but their own property! To establish equality between people at last! That's what progress really is!"

"By God, you only hear that from oddballs! Don't you see how ridiculous you are, Nikola, Nikolai Levontyevich Ustinov? Where did the revolution come from? It happened when everyone began to want at least a little bit of something for himself! Either a little bit of land, or a few more rubles! You have to start with something! Just go and tell the masses that they won't get anything from their revolution—not land, not rubles, nothing! Who would be for the revolution then? No one! They'd all say to hell with it! Any change in human life, any, has the same source—the desire for property! Just look at the animals—they don't need personal property, so they live on through the ages in exactly the same way, without changing a thing! Is that what you want, to live like an animal?"

"Like Barin here?"

"Like him!" agreed Grishka Sukhikh, glancing at the dog. Barin pricked up his ears. They were talking about him! Why? He wanted to know, but he couldn't understand a thing.

"No, Grigory," said Ustinov, "you can't look at men that way, only from their dark side. It's true you can't establish justice with an empty belly, but that doesn't make it right to put your belly higher than your head!"

"No, you can't," Sukhikh agreed. "If I put my belly in first place, I'd do nothing but feed it till it was full, no matter how much it asked for! That's the point—I still think with my head, and I understand that everything that we humans do is done in order to take things from one another. Just look at your Lebyazhka Forest Commission—isn't that exactly what it's doing? It wants to divide up the former property of the Tsar as it sees fit. Do you remember how the people went with their icons in '05,* and what the Tsar did then? He ordered them to be shot at! He was afraid that the people would demand something from him, that they would con him out of something or beg something from him in the name of Christ. When the time came, they shot the Tsar and all his children, and for what? They were afraid that if he stayed alive he'd demand that they return everything they took from him! It's all just dividing up the goods, brother! Who was first to take power away from the Tsar? The bourgeois!† And before they knew what was happening, we, people of all different kinds, toppled them and took what they had taken and all their property to boot. And now we, the farmers, have to watch out so that someone else—jailbirds, the proletar

---

*On 9 January 1905, a crowd of over 100,000 peaceful demonstrators was fired on by police and troops, with the loss of several hundred lives.

†Refers to the assumption of power by the Provisional Government.

iat, or, even worse, the Ignashka Ignatovs—don't take what is ours away from us!"

"And why do you need more than anyone else, Grigory? What good is it to you?"

"I don't need any more or any less than what is equal to my strength and my skills! I can do the work of any three men, you know I can! And since you know that, you should admit that I should, in fact, have as much as three men! There's nothing worse than being poor, and not working as hard as you are able is poverty, too. It's the same with letting your skills get rusty!"

"All right!" Ustinov conceded. "Like they say in the stories, 'Fine, if that's the way it is!' You live like you're the only one on earth, and everything seems clear to you. But you aren't alone. There are lots of other people living all around you. Do they understand your way of seeing things? Will they agree with you? And if they don't, how can you ignore them? How can you refuse to try to agree with them somehow?"

"Well, Ustinov, I have my choice! If I want to agree with people today, I will. If tomorrow I don't, then I won't. And the next day, if I feel like it, I'll be against them completely!"

"That's not honest! That's unthinkable!"

"Don't people treat me the same way? That's why they thought up that fairy tale of 'all for one, and one for all'—all the better to fool a body! But I won't pretend that I'm a friend and brother to people. People never thank someone who sacrifices himself for their sake. They'll even ridicule him and complain, 'He didn't do the right thing, he wasn't with the people all the way.' I despise a man who serves the people and doesn't want to kill anyone for his ingratitude or, at the very least, bust someone's face in!"

"We'll never become human beings that way, Grigory!"

"Right! Who needs it!"

"Don't you?"

"No, it's stupid! A human being is one thing for you, something entirely different for me. We'll never be able to agree about just what a human being is supposed to be. Ask Ignashka Ignatov, he'll say, 'Everyone should be just like me, maybe just a little different!' That's what he thinks about mankind. He always thinks he is better than you. Suppose I kill you, and then I tell Ignaty, 'Keep your mouth shut, Ignaty, or it will go bad for you!' It would be easy for him to keep his mouth shut. How could it be any other way if he is so much better than you? Why should he risk the good for the sake of the bad?"

"Who cares about Ignashka?"

"All right, let's say I kill Ignashka and then tell you if you say anything to anyone, I'll kill you, too! Well? What do you say about that?"

It grew quiet in the cabin. Barin froze in the corner, and the two men didn't move a muscle either.

"I would turn you in, Grigory. Yes, I would!"

Sukhikh felt around with his leg for the small stump that served as a stool and sat down.

"You know, anything really stupid is interesting! To give up your own life for a piece of filth like Ignashka, even after he's already dead and buried—isn't that stupid? And now isn't it curious to hear such a stupid thing coming from such a smart man?! Ver-r-ry interesting, by God! I'm obliged to your wife, Domna Alexeyevna, for not hiding anything and telling me where you were. There were a number of fools at your house. Some of the Zhigulikha and Kalmykova peasants have left already, but others are still waiting for you to come back. But I was able to find you within the hour! I'm obliged to Domna Alexeyevna for letting me have such an interesting chat with you!"

Ustinov didn't answer. He was wondering just what had happened between them and when. When had such hatred for him flared up in Grishka? And what kind of hatred could Grishka try to extinguish with friendship? "He hates me, but he wants to be friends with me for life?"

Sukhikh was of pure Kerzhak stock, while Nikolai Ustinov was of mixed blood, descended from a Kerzhak lad and the Poluvyatsky maiden named Natalya, but both men were native sons of Lebyazhka, both genuine Siberians descended from the first settlers. Accordingly, they had never quarreled or offended each other in public. It was as if they were kinfolk, or something even closer than that. In fact, they had never quarreled or offended one another at any time. When they were still lads, they had avoided being competitors and never compared their agility and marksmanship when they pushed the girls high into the sky on the swings or played babki and gorodki.* If it happened that one of them appeared at a party in a fancy velveteen shirt and new boots with shiny galoshes while the other was plainly dressed, the one would not show off in front of the other. Instead they would avoid one another, and whoever was wearing the galoshes, pretty as a picture, would put his arm around his girl and move away. Nikola Ustinov always had fancier clothes, and so that was what he had had to do. If the two lads met on the street, both were quick to doff their caps.

"Hello there, Grishukha!"

"Howdy, Nikola!"

"How's life treating you, Grishukha?"

"Not bad, Nikola!"

They would slowly go their own way, just like full-grown men. The other Lebyazhka lads took note of this custom. They very much wanted Nikolka and Grishka to get into a fight, especially since Grishka had thrashed each

---

*Traditional Russian games both involving the tossing of objects.

of them at one time or another. He was strong and quarrelsome, too, but he had never once laid a finger on Nikolka. Whenever Nikolka came to the village square or went to the village grain barn in the meadow, one of the lads would whisper in his ear, "Nikolka, Grishka Sukhikh said he's going to punch you in the nose in front of everyone! He called you all kinds of names!" They probably said exactly the same thing to Grishka. But the two of them never did become enemies. Though there was never a real friendship between them, they never laid a finger on each other or spoke a bad word about each other.

Grishka Sukhikh came from a huge family. Because they had fields in many different places, and some of the brothers had already gone out into the steppe as far as the Kirghiz lands and sown more than one desyatina there, no one knew exactly how much land they were working. But the family never prospered more than others. The Sukhikh clan plowed too hurriedly, and their seed was full of weeds and sometimes even contaminated with ergot. They harvested later than anyone else, just barely before the snow came. It was fruitless labor. When Dormidont Sukhikh, Grishka's father, died, the household fell to pieces completely. The brothers divided the property with so much fuss, uproar, and bickering that they had to call in Ivan Ivanovich Samorukov to settle their arguments.

Grishka, the youngest brother, received the smallest allotment of land and the smallest share of the property, but five or six years later he had joined the ranks of the richest of the Lebyazhka farmers. Almost immediately Grishka sprouted his shaggy fur and turned into that hardened peasant for whom there was no match in all the neighboring villages of forest and steppe. When his young wife died, Grishka moved out onto his isolated freehold and brought a new wife there from somewhere far away. His new wife never took a single step away from home and hid her face in her kerchief so that no one knew what kind of woman she was or even what her name might be. Grishka lived on his freehold like a bear in its den, leaving it only now and then to go to one railroad station or another to trade his goods or to go drinking and brawling with his friends, about whom nothing was known either. That was all that Ustinov knew about him, and he could find no reason for Grishka's enmity and hatred toward him.

Rolling a cigarette and then offering his tobacco pouch to Ustinov, Sukhikh said, "I got my hands on some Turkish stuff myself this time, not any easy thing these days!" After a pause, he added, "You're always searching for something, Ustinov! You're always looking for freedom, equality, brotherhood, and all sorts of justice, and it's always surprising that, as smart and clever as you are, every single day you walk right past the only place where all of that is to be found! You walk right by without even noticing!"

"Where is that?"

"Wherever I am—me, Grigory Sukhikh! I told you once, and I'm telling you again: let's show a little charity toward each other instead of anger! Let's have a real friendship! That's the only thing that's holy. The rest of the world is nothing but greed, fraud, and robbery! It's only in real friendship that there's no strong and weak, deceiver and deceived, lord and slave! Why were the saints saints? Because they knew how to stand up for each other! We've waited too long, Nikola, you and I. We should have started when we were kids! Let's not wait any longer—better late than never! Let's swear an oath of friendship, with blood or whatever! Well, Nikola? Don't ruin me or yourself by refusing! I can't take it! You're smart, you should understand that a friendship between two people means great freedom! The two of them are bound together by an invisible chain—that's their law and their rights, and they don't know any other laws. Friendship frees them from all others forever, and for the rest of their lives they can do whatever they want!"

"All that comes to you from the Old Believers, Grigory!" Ustinov surmised. "If you think about it, they were looking for that same kind of closed brotherhood, but they didn't find it, and they went into the fire!"

"I don't care where it comes from, Nikola! If it's in me, then it's mine! That's how I've looked at people ever since I was born!"

Sukhikh thought that Ustinov was inclined to agree with him on this last point, if only just a little, and he fidgeted on his seat, his eyes now staring intently, now closed altogether, and kept repeating his opinions.

"Nikola, don't go looking for fairness and friendship in everyone! That's stupid, and you've been doing it since you were a boy! When you look for it, look only in a single person, in Ivanov, in Petrov, or in Grigory Sukhikh! Then you might find it, though not always! I'll tell you this—two or maybe three friendships, now that's a holy miracle! There's nothing higher than that, and never was in all the ages! That's the most important thing in anyone's life, peasant's or pirate's! Just think about it: say three of us have done a bit of work, we've been at it to the last drop of strength! That's already a fine thing, you know how it is! Then we all take a rest, stare up into the sky, and listen to the birds sing in the heavens! And it's good when you're not doing something by yourself and you're living in two or three bodies at the same time, listening to the birds with six ears! Then we friends warm up around a fire, and from each other, too, and then we're ready for a little fun. That's what we feel like! So we harness up some fast horses, dress up a bit, and raise hell for a hundred versts all the way to the railroad station. We find some women, order some musicians, take a ride on a troika! And then show off a little, maybe get into a fight, break some shopkeeper's window, or find some other amusement!"

Grishka paused to catch his breath, thought a moment, and, imagining a conversation, screwed up his eyes.

"'Well, we've had enough fun, my friends! It's time we gave that a rest.' We go riding home at daybreak. The sun comes up and shines on us, we sing a song, and give a good spit at everyone else in the world! That's all the good they are to us, just to spit at! They don't know what is going on! They're all stupid, empty, and worthless! We're the only ones who live life the way it should be lived and take what we want from it! The three of us feel like one person! If one dies, then the others will follow him without blinking an eye! That's something holy for you—that's your justice, that and nothing else! And freedom! And equality! And brotherhood! It's a simple thing, but no one has what it takes to see it. We three are the only ones!"

"And if someone gets in your way, you'll kill him?"

"What do you mean? So you, Nikolai Ustinov, won't kill anyone?"

"Never! That's revolting!"

"But the war between the Reds and the Whites is starting up in our parts now. And I know that you'll be for the Reds! You'll do it for the sake of justice for the masses. And then you'll have more than one murder chalked up to your account, Ustinov! When the scale of things is that big, you won't get by without killing one or two people! No, you won't! Half the world is turning into your enemy now! Now just add it up on your fingers, which of us is the better and more righteous? And more just? I knock off one or two people who got in my way, and it's easy enough to understand because they got in my way. But you go to war with half the world and kill people who have never done anything to you and never would in their whole lives! You're a smart man—you'll kill a bunch of them before you get dropped yourself! You'll die without ever knowing justice or even that little bit of brotherhood I have with my one or two friends! What a bore!"

"When people are sent to war in great numbers, they are not murderers. They fight for the good, that is, for justice, for the state."

"Well, right now there are Whites, Reds, Greens, and, for all I know, Blues fighting in Russia—what good will they bring to the state?"

"They're fighting to build a life. For many years to come, the winners will arrange life the way they see fit!"

"The way they see fit?"

"How else?"

"This way: kill everyone right now who doesn't agree with your way of doing things! Right away, without waiting a day longer! And what about tomorrow? What will be your way of doing things tomorrow? You don't even know yourself! Maybe it will be nothing less than your right being my wrong, or the other way around . . . That could happen just as easy. In other words, there'll be the same old thievery and fighting the whole world over just like there was before. You will kill people nobly and scream that Grishka Sukhikh is a thief and a brigand! He did the work of three men and earned his property with his labor, so he's a thief! I know. I've read the newspapers. In the White papers they write about the atrocities and usurpations of the Reds, and in the Red papers, about the atrocities and usurpations of the Whites. I'm telling you again, Ustinov—you'll have to chose between one or the other for yourself. Whichever one suits you the most. For the time being, you sit in your cabin, broken-down as it may be, with one eye on your dog and one on me. You're trying to figure it out: 'Is Grishka Sukhikh really threatening to kill me? Or is he just saying that, and is everything really just fine and dandy between us?' But tomorrow you won't think anything of the sort. You'll make up your mind and begin to bash and shoot people, and the only thing you'll dream about will be how to bash more of them!"

"I don't dream about that, Grigory, and I never will. I'm no military specialist or some hero out looking for a war. I'm a farmer! But what if this war concerns all of us? Down to the last man? It will be sure to touch you, and you will choose. I know what side you will choose, too. I have no doubt about that."

"It's simpler for me than for you, Nikola. Whoever touches me first, that's who I'll fight against. And with all my strength! If no one touches me, then I won't lay a finger on anyone, by God! Except you . . . But I have entirely different reasons for that! So, Kolya Ustinov, Nikolenka, first of all you decide: are you my friend or my enemy?! You'll never have such an enemy or such a friend! Listen to me, let's join hands so we won't attack each other! Neither of us is afraid of dying! We think differently about justice— that's nothing, a trifle! You're not like the other peasants in Lebyazhka, not ignorant and dimwitted, and neither am I! How can we refuse to stand up for each other? Do you want Grishka Sukhikh to fall on his knees and beg you? Well? Be done with the piss-ants and join up with me! I want to save myself from being your eternal enemy and save you from the piss-ants and the grave! If the war comes tomorrow, we'll go into the Altai Mountains together! There'll be just the two of us. We'll build us a cozy place to live and drink spring water. We'll leave behind all this squabbling and scrambling after things, and however it turns out, we'll come back to Lebyazhka cleaner than anyone, unstained by all the grabbing and fighting, and together we'll make ten times more than we had before! Well? Do I have to go down on my knees?"

And Grishka Sukhikh, huge and shaggy, began to slip from his seat. Stretching out his neck and flattening his ears, Barin couldn't understand what was going on. Ustinov shuddered. He couldn't allow Grishka to get on his knees—later Grishka would be sure to remember it bitterly! You couldn't knock his stubborn malice out of him with a stick, and there was no need to add to it.

"Stop it, Sukhikh, stop it! Maybe neither of us will find anything at all. I won't find justice for the whole world, and you won't find it for your two or three friends. Fine! So let each look for his own! But all the same I think it's better to look for great things rather than small things in life, and I'll die believing that. But don't touch me with your hands—or your knees either!"

Sukhikh got up from his seat, knocking his head on a beam in the ceiling, and Barin stirred and sighed with quiet happiness. Both he and Ustinov understood that Grishka would be going away now. But instead of going away, Grishka leaned against the wall, his head hanging, his arms folded on his chest, and stood that way for a long time, waiting for something or remembering something. Then he sighed loudly and angrily threw his cigarette butt in the corner, almost in Barin's face.

"Nikola, why didn't you choose Zinaida for your bride? Mrs. Pankratov?"

"What?" Ustinov asked in bewilderment. "I didn't, and that's that. I never wanted to."

"You're lying!"

"I'm not lying, and it's none of your business anyway who I chose and who I didn't!"

"You're lying if you say you never wanted to! Admit it!"

As Grishka stepped away from the wall and came closer to Ustinov, Ustinov suddenly believed it: "He really does want to kill me!" Giving a start in the corner, Barin shifted his weight onto his hind legs. The muscles in his front legs swelled as he got ready to jump Grishka from behind. For a moment Ustinov was not sure whether to stop Barin or let him jump, but he said, "Quiet, Barin!"

"Don't lie to me, Ustinov!" Sinking both hands into his shaggy hair, Grishka sat down. "Tell me honestly how it was! You wanted to marry Zinaida, but I stopped you! Well? Won't you at least admit that much now?"

"Not at all! It never even crossed my mind, Grigory! I've never gotten in your way!"

"How can that be when Zinka had eyes only for you when she was a maid? No one but you!"

"I never knew that. She married Kirill Pankratov, after all, so what's it got to do with me?"

"Oh, my God!" groaned Grishka, rocking back and forth on his seat. "How did it happen? I backed off from Zinka because of you, Nikola. For some reason all my life I couldn't bring myself to insult you, let alone kill you! I couldn't even do it to save my own life! Maybe it's because you were always so educated and worked with the inspectors and surveyors, or maybe it's for some other reason, I don't know, but I just couldn't!"

"She wouldn't have married you, Grishka, never!"

"She would have! Alive or dead, but she would have! She kept a sharp knife in her boot under her skirt, and she threatened me with it, and to use it on herself if she had to! I wasn't afraid of that knife! She wouldn't look at me, but I would have made her see me even through closed eyes! But I was afraid of only one thing—that she loved you and you loved her! I was afraid, and it was the only thing I couldn't overcome! And you? Didn't you know how Zinka looked at you? Didn't you know how I looked at her? You wouldn't have blamed me in any way? So what a fool I was to be afraid of you and to step aside! I tried to drive away my fear of you, but I couldn't! I wouldn't have cared if all Lebyazhka judged me, but I was afraid that you would!"

"Wait a minute, Grigory! I married Domna Alexeyevna, and Zinaida married Kirill. So didn't you understand after that? Haven't you understood till now?"

"Dear God, how does this kind of thing happen to people? She married the wrong lad, but was that snot-nosed Kirilka Pankratov even a lad, let alone a man? He's almost a woman himself, but Zinka married him, that's the way it was with her. You married Domna Alexeyevna, and that was your fate, too. And I got married to a girl I found at the railroad station, a pretty one, from a good family, and I worked her to death in three years, so what? Do we really have to look for a reason for all this?"

"There ought to be a reason!"

"A lot of things ought to be! Those are empty words! You should look at things the way they are!"

"And so you have."

"Yes, so I have! I've taken a good look at everything as it is! And at everything as it was! And the way everything will be! No, I didn't know I was such a fool! Not until today! Such misfortune! I was always a friend to you just the same, Ustinov. You weren't one to me, but I was to you! I asked you to be my friend with that same loyal friendship and trust that I was just explaining to you, the kind that got stuck in us Kerzhaks by the Elders Lavrenty and Samsony Krivoi. The Elder Samsony Krivoi betrayed the saintly Lavrenty. He deserted him and led many people away from him, and that was good for them. But after he'd left Lavrenty, Samsony Krivoi's own conscience tormented him till his dying day. Isn't that the way it was, Ustinov?"

"That's the way it was, Grigory."

After sitting a while longer, breathing heavily, calm and somehow even shy, Sukhikh shook himself, fumbled for something in his shirtfront on his hairy chest, wearily stretched out his hand to Ustinov, and said, "I brought you one more piece of paper, Nikola!"

"Who's it from?" Ustinov asked, taking the paper.

"From me!"

Grishka Sukhikh rose from the stump, hastily muttered, "See you around, Ustinov," squeezed through the doorway, and was gone. Barin, who didn't believe he had left, approached the doorway cautiously and sniffed the threshold. And he was right—Grishka was still there behind the door. What was he doing there? What was he thinking? What had he decided? Looking through the window, Ustinov saw Grishka's horse still standing with its reins hanging over the new row of beams on the well frame that Ustinov had built the day before. It was as quiet as if the entire cabin had been lowered into that well and not a sound could reach them from anywhere. The only sound was a cautious rustling from somewhere above, the wind in the weeds sprouting on the cabin's sod roof.

Barin looked at Ustinov. "What's going on?"

"Just wait a bit," Ustinov said.

The weeds up on the roof rustled.

"You're a bastard, Nikolai Ustinov!" Grishka Sukhikh said through the doorway, pushing aside the squeaky door on its one hinge. "You're a bastard, and I don't believe you one bit! Why are you lying to me?"

"Who's lying to you, Grigory?"

"You are, Ustinov! Even now! It's mean, and it makes no sense. Why are you doing it? Even after Zinka had already married her snot-nosed Kirilka, didn't you spend the night at her house? Didn't you? Have you forgotten that?"

As Grishka Sukhikh slammed the door, it broke off its one remaining hinge. Ustinov watched Grishka jump on his horse and heard the sound of its hooves as he rode off. Barin jumped up and went outside. After running around to take a look for himself, he returned satisfied. "Our guest has really gone!" he confirmed.

Ustinov unfolded the piece of paper that Grishka had left.

To the Comrade Members of the Lebyazhka Forest Commission, from Comrade Grigory Dormidont. Sukhikh.

For your information and knowledge, I am informing you of this drawing of my claim within the territory of the second sector of the former Lebyazhka Royal Reserve, which is now the property of the people. The drawing shows the boundaries set by me, namely, from the western side of the steppe to the edge of the pine forest along the road to the former forest marker No. 27; from this designated post along the clear-cut line back to the steppe, that is, to post No. 8; and from post No. 8 back to the same road.

There followed a rough sketch showing the marker posts and the clear-cut that formed a triangle enclosing six or seven desyatinas of forest proper. Written below the drawing was a warning:

For your information and knowledge, I am informing you that I absolutely forbid the entrance across the stated boundaries of any livestock, large or small, and any persons of any kind, and for violation of this I will shoot and maim the same as for infringement of personal and public property and rights.

Signed, Comrade Grigory Dormidont. Sukhikh.

This and That and the Other

In the autumn sky of 1918, there seemed to be every possible shade of color, every kind of cloud shape, and the barely discernible sound of someone's breathing. Ustinov just could not believe that no one lived in that immense space. Could there be such freedom without anyone to enjoy it? He could not believe it, especially since the sky was so close to the Earth, which was always ready to lend it some of its own life. Of course, Ustinov had no desire to go up into the sky himself. It was an unfamiliar place, and he had a lot of work to do at home. Perhaps if no one on Earth had any need of him—but when would that ever happen? Or maybe if he got old and weak or forgot how to plow and sow and tend the Earth, and the Earth whispered to him quietly, to avoid embarrassing him in front of others, "Listen here, Ustinov, get away from me, go off somewhere!" But there was little chance that Ustinov could fail to please the Earth while he was still alive, none at all, really! He suspected that there was little life in the heavens, no voices to be heard, and that from one edge to the other the whole wide expanse of the sky was saddened by this loneliness, by this yearning for some living soul, for the tiniest little insect or foolish little dog. It was this sadness that had made the heavens so pure and beautiful, and the heavens passed their sadness on to anyone who looked long and silently at the sky.

It is a good thing that a man can see where the sky ends and can therefore feel that there is also an end to this sadness, even though the heavens really have no end. Every living thing, everything that grows and grows old, has an ending. Some people say that even rocks grow and age, but when there is nothing at all, what is there that can come to an end, and where would that end be? And so the colors poured from the sun to the Earth, colors untouched by any existence, undisturbed by any sound or echo, not knowing the reason for their beauty and plenty, knowing nothing, seeing nothing, with no knowledge of knowledge.

A streak of red ripened in this infinite space, a huge flag—whose banner was it? A fire blazed—but just what was burning? There was an arc of dark silver, with bright highlights here and there, stretched out over something or other, but what? The sky-blue color, well now, that was simply an everyday thing for the heavens, like the yellow floorboards in a Russian house. These heavenly floorboards were swept clean, and little clouds crawled across them without leaving a trace behind them, like chubby bare-bottomed babies. Sometimes smoke moved across the dark blue without leaving a trail of soot or embers.

The work of some other mind entirely was being accomplished there, one not human, of unknown origin. But Ustinov thought that it was not such a bad thing, really, to live for the sake of some other, unfathomable intellect. After all, Morkoshka, Solovko, Grunya, and Barin all lived because of Ustinov, their master, as did his children and grandchildren. Many people were leaning on him, and it would be much worse if it turned out that Ustinov himself had nothing to lean on in turn, if the whole wide world rested on his shoulders alone. He needed no more or no less than anyone else in the world. The world had been created quite nicely without his help. He could never have done it himself. He could not have made the sun, the Earth, the soil, or the birds. There would be no joy in doing everything in the world yourself, without anyone's helping hands! If nothing in life is a gift, then all that is left is mechanical labor, nothing but a workshop or factory in which people hammer and forge their lives day and night without taking a break for food or sleep, without any time for living. You don't look a gift horse in the mouth. But if everything in life is a task and nothing is a gift, then life is nothing more than an occupation, and you'll inspect every tooth and hair in it and never be satisfied.

It's another matter entirely to understand that you are put to a task that is not of your own making, but which is the most important thing. When you're in your field, it is impossible to imagine that anyone is closer to the task at hand than you, the peasant and plowman. It was not Ustinov alone who understood this. Whenever he took a breather from his labor and had a few minutes to look around, every farmer understood it the same way. Of course, the farmer is too busy to take much time to ponder over why things in the world are done one way and not another. It's not his business—let others who are not farmers figure it out. A farmer's main concern is with things that have already been worked out. He has no need of things that are not settled already.

Nevertheless, all his life Ustinov had wondered how the color green had come into the sky. After all, any bit of green was an earthly thing. The green grass and the green trees have their beginning in the earth. If seaweeds grow in water, it is only because their roots have found the earth or because they are nourished by spores of earth dissolved in the water. If mold grows on a wooden roof, it means that the wood has already returned to the earth. The wind has carried the spores of earth to it, and it has begun to rot, to turn back into soil. But why does a shade of green sometimes appear high in the sky? What is it telling us? Ustinov thought that maybe it tells us that the sky and the earth are harnessed together like a team of horses, that they really aren't as far away from each other as they might seem to be at first. The birds should know something about this subject. Born on the earth but living in the sky, they feel equally at home in both places. It's a pity a man can listen to the birds but can't understand them. It is not given to him to learn anything from them.

No longer a boy, Ustinov didn't have the time to occupy himself with such questions. He didn't dwell on them—they just came to him from those childhood days when he had been walking on his own two feet but the time hadn't yet come to ride the horse during the harrowing. Ustinov remembered that in that brief period of his life his only occupation had been to look around endlessly and wonder where the sun comes from, why birds fly, and why the sky is above us and the earth below us and not the other way around. A grown man, of course, has other cares, real ones—to double the fallow, to repair the well, to build a new cabin. But now, strangely enough, the peasant Ustinov had yet another care—how was the Lebyazhka Forest Commission, the LFC for short, getting along without him? Had it perhaps made some new mistake? That was the least of it. He remembered Grishka Sukhikh, what he had said and how he had said it. It didn't matter if you agreed with Grishka or not. He was not the kind of man you could just send to hell and ignore. Not him!

Ustinov was up to his chin in problems, and now one more appeared. As he was hewing the fifth row of beams for his cabin, it suddenly hit him like the butt-end of the axe: "What about Grunya?" The last time he had ridden to the mill with her, Grunya had limped with her left foreleg. He had thought at the time that he would have to watch her to see if she favored that leg when she worked, if her eyes had become cloudy like a sick person's, or if the skin on her neck and back was quivering too often. He had thought about it, but he hadn't done anything. Either the Commission got in the way, or else he had come here to his field with Morkoshka and Solovko and had forgotten to worry about Grunya. "Some farmer you are, Ustinov!" he scolded himself angrily. "You worry yourself about the

Commission, about the birds in the sky, and about Grishka Sukhikh, but what about Grunya? Doesn't she mean anything to you?"

And so the day after Sukhikh's visit, Ustinov, preoccupied with his problems, was urging Morkoshka and Solovko along with his whip on the road back home. Driving quickly and somehow idly, without conversing with Barin, who was running beside the wagon, he just moved through space. When he got home he went into the house for a minute, nodded to Domna and his daughter Ksenia, and gave his infant grandson a gentle pat on the bottom without stopping to play with him. Instead he went straight out into the yard, to Grunya. Her left foreleg was swollen, though not very noticeably. Ustinov called out to the neighbor boy and had him ride Grunya back and forth along the street. Watching closely from the side, Ustinov saw that Grunya was indeed limping. He took the boy's place on Grunya's back and rode for a while himself, listening to the sound of her gait. It was true, Grunya had gone lame. What a business! Ustinov went back home, tossed Grunya's reins over the garden fence, and sat down on the porch.

Grunya had rheumatism, and there was no way to treat her. She was already too old. There was no joy in old age because there was no way back out of it for anyone. In old age even a pimple was an illness. No hurt would heal—it could only get worse, whether it was a wrinkle, gray hair, or rheumatism. And Grunya had always had shortcomings. Her forelegs had always been on the weak side. Her legs were improperly formed—not bowlegged, but bent in the pastern. A chain is only as strong as its weakest link. That was true not only for Grunya's forelegs but for his whole household as well. It seemed that his horses had become the weak link, and he had nothing in reserve. It was not the first time he had suspected that Grunya's legs were bad and had asked himself how long Solovko would keep pulling a full load. Today he was fine, but what about tomorrow?

If Ustinov had been at home these past years instead of in the war, he would, of course, have acquired another gelding. But that was no excuse either—he should have given serious thought to his horses as soon as he had returned from the front in the spring. It would not be easy to buy a horse tomorrow on such short order. Horses, too, had been drafted into the army these past years, and workhorses were in great demand. Besides that, the peasants were unwilling to sell anything these days when money had no value and none was foreseen in the near future. It was easier to buy a one- or two-year-old, but the risk was great. You had to pay for the horse, and then feed it and train it, and what would happen if tomorrow Grunya up and quit working altogether? Four horses in the yard, but only two workers among them. And there would be only one left if Solovko somehow became disabled. These thoughts got Ustinov so angry at himself, a fool, that he began to whip Grunya. He couldn't whip himself, but he had to whip someone for the mess he was in!

When Grunya began to thrash about and pulled a stake loose from the fence, Ustinov grabbed her bridle with one hand and with the other gave it to her still harder for that. She neighed quietly, and the skin on her back twitched. Her white upper lip was raised, exposing her yellow, thoroughly worn teeth, and she got some more for that, too.

"Nikola, what are you doing out there?" Domna hollered from the porch.

"I'll be right there," Ustinov answered without turning around and whipped Grunya again for this disturbance. Then he threw the whip on the ground. "And what will I do now?" he asked himself. He certainly did not want to go inside and tell Domna about Grunya's foreleg. He stomped around the yard for a while and finally went—to the Commission, to the Pankratovs' house.

Zinaida, making noodles in the kitchen, was absorbed in her task, and her face and arms, with her sleeves rolled up above her elbows, were covered with flour. Ustinov greeted her and went into the other room without waiting to see what kind of look she gave him. In the comfortable and familiar room, the members of the Commission were sitting around the table, on which there were various papers and the huge abacus that Zinaida had borrowed from the Kruglovs without asking permission.

"Ah-h-h," said Kalashnikov slowly when he saw Ustinov. "You're back—that's good!"

"I'm back!" Ustinov replied, sitting down on a stool. "Is there any news?"

"Of course there is!"

"A lot?"

There turned out to be a fair amount of news. The Lebyazhkans had brought the construction of their new school to a successful conclusion. The leftover lumber had been traded in the neighboring villages for notebooks and ink for the schoolchildren. They had settled their dispute with the men from Zhigulykha and Kalmykova and had given them some lumber, and in return they had promised not to touch the Lebyazhka forest for the time being. If they had to cut wood, they would go to the Barsukova forest instead.

"And what did the men from Zhigulykha and Kalmykova want me for?" Ustinov wanted to know. "Why did they wait around for me for so long?"

"I guess they just couldn't get it out of their heads that they had to talk to you."

"About what?"

"About justice. They all said that you knew more about justice than anyone else."

"The sly bastards!" Ignashka Ignatov jumped up from his stool. "So they wanted to chat with you about justice, did they? Well, we're not fools either, so we up and hid you! An' yesterday they got tired of waitin' and went on home! But who told you they went home already?"

"Nobody. I just showed up on my own."

"They went off saying you tricked them, Ustinov," Polovinkin said gloomily, blowing his nose on his sleeve. "You made your speech that night and had them pull back from the forest, and then the next day you disappear like a gopher. They waited, and then they said it was a trick! 'We ought to kill your speechmaker for such a trick!' "

"Just how many folks want to kill me these days?" Ustinov sighed. "Is there any other news?"

There was more. The Forest Commission had confiscated a still from the Kruglov brothers and had given a stern warning to all the other moonshiners.

"You don't say!" Ustinov was surprised again. "Has the Commission taken control now? Is it enforcing the law?"

"What of it?" Ignashka spoke up again. "When the authorities is all but disappeared and we've got a guard of twenty-four armed men, we have to be in control, don't we?"

"Why twenty-four? Weren't there ten men in the main guard?"

"We've already called up everyone. The main guard is still just that, but we made everyone arm themselves!"

"And why don't I see Comrade Deryabin here with you?"

"He's got business!" Kalashnikov answered. "We're waiting for him. We're not doing any work here right now. We just got together out of habit."

Ustinov sat without saying anything. He had gone to his cabin to get away from people, and a week later he had come running back. Why? He didn't feel right around people. He wanted to be alone, but that didn't work either. A man needed to be with people, and that was that! His cabin in the fields was waiting for him. Grunya, soundly whipped, was waiting for him, shifting her weight back and forth on her legs and thinking, "What will my master do with me now? How will he treat me?" Domna was wondering, "The man went out into the yard and disappeared. Where can he have got to?" And maybe Domna was also thinking, "It would be fine if I had only the Commission to worry about. But Zinka Pankratov is also there day and night with the Commission. Is there something going on there?"

Zinaida had already wiped the flour off herself, come out of the kitchen, and sat down by the window. There the sunlight on her face was silently searching for troubled wrinkles, some sign of fear, or an uneasy smile, but it found nothing of the sort. Zinaida looked stern, even angry. She had quarreled with Ignashka about something or other and paid no attention to Ustinov. But in a minute she would begin to talk to him, and then she would fix her eyes on him and listen to him without blinking or breathing.

Trying to prove some point to Zinaida, Ignashka got heated up and began to swear in the name of God and cross himself.

"You swear in God's name, but do you believe in God, Ignashka?" Zinaida asked him.

"What do you mean? Of course I do!" Ignashka assured her.

"And does God have faith in you?"

"Well, I don't know nothing about that, Zinaida Pal'na!" said Ignashka with a shrug. "I can't answer for God. How would I know?"

"Don't you feel God's own faith in you?"

"Not much, I guess, not really . . . "

"Why not?"

"He don't have much reason to be looking at me! There's lots of others in the way!"

"What do you mean?"

"You figure it out. Say I light me a candle, a one-kopeck candle, and then some merchant puts one down that weighs a pood! Now tell me which candle God can see better from way up on high there, mine or the merchant's? That's how it is!"

"So nothing is holy then? But there are saints, aren't there?" And then Zinaida asked Ustinov, "What do you think, Nikola, are there saints or not? Real ones, I mean?"

Ustinov said nothing. He wanted to wave his hand, to get up and leave, but he didn't. After thinking for a minute, he said, "Yes, there were saints. A lot is said about them in the Bible and other holy books. And someone said it, didn't he? It didn't just come out of thin air, did it?"

"Since there are so many bad men in the world, I've been thinking that the opposite must be true, too—there have to be saints as well. If it wasn't so, then thievery would have won out over everyone a long time ago and destroyed us all. But we're still alive, still people!"

"That's right!" Kalashnikov agreed with Zinaida. "And more than that, we want to establish equality and brotherhood between us all for centuries to come! In other words, we want to take the cooperative path that was proclaimed almost a hundred years ago in England, in the city of Rochdale. It's a famous city, where the very first consumers' society was formed, and where they put together a set of rules for themselves sure to continue and progress until the whole of mankind adopts it as a way of life!"

"I agree with Kalashnikov completely," said Ustinov. "If you look at how much has been made in nature—the sun, the earth, the rivers, the meadows and forests and fields, and us too, human beings—then it's clear that there really isn't much left to be done to establish justice between people, to finish what has already been begun!"

"You and Kalashnikov have something like a religion!" Zinaida remarked.

"Not really, but still . . . "

"Well, I got no use for England!" Ignashka announced. "What do I care what people think up there? The soldiers coming back from the war were always cussing the Englishmen. They said if it weren't for them we wouldn't have got mixed up in this war with Germany! Phooey! That's what I think of England and the city of Rochdale!"

"No, men, we can't spit on other countries like that," Ustinov protested.

"But what's it to England if Ignaty is against her?" Polovinkin asked. "Ain't it all the same to her? You spit on her, but she don't care, Ignashka! Go ahead and spit!"

"It's just the opposite, Ignaty," Kalashnikov argued. "You need to look and see where and how things are done wisely, and then use that wisdom in your own life, even if it comes from foreigners. You can't do it any other way. Isn't that right, Polovinkin?"

"No, that's not true at all," answered Polovinkin, spreading wide his hairy fingers. "Just what is this cooperative of yours? It goes around all black and blue, inside and out. The rich bourgeois beat on it from the outside, and on the inside the common members get stomped on the same way. Wasn't that the way it was with our own Lebyazhka consumer co-op and the creamery co-op?"

"It was, but that wasn't the whole story!" said Kalashnikov hotly. "Didn't it save a lot of poor folk from ruin and give them help? And didn't it build real human cooperation between us Lebyazhkans? It all boils down to the same thing: you have to keep what is good for life and throw out what is bad, and then the cause of the people will move forward! Because the people are great! They can do anything and attain anything—all they need to do is choose their road carefully!"

Zinaida spoke up again. "Didn't the people in England find some truth?! And maybe you will also find some in your Commission? I want truth so much that I wouldn't begrudge my own life for it! If I knew where it was, I would give up my whole life for it. I'd say, 'Here, take it all, I don't need anything in return, nothing at all!' Everyone knows where there's war and murder, but no one knows where the truth is!" Looking at Ustinov, Zinaida asked him loudly and stubbornly, "So which of the saints do you know about, Ustinov? Whose story can you tell? You said there really were saints on this earth, so which ones do you know about?"

"I don't know about any of them very well," said Ustinov, embarrassed. "Ask Kalashnikov there, he used to work in the church."

"But don't you know about any of them at all?" asked Zinaida, not giving up.

"Well, I remember the story of Alexei. I've read about the Man of God."

"So tell us about it, tell us why Alexei became the Man of God."

"He renounced the world."

"How?"

"He lived with his rich parents in comfort and plenty. His parents married him off. But the very night when he was to share the marriage bed with his young bride, he up and left home and became a beggar."

"Oh, so he didn't love his bride? Maybe he even hated her?! He could do that only if he hated her!"

"No, he did it for the sake of holiness."

"How can there be anything holy in that? He shouldn't have gotten married. Didn't he think of how she would feel that night if she loved him?"

Ustinov paused in confusion, as if he himself were responsible for the behavior of the Man of God.

"Just listen, Zinaida!" Ignashka said sternly. "You ask questions but won't let the man answer! What happened then, Nikola? Did they both lose that first night together for no good reason?"

"After that Alexei spent seventeen years in poverty and wandering, and then he came back home."

"And did his parents greet him at the door, or had they died already?" Zinaida asked again. "Not a word from him for seventeen years! What sense does that make?!"

"He didn't say a word to his parents this time either. He settled in the cowshed out in the yard, like a beggar. Every day he saw his mother, who had never stopped tormenting herself over him, and he also saw his bride, who had stayed under her husband's roof and had suffered and sobbed along with her mother- and father-in-law."

"Did things go on like that for long?"

"For another seventeen years."

"Seventeen more?!" exclaimed Zinaida in complete amazement. "Isn't a saint ashamed to behave like that? His mother is suffering, his bride is half-dead with grief, he sees their tears for seventeen years, and he doesn't care?"

Then there was the sound of footsteps, and the door from the kitchen opened. Kirill Pankratov appeared, with wood shavings in his blond beard, and said sternly, "Zinaida! Stop lazing around listening to stories! Is the soup done yet?"

Kirill tried to be strict with his wife, especially in front of other men, but it didn't seem natural for him. This time, however, it did. He must have been very hungry after working in his shop since early morning.

"Go on, Zinaida!" Ustinov said after a pause. "I can finish the story later."

"Don't talk drivel!" Zinaida suddenly snapped at Ustinov. "Finish it now that you've started. The soup can wait a minute!" Zinaida got up from her stool, but instead of leaving the room, she leaned her shoulder against the stove. "Well?" Making a sign to her husband, she said, "In a minute, Kirill, in a minute!" As Ustinov and everyone else in the room fell silent, Zinaida added to her husband, "You come in here too, Kirill! Just think, Kirya, this saintly man hid from his parents and his bride for thirty-four years, tormented them with his absence, and lived in their own household without telling them who he was! She must have loved him if she missed him so much. Did she really have nothing better to do than cry for her missing husband? A woman is a person, too. Is she supposed to kill the life in herself and not even resent it? What happened then, Nikola?"

Kirill shyly squeezed into the room and stood next to his wife by the tiled stove.

"Well, tell the rest of it then, Ustinov!" Kalashnikov said. "What happened next?"

"In the end they figured out who the beggar in the cow barn was. But just as soon as they found out, he died. They buried him with great honor, and he was made a saint. That's what happened."

"I think that's strange!" Zinaida loudly sighed.

"What do you mean?!" Polovinkin responded to her sigh. "What are saints like? They're just the opposite of us, or at least me, anyway. The most important thing for me is to live my life, but he didn't care if he was born or lived at all, as long as he lived on in people's memory. And that's all there is to it!"

"It's still strange! And I don't agree with it! So what if he left behind a holy memory? What if I'm praying to him sometime, and then I suddenly think, 'Dear God, look how much suffering he brought to people in his lifetime, to his parents and his wife and maybe to a lot of others besides!'"

"That's just the way it is with saintliness, it all comes from suffering. Where else would it come from?" Kirill asked suddenly and quietly, looking at his wife.

"Where does saintliness come from?" Zinaida shrugged. "From kindness! When he was rich, Alexei the Man of God should have helped people with a piece of bread and a good example. Let him take from himself and give to others; let him suffer himself! But why does he have to lead other folks into such suffering? I can't understand it! It's like he was a criminal! If some criminal would have killed Alexei, it would have caused his parents and his bride just as much pain as he caused them himself. That's just what they must have thought when he disappeared, that some bandits got hold of him and killed their son and husband!"

"The work of a saint is a thing of greatness . . . ," Kirill said again, even more quietly. "It is a great thing and takes a very special talent, and what is great and takes great talent cannot happen without people suffering. It comes only through suffering and renouncing life."

"One has to be born for something so great and special! But if someone is born just like everyone else, maybe even stupider than others, but then all the same takes on something bigger than he is, the first thing that comes of it is torment and suffering for other folks. He doesn't know how to do more than that; he's not up to it. Isn't that how it was maybe even with Alexei the Man of God? The only way I can understand it is that he wasn't born for greatness, but he still wanted it in the worst way! So he figured he'd get his greatness, his sainthood, through the suffering of his parents and his bride. He didn't think about any more than that. That's the way they should paint him in the icons, with a tiny little head!"

"What you won't say, Zinaida!" Polovinkin exclaimed.

"And I'll say it again!"

Giving Zinaida a sharp push on the shoulder, Kirill said as sternly as he could, "Let's go eat!"

The Pankratovs left, and everyone else in the room felt uncomfortable.

"Everyone keeps talking about the truth," said Polovinkin. "Everyone's been jabbering about it up one side and down the other, but no one's made a bit of sense!"

"You can't make truth out of silence," said Ustinov with a sigh.

"What's truth got to do with our Commission?"

"Isn't it the business of every commission on earth? All that are and ever will be?" Ustinov answered.

"I don't agree!" Polovinkin protested angrily. "What's going on here? You, Kalashnikov, and Ustinov especially, you've learned how to talk so fine! Maybe you don't even know what's what yourselves, but you still show off with how much you know. Ain't you just blowing your own horn?"

"That's the truth, that's just the way it is in the Commission, just like Polovinkin says!" Ignashka was so excited that his scraggly mustache started wagging. "You make out like you're all such wise men and beat around the bush without ever getting down to business! And Kalashnikov here goes on and on about England like he was some kind of English spy!"

"I didn't talk about it at all!" Kalashnikov defended himself.

"All right, you were talking about the co-op shops, but what about Ustinov? Ustinov, you show up and talk and talk—nothing can stop you! So you gave a speech to the Zhigulykha and Kalmykova woodcutters, and that was just fine, but after that you just can't let it alone! You still talk and talk!"

"I can't believe it, Comrade Commission Members!" Ustinov was so surprised that his face, even his whole head, reddened under his blond hair. "I can't believe what you're saying! How long have I been away from the

Commission? I've come back now, but haven't you been discussing the Commission's business and getting something done even without me?"

"Stop playing the fool, Ignaty!" Kalashnikov said angrily.

"Stop doing what? I got nothing to stop doing! Polovinkin and me are telling it right! We're being straight and honest about it—we're not hiding nothing. You got no use for what me and Polovinkin's got to say, you only listen to yourselves! You're such big shots! Polovinkin ain't said ten words in this Commission, you can count them on your fingers, and when I try to say something, you don't like any of it!

"And why? Here's why! Thanks to Ustinov and his secret efforts, our Commission's been split and divided into the smart ones and the stupid ones, and that's no good for nothing! We ought to be together in everything every day! We're supposed to be an example of togetherness and common sense to everyone, or else there's no telling what will happen. It's terrible to even think about it! It'd be a disgrace, counterrevolution even! If we, the Commission, let ourselves go so far as to let one of us use two voices and a thousand words, but another one no voice and not a single word, if we give that kind of example to folks, then how far will the simple citizens go? Huh? Don't no one have nothing to say? That's just great!"

"Now just wait a minute, Ignaty!" Polovinkin said with lowered eyes, "you can't . . . I didn't . . . "

"Why should I hold back, why?" Ignashka turned on Polovinkin as well. "I'm not going to! You do it, but I got no use for it! Ustinov here keeps muddying up the truth. He's always getting carried away with something, with Aleksei the Man of God, or who knows what else! But I cut right through to the truth without any of it. I wait and wait, but once I start to cut, boy-oh-boy!"

"You're really something, Ignaty," Kalashnikov broke in again. "Just stop and think about it, and you'll see. You've got so-o many things to say, but how many things have you done? Can you tell us?"

"Can you ask me what I've done?!" Ignashka asked with his eyes widening and his finger jabbing at Kalashnikov. "Have you no shame? How can you ask that, Petro?! I never thought you'd have it in you!" Ignaty got up from the table, quickly paced the length of the room, stopped in front of Kalashnikov again with his arms crossed on his chest, and launched into a long speech:

"Just what could you do here without me, Comrade Chairman?! When the Lebyazhkans went rushing off to cut down the forest, just who reported that fact to you? Ignaty Ignatov told you about it! If he hadn't done that, you'd have just sat here behind this very table without knowing a thing, counting up your figures and writing them down on different pieces of paper. And thanks to me, everyone went into the woods and caught Sevka Kupriyanov, that no-good son of a bitch, and brought the forest into order! It was you who was stupid that time—you untied Sevka and let him go along with his pup, Matveyka, and I ain't taking any of the blame for that!

"And another thing—when the woodcutters from the steppe showed up, eighty-seven wagons of them, with a water barrel on the last one, who raised the alarm for the rest of the Commission? Who was it got you up out of your warm bed, Nikolai Ustinov? You're keeping your trap shut now, eh? You still got a drop of shame left in you and admit that it was me who got you up? And that if it wasn't for me, you wouldn't of had to make any speeches to the woodcutters? Do you admit that, too?!

"Here we all sit in the Pankratovs' house, holding meetings day and night, while our mistress, Zinaida Pal'na, feeds us kasha, but just whose idea was it to come knocking at the Pankratovs' door, to come to this house that's so clean and tidy and doesn't have any kids running around in it? It was my idea! If it wasn't for me, we'd all be sitting at the assembly hall along with the village clerk, and every citizen off the street would be coming in and bothering us and our important work whether he had any business to or not!

"No-o, sir, the people knew what they were doing when they elected Ignaty Ignatov into the Commission! I'm going to go out right this minute and explain to people just what I've done in this Commission and how much I've justified the faith they have in me! Could you try to do the same, Kalashnikov? Or you, Ustinov? Or even you, Polovinkin? No, I won't give up so easy! I've had enough! My patience is used up, too, and here's what I'm going to do: Comrade Deryabin will be here any minute, and as soon as he comes, I'm going to explain to him just how things are! Just as soon as he comes!"

After Ignashka had sat down on his stool again, dug around in his pocket for his comb, and begun to groom himself, Kalashnikov retorted, "We'll have something to say, too! We'll tell Deryabin all about you, about how you accused the Commission of misconduct! Then we'll see just what is what and who is who!"

With a start Ignaty returned his comb to his pocket and protested, "I didn't say nothing about the whole Commission! I was only talking about certain people in it!"

"All right, Ignaty! Weren't you talking about Ustinov?"

"About him? Of course!"

"About me?"

"About you? Well, sort of ... "

"And about Polovinkin?!"

"Not at all, not about him at all!"

"What do you mean? Didn't you criticize him?"

Ignashka answered boldly, quickly, and unhesitatingly. It was Kalashnikov who was embarrassed questioning him. An educated man and a leader,

Kalashnikov had headed the cooperative in Lebyazhka for many years, and now he was the head of the Forest Commission as well, but he was shy. Solidly built, with a firm step, thick hair, and a deep, husky voice, he was getting on in years but was not old yet by any means. But he could suddenly turn shy in mid-stride or in the middle of a sentence, not because of fear or some threat, but because of his own sense of doubt, a childlike simplicity that would unexpectedly seize him and soften his large, rough-featured face with a gentle, youthful smile. At such times you couldn't be sure what was going on in the man's soul, especially because he would hastily cover that smiling, perplexed face with one or even both hands and sit by himself, thinking about something or other. After he had gathered his thoughts, he would show himself to the world again, open his arms wide, and begin to talk quickly, moving his hands up, down, and to the sides, sometimes freezing them in some strange and playful pose.

That's what happened now. Kalashnikov hid behind his palms, and when he came out from behind them again, Ustinov said point-blank, "Petro, I don't understand something here. Are you still the Chairman of the Commission, or has Deryabin replaced you?"

Kalashnikov blinked and asked hesitatingly, "What do you mean? I am the Chairman! We haven't changed places. But, nevertheless, we'll decide this question when Deryabin comes. Ustinov, why don't you sit at the table and have a look at those papers? There's a lot of them there."

Once more Ustinov did not leave, but, sighing, began to leaf through the papers of the Forest Commission. The Commission had established the rate of timber output by doubling the figures calculated from the results of the last forest inspection, but nothing had been written in the document about how and why this had been done. Among the papers was also the Commission's decision about the coming summer of 1919:

> The grass in the forest is to be mowed after the hatching of the grouse and other ground-nesting birds so as not to damage the nestling-bird population, that is, after the 20th of July.
>
> In order to prevent damage to sapling trees, the forest grass should in general be mowed only in case of extreme need and only in wide clearings.

Ustinov read the Commission's resolution against the distilling of moonshine and the act of confiscation of the Kruglov brothers' still. And then he came across yet another and most curious document, a resolution on the reconciliation of the Zhdanovs, husband and wife. From this document Ustinov learned that Yelena Zhdanov had brought to the Commission a complaint about her husband, Alexander Zhdanov, because of his crude behavior, drunkenness, and physical abuse. The Commission had summoned and heard both of them out and had ordered the couple to be reconciled.

"What is this about the Zhdanovs?" Ustinov inquired. "Seems a bit strange to me, Petro! Is this really any concern of the Forest Commission?"

"And why not?" Kalashnikov asked with a shrug. "Keep looking, there's another piece of paper there that explains everything!"

Indeed, there was another document, written in Kalashnikov's attractive hand, LFC Record No. 17, which offered an explanation:

> Recently it has been noted that there is an ardent desire on the part of many of the citizens of the village of Lebyazhka to turn to the Forest Commission, which they have unanimously elected to office, with various questions that have no direct connection with the affairs of the forest, in particular, questions concerning the division of family property, the Mutual Benefit Fund, the construction of the new school, the apportionment of obligations for community work, and so on and so forth. In the absence of local authority accessible to the citizenry (with the exception of one able-bodied and one quite ailing policeman of the somewhat uncertain Siberian Provisional Government), the Commission, in response to the desires of the working people, considers it essential to decide these and other issues of civilian life and community organization to the extent of its abilities.

Ustinov finished reading and was about to ask for further clarification when Ignashka, who had been looking out the window all this time, announced, "Like I said, here comes Comrade Deryabin!" Taking up his comb again, he continued to groom himself. He had even gone over to look at himself in the mirror on the wall when the door to the kitchen opened up wide enough to let through Zinaida Pankratov's clenched fist. She was in a rage, with lips pressed tightly together and scowling eyebrows.

"Ignaty," she called out quietly, "just you wait, you rotten louse, I'll get you for what you said about Alexei the Man of God, and for everything else you said to me—I'll get you! I'll beat you to a pulp! I'll smash your stupid head with an iron pot and rip your tongue out! I'll . . . You just wait and see, Ignaty!"

The door slammed shut, all the members of the Commission sat in bewilderment, and Ignashka, swallowing hard, kept his eyes fastened on the door.

"Hello, Comrades!" said Deryabin, walking into the room. "Ah, Ustinov, so you're back with us now?! That's good! So what's going on here with you all?"

As always, he was poorly shaven, pale and thin, with a soldier's cap set awry on his head, a military overcoat thrown over his shoulders, and a cigarette butt in the corner of his mouth, like a soldier from the front-line trenches who had just been under an artillery barrage, but instead of being dull and miserable, he was light on his feet. He sat down next to Ustinov just as he was, in his cap and overcoat, and, without taking the cigarette out of his mouth, asked again, "So what's going on here with you all?" Chewing on his cigarette and repeating his question, he glanced around to see if they had understood him.

Ustinov, who hadn't understood, looked at him attentively. Their eyes met briefly, and Deryabin quickly switched his gaze to Ignashka.

"Nothing is going on here," answered Ignashka, who had understood immediately. "Everything is fine . . . " Then he laughed and added, "We were all simply waiting for Comrade Deryabin to get here, every last one of us.

Kalashnikov cleared his throat and said, "Comrade Ignatov here feels insulted . . . "

"Ignatov? Don't take offense, Ignaty. Just do your duty as a Commission member. Understand?"

Ignashka nodded, "Of course I understand!"

"All right, then! Well, I just made another inspection of the forest guard. From top to bottom, you might say, down to the last simple guardsman. I checked all of their weapons and their ability to use them. And I must say, our guard is dependable and fit for battle. Our people understand the job that needs to be done. They're good people in every way. Except for one thing—they have a poor leader. We made a mistake when we appointed Leonty Yevseyev as leader of the guard. That's a good lesson for us, and we'll have to remember it in the future. He's one of our own, and we thought we knew the man, but it turns out that we didn't."

Leonty Yevseyev was indeed known by the people of Lebyazhka and other villages. He had served well in the Tsar's forest guard. If one of the peasants came to him and complained about his hard lot, Leonty would take him into the forest and point to a pine tree—"Cut down this one right here! But you didn't see hide nor hair of me, understand?" Of course, the peasant understood perfectly. Now Leonty was the leader of the Lebyazhka people's guard for the protection of the forest. But people had noticed that recently he had begun to ramble absent-mindedly when he talked, and more than a little. Someone would ask him, "Leonty, what's the best way to get to the ninth sector of the forest, to the northern side?" Leonty would lay a finger along his brow. "Since the people asked me to guard their forest, I will deal severely with woodcutters and bring them to the village assembly without asking questions!" "That's fine," they would say, "you do just that, but how can I get to the ninth sector?" Again, with his finger along his brow, "Go past Gulyayev's meadow!" "Which Gulyayev, Andryukha or Pyotr? They both have meadows in the forest." "Well, Andryukha fought in the war, but Pyotr never did!" "What has the war got to do with it, Leonty? I didn't ask you about the war!" "You know, in July of '17 they almost put Andryukha Gulyayev in front of a firing squad." "That's fine for Andryukha, but I need to know how to get to the ninth sector!" "It's simple! If we had an azimuth here, it would be even simpler. Maybe you don't understand, there's this sort of an arrow called an azimuth." "You just won't quit! And an azimuth isn't an arrow at all. You can only figure direction by the arrow on a compass. How do I get to the ninth sector, Leonty?" "You think an azimuth is something more than an arrow? I don't believe you!" "Don't believe me then, for God's sake, just tell me where the ninth sector is!" "You see, there's this huge mag-nut in the earth, and that's why an arrow is always more important than an azimuth! And just between you and me, the scientists say there isn't a God any more!"

That's how Yevseyev was doing his job in the forest these days. At home he was a man like any other, not a bad farmer, and well-mannered with his family, but in his public service he would get a swelled head, talk nonsense, and then get angry when no one listened to his explanations. Wasn't he the leader of the forest guard, everybody's senior? Now Deryabin gave a long and detailed account of all of Leonty Yevseyev's useless and senseless talk. He put his cap on the table as if he were reading from it, opened his overcoat wider, and in a businesslike manner told about the Gulyayev meadow, and the "mag-nut," and the azimuth, and how Leonty Yevseyev had explained it all.

Ustinov and Kalashnikov listened to him in silence, their eyes on the floor. So did Polovinkin, glancing from time to time first at Deryabin, then at Ustinov.

Ignashka, sitting across from Deryabin, watched the speaker's lips closely and was loudly indignant. "That's right! Look what Citizen Yevseyev has come to!" And when Deryabin had finished his story, Ignaty slapped himself on the knees, rose up on his stool, and commented hotly, "Yes, yes! That's right, Comrade Deryabin!"

"What's right?"

"Well, before you got here, I was speaking out against all these harmful and senseless words, too, the kind it's impossible to even listen to!"

"Why impossible?" Deryabin asked in surprise.

"It makes you sick to hear them!"

"Words directed against the people? Against the Forest Commission? All the same, why is it impossible to listen to them?"

"Against the people and, it seems, against the Commission, too!"

"For example?" Deryabin asked sternly.

"Take Kalashnikov and Ustinov here, and Polovinkin, too. One spits out a pile of words you can't understand, that make no sense at all, and the other repeats them with a straight face like some kind of fool. Like he's reading from a book. It's like a fog on the brains for regular folks."

"What kind of folks?"

"Well, Comrade Deryabin, for folks like me!"

"Like you . . . ," sighed Deryabin. He drummed his fingers on the table top, put his cap back on his head, and cleared his throat. "I spent so much time talking about Leonty Yevseyev and about everything that I had to hear from him because he has to be fired, relieved of his duties as the leader of the forest guard. Immediately."

"Immediately!" Ignashka chimed in, almost shouting.

"And that being the case, I'm reporting to the Commission that I've already relieved him of duty. And so there won't be any redundancy in command, bureaucracy, and red tape, I have also done away with the position of leader of the guard. Is that clear to everyone? From now on, the forest guard will be directly subordinate to the Commission, without going through a leader. And within the Commission, it will be subordinate to me, I think. Since I have been involved with it every day for some time now, nothing will change, actually. Everything will go on like it was before. Well, do I see that there are no objections to the question under discussion?" Deryabin looked around the room and settled his cap more neatly on his head. "Do you have some comment to make, Comrade Ustinov? Or did it just seem that way?"

"I've been away for some time, and it's not quite clear to me yet just who the Chairman of the Commission is now. Is it you, Deryabin, or is it still Comrade Petro Kalashnikov?"

Kalashnikov blushed and squirmed on his chair, Polovinkin let out a resounding sigh, and for some reason Ignashka laughed.

"It's a proper question, Ustinov!" Deryabin nodded. "You should have been informed. This is how it is within our Commission: Kalashnikov is the Chairman just as he was before. Even more than that, he's like our president; that is, he represents the Commission at the village assembly, in negotiations with other villages and with individuals. In general, he is our main rep-re-sen-ta-tive. I'll be the chief in matters of business. All complaints, petitions, and so on will be directed to me. I'll read them carefully and decide what should be done; then I'll report to the Commission for final approval. And, like I said, starting today the forest guard will be under my direct supervision. I have more work to do than anyone else. Other members may sometimes be absent from the Commission, but I am here every day, sometimes even all night. I am on duty twenty-four hours a day. Yes, Comrade Kalashnikov?"

"It's amazing that Comrade Deryabin even finds time to sleep!" Kalashnikov added his support. "During the day he is either in the forest, or with the guard, or away somewhere performing other public duties, and at night he reads and writes documents in time for us to look at them and approve them later. The man is living without sleep, by God!"

"Exactly . . . ," Deryabin nodded again. "As for Comrade Ignatov, his purpose in the Commission is for special assignments, to be a courier and scout, to reconnoiter. Comrade Polovinkin, on the other hand, has no special duties, and finally there is you, Comrade Ustinov. We consulted with each other and decided that you will be our main specialist in affairs concerning the forest, and also, based on your speech to the woodcutters, you will conduct certain negotiations."

"What sort of negotiations?"

"I see you have a file of papers there in front of you. Did you acquaint yourself with them?"

"Yes, I did."

"Did you read Record No. 17?"

"Yes, the one about the various new responsibilities of the Commission."

"Exactly! And No. 21?"

"I didn't come across that one . . ."

"Read it. Then we won't have to explain anything to you." Deryabin quickly opened the file to the right page, and Ustinov began to read Record No. 21.

> Heard: concerning acts of resistance to the Forest Commission.
>
> The future accomplishments of the LFC as well as its current day-to-day operations are greatly impeded by the behavior and even agitation of certain citizens, namely:
>
> 1. Sukhikh, Grigory Dormid., who has stated: "Let every man cut and haul as much as he is able. That's the way things are in life, and the only way they can be."
>
> 2. Yankovsky, Dmitry Panteleym. (known as Kudeyar). Proclaims the end of the world to everyone, by which reasoning there is no sense at all in preserving the forest or establishing any kind of social order among the citizenry.
>
> 3. Smirnovsky, Rodion Gavril. Although an educated and respected citizen with the former rank of army officer, he has scorned the Forest Commission in every possible way, thereby giving a bad example to many other citizens.
>
> 4. Samorukov, Ivan Ivan. Has held the title of Finest Man in Lebyazhka for decades and still maintains his personal influence among the citizenry.
>
> Be It Resolved: to determine the specific intentions of each of the above named persons. Afterward either to take action against them or enlist their services for the benefit of the Commission.
>
> The execution of this resolution is to be carried out by Commission Member Nikolai Levont. Ustinov upon his return from the fields.

This was all interesting to Ustinov. He vividly pictured himself meeting with Smirnovsky, Kudeyar, and Ivan Ivanovich Samorukov, people he should have talked to a long time ago. Pushing the file away, he said to Deryabin, "Well, I've already met with Grishka Sukhikh! At my cabin in the fields. There's no need for any more talk about him!"

"And rightly so, indeed!" Deryabin replied. "And did Grishka come to you with this particular piece of paper?!" Deryabin quickly leafed through the file. "This one here?!" It was Grisha Sukhikh's letter to the Commission, designating the portion of the forest that he considered to be his own and threatening anyone who trespassed on it.

"Well then, how did you decide to answer Grigory?"

"Here's how!" said Deryabin, stabbing his finger at a corner of Grishka's document, where in Kalashnikov's hand was written: "Categorically put a stop to this. Entrust to Com. Deryabin personally."

"I see . . . ," Ustinov nodded. He didn't even want to ask what was meant by "categorically put a stop to this."

"Well then," said Deryabin, "all the members of the Commission are free to go now. I'll stay on here awhile with the paperwork and prepare for our next meeting, which I am scheduling for the morning."

When a few minutes had passed, but no one had got up, Deryabin looked at first one, then another, then glanced at Polovinkin, fidgeting on his chair.

"We've left something unsaid here, by God!" Polovinkin said. "We've cussed at each other, even insulted each other. We've been looking each other over from head to foot out of the corners of our eyes, but we haven't said all we need to! Not at all!" And then he grinned, his face brightened, and he shouted through the door, "Zinaida, Zinaida Pal'na!"

Zinaida came into the room. "What?"

"Tell us a story, Zinaida!" asked Polovinkin with a bow, half rising from his chair. "About the maiden Yelena, the story about her! I haven't heard it for a long time, and you tell it good!"

"What are you thinking of, Polovinkin?" Zinaida asked in surprise. "Because of the story about Saint Alexei, here I was just threatening to throw Ignaty out with the garbage, and before I've even had the time to keep my promise, you want another tale! Isn't that a bit funny?"

"It's not funny," Deryabin replied, almost tenderly. "Go ahead and tell it, Zinaida, humor the Commission that's gathered here in its full complement!" Deryabin got up from the table, took off his coat and cap, hung them on a nail on the wall, and sat down again. "Humor us, Zinaida!" he repeated. "I ask you on my behalf and for all the others!"

"All right," sighed Zinaida. "If so many of you ask, how can I refuse? But on one condition—don't get mad if I don't tell it the way you want."

▲▲▲

This is the way it was, then . . . The maiden Yelena was a real beauty, with blond braids, blue eyes, and a delicate rose complexion. She was known for her skillful embroidery. On rough homespun or the finest store-bought fabric, she could embroider a pattern as pretty as a picture! It was a wonder to behold! She already had a sweetheart, a Poluvyatsky lad named Lukyan. All that is told about him is that he had a thick head of light-brown curls.

But this is what happened: Yelena's parents, and the other Poluvyatsky folk, too, all told her to marry herself a Kerzhak! They insisted, "We have to marry you off to the Kerzhaks; we have no other choice." She was the most beautiful maiden and the first to marry a Kerzhak. The task of beginning the kinship between the Poluvyatsky people and the Old Believers was placed on her. "Do it, Yelenushka, for the sake of all of us! None of the Old-Believer lads will be able to resist you. All you have to do is give your consent, it's as simple as that! And then all of us will be saved, and we can all stay here in our own homes!" That's how they put it to her the first, and the second, and the third, and even the hundredth time. And so, having bid farewell to her Lukyan, she gave her consent, and everything turned out just the way it had been foreseen. Other Poluvyatsky maidens also went over to the other side, and other Kerzhak lads could not resist them, and the weddings that took place were the beginning of the Lebyazhka of today.

But there was a cloud on this new horizon. The unlucky Lukyan went off to work in the distant mines, deep, dark, and dank. He went of his own free will to dig and delve in the earth, to the place where people go only in chains as prisoners in Siberian exile, their heads shaved and their flesh branded. Fine, if that's the way it is. Fine, if the fate of only one soul had been sealed in doom. Then maybe this tale would never have been told, and that would have been a good thing. But that is not what happened.

Yelenushka's husband, young, stern, and gloomy, was a carrier by trade. At that time they had just started up a saltworks at Lake Kotyol. They began to extract salt from the lake, and the merchants knew just what to do. They called on the peasants with horses to come and haul away the white salt and sell it to villages far and wide. Back then salt was in short supply, just like it is these days. Many men went into the salt business, and so did Kuzma, Yelena's husband.

One day when Kuzma was washing up after coming home from his business, his young wife gave him a little hand towel that she had embroidered while he was gone. He dried his hands and looked to see what kind of needlework she had done. It was beautifully and very skillfully done, but Kuzma found no joy in it. He sat down to eat and sprinkled his cabbage soup heavily with salt, but all the time he was looking at the hand towel.

"Yelena?"

"Yes!" his young wife answered. "What do you need?"

"I want to know what is embroidered there on your towel."

"Where?"

"There on the border."

"There? Oh, it's just a little pattern, not anything in particular . . . "

"No," said Kuzma, "you haven't embroidered a pattern there."

"What do you think it is?"

"You've embroidered a picture of Lukyan's curls! Am I right? While you were embroidering, weren't you thinking about him and remembering him the whole time?"

"I was thinking about him . . . ," said Yelenushka. "I was remembering."

And then Kuzma took the towel, rolled it up tight, and whipped his wife with it with all his might. And he was a strong one, that Kuzmin!

Yelena didn't shed a single tear. After taking the beating without a word, she even admitted to Kuzma, "I have done you wrong. I didn't mean to, but I did, it seems."

Fine. Time passed, Kuzma went back to his salt trade, and Yelenushka, the young wife, made a new towel. She worked hard at it, looking at it with eyes now open wide, now half-shut in a squint. Her stitches were so tiny that by itself a single one was invisible. Yelenushka had white and nimble hands with slender fingers and sharp nails. As she added one deft stitch to another, a picture grew from her needle and thread: a tower with a small window from which a fair maiden was looking out far, far into the distance.

Kuzma, her husband, came home, wiped his face on the new towel, and noticed that embroidered tower with the fair maiden. He sat down to eat his soup, sprinkled it with salt even more than before, and called his wife, "Yelena?!"

"Yes? What do you want, my husband?"

"Who is that sitting there in your tower? Who is that maiden with the blue eyes and the long blond braids?"

"I don't know who that is; I don't know her name. It's just some maiden, no one in particular," Yelena answered her husband.

"Well, then I'll have to tell you myself: it's you in the tower, and no one else! And you're looking off into the distance—you can't keep your eyes off it. Who do you see there?"

Yelena was silent. Then she lowered her head and quietly confessed, "I have wronged you once again, my husband! I stitched without anything on my mind, but it turns out I was thinking of something."

But Kuzma was already rolling and twisting that new towel tightly into a whip, and he beat his wife with all his might.

Kuzma went off to the salt trade for a third time, came home, washed, dried himself with yet a third towel, sat down to eat, salted and salted his cabbage soup till it was hardly fit to eat, and called, "Yelena?!"

"Yes," she answered, "what do you want?"

"What are these two birds that fly so prettily in the sky? Why are they flying?"

"They look like ordinary birds!" answered Yelena.

"And why can't these birds sit on the ground? Or on a roof or some little branch?"

"They can't sit on the ground," Yelena answered. "They want to fly."

"So the two of them can be together in the sky?"

"Maybe so, my husband. So they can be together . . . "

"And if these two little birds were christened as people, what would they be called? It looks like one birdie would be called Yelena, and the other? Well, why don't you say anything? Why are you so silent when I have already guessed the riddle of the story you've embroidered on your towel?!"

Bowing her head on her breast, Yelena said softly, "Maybe you have guessed it, maybe so."

And once again her husband rolled the towel up tight, dipped it in the bitter white salt, and beat his wife with all his might until he fell into a frenzy. And when he returned to his senses, Yelenushka, his wife, was already lifeless. Then Kuzma left the house without even putting on his cap, ran far away, and was never heard from again.

The beautiful and skillful maiden Yelena and the Kerzhak Kuzma had no children. So their family died out, and they have no living kin on the face of the earth. That's the way it was . . .

▲▲▲

Zinaida was quiet for a moment.

"Did I tell it right, men?"

"You told it right, Zinaida!" Pyotr Kalashnikov nodded, lost in thought. "Your voice sounded fine. I liked the part about the tower most of all. I don't even know just why. And the part about the birds worked fine, too!"

"That was something!" Ignashka remarked. "She half whispered that part. Was there somebody here who made her feel shy? God only knows! You know, some years back I heard Zinaida here tell this same tale at Terenty Lebedev's house. She was telling it to the women, and boy, did she ever tell it then! And believe it or not, every last one of them was sobbing and crying a river of tears! Do you believe it? It's the truth, by God!"

"Why wouldn't we?" Deryabin shrugged. "We all believe it!"

"But Ustinov didn't care for the tale!" Zinaida's statement was a question that she answered herself, "Not at all!" She was still sitting on the chest by the window as she had been while telling the story, her hands on her knees, shaking her head whenever a wisp of hair fell on her temple or got in her eyes.

"I liked it, Zinaida Pavlovna! Thank you! You told it well!" Ustinov said.

"Not likely! I shouldn't have agreed to tell you the tale! It was a waste of time. It's a woman's tale. A man just can't understand it, and a woman doesn't know how she should tell it to a man—loud or soft, short or long! No, I shouldn't have agreed. I'm always doing that. I do something, then afterwards I think that I shouldn't have done it, I shouldn't have said it!

Sometimes I wish I could live a day over again so everything could be the way it should have been. And not just one day, but my whole life!"

"What's this?" Deryabin drummed his fingers on the table top. "Even in this tale life doesn't go smoothly—it's not arranged according to human wisdom and knowledge. So what can be said about real life if things don't work out even in a fairy tale?! We should understand that life is no good anywhere! It's no good, and all of it, everything on earth, must be done over! Every last bit of it must be driven, driven, driven to change! There is nothing else to do. That is the most important business of our time!"

"But how do we change it, and into what?" sighed Ustinov.

"How, and into what? The work itself will tell us! If you don't act, you can't see it, but once you start, the work itself will show what and how and why. We need to drive on hard! Without stopping to take a breath! The first step is the hardest!"

"What a lot of different things we have talked about today!" Ustinov sighed. "What a lot of this and that and the other!"

Rodion Gavrilovich Smirnovsky

One of the Lebyazhka men, it was said, wanted to sell a workhorse, a six-year-old gelding with a good disposition, a horse that would do an admirable job. The second the news reached Ustinov, he was ready to go running off at full speed to see that gelding, but—what a situation!—it was Sevka Kupriyanov who was selling the gelding. Ustinov paced around the house collecting his hat and fur jacket, then stopped as if rooted to the floor, sighed, blinked, and went back to the kitchen where he had been repairing Grunya's collar. He would have to pamper broken-down Grunya somewhat. He would fix up her equipment a bit. In a light and well-fitting harness that didn't chafe or pinch her anywhere, maybe she would agree to work a little longer.

Sevka Kupriyanov was selling his six-year-old gelding because his son Matveyka had firmly announced that he would no longer stay in Lebyazhka. He was going away to the city. If they wouldn't let him go, he would surely beat Ignashka Ignatov to death, and then he would have to go away anyway, even if it were straight to prison. He could not forgive Ignashka Ignatov for the ridicule he had suffered after the cutting of that absurd, useless tree. Ustinov had participated in the insult less than the others and had not tied up the Kupriyanovs, but he still couldn't just walk into the Kupriyanovs' house and, as if nothing had happened, take a look at the gelding they had for sale. It was impossible!

After some thought, Ustinov felt sorry for Sevka. What could he do? If he didn't let his son go, Matveyka really would bash Ignashka's head in, and that's all there was to it. But how could he let him go? Now, when the Lebyazhka peasants were hiding their draft-age lads in field cabins and bathhouses, Matveyka Kupriyanov wanted to go off to the city! He wasn't draft-age yet, just barely sixteen, but he was a full-grown lad, and no one in the city would bother to ask. It was practically written all over him—"fit for military service!"

With such sympathy for Kupriyanov as a father, Ustinov felt it even more improper to go to him. Could he send his son-in-law Shurka instead? But that was also a losing proposition. God only knows what nonsense Shurka would come up with, and when it came to asking the price of the horse, he would slap Kupriyanov on the back and say, "You're a good man, Kupriyanov!" Figuring out what was going on, Kupriyanov would slap Shurka on the back. "And you're even better!" After that, Shurka would start to embrace him like a young wife and say, "What's a price, Kupriyanov? A price is a trivial thing, Kupriyanov. The important thing, Kupriyanov, is everlasting friendship, that's what!" Shurka knew only too well what was important in life and what wasn't—here he was living with his three children at his father-in-law's. He could never manage to set up his own household.

Another man would have sent his wife to talk to Kupriyanov's wife, but Ustinov didn't like that approach either. That never worked for him. Domna was too proud to go snooping around and to pretend that she had come by for no particular reason. Or maybe she simply had no talent for such things. Ustinov was no good at pretending himself, so he couldn't teach his wife anything about it. If someone borrowed a fiver from him and didn't pay it back on time, he could never demand his own. He would even feel embarrassed around his debtor and shun him to avoid the impression of following him for the sake of the money. That was a flaw in Ustinov that always weighed on him. Then he remembered that the Forest Commission had instructed him to have a talk with Rodion Smirnovsky and that Smirnovsky's sister was Sevka Kupriyanov's wife.

The Lebyazhka folk went to see one another for business or pleasure at any time of day or night, without knocking or invitation. If the thought popped into your head, or you hadn't seen someone for a while, or there was some other reason, you just went right ahead. It was considered impolite to keep your door hooked. If you have nothing to hide, why fear prying eyes? Locks—heavy, rusty ones—were hung only on barns, and even though opening them would have been simple with any old nail, still, the bigger the lock, the more a thief would think twice. But even the smallest lock on the door of a house would mean that someone rich and greedy lived there and that his wealth gave him no peace of mind day or night. When they weren't going to be at home, all normal, law-abiding people would lean a log against the door to show that there was no one there to talk to, no one to share the latest news or lend a match or a pinch of salt. The same custom prevailed at the Smirnovskys', but people were shy about visiting Smirnovsky even if they really did have some business.

The Smirnovskys' yard was special; there wasn't another like it for a hundred versts around. It was divided into two halves—one for the animals, the other for humans. The human side, sprinkled with sand, had gymnastic equipment set up in the middle of it. There were horizontal and parallel bars, rings hung from tall trestles, and a smooth pole for climbing. Every single day in the summer, and sometimes in the winter as well, Smirnovsky's sons, Gavrila and Anatoly, worked out on this equipment. Their father also did a few exercises, and with no less agility than the youngsters. To walk through all this tidiness, through this sand-sprinkled yard, the same way you walked anywhere else would be impossible. First you had to pull yourself together, straighten your shirt, set your cap more neatly on your head, and perhaps assume a stride that was, if not military, at least firm and brisk. A peasant didn't need all this. It would be easier for him to waddle through the whole of Lebyazhka from one end to the other than to walk five sazhens with such a half-military step. He had marched his fill in the army, and now that he was home it was the farthest thing from his mind!

The Lebyazhka folk were shy around Rodion Gavrilovich Smirnovsky. True, he was a peasant the same as they were. He plowed and sowed and looked after livestock, but he had also been an officer, a real officer—not a noncommissioned officer or even a sergeant major, but a lieutenant. He had gone to officers' school, and, most important of all, he had had a long career. He was not just "Your Honor," but also "Your Worship." And he had not been just any old lieutenant either, but the genuine article. Ten or so men in Lebyazhka, Ustinov among them, had served with him in the war, and they knew him from their own experience, not from others' stories. He was an amazing one, that peasant-officer! They might be marching to the rear, in mud up to their knees, utterly dejected, with no field kitchen or tobacco, and with all the officers as evil-tempered as dogs, but Platoon Commander Smirnovsky—and by the end of the war, Company Commander Smirnovsky—marched along easily, handsome and clean-shaven in a clean overcoat and boots only slightly smudged at the ankle.

Such natural-born soldiers, and such officers especially, aren't kept long in the ranks and at the front. The higher-ups notice them and take them away to be orderlies or adjutants, to serve as standard-bearers and in honor guards, to stamp around in parades and during the visits of generals. But Smirnovsky always served with his unit. His expectations for his subordinates were strict, and, by the same rule, he never indulged himself. He served splendidly and never looked for an easier or more comfortable position. Wherever his men were, that's where he was, too.

Most likely this was a Smirnovsky family trait—all of them had been veterans for generations. Everyone in Lebyazhka was amazed that they hadn't abandoned farming and joined the officer class. In recent years it was not only the aristocracy that made up the officer corps. As time went by, it contained more and more people from the other social classes. What kept the Smirnovskys in Lebyazhka? The Smirnovsky men would serve a year or two beyond their regular hitch, and then, having attained the rank of sergeant major or even ensign, they would always return home, hang their Crosses of Honor and other medals on the walls of their homes, and take up farming again like everyone else.

When they were asked about it, the Smirnovskys would say, "An officer from the peasantry is still a man of common birth. As long as you are a good sergeant major, a gentleman officer will think you are a good man and brag about you in front of his friends, put you in for medals, and have a shot of vodka with you, maybe even more than one. But if you are equal to him in rank, then you are already his enemy. He will trip you up when he can and offer you his hand only when no one else is looking. You'll never find an empty place at a staff meeting—you're always told, 'Excuse me, but this seat is taken!' "

"But then why do you Smirnovskys bother with the military? Service means rising in rank as high as you can, so what good is it to you if they shut you out? Why don't you just say the hell with it?"

"We couldn't do that either! All our grandfathers and great-grandfathers served and fought!"

Rodion Gavrilovich Smirnovsky was now just past forty, but he had managed to distinguish himself in two wars—one with Japan and one with Germany—and had risen in the ranks higher than any of his forefathers, all the way to lieutenant. At the beginning of the war, his fellow Siberians took pride in their commander, but toward the end, when political meetings with slogans like "Throw Down Your Arms!" and "Down with War!" were being held all along the front lines, the same soldiers began to look askance at him. He didn't attend political meetings and did his duty as he had before, as if nothing had happened, as if nothing had changed. He had spoken out at a meeting only once. "If I am ordered to leave the front, I will leave," he had said. "If not, I'll stay in the trenches even if I'm the only one left. I won't force anyone to do the same, but don't try to make me do otherwise either!" They had whistled at him in derision and called him various names, but he took no notice and walked away, sharp and smart.

Then came the Treaty of Brest-Litovsk. The Siberian regiment, despite all its meetings and despite its being only at a quarter of its normal strength, held its positions longer than any of the other regiments did, but then it decided to form a single convoy and make its way back home. Then the soldiers remembered their lieutenant and elected him Chairman of the Regimental Committee, that is, commander of the convoy.

"It's settled—we'll evacuate to Siberia!" Although Smirnovsky agreed, he stated his conditions. "But we won't do it as slaves in revolt! The great armies are in retreat, and we will retreat, too, but we'll do it under the strictest military discipline. Those who agree to this will board a train tonight and move eastward, and those who don't agree—well, I won't force them!"

Various commanding officers stopped the convoy in the forward staging area, and some tried to divert it to the south, to Rostov, explaining that the Siberians could go nowhere else but into the valiant White Volunteer Army. Giving them a proper salute, Smirnovsky insisted that the Siberians' business awaited them, not on the Don or Kuban Rivers, but on the Irtysh and the Ob. Then he speedily confirmed their itinerary, demanded a locomotive, and parade-marched back to his railroad car. When the train lurched forward, he saluted smartly again and waved his hand in farewell. Whenever the Reds stopped the train, he went out to meet them and explained what regiment they were and where they were bound. They could see that he was one of their own and not some kind of counterrevolutionary. The Czechs stopped the convoy in the Urals, where they seemed to be in control already. Once again the ostentatious officer stepped out of the train, though this time without epaulets, so that at first glance you might take him for a lieutenant colonel. Once again he explained that the Siberians understood perfectly where they were bound and why. He ordered the doors of the boxcars to be opened wide, and the Siberians, in full battle gear and with machine guns, peeked out gloomily at the station buildings, the early spring sky, and the Czechs. The convoy continued on its way.

Finally they arrived at Ozyorki, a tiny station, but for the Lebyazhkans truly the most important railroad junction in the whole world, for here they would get off the train and continue their journey on horseback. When the convoy came out to bid farewell to Smirnovsky, the soldiers tossed him into the air, made speeches, and swore their eternal devotion to him, and a portion of this praise even spilled over onto all the other Lebyazhkans. But when the eight front-line veterans returned to Lebyazhka and scattered to their separate houses, they forgot all about Smirnovsky. Whether he was dead or alive, everyone else had his own cares and chores in his garden and fields. Does it make any difference to your work who your commander was in the war and how he performed his duty? What is more, Smirnovsky didn't show himself much in public, and, though quietly, they began to call him what they had before, "Officer! Your Honor!"

And so Ustinov grew hesitant as soon as he entered Smirnovsky's yard and set foot on the sand-covered ground, hardened by frost and powdered here and there with snow. Although it had never even crossed his mind to call Smirnovsky "Your Honor," he still felt uncomfortable. He had completely forgotten about his commander! It was as if Ustinov was supposed to attack, but without orders. If only Smirnovsky would come out onto his porch and order, "Come here to me, forward march!" But in the quiet garden it became entirely unclear what he was supposed to say to Smirnovsky. It would be awkward to ask about Sevka Kupriyanov and his gelding right away, but if he waited it would be awkward to change the topic of conversation later. "It's the Forest Commission's fault!" thought Ustinov. "They sent me to talk to him, but they didn't say what I should talk about!" And so he very quietly retreated to the gate, let himself out, and continued walking along the street as if he had never intended to visit anyone. He decided on another plan, to go straight back to the Commission, which he knew was still in session.

When he walked into the Pankratovs' main room, he began to speak with angry abruptness. "Here's how it is, Comrade Commission Members! We need to send for Smirnovsky and offer him the command of the forest guard!"

"What?" Dumbfounded, Deryabin shook as he stared at Ustinov. "Yesterday we decided one thing, but today it's an entirely different thing? Why?" He paused a moment and added, "Smirnovsky would never agree to it, anyway! He doesn't want anything to do with us or the rest of Lebyazhka—that's an officer for you!"

"He won't agree!" Ustinov concurred. "However, his refusal will be just as useful to us as his consent. Otherwise, every citizen of Lebyazhka will find fault with us and ask why we didn't offer such a man the leadership of the armed guard."

"And what if he does agree to it?" Deryabin asked.

"Then we'll have absolute order, and neither our people nor the woodcutters from the steppe will even dare to stick their noses in the forest! And it will help show that the Commission carries authority with all the people!"

"You've come up with some fine words this time, Ustinov!" Deryabin said in surprise. "But I'm sure he'll refuse!"

"Then when he does, I can fulfill your request; that is, I can tell him not to interfere in any way with our Commission. There was no way to broach the subject before!"

Deryabin could not deny this argument, and both Ustinov and the Commission knew it.

"And if Smirnovsky agrees, there's no need to worry that he will start meddling in any of the Commission's other affairs!" Ustinov added. "He won't! He'll perform his duties, and nothing more!"

Drumming his fingers on the table and glancing at some paper or other, Deryabin ordered, "Ignaty! Run over and bring back Smirnovsky!"

"But he won't come, Comrade Deryabin! Never!" Ignashka answered.

"Ignaty! Run over and bring back Smirnovsky!" Deryabin repeated.

Ignashka grabbed his cap and sprang through the door. Deryabin buried his head in his papers, still drumming his fingers on the table. Kalashnikov paused for a moment, tousled his thick hair, and began to explain the statutes of some cooperative or other. He talked in detail for a long time, but he was the first to nod toward the window. "They're coming!" Smirnovsky was striding smartly along, with Ignashka now running in front of him, now lagging behind. A minute later the door swung open.

"Here he is! And you said . . . But I . . . ," Ignashka reported.

"How can I be of service?" asked Smirnovsky with a salute. Not a tall man, but well-proportioned, he wore a slightly military, city-made gray suit, a topcoat, and a green service cap without insignia. His voice was a little husky, and his narrowed, slightly Kalmyk eyes were stern.

As Deryabin looked at Kalashnikov, Kalashnikov said, "Sit down, Smirnovsky! We called you here to have a talk!"

Smirnovsky took off his cap, undid the top two buttons of his coat, and sat down. They were all waiting for him to ask what they wanted to talk to him about, but he said nothing and only looked at each of them in turn, shifting his glance from Kalashnikov to Polovinkin, from Polovinkin to Ustinov, and so on around the room.

"Well then, Rodion Gavrilovich," Kalashnikov said at last, "we have a request for you. From the Forest Commission, more precisely, from the whole community of Lebyazhka . . . " When Smirnovsky nodded but still said nothing, Kalashnikov caught his breath and continued, "Here's our request: we want you to take on the leadership of the armed forest guard. We are trying to stop it, but people are still cutting wood in the forest, and now not just for themselves, but also for sale to the villages on the steppe. If you give it a try, we are sure that there will be no more of it."

Before answering, Smirnovsky paused to see if Kalashnikov had anything more to say. Then he said, "I cannot honor your request!" He gestured abruptly. "No!"

"Why, Comrade Smirnovsky?" Deryabin asked.

"I'm afraid of weapons these days!"

"Afraid?!" asked Deryabin in amazement. "You, afraid?!"

"Afraid!" Smirnovsky repeated.

"But how is that possible, Rodion Gavrilovich?" asked Ustinov, stretching out his arms. "It's hard to believe that from you."

"I'm afraid because an unbelievable fratricide is going on all around us. Every shot fired now is like a match put to a powder keg. These days no one can even have an argument without shots being fired. One day we cuss at each other across the fence, the next we're shooting at each other across that same fence! One day you arrest a woodcutter in the forest, and the next day, when war begins, he'll remember the insult."

"Understood!" nodded Deryabin. "One day we arrest Kupriyanov and his son, and the next they . . . The Kupriyanovs are your relatives, aren't they?"

"Kupriyanov will restrain himself. I'll persuade him not to let his wounded pride get out of control. But can you persuade everyone? Will you on the Commission be able to restrain yourselves? Today you might quarrel only with words, but what about tomorrow? Maybe then you'll quarrel with weapons?"

"What'll you say next, Rodion?" Kalashnikov shook his head in dismay, his whole body swaying on his stool.

"There's no call to talk like that, Rodion Gavrilovich!" Ustinov supported Kalashnikov. "Such a thought shouldn't even enter your head!"

"It really hasn't!" Smirnovsky reassured him. "But then in '17 when the great change began, it never entered my head that Russia would be ablaze for a year, and maybe two, with a fratricidal war!"

"Aha, I understand this point of view, too, Smirnovsky!" said Deryabin. "You always wanted to bring the war to a victorious end! But I ask you, what good would this victory have been to the people?"

"It would have prevented us Russians from fighting among ourselves, our regiments from withdrawing from the front only to fight a civil war in our own fields . . . And even so the Germans would have lost fewer people than they did when their defeat was postponed for another whole year. It would also have decreased our allies' losses. We left our allies with the calculation that they would win a victory for us in any case! If Germany had won, she would have left no trace of us or our sense of justice, no trace of the Whites, and even less of the Reds! It would have prevented Russia from falling to pieces, and the Kuban and the Don Cossacks would not have separated themselves from her, given Kaiser Wilhelm a free victory parade, and made a deal with him to make war on their own Russian people! It would have prevented anyone, either the Japanese or the Czechs, from occupying Russian soil and deciding our internal affairs with weapons in their hands. Well, am I free to go?" Smirnovsky stood up and put on his cap.

"As you wish!" Deryabin answered. "If you can't stay a few minutes longer."

"I can stay a few minutes."

"All right!" Ustinov was glad. "But, Rodion Gavrilovich, you've forgotten that a man has his limits and that once he's reached them, he can't do the same thing he did yesterday. That's the way it was with the war. Once a soldier no longer understood what he was fighting for, it was impossible for him to go on. A soldier will accept even the worst war if he understands what it's all about!"

"There is no limit, Ustinov," Smirnovsky disagreed. "Yes, there is a limit to understanding and thought—there a man has his back to the wall. But he can go on doing either good or evil to his dying breath!"

Leaning back in his chair, Deryabin looked attentively at Smirnovsky and said, "Thank you for continuing our conversation, Lieutenant! Sometimes the son of a peasant can even out-bourgeois a bourgeois! I'd like to ask you if you mean that we, the working class, did the wrong thing by not asking the bourgeois imperialists when the best time to oppose them was? We should have asked, and they would have answered that we should beat the Germans first! But did the imperialists ask us about anything when they threw us into this war, the worst slaughter in the history of all nations? So who is to blame first? Who is responsible? Shouldn't someone get rid of the guilty party? It's never too early to do that!"

"But there's no reason to ask the capitalists. Shouldn't you be asking yourself what you should do? And tell me, Deryabin, did you yourself ever see an imperialist during the war, in the trenches or in combat?"

"No one ever saw them! Maybe once in a while someone's son would stick his nose in the trenches just for show so they could write about it in the newspapers. An imperialist is always safe at home or in some bank vault behind iron doors!"

"Exactly, Deryabin! And when the working class rises up against the imperialists, he will still be sitting there, and again he'll send the workers to defend him. A war against the imperialists is always a war between workingmen! You should never forget that when you call people up for such a war! And you can't help but be afraid. I'm afraid! Maybe I'm not afraid of anything else, but in this I'm the biggest coward of all! I'm not afraid of the war as much as of the life that will come after it! Even after it is over, we will see each other as enemies. Instead of mutual faith, we'll have mutual suspicion! And it will be like that to the end of our days! Ustinov!" Smirnovsky called out sharply, like a commander during military maneuvers. "Could you fight against me? Or even worse, fight against me and then later live as my neighbor? Fight, and then later have our children go to the same school, sit together at the same desk, both thinking and remembering to themselves, or even out loud, how one's father had killed the other's? Well, Ustinov?"

Ustinov heaved a deep sigh, but said nothing. He had to think it over first.

"Well, I'm ready to fight against you, Citizen Smirnovsky, or against anyone else, at any time!" Deryabin had taken the floor. "Even against other workingmen, if they've taken up with the other side, the wrong side. You know how it is in war—there are only sides, not people, only raw power! And there's no talk about who's on what side and how they wound up there. You've said a lot about the Brest-Litovsk treaty and civil war. But life is made up of actions, not words. And actions come from choosing sides, from different classes. I'll repeat my question: why did the bourgeois bring me to the point where even the fanciest words are useless to me and I have only one alternative—to fight him? Did I declare war on him? No, he declared war on me! He used the land like a noose around the neck of the peasant, and when the peasant cried out, 'Help, I'm dying!' he stopped him from crying out and sent anyone who did into exile, to us here in Siberia! Wouldn't it be more just to exile just one landowner to Siberia, divide up his lands, and settle a hundred or a thousand peasant families on them in Russia?

"And don't make yourself out to be so honorable, Lieutenant," Deryabin went on. "Don't pretend that I'm the first to organize bloodshed! When the people went prayerfully to the Little Father, the Tsar, in 1905, all it took was a wave of the Little Father's hand, and honorable lieutenants just like you gave the command to fire. If that had been the only time, it would be one thing, but all the army ever did was suppress the people! What is left for me, one of the suppressed, to do? Am I right?"

"If the army had carried the honor, glory, and power of its nation to other nations, I would still be in it. But I am not in it now and cannot be! Because these days you are right!"

"Well then! To win a victory for your own bourgeois in someone else's country—is that honor? And to do it as their slave, is that honor either? Now the Russian and German peasants have become brothers to prevent such a thing from happening, and they've all done away with their generals or are about to do so."

"They've become brothers—the Germans are in Rostov-on-Don! And the Ukraine has been torn away from Russia, and so have Finland, and Estonia, and Lithuania. And Poland. And Kars. And Batum! And what's more, we will pay six million marks in compensation. They became brothers with the Germans, but with the hope that the allies we betrayed would win a victory without us! They would rout the Germans, and then we would breathe more freely too!"

"And why did all this happen? The German soldiers weren't able to deal with their generals and landowners in time, that's why. But we will put an end to capitalism completely in our country, and then we'll go help them! So, Lieutenant Smirnovsky, thank you again for talking with us! You're doing the right thing in refusing to work with us! The right thing, indeed!"

"One thing's sure," Polovinkin, who had been silent the whole time, said slowly. "We started out with the forest guard and finished up with who knows what, even the treaty in Brest and the year 1905! If we're going to do our business that way, talking about all sorts of different times, we'll never make any sense! We'll never get beyond the question of Leonty Yevseyev. Should we call Leonty back to the job of commander of the guard?"

"You've made a mistake, Rodion Gavrilovich," said Ignashka. "You've made a mistake, and I feel sorry for you!"

Smirnovsky got up and stood for a moment, then saluted to no one in particular, saying good-bye only to Ustinov. "Good-bye, Kolya! Do you remember serving together?"

"I remember, Rodion Gavrilovich!"

"Take care of yourself, and come and see me if you get the chance!" Smirnovsky left quickly, with the same measured stride.

Deryabin was quiet for a moment, then said to Ustinov, "Good work, Comrade. You were right about calling in the lieutenant! We did so and learned all we need to know, and now you won't have to bother with him anymore!"

"I still have one piece of business with him."

"You do?" asked Deryabin in surprise. Then he asked Kalashnikov, "Tell me, Petro, Mr. Chairman, who was in the right, me or Smirnovsky?"

"You were, Deryabin . . . ," Kalashnikov nodded. "But you could have touched on the subject of the working class's path to justice, that is, the cooperative path—"

"All right!" Deryabin interrupted him. "And who do you think was right in our discussion, Ustinov? Will you tell me?"

"It's hard to say. If I have to choose, I'd say your views are closer to mine. However—"

"Closer! Then why do you still need to talk to Smirnovsky? What kind of business could you have with him?"

"I have personal business with him . . . "

"Personal! Well, well!"

Comrade Deryabin was quick and clever. He had come home from the front long before and had not heard the political speeches in the trenches in '17. He had not torn the epaulets off the shoulders of any officer or elected Socialist Revolutionaries or Bolsheviks into the Regimental Committee or any other committee. But as soon as you started to tell him about any of this, he would begin to correct you, "No, it didn't happen like that, it was this way . . . " And he made sense, too! Or he would begin to tell you about the suffering of the landless peasants in Russia, and again, in detail. Everyone in Lebyazhka was amazed. Where did the man get all that? Of course, he had received quite an education from Andrei Mikhailovich Kuzmenkov.

From the beginning of the war, Deryabin had served in a field telephone unit with Kuzmenkov, a worker from Tver, and they were discharged at the same time—Deryabin because of shell shock, Kuzmenkov because of illness. In the spring of the past year, Kuzmenkov had come to stay with his friend, to drink milk and eat well, to regain his health, but it was already too late for that. He repaired sewing machines and cream separators for the women and mowing machines and hay balers for the men. He soon died, but he left his thoughts and quite a number of books to Deryabin. But while Kuzmenkov was a quiet man of few words, either because of his illness or his own nature, and always smiled at everyone as if he were embarrassed about something, Deryabin always spoke quickly and loudly whether he needed to or not. Always serious, he could spend two whole days without a break at his books, and now at the Commission's paperwork. That's the kind of man he was. He knew how to borrow not only from Kuzmenkov but from many others as well. He had a talent for catching a thought on the wing and then working on it and developing it toward some end. Now he leaned back in his chair and made movements with his arms that resembled the exercises noncommissioned officers used to torment soldiers on the parade ground.

"What about you, Polovinkin?" he demanded sternly. "And you, Ignaty? What about you two?"

"What d'ya mean?" Polovinkin asked.

Giving a jump on his chair, Ignashka asked, "Me? I didn't do nothing! I was just . . . "

"What do you mean, 'nothing'? I'm asking you what you thought about my talk with Smirnovsky."

"What is there to think?" Ignashka jumped up again. "Who is Smirnovsky, anyway? He went from rags to riches—and not to such great riches at that—but he's so proud. He's got more pride than he knows what to do with!"

"And just what rags did he come from? Can you explain that, Ignaty?"

"The usual. He's from peasant stock, from the big-footed old Siberian types!"

"So you think the working peasants are like filthy rags? Is that it?"

"I didn't say no such thing, Comrade Deryabin!"

"Just remember, Ignaty, that the filthy rags are not the peasants or the workers, but the rich people that many, out of human stupidity, would like to join! Have you got that?"

"Well, still . . . I wouldn't mind being rich . . . For two weeks or so, maybe three . . . But in general, I understand, Comrade Deryabin!"

After thinking for a while and listening to the others, Polovinkin said, "Smirnovsky never wants to be like everyone else! It's pure hell for him, it's death!"

"So it is; you're right there! When a man cuts himself off from the masses, from the majority, there is no truth left in him, and there can be none! There can't be anything but arrogance and crafty lies. Lies so crafty that it's not easy to expose them!"

"But what about the saints?" asked Ustinov. "They were always alone, but they brought the majority of the people to see things their way. Is there no truth in the saints?"

"Nothing but lies!" Deryabin insisted. "What is truth, Comrade Ustinov? One person understands it this way, another that way, but where and what is it really? It exists only in what is good and just for the people, that is, for the majority of the people. Now since the people are demanding to take the land, the factories, and power into their own hands, that is the holy and highest truth—there is no other! Time will pass, and the masses will dictate some other conditions for life, and then that will be the truth. And that's how it will always be. Do you get it, Ustinov?"

"Well, it used to be that people would burn other people at the stake if they didn't believe in their God. Who possessed the truth, the majority, or those who were burned?"

"Here you need to determine where the people are acting on their own and where they are being pushed into a crime by some evil force."

"What kind of evil?"

"Different kinds—monks, sorcerers, capitalists."

"And who will determine this? Will you determine where the people are acting on their own and where they are incited by someone else, Deryabin?"

"Why not?"

"But if you can do this while others can't, aren't you separated from everyone else, just like that saint?"

"Never! I will never stand apart from the people. I will always be with them, in the depths of their souls, because I can feel, I can sense what comes out of their true selves and what evil ideas are foisted on them! My own personality means nothing in this, I am a zero!"

"That's a bit strange! Just who are you in our Forest Commission? A zero? Or the main working member, the commander of the forest guard, and, it seems, our leader? And if you, our leader, are a zero, then what are we?"

"You haven't quite understood me, Ustinov," said Deryabin, drumming his fingers on the table. "If I am directing things, if I have accepted this responsibility, it is only because I understand that I am a zero before the people! That means that I more than anybody else should be a servant of the people, only a servant! Serving and leading should be twin roles, merged into one. Is that hard for you to understand, Ustinov?"

"Of course not! That night when the woodcutters from the steppe appeared so suddenly and you were about to give the command to shoot at them—who were you then, a servant and a zero? Or were you the leader at that moment? The steppe folk are also the people, and noticeably poorer than we Lebyazhkans are! No doubt, they need the forest more than we do. Our own Lebyazhkan woodcutters have already gone so far as to chop wood for sale. 'Soon,' they say, 'the war will start, and then the steppe men will cut our forest anyway! So it's better to sell a man one timber now than to give him ten for free later!' But that man can't wait for the war. He needs lumber to fix the roof of his cabin today, and so he comes to the Lebyazhka forest, and there a simple Lebyazhka peasant greets him with gunfire. And doesn't he give the signal to fire with a wave of his hand, just as Tsar Nicholas waved his from the palace window when they shot at the people in 1905?!"

After thinking a bit, Deryabin said pensively, "During the talk we just had with the lieutenant, you didn't miss a thing, did you, Ustinov?" Then with sudden animation, he got up from the table, took three steps, turned, and pointed at his empty chair. "Sit in my place then, Ustinov! There it is. And there's all the paperwork. There's the list of the members of the guard, that paper there, hanging over the edge of the table. Take on the job! I'll help you familiarize yourself with what's going on, and you can do everything your own way. You can deal with everyone intelligently and honorably—your own Lebyazhkans, and the steppe folk, and the moonshiners, and Grishka Sukhikh! Everyone!"

In the resulting confusion among the members of the Commission, Kalashnikov stopped Deryabin. "Now wait, Vasily, don't be in such a hurry!"

"Did you think that's what I meant?" Ustinov asked in complete confusion. "I didn't mean that at all!"

▲▲▲

Back in '15, the regiment in which Ustinov had served was being regrouped in a small town in Grodno Gubernia, and in that town there had been a statue of a mermaid in a small, shady garden. A little maiden seemed to be standing and gazing into the water, but she was made of iron and must have weighed at least seventy poods. To make her dive head first into that round pool, you'd have to knock about twenty bricks out of the base she was standing on—not something you could do with your bare hands. So the soldiers sneaked an iron crowbar out of the barracks and cleverly dumped the mermaid into the water. Let her follow her eyes! The city authorities tried to fasten their mermaid to its base with iron rods, but those didn't help. The soldiers all worked together to pull out the rods and threw the little mermaid into the water anyway, disfiguring her eyes, ears, nose, and other parts with the crowbar. There was no end to the bother caused by this troublesome maid. There were more arrests and orders and arguments between the mayor and the regimental commander than you could count! A policeman was assigned to guard the mermaid. The soldiers generously passed the hat, everyone pitched in a few kopecks, and they bought the policeman a bottle. The policeman went away for a quarter of an hour, and that was all it took. The soldiers were skilled at it, and the entire regiment lent a hand.

The whole affair ended with the regimental commander placing a guard in front of the mermaid. The soldiers had to defend her against themselves, and any guard lax in his duty was court-martialed under the articles of war. Although the soldiers left the mermaid alone then, they also laughed at their regimental commander. Just think of it: he had put a guard with a fixed bayonet in front of a naked iron woman, and the guard was changed in the afternoon, at midnight, and at dawn, with full formalities, with a password and presentation of arms! Wasn't that ridiculous? Ustinov had only looked at the mermaid from the sidelines and had taken no part in her fate. Once or twice, to be like everyone else, he had thrown a five-kopeck coin into the hat for the town policeman so his comrades wouldn't say he was stingy and unsociable.

But in '17, again while they were resting in a town near the front, it was no longer possible to get off the hook with a few kopecks. Because the soldiers' food allowance had fallen short of their needs, they began to loot the stores, first grocery stores, then all the others as well. The amount of food they got this way was pitiful, but they smashed things, scattering a lot of broken pieces of glass, wood, and bricks. If they had just taken what they needed and carried it away quietly without saying a word, it would have been like stealing. Only a thief does such a thing quietly, but if it's done loudly, while smashing glass and making lots of other noise, it turns the soldier into a kind of hero. It answers some inner need, something in his guts. At home in Russia, a soldier had always loved to smash something or other to bits, and abroad, in Austria, he was for some reason especially fond of goose down. As soon as he appeared, feather beds would be disemboweled and scattered around the towns and villages. Was this perhaps because he never got to see his own feather bed?

Because of this behavior, the Austrians and Germans called the Russian soldier a barbarian, but the years passed, and there turned out to be no justification for this label. When the Germans appeared in Russia, they didn't bother with feather beds. They took the grain supplies and livestock and drove people off to work for them. So which is the most barbaric—to let some feathers fly to work off your foul mood, or to condemn those you have defeated to starvation and slavery?

During the looting of the grocery stores and bakeries, Ustinov was at first on the sidelines again. He walked around the town and watched what was going on, and nothing more. His fellow soldiers began to look askance at him, and once he overheard someone having a smoke and saying that this Ustinov must be some sort of spy, and if not a spy, then some other kind of counterrevolutionary!

It had been a day of desperation. There had been a political meeting where they had voted on two slogans, "Onward to Victory!" and "Down with War!" Trying to blow up the railroad bridge, the Germans had ventured an exchange of artillery fire, and the whole population of burghers was frantically crowding the trains to evacuate the town. The soldiers threatened them with their fists, and some with their weapons, reminding them of the burghers' speeches, and money, and some fires or other. Ustinov watched and watched, and then he drew his revolver—he always carried a revolver at that time—and bang! He shot a gray draft horse that was clumsily pulling a light carriage. The carriage held a very fat gentleman wearing a derby, a lady so slender she was almost waistless, two or three small children, and a large collection of various bundles, valises, and other luggage. The coachman threw down his reins and ran away, the lady began to shout, and the gentleman covered his face with his derby, but Ustinov didn't even see what happened to the horse. He had turned on his heel and gone back to the barracks.

That put an end to the soldiers' talk that Ustinov was not one of their own or was even some sort of counterrevolutionary. He had become the same as everyone else around him, and his comrades liked him as they had before. Only in Lieutenant Smirnovsky's eyes did Ustinov notice some sort of coldness or distance. But, nevertheless, after that incident life took its course. It was a soldier's life, without rest and full of endless discussion, but it went on.

Once again Ustinov needed life to take its course—not the course that he had wanted and achieved by shooting that horse, but, nevertheless, some step had to be taken, and he knew that he would not be able to pass by Smirnovsky's house a second time. Drawn there, he was worried by only one thing, finding a fitting opportunity to discuss Sevka Kupriyanov's bay gelding with Rodion Gavrilovich. This time the sand-sprinkled yard and the gymnastic equipment didn't stop him. He went into the vestibule, coughed audibly, and tapped lightly on the door.

"Who is it?" someone asked, and Rodion Gavrilovich appeared barefoot at the threshold. He was wearing store-bought suspenders, a white shirt, and army riding breeches. "Ah, it's you, Kolya!"

From a bird cage in the window of the quiet, tidy house, a pair of goldfinches stared at Ustinov from their perch and wondered, "Who could that be?" When the two men had exchanged greetings, Ustinov asked, "Why is it so quiet? Where are your sons? And your wife?"

"My sons are out fishing on the lake. They want to stun the fish while the ice is still thin. They went off and took their mother with them so she can visit with some folks along the way."

Having seen the three Smirnovskys pass by on the street, Ustinov already knew this. He had thought, "Now's my chance to go see Rodion Gavrilovich!" He was just checking the correctness of his assumption.

"Come into the parlor, Kolya!"

Ustinov hung his hat and coat on a nail and went in. Smirnovsky stayed in the kitchen, quickly pulled on a pair of soft deerskin boots, took an old leather boot out from under the stove, and, using it as a bellows, began to revive some coals for the samovar.

"But I don't need any tea!" Ustinov said.

"You will! I'll treat you to some real tea!"

"You got your hands on some?"

"After we came home with the convoy, I opened up a trunk, and what did I see but packets of tea, cigarettes, and even a woman's brooch! That's how I came across it!"

"The men put it there," Ustinov silently guessed, "as a sign of respect for their convoy commander. The soldiers loved Smirnovsky!"

"We had everything back then. You remember yourself, Kolya. Didn't we have everything?"

"All the same, they did the right thing with their presents!"

"I'm not so sure! You never know if it's a friend or an enemy who is giving you a present." Smirnovsky tossed some coals into the samovar and began to fan them again with the boot while Ustinov examined a print from an engraving hanging on the wall between the two windows of the room. A great battle was depicted, with cannons in clouds of smoke, and in one cloud, with sword raised on high, was Peter the Great. Below the picture was a text written in old Russian ornamental script:

FOR THE RUSSIAN ARMY KNEW THAT THE HOUR HAD COME WHEN THE FUTURE OF THE WHOLE FATHERLAND HAD BEEN PLACED IN THEIR HANDS: RUSSIA WOULD EITHER PERISH OR BE REBORN FOR THE BETTER. AND THEY WOULD THINK THAT THEY BORE ARMS AND TOOK THE FIELD, NOT FOR PETER'S SAKE, BUT FOR THE STATE ENTRUSTED TO PETER, FOR THEIR RACE, FOR THE RUSSIAN PEOPLE, WHICH UNTIL NOW HAD REMAINED STANDING BY THE STRENGTH OF THEIR ARMS AND WHICH NOW WAITED FOR THEM TO DECIDE ITS FATE.

> Address of Peter the Great to his troops on the eve of the Battle of Poltava,* from the 26th to the 27th of August 1709.

Ustinov read the inscription slowly, pausing in thought over those words that he didn't understand right away. When he had finished, Smirnovsky brought in the samovar and set it on the table.

"You know what I like to read about Peter the Great more than anything else, Kolya? It's not what has been written about him, but what he wrote and said himself! He uses marvelous words: 'to search out victory!' 'we strove to save ourselves,' 'we ran forward at a great gallop,' or here's another one: 'the road of fasting'—that means a hungry road, without

---

*A decisive victory by Russian tsar Peter I against Sweden in the Northern War (1701–1721), which marks the beginning of Russian influence in Europe.

provisions or fodder. It's a pity expressions like that haven't stayed with us! These precious words would have been especially useful in the army. But then what sort of people are we? We Russians don't take care of what we have and we boast about what we don't have! No one knows when we will ever change. Maybe never! No, read it one more time, Kolya: 'Russia will be reborn for the better!' That Tsar knew how to work with words as well as ships and cannon! You can see the man in his words, through his words! But would you like a little vodka, Kolya?"

"I really don't feel like it, Rodion Gavrilovich."

"A small glass? Just one?"

"No, I don't feel much like it . . . "

They talked for a while about the weather, the harvest, and the chaos that surrounded them on all sides. Smirnovsky spoke with great anger about the Czechs. He said they didn't do much in the war. They had surrendered to the Russians and had been regrouping in the rear for action against the Germans, but they never saw that action, and now they were mixed up in the civil war. And they were cruel—worse than the Germans! They pillaged, and flogged, hanged, and shot people! They were not just allies to the Whites, they were the whitest of the Whites themselves! They worked for whomever gave them the most or even promised the most. And they might be the deciding force in the civil war. More and more interventionists, from many different nations, were crawling out of the woodwork to help them. Without them the civil war would already be over. Ustinov maintained that as soon as the Czechs and their own Whites got as far as the central Russian provinces they would be stopped. The peasants there had taken the land as their own, and they would defend it with their lives. They would never let it go back to the landowners.

"But what about Siberia?" Rodion Gavrilovich asked. "What will happen to Siberia, Ustinov? The Japanese are in the Far East and east of Lake Baikal almost all the way to Chita. There's a British battalion in Omsk, and without newspapers you and I have no idea who else there is. What will become of Siberia? Will it perhaps be split off from Russia?"

"Never, Rodion Gavrilovich!" Ustinov answered. "That would be impossible!"

They were silent for a moment. Ustinov thought that perhaps the time had come to find out something about Sevka Kupriyanov's gelding. If he waited any longer, it might be too late! But it wasn't the right moment.

Pouring some tea for himself and his guest, Smirnovsky asked, "Well, what are you looking for these days, Kolya?"

Ustinov sighed, "In what way?"

"In life."

" 'In life'? I don't really know, Rodion Gavrilovich. I keep looking and looking, but for what, I'm not sure. But I've come here to find out how you are. Have you found anything? Have you had any luck?"

"Me? I've been fine until just recently, Kolya. Everything has gone well. I've looked for honor. Always."

"What kind of honor?"

"My own. What other kind is there?"

"These days there are many kinds: the honor of the army, the honor of country, the honor of the Revolution—I could go on and on!"

"None of them mean anything without your own honor. That is the only honor that assigns the other honors their proper places—this one in a good place, that one in a bad place, a third in the highest place. Then life falls into order."

"Even though you're real peasants and not Cossacks, you Smirnovskys always took up military service. Why? For the sake of your own honor?"

"I've seen you in war, Kolya. You are a brave man, but still things have to be explained to you. We Smirnovskys don't need any explanations. Courage is in our blood. We are born brave; that is, Kolya, we're not afraid of death. From childhood on, people make such a song and dance about their own deaths! They will tell everyone stories about it, nurse it, continually predict it, crawl on their knees before it, betray people because of it. They live like its slave. And all in vain!

"Awareness of death is given only to men, and they need to make use of it like men, and not to sink even lower than the animals, who know nothing about it! Kolya, a man's consciousness of his own death, his knowledge that he is not immortal, raises him above all other living things. So while he is alive, he should be a man and do a man's work. Because an animal doesn't have this consciousness, its life may be brutish or swinish or as carefree as a bird's, but it has no work to do. Can you imagine, Kolya, that your cow or your horse would labor for you as it does now if it knew that in ten years it will die? No, that isn't how it would like to spend the rest of its life! This is the way things are arranged in nature, Kolya.

"Great people have understood this arrangement, even Tsar Pyotr Alexeyevich, Peter the Great. But the insignificant and the ignorant have not understood, and they never will. And if I, a peasant and soldier, have understood this and recognized it just as the greatest of people have, then this is to my merit and honor. Because I know the value of it, no one can make me his slave, and there is no lord above me but the Lord God Almighty! And it also seems to me that if there are no brave men among the peasant class, or the working class, or the merchant class, or the educated class, or the aristocracy, or any other class, then there can be no nation, no people, and no true government either! Every class is put to the test in its own way, and such an ordeal cannot be endured without daring and courage!"

They drank their tea a while longer in silence, each with his own thoughts, and then Ustinov asked, "Are you trying to convert me to your own faith, Rodion Gavrilovich?"

"You didn't understand me very well, Kolya. Courage is the kind of faith you can't draw anyone into—it's useless to try! It comes by itself to whomever is ready for it. Were you afraid I was trying to convert you, Kolya?"

"No, I wasn't. Everyone has his own unshakable faith! Grishka Sukhikh just came to see me in the fields with his religion, preached it to me, and even threatened me, 'If you don't accept it, I'll kill you!' I didn't believe that he would kill me. But why, Rodion Gavrilovich, does everyone with a faith of his own have to shove it at other people? And why doesn't he do it to his own father, or his son, instead of some person who has nothing to do with him?"

"What do you mean? Many words and thoughts come to us from our fathers! Many indeed!"

"Did what you just said to me come from your father?"

"No, my father didn't teach me those words. But they came out of the way he lived and the way he taught me to live."

Just as Ustinov was about to ask how Rodion Gavrilovich's father had taught him to live, the voice of an old man, already as squeaky as a small child's, came from the kitchen: "What are you saying there about your father, Rodka? Is it good or bad? What brought him into the conversation?" And Smirnovsky Senior, Gavril Rodionovich, his bony bare feet slapping against the yellow floorboards, came into the main room.

"Why would I say anything bad about you, Papa?" Rodion Gavrilovich said with a touch of embarrassment. "Sit down and have some tea, Papa."

"I'll join you, but I don't want any tea, I've had mine today, and then some. I just came out to see if that ain't Kolka Ustinov who's come to visit. Is it him?"

"It's me!" Ustinov nodded. "You recognized me all right, Gavril Rodionovich!"

"Of course I did. I still recognize my own Lebyazhkans! Sometimes even from a good piece away! So, were you off fighting in the war for long this time, Nikolka?"

"More than three years, Gavril Rodionovich!"

"Now that's a lo-ong time! And how is it you fought so long and didn't win? Is it the Tsar's fault? These days no matter what goes wrong, it's always the Tsar's fault! If our neighbors', the Gladkovs', cow gives no milk, what does the missus say? 'The hell with you, and the Tsar, too!' I've heard her say that to her cow and then smack it on the nose with the empty milk pail!"

"But the Tsar is guilty, Gavril Rodionovich. How can we not blame him for being unable to run the government?"

"A Tsar does what he has to, and a soldier does what he has to! No, we didn't do it that way in our time. We didn't behave like that when we hit the Frenchies at Sevastopol,* and the English, and some other country, I don't remember just who else was there with them."

"But, Papa, didn't you give up the city of Sevastopol to the same ones you hit?" Smirnovsky Junior reminded his father.

"Rodka! Don't argue with me!" Gavril Rodionovich said, slapping his son on the knee, his face reddening. "They took Sevastopol, it's true, but soon they gave it right back to us. They were in a hurry to clear out! Isn't that to their shame more than ours—to take a city, spill their own blood, stack up whole regiments of corpses like cordwood, and then give it back? How is that? That's the same way Bonaparte—a pox on him!—wandered around Moscow, and then wound up back over his own border just barely alive and without his hat. But then what good's it to him anyway—what's he going to do, go back for it? And I might be asking the two of you: how many cities did you give up to the Germans and never take back?"

"Many of them, Papa!" Rodion Gavrilovich sighed.

"That ain't no good! We didn't do it that way, I tell you. We did just the opposite. We looked for cities to take in faraway lands! We met the Turk in the Balkans,† and didn't we give him a fight? We'd go into some country, and the same day we'd give it to him in the chops! He'd retreat to another place—there's lots of little nations there, all with their own tongues—and we'd march through it in a week's time and catch up with him, and we'd give it to him in the chops again! He'd go off into a third country, and we'd go in after him! He'd go on home, and we'd follow! Our Thirty-ninth Regiment, what was formed in 1796, got the Banner of the Order of St. George for that campaign, and we already had insignia on our caps from fighting the Turks back in that time, and they say the lads that served after us won the Order of the Silver Trumpet for the regiment! That's really something! But now? Look how many medals Rodka brung back from the war, the St. George and other officer's medals, too, but so what? He won the St. George, but surrendered cities! That's a fine thing! It's a crying shame!"

Without saying a word, his son looked out the window.

"Just how old might you be now, Gavril Rodionovich?" Ustinov asked.

"Oh, I'm old, Nikolka! I've gathered so many years I don't know what to do with them all! Death won't be able to hold all my years, a pox on her! And you know, she never came near me, not with the Turk, not with the

---

*A major battle site in the Crimean War (1854–1856) between Russia and allied France, England, and Turkey.
†Refers to the Russo-Turkish War of 1877–1878, fought ostensibly on behalf of fellow Slavs in the Balkans.

Frenchies, not with anyone! It's a pure wonder I haven't yet stared her in the face to this day!"

"And that's good, Papa," Rodion Gavrilovich smiled at his father. "Live a while longer!"

"And I would, too! And I wouldn't be shy about it if I could still climb up into my bunk by myself! That's the problem—it's easy to climb down, but up, I just can't do it. If I could still climb up, I'd keep living a bit longer!"

"You should make yourself comfortable down lower, Gavril Rodionovich." Ustinov advised. "You could make up a bed on a bench, or a cot, or on the floor. Look how nice and clean your floor is!"

"On the flo-or? On a bench? On a cot?" Gavril Rodionovich screeched. "What are you saying, Nikolka? It's shameful! Floors and benches and cots are for children, and gentlemen, and travelers of some kind, or billeted soldiers, that's who! Did you ever see a stranger sleeping on the high bunk, Nikolka? Never in your life! Only the master of the house sleeps there, and no one else! Am I no longer the master of my own house? Is that it?!" Staring angrily at Ustinov with his moist but still lively eyes, Gavril Rodionovich got up, snorted through his very sparse little beard, and returned to the kitchen.

"Should I help you get up on the bunk, Papa?" Rodion Gavrilovich asked.

"No! I'll sit here a spell on the bench, like some sort of guest, that's what!" And he shut the door to the kitchen noisily.

"Did I offend him?" Ustinov asked the younger Smirnovsky.

"Don't worry about it. Let him sit on the bench for a while and move his legs a bit. It's not good for him to lie around in bed.

"He's a man of the old school, is Gavril Rodionovich!"

"Well, Kolya, I'd be more than happy to live my life the way he has! And to die with such an awareness of the life I've lived!"

"And I, Rodion Gavrilovich, would like to ask you again—haven't we had enough killing, enough death for our own people and for others, too? The death of both the brave and the not so brave? Enough educated bloodshed, like when the Socialist Revolutionaries, gentlemen themselves but defenders of the people, shot at other gentlemen who were monarchists? Before the war there were three such murders a day. And hasn't there been enough uneducated, ignorant bloodshed, too, like when we soldiers did in the bourgeois behind the front?

"So didn't we set an example of peace when we threw down our weapons and said, 'The hell with them, let someone else pick them up if they want; we've got more than enough peaceful business of our own waiting for us at home'? That's what we figured, but then you turned up, the brave officer, Rodion Gavrilovich Smirnovsky. 'No, men,' you said, 'you're doing the wrong thing! Go back and fight for victory!' It's true, you were better than the others. During the war you were always in the trenches with the men, and now you don't want to fight against us, just against the others, against the Germans or the Turks! But all the same, your courage won't give you a minute's rest, your hands itch for a weapon, your soul aches for it. You need to be a hero, and so no matter how you look at it, you always stand apart from us peasants. A hero always stands apart, and he can't join the Forest Commission, or even go help the rest of his own village build a school . . ."

"I didn't go to help build the school only because I didn't know how the other people would react to me. I didn't know who would see me as a friend and who would already consider me his enemy. I didn't know who would offer me his hand and who would turn away, turn away just like the gentlemen officers turned away from me at staff meetings. It's a hard thing, Kolya. And I'm not the only one whom courage won't give any peace—it won't give you any, either."

"Me?!"

"You! If it weren't for that, you wouldn't be thinking about any bold action! You would sit at home, with no use for commissions of any sort. You'd sit and wait, let be what may be, as long as you survived! But sitting isn't for you! You can't keep quiet. You'll go and make speeches to wood-cutters from the steppe!"

"I'm not a brave man at all, Rodion Gavrilovich. I just did it when there was a great need for it and no other alternative. It's another thing with you. When war really does start up all around us, you'll lead many thousands of men into it! Who's leading them in the civil war in Russia right now? The lieutenants! After that you'll be what you want to be, a hero with a life of glory!"

"We won't live to see heroism, Kolya! None of us!"

"No?!"

"No, and that's a fact! Which officers from this German war are still alive? Neither those who started it nor those who joined it at the very beginning. They've all been killed. Only the second or sometimes even only the third echelon is left. I'm alive only because I spent almost a year in officers' school during the heaviest part of it. You survived because twice you were pulled back to regroup. And what kind of heroism can there be, anyway, in a war of fratricide? We'll all be tainted by the burning and by the murder of peaceful citizens, and that will be the least of it. What makes a fratricidal war more horrible than any other, Ustinov? In every village and city it will take the heads of the brightest people first of all, the heads of the truest citizens! It will take yours. And Kalashnikov's. And Deryabin's, for his love of action."

Smirnovsky pushed away his teacup, stood up, and paced quickly around the room, his soft deerskin boots not making a sound. He pulled at his suspenders and asked, "Are you looking for a teacher, Kolya? Maybe even me?"

"I'm looking . . . It would be good to find one."

"But if one has lost his way, what kind of teacher could he be?"

"The saints also strayed a lot, but they taught nevertheless. It depends on why a man has strayed—because of his own unworthiness or because there is too much humanity in him, more than in other people."

"No, Kolya, I won't be anyone's teacher! I can't do it!"

"Have you had a teacher yourself, Rodion Gavrilovich? If your father didn't teach you those words you just spoke to me, then who did? Captain Zurabov?"

"No!" Smirnovsky shrugged. "Zurabov refused me. Exactly the way I'm refusing you now. He couldn't be my teacher."

Captain Zurabov had been a well-known officer in the regiment, and, it was said, Smirnovsky's friend. Even though he was from an honorable family, of first-rate bearing, and a man of no little bravery, it was noted that his superiors didn't regard him with much favor. Only when the top brass came to inspect the battalion was Zurabov trotted out with all his medals on his chest, pretty as a picture. Unbelievably strict with the lower ranks, Zurabov was sent to sit on the military court at the end of the war. After he had had a lot of soldiers shot for disobeying orders and deserting, the soldiers grabbed him, put him on trial in their own court, and shot him.

"Before he was shot," Smirnovsky said, "Zurabov asked for only one favor—to see me." Giving Ustinov time to remember and think, Smirnovsky had said nothing for a while. Now he offered his own memories. "We met. And this is what Zurabov said:

" 'We, the landowning class, for the sake of the history of Russia, for the sake of the God of Orthodoxy, for the sake of all that is human in us, were bound to watch over Russia carefully. But we did not watch over it. We were unable to do so. We could not find the strength in ourselves to restore the throne, to modernize it, to offer it a helping hand. We made ourselves slaves to it; we groveled before it, powerless and depraved, endlessly thirsting for rewards, honors, titles, and prosperity, even though there was not a drop of prosperity left in the throne itself, but only a ghostly illusion of it. The Socialist Revolutionaries shot at the Tsar, and we cursed them, and that was a great shame to us. It was not they, the enemies of the throne, who should have shot at the Tsar, but we, his friends, to save him and the throne from shame and dishonor, just as our ancestors saved it from such misfortune more than once! There can be no greater sin and human degradation than to serve a phantom, to flatter it and spout praise for it in front of someone who knows the real truth. It is for this that our punishment has come— to be burned and to have our ashes scattered to the winds! But if only that were the end of it! I see something else: won't all of innocent Russia be consumed by the same fire in which we sinners will burn? How much human innocence has always burned with the sinners? That is my torment and terror and revenge.

" 'You, Smirnovsky,' Zurabov told me then, 'are also an aristocrat and a gentleman, only from the peasantry. Forgive us for being mean and hypocritical, for not shaking your hand at staff meetings! Forgive me for being your friend for years but not allowing myself to talk to you like this until my last hour on earth, and forgive me for pinning my hopes on you. Curse my ashes, but do me one favor! Do what we failed to do—don't let Russia burn along with me!'

"That's how it was, Ustinov . . . His cell had a low ceiling, just over two arshins, and Zurabov, you remember, was a tall man. As he talked to me, he was all hunched over, and then he got down on his knees in front of me. That's how it was, Kolya."

As the goldfinches chirped at one another in the kitchen and Gavril Rodionovich began to cough, Ustinov asked, "But wasn't he your teacher after that, Rodion Gavrilovich? Didn't he leave you a testament?!"

Smirnovsky, who had been pacing around the room all this time, sat down again, rested his arms on the tabletop and his head on his arms, and, looking at Ustinov with his Kalmyk eyes, explained, "But, Kolya, leaving a testament is denying someone, is refusing to be a teacher. What does a testament really mean? It's the same as saying, 'Go on, go on alone, as you wish, as you are able, but I'll stay here. I refuse to go. I won't be with you! That way is East, that way is West—go!' But everyone already knows that, even the birds in the sky and the tiniest mouse in the fields. But how do you get there? How do you keep from losing your way between the one and the other? I'm just as ready to tell you as Zurabov was to tell me, 'Go, Ustinov, go, Nikolai Levontyevich, do what I was not able to do, put right what I have botched up! Go, my dear friend, my hopes are on you!' That's the arrangement we people have. Someone dumped this burden, this testament, on Zurabov. He handed it to me, and I pass it on to you . . . And whom will you pass it on to—Ignashka Ignatov?"

"What are you talking about?!" asked Ustinov in alarm. "I'm a peasant, Rodion Gavrilovich. My task will always be the peasant's task, to plow and sow! I will never shove this duty off on someone else, I swear! My work is my steadfast bargain with life itself. I will do my job, and in return life will not bother me with things that do not concern me. If life breaks this bargain, I'll push even life away! All that's required of me is to be a faithful subject, sometimes even a slave, to the life of the peasant! But in everything else I'm as free as a bird—if I want, I'll join the Forest Commission; if not, I won't; if I want, I'll look for a teacher for myself, or I won't look for anyone, as I wish! And don't try to deprive me of my own free will!"

Rodion Gavrilovich smiled. Folding his hands behind his head and swaying his strong, tense body from side to side, he said, as if laughing quietly at
some secret, "You'll never push life away from yourself, Ustinov. There's no
sense in even trying! You're up to your neck in it right now, and you need
more than just your fields and your livestock. You need the Forest Commission, too, and in the worst way. Not only that—time will pass, and
you'll even need the war, believe me! Especially because you are a capable
man, a born leader. You need to touch everything in the whole wide world
with your own two hands and to remake something or other to your
own liking.

"Do you remember your training with the machine gun? Twice they assembled it and disassembled it for you, and the third time you could already
do it yourself. Quietly and carefully, as if you were blindfolded and working
only by touch, but you did it. No one who didn't see it with his own eyes
would believe it. In machine gunners' school people spend months learning
how to do it! Zurabov didn't believe it, but I had witnesses and won the bet!
If a man has the gift to succeed in such an unfamiliar task, then he's not the
man he thinks he is!"

But at that moment Ustinov was not at all interested in Zurabov. He was
recalling something else that had come alive in his imagination as if it were
happening right at that moment. Once when he was a little boy he had
grabbed on to the carved ornament on the peak of the gable of his house
and had felt that he would surely slide down and fall to the ground, smash
himself to pieces, and die. And he did slip and fall, but he was wrong about
one thing—he didn't die. Then everything had happened without a sound,
but now it seemed as if Smirnovsky were laughing at him and taunting him
out loud, "Give it up, Kolya, don't try to hang on to yourself, let go . . . You
won't be able to hang on, you don't have the strength!" Ustinov got angry.
He didn't completely understand whether he was mad at himself or at
Smirnovsky, whether it was because he felt confused or because Smirnovsky
was laughing, briefly and quietly, but sure of the reason for his laughter.

"Don't try to turn me into something other than a peasant, Rodion!" His
angrily flushed skin visible through his shock of blond hair, Ustinov jabbed
his finger at Smirnovsky and shouted, "I'll never forgive you for that—no
one has given you the right, neither God nor anyone else!" Ustinov lowered
his voice, but he continued as angrily as before. "You want me to be someone else instead of a peasant? Not on your life! If you think my being a
peasant is unnatural, then I'll tell you what I think: your heroism is unnatural! Just what is a hero? Someone who boldly and bravely and enthusias-
tically kills other people, that's who! They always point at the simple
citizen, the peasant, and criticize him, 'You do a bad job of killing—learn
something from the hero!' There is no justice in that, and there never can
be! Aren't we fed up to the teeth with killing each other? I know that you

are against fratricide, but at the same time you wait like a hunter for your chance to shoot! Once you understand who you're supposed to have in your sights, you'll take aim again and again. Why are you worried now, why don't you show yourself in public, why didn't you come to build the school with the rest of the people? I'll tell you why—you've hit a snag, you don't know which people you're supposed to shoot at! So go ahead and worry, hero, but don't try to drag a peasant into it! That's why the soldiers turned away from you in the trenches—your heroism made them sick!"

Ustinov fell silent, and it grew quiet in the house. The only sound was that of the goldfinches chirping at each other and fluttering their wings in the kitchen. In this silence Ustinov rummaged quickly through his own memory, and then, as it came to him, he shuddered and grabbed his head with both hands. How did it happen?! He had told Smirnovsky the same things, he had made the same accusations, as Grishka Sukhikh had made against him not long before. How did he miss the parallel?

Smirnovsky, too, paused, staring deeply at Ustinov for a long time, then asked, "Kolya, why do you talk to me this way? Why do you shake your fist at my soul? That's the way life is. Did I think up the war? Did I decide that there can be no life without birth, and none without death, and that there has never been any without death in battle? And if you can't escape death anyway, then why not die in battle? Will the commandment 'Thou shalt not kill' ever be so completely obeyed by everyone on earth that power, whenever it appears, will have no weapon other than prayer? In other words, that power will also become powerless? And even to be able to say, 'Thou shalt not kill,' first you have to be strong, because those words on the lips of the weak would be ridiculous and useless. All great men who have said, 'Thou shalt not kill,' all the writers who preach it—take note, Kolya, all of them— were born in powerful nations with an influence on the world!"

"All right, all right, Rodion Gavrilovich," began Ustinov, noticing how Smirnovsky's delicately formed and slightly curved upper lip was twitching, but Smirnovsky didn't let him continue.

"I beg your pardon, Kolya! I don't criticize you for wanting to plow well, neatly and properly, so why should I be criticized if I want to fight honorably? Against men, not against women and children and old men! Against those who deserve to have me make war against them, not against those who just happen by!" Then, trembling all over, Smirnovsky dropped his head on the table and half cried, half groaned, "Do you know what else I'm afraid of, what else torments me, Kolya? It's not the war. I'm afraid that neither you nor I nor anyone else will have any need for valor and honor, that we'll renounce them. But what will we put in their place? Maybe nothing? Maybe baseness and the endless fear of death? If you take valor and honor away from a man and tell him they are useless to him, what will he have left?"

"All right, all right, Rodion Gavrilovich," Ustinov began again, and this time he was able to finish his thought. "This war will not pass anyone by. And it won't pass me by, I know. And when it becomes impossible to do anything else, I will go kill. I know. Forgive me if I offended you . . . The war is breathing down our necks, day and night. You can't get away from it. It won't let you think."

Smirnovsky got up and stood still for a moment with his hand covering his face. Then he went over to the window and, looking through the steamed-up glass, asked, "Do you know why I take what you say so hard, Ustinov? I've seen you in action. You're a brave soldier, a bold man. But just now a woman came to see me. Intelligent. Beautiful. A woman with understanding. And—can you imagine?—she said the same things to me that you are saying now. Almost in the same words. A woman has a right to speak this way. She has a right to ask you and me just how we men should live now and what we should do as men. But how are we to answer, Ustinov?"

"What woman?" Ustinov asked with a shudder.

"Zinaida Pankratov. She came to see me."

"Why?"

"She was asking for a book. A book that would prove that killing is necessary and that people cannot exist without it! She couldn't believe that I, a military man, didn't have such a book! Why are you looking at me so strangely, Kolya?"

They stood for a while longer without speaking and then went into the kitchen. Smirnovsky was about to see Ustinov out, but Smirnovsky's father beckoned to Ustinov with a crooked finger.

"A while back I was sitting like I am here on this bench, only outside, and who do I see come a-walking along but Vansha Samorukov!" said Gavril Rodionovich to Ustinov, as if their previous conversation were continuing without a pause. "I says to him, 'Vansha, what's got you all so lopsided? How come your right shoulder keeps moving in front of you more and more, and the other one more and more behind you? Or are my eyes not seeing straight in my old age?' He says to me, 'You're right, Gavrilka! It's true, and not only is one shoulder sticking out in front and the other behind—if you take a good look, you'll see one of them is higher than the other, too!' So then I asks him, 'Vansha, tell me, with these shoulders of yours, do you climb up onto the sleeping bench by yourself, or does someone put you there?' He says to me, 'I do it by myself!' I says to him, 'You're lying, Vansha!' So anyway, we both went to his house to see what was what, was Vansha telling the truth or not? So we both goes into his house, and I didn't even have time to cross myself before, one-two-three, Vansha throws off his hat and coat and—what do you think?—he's already up on the bunk! So I tell Vansha, 'If you can still do that, you're going to live for a lo-ong time yet, Vansha!' 'That's nothing at all, Gavrilka!' says Vansha.

'This fall when the village was building the school, I cut out a dovetail on a log six vershoks thick, believe it or not!' Well, that was more than I could believe. 'You've told a whopper that time,' I told him, 'You're bluffing!' I told him, and came on home. But then at home I got to thinking, what if Vansha wasn't lying about that dovetail? What if he was telling the truth? He was telling the truth about the sleeping bench, he wasn't lying, I saw it with my own two eyes! We've been friends since we was kids, and now all of a sudden I don't believe him no more? It's true, Vansha didn't serve in the army, whereas I, God be praised, fought and killed me a bunch of Turks, but still, we're friends, and all of a sudden I don't believe him? You tell me now, Nikolka, do you know? Did you see Vansha Samorukov cut out that dovetail with your own eyes?"

"Yes, Gavril Rodionovich," Ustinov said, "I saw it with my own eyes."

"And the log was six vershoks thick?"

"Maybe even thicker! Everyone saw him do it!"

"Everyone!" said Gavril Rodionovich, clutching his head. "Everyone saw him, but I didn't believe my friend! It's shameful, Nikolka, so shameful! I've got myself in deep! Ay-ay-ay!" Stamping his foot, Gavril Rodionovich shouted, "You, Rodka, why do you stand there like a post? Why aren't you helping your father get up in his bunk, away from this shame? Well?"

Rodion Gavrilovich lifted his father into the bunk.

"Good-bye, Kolya," he sighed. "More of Peter's words come to my mind: 'I know no refuge for myself!' Maybe he was talking about you and me? I am sure it was about me."

Ustinov nodded, stood a moment, and offered Smirnovsky his hand. "Good-bye, Rodion Gavrilovich!"

As he was walking away, Ustinov thought, "Such things we talked about! Such grand things! But what about the gelding?"

Personal Property

Before the war and in its first years, the census takers would come to Leb-yazhka in early winter. These statisticians, as they were called, brought amazingly long blank forms, crisscrossed by thick and thin lines. They went around to each and every house, writing down who had what—how many pairs of working hands each family had, how many members of each gender and age, how much real estate and personal property. Well, of course, real estate is always sitting there for all to see—the house, the barn, the shed, the bathhouse. You can have them insured against fire, and then the Sala-mander Insurance Company will put its little round metal sign on your gate, with a picture of a salamander on it, a long-tailed creature neither quite snake nor lizard. Probably it's a creature that doesn't burn and maybe won't drown either. Every year the census takers asked about the harvest— how many desyatinas each farmer had sown and how much he had reaped from each desyatina. That led to a particular kind of conversation.

Taxes were assessed according to the number of desyatinas cultivated. The number of desyatinas for cultivation was distributed among the house-holds of the village by the village assembly. These facts were a matter of public record; but all the same, if, for example, a peasant had milled 300 poods of wheat, he found more satisfaction in telling the census taker that the crop wasn't much to look at that year and that he had only 200 poods— well, 220 at the most—stored in his barn. And really, he argued, why should you count the poods that you would use for feeding yourself and for next year's seed? When you know that regardless of what happens they won't be there in a year's time, it's as if they didn't exist. It's not like having a reserve supply or goods for sale. It's as if the grain weren't there at all. It's like air—it exists and you use it, yet it isn't there either. Besides that, for some reason those yet uncounted poods looked better than the others.

The census takers explained that the peasants should give accurate figures because these figures were a part of the inventory of the entire country and because the country had to know what the actual harvest was and what supplies were on hand. The peasants were more than willing to agree with the census takers, but they still did things their own way. Why did the whole country have to know how much grain you had put in this bin and that bin? A man doesn't go peeking into his neighbor's barn, but the government sticks its nose into your barn without a second thought! That's not polite! Things went much the same with personal property. You couldn't get away with not owning up to a working horse since it was registered with the volost, but cows could easily be mixed in with the village herd. As far as small livestock and poultry were concerned, well, you could just say you had never seen a sheep, pig, chicken, duck, or goose in your life and didn't even know what the words meant. There they all are out in the yard, bleating and oinking and clucking and quacking and cackling, and it's easier for them to be fruitful and multiply if they are not recorded on a single piece of paper in the whole wide world, and it's easier for you, too.

But it was not because these raucous and numerous flocks were not entered into the serious economic statistics of property that Ustinov always raised so many varieties of livestock in his yard. Besides the admitted economic advantage, there was another reason—in each and every chicken, no matter how small, there was a little bit of a living soul. When Smirnovsky had tried to tell Ustinov that he was no longer a real peasant, Ustinov felt very insulted. In this bad mood he went to see his beasts, both great and small, to find out whether what Smirnovsky had said about him was true. All these living creatures would know whether he was ruined as a farmer or still hale and hearty. Of course, even the most genuine peasant might show signs of cracking under the stress of war and now of the Forest Commission. Besides that, all his farmyard creatures would blame him for not saying a single word about Sevka Kupriyanov's gelding. A task left unfinished was worse than one not begun!

Grunya had begun to limp more noticeably despite their attempts to treat her, and her eyes had a more mournful look. Perhaps she felt too insulted after her undeserved beating, or perhaps her left foreleg was really hurting her more than she could bear. Whatever the reason, her master should now be thinking as hard as he could about how to obtain another working horse. Everyone needed him to solve this problem as soon as possible.

Only if there were enough working horses would there be enough to eat for everyone, for people, calves, piglets, and the barnyard fowl, for all living souls.

Whatever the reason for Grunya's behavior, Ustinov decided to take a look at all his animals one at a time. Grabbing an axe, a hammer, and some nails in case something needed repair, he began with the henhouse. But first he stopped by the house to stuff his pockets with bread crumbs and crusts, and only then did he open the henhouse door, throw a handful of crumbs on the floor, and call out, "Chick-chick-chick!" What a noise and uproar there was then!

For some reason he always forgot that you never have to call chickens. All you need to do is throw some crumbs or even just wave your arm as if you were throwing some, and they are already flocking to you as fast as they can, rushing and crowding, even standing on one anothers' backs. It's not a flock so much as a free-for-all. They are terribly dimwitted birds, most likely because they are so clever and independent when they are new-born chicks. Just as soon as they're hatched out of their shells, they're already running off to find themselves some kind of crumb or bug to eat. Their mothers have no worries about their little ones. All they have to do is cackle, "Follow me, there's some manure around the corner, we'll dig around a bit and, God willing, we'll find something to peck at!" A creature that is born smart and capable will become the stupidest. Its mind won't mature, and it will remain a child all its life. Such creatures have no real sense of motherhood either. There is no need to look after the little ones—they will grow up by themselves. After all, mothering requires the intelligence and teaching ability that these creatures lack. There's no need even to mention fatherhood among the chicken species—there's not even a hint of it. There are hordes of chicks, and since the mother cannot be everywhere at once, the young, small as they may be, are born as adults.

Ustinov fixed the loose perches in the henhouse and replaced one that had worn out. While he was working, he thought about how he could make nests for the hens so that their eggs wouldn't be ruined after laying. He had some chickens that would peck at their own eggs as well as those of other chickens. What had to be done was to make a hole in the bottom of the nest and camouflage it with some twigs so that the egg would fall through into a padded box where only a person could get at it. It was a simple thing at first glance, and it was hard to know why someone hadn't thought of it sooner. But would a chicken lay an egg in a nest that had a hole in it? They were foolish creatures, but their natural habits still weren't completely foolish. At any rate, he had to make such an egg trap.

Before the war Ustinov had had a red-feathered rooster named Drach in his yard, a hooligan and a terribly pugnacious bully. His chest was always puffed out, and he had a peculiar voice. He would start out hoarse and muffled, "Cock-a, cock-a," and then, having taken a deep breath, he would roar out, "Doodle-doo!" so loudly that the windowpanes in the house would rattle. Several times this wild exclamation had so startled Morkoshka in his stable that he bumped his head on his crib, especially if Drach had come into the stable to peck at the manure and Morkoshka had been dozing and hadn't heard his quiet "cock-a, cock-a," and then the "doodle-doo!" blasted him right in the ear. Drach had even been a father of sorts—suddenly he began to call the chicks to himself like a commander with his troops. Once it happened that a large hawk swooped down and grabbed a chick in the yard, but because the chick was almost a full-grown chicken, the hawk had trouble lifting it off the ground. On the spot in an instant, Drach jumped on the hawk's back and began to tear at it with his talons and to stab the back of its head with his beak. The hawk let go of the chick and managed, though with great difficulty, to rise into the air with Drach still on its back. At an altitude of two or three sazhens, Drach let out a wild shriek of terror and flung himself earthward with a clumsy beating of his wings. As soon as he touched the ground, he rushed off into Barin's dog-house and hid there till evening without making a sound. He would have liked to peck the hawk in the neck just a couple more times and to squeeze its back a bit more with his talons. Then he could have celebrated his great victory back on earth, but how sadly and shamefully it had all ended! Drach didn't suffer from his humiliation for long, however, and the next day he was again sticking out his powerful chest and roaring out his "doodle-doo!"

While Ustinov was still tossing crumbs to the chickens and thinking about Drach, the little swinging door opened, and a pig's head pushed itself through into the henhouse and gave a loud oink. It pushed some more, and a small pig appeared, a six-month-old shoat from the spring brood. It quickly pushed away the chickens, which, even more alarmed than before, rushed up to their perches or sought safety in the corners. The pig made quick work of the crumbs on the floor and then gave Ustinov an angry and ill-tempered look. "That's not enough for me! Give me some more!" "I don't have any," Ustinov shrugged. "You're lying! Take your hands out of your pockets! What have you got there?" "Well, if that's the way it is . . . " Ustinov tossed it another crust, and as soon as he did, the door was raised again and another piglet, noticeably larger than the first, poked its head into the henhouse as far as its ears. Too big to get all the way in and exhausted by humiliation, anger, and greed, it could only shout loudly enough for the whole barnyard to hear, "Oh, you scum, you're stuffing your faces without me! You're bastards, the lot of you!" Ustinov ran outside and tossed the loudmouth a small crust. It turned around, caught it, devoured it noisily, and then stuck its head back through the door to continue cussing out its comrades in the henhouse and its master along with them.

For a pig there is no greater misfortune than only watching as others eat. This is sorrow, despair, shame, and humiliation. It will suffer a martyr's torments, then rush at the others' food through hell or high water, pushing away anyone else who is there. For a pig, devouring, gobbling, and gulping are the same as soaring in the heavens and singing for a bird. A pig will gobble a mouthful, oink, gobble another mouthful, squeal, take another noisy mouthful, and then, like a watchdog on a chain, snarl out of pure pleasure. It's a real song of gluttony! A pig will sing out in every possible voice it has, tearing its hair and almost going mad with impatience until its master pours something in its trough. If pigs could reach their heads, every last piglet would be bald by the time it was three months old, if not sooner. A pig will eat anything it can chew, and the black-and-white and all-black Lebyazhka boars had teeth that could grind anything but rocks!

"Well, the hell with all of you," Ustinov decided. "I won't go to see you pigs! I'll go straight to the sheep!"

On the way he remembered his fine sow, Bunka. Bunka had lived in his yard at the same time as Drach, but she had been submissive, kindhearted, and always in farrow. She was a real expert at bringing piglets into the world. She didn't give birth to them so much as hatch them out as a chicken did eggs. She would lie on her side for a while, grunting, and when she got up, there would be seven, eight, or even ten little piglets already swarming around and butting each other with their snouts.

Ustinov had been very foolish not to make a serious effort to breed Bunka, which would have made a lot of sense, but he had just laughed at Bunka and, even though he always meant to, had not even kept a record of the number and size of her litters. He thought of it again only after he was already at the front, and he wrote to Domna two or three times to tell her to keep records, at least out of curiosity if not for breeding purposes. But did Domna really have time for such things in those years? Meanwhile, Bunka had one last litter and died. It was an everyday thing for Bunka to give birth to piglets, but the last time it wasn't so easy.

While clearing the manure out of the sheep shed, too small to be a proper sheep barn, and bringing in a new piece of salt, Ustinov thought about sheep. When God and nature distributed characteristics and abilities among living creatures, each received something different. Some got strength; others, cleverness and agility; others, loutishness and carelessness; and sheep were given timidity and fear. Rodion Gavrilovich Smirnovsky believed that animals live without knowledge of their own deaths, but this was not quite so. A sheep always lives with the fear of death. As sheep push against each other in a half-lit corner, you can hear their communal rustling and breathing, the frightened stamping of their feet. And in the rustling and the breathing and the stamping, and especially in their eyes, there is fear, fear, fear. And of what? Of some beast, though there is none near, of their master, though he has not hurt them, but has watered and fed and protected them. No, for a sheep, fear needs no object or shape. It is dissolved in the air, in every splinter of wood and every stone, in every sound, in every little breeze, and in the very shining of the sun itself. A sheep senses the end of the world in everything. It looks at any object in terror, its eyes bugging out, waiting for the thing to come to an end, to disappear, or for itself to disappear at the mere sight of it. A sheep stands in its shed, chewing quickly, as if it were chewing a mouthful of grain for the last time in its life, and then suddenly it freezes and trembles all over, as if something had grabbed it by the throat from inside or as if it had been stabbed through the heart with a knife. It senses invisible terror, not only everywhere around itself, but also inside its every corpuscle. Then its throat is released, and its heart, untouched, beats once more. Opening its eyes, the sheep sees what had been there before. It is alive; it has not disappeared; nothing has happened to it; no end of any kind has come to it, no . . .

But there is still no joy in its open eyes. Now it is afraid, not because it is dying, but because it is still alive—life for a sheep is only the expectation of death. So it stands and trembles, forever waiting for something to be afraid of, something to flee from, ready to run to the wall and press itself against it, trembling. If there is nothing to be afraid of, then it is afraid because there is nothing to fear. And so it exists, in fear of death, in fear of life, and maybe in many other kinds of fear known to no one but itself, or known only to some solitary thing, an insect, or one unseen little mouse, or a person living all alone, or maybe one already dead. The sheep feels and suffers all these myriad past, present, and future fears. Filled with them, it has no inkling that there is any other kind of life.

Sometimes a little lamb will kick its legs and gambol about, but its mother sees no reason even for the joy of her own child. She does not accept it and is amazed as if by some ungodly thing, strange and unbelievable. Somewhere under her thick wool she burns with embarrassment and turns her head so she doesn't have to look at this stupidity and shame. She turns away and waits to see if some cruel punishment will come to her for even having seen it, for having given birth to such a mischievous lamb or even two.

It would seem that such timidity would rather hide somewhere by itself, far from everyone in a dark corner where no one can see it, but a sheep is even less itself without its flock. Its own timidity and fear are not enough for it. It needs to tremble, not alone, but along with the other sheep. It squeezes into the pile, into the middle of the communal trembling, finding safety in numbers. The more fear there is around it, the better it feels, for then it is not the only coward. It does not stay at the edge of the flock but pushes into the center, where it won't be the first that the shepherd will hit with his crook or the sheepdog nip in the haunches, and, if there really is a wolf around, where it won't be the first it will grab by the throat. It wants only to push its way through to the very center, where bodies press against it from all sides. It wants the flock to take hold of it and to carry it away somewhere. It would seem that there would be nothing to breathe in such a crush of bodies, but it is easiest of all for it to breathe where there are living bodies but no life. That is what the sheep hopes for. It doesn't know how to run away, or hide, or defend itself, or calm itself, because only if it were by itself could it learn all that, but when it is left alone it only wanders mindlessly, searching for its flock. That's the kind of life nature has given to this creature. With its timid and beautiful eyes, a sheep always looks at the world that is directly in front of it. It never turns its eyes to the side—what if something terrible should suddenly appear there? Beneath the cozy wool that keeps it warm in winter and cool in summer, it lives a chilly and un-comfortable life. Couldn't it give itself a rest from fear and trembling at least once a week, say on Sundays?

Ustinov counted his sheep—they were all there, eleven head. They looked at him as if they were trying to remember who was standing in front of them. Was it perhaps the master, who gave them food and water, sheared their wool, and herded them into the shed? Or maybe it was not him at all? Fear had knocked the slightest memory out of their heads. And without meaning to, Ustinov himself looked at them with a sheep's gaze, without recognition. The count was right, there were eleven heads, but if two of his own sheep had strayed away and two strange sheep had joined the flock, he would not know it because they all looked alike. Well, he knew the one-horned ram was his, and the three sheep that were younger and smaller than the others; he knew those three belonged there, but you couldn't tell about the others. They all had the same faces and the same fear.

Ustinov tossed a piece of bread into the sheep pen, and the sheep jumped back away from the crust to where it was darker and harder to see them, where they were hidden from casual glances. When he moved away to the side, the sheep returned to the doorway in a clump, leaned against the old darkened rail that blocked off the entrance, and stood without moving. The pigs would walk under this rail without thinking about it, and the cows would step over it, but the sheep would stand in front of it on their slender and nimble legs as if before an obstacle. They could be dying of hunger or thirst or frightened to death, but they would not pass this crossbar. So be it. Let the sheep be there, fenced off from the world by a thin pole, a single fear with eleven heads on forty-four little hooved legs. Ustinov hurried on to his cow.

The Ustinov household had its own particular bovine history, and not a simple one at that. Fifteen years earlier all the Lebyazhkans had kept only one breed of cows—unpedigreed Siberian stock, white with black mark-ings, shaggy, big-bellied, evil-tempered, larger than a good-sized ram, but not by much. Such a cow was about as easy to provide for as a sheep. You only had to toss it an armful of hay on a rainy day; the rest of the time it took care of itself. It would go off to the lake, wade into the reeds up to its shoulders, and feed there all summer, and sometimes in the winter, too. This Siberian cow, a nomad by blood and habit, knew nothing about shelter. The Kirghiz had driven herds of its not-so-distant ancestors across all the Siberian lowlands, and the Tatars had kept them in the reeds almost the year round. In a shed or even in a corral, it felt imprisoned, and it couldn't stand captivity. It would jump over a fence like a goat, and if it could get its head through some opening, then it would invariably get its whole body through. It didn't care where the opening led, as long as it led somewhere. It had small, sharp horns and teeth that could bite like a dog's and give you a wound that was hard to heal. If the mistress milked it, fine; if not, no problem either—its udder wouldn't dry out because there was almost nothing there to dry out. Only during the fiercest frost, when it was hard even to breathe and the hungry wolves were at their most ferocious, did this Tatar horde flatten itself against the outer wall of the house, warming first one side and then the other, and give the master a mournful look: "Forgive us worthless creatures, we'll never go wandering off again." Of course, the master would toss them some hay and scatter some straw on the ground, on which they would curl up like dogs. But you couldn't believe their promises, for as soon as the frost let up there wouldn't be a trace of them. Maybe a goatlike little cow would come running up to be milked and butt someone in the yard, but then it would go off again who knows where.

These beasts had yet another damnable habit: they liked to chew on dry wood to sharpen their teeth, and they would pick someone's house for this purpose. You would be sitting in your own home, drinking tea or something, and suddenly the house would begin to shake and be filled with a grinding sound, as if someone were trying to tear it apart down to the last log! That meant that this Tatar horde had taken a liking to your house and wouldn't be leaving it alone soon. And to top it all off, practically every living creature from every street around would follow the cows to the very same house. Pigs would come to root around the mound of earth at the base of your walls; chickens would follow the pigs and set up a noisy colony in the same place. After the chickens, the geese would make camp and honk and cackle all night under your windows. And when the geese were getting ready to return to the lake at dawn, first, trying to decide who would lead, they would sound off by number about ten times, and then all the same they would line up in single file behind the senior gander for the procession back to the lake while the water was still cold and steaming with mist. In the midst of this sea of the most diverse animals and birds, your house would seem like Noah's ark or a little island of human life. You could live on this little island in this hubbub, uproar, and gnashing of teeth, and wade through manure of many sorts and smells, or you could do something about it.

And so it was inevitable. Those cows once chose Ustinov's house and began to chew on it from two different corners at the same time, and all the other livestock from about thirty different households joined them and brought along all their needs, squabbles, arguments, shouting, cussing, and friendships. Although Ustinov was cordial and friendly to all living creatures, domestic animals in particular, even he ran out of patience. What didn't he try to rid himself of his uninvited guests, the instigators of this whole mob, those toothy little black-and-white cows! He smeared tar on the butt-ends of the logs at the two corners of his house, but that didn't help. He put a sturdy fence up around the house, but in a day or two the cattle broke this fence down. Finally he hammered a good hundred horseshoe nails into the logs. It made him sick at heart to risk injuring a neighbor's livestock. But it never even came to that. The cows wouldn't touch the logs where the nails were, but you can't stick nails in a whole house, so they would just chew somewhere else.

During this attack Ustinov decided to get himself a domesticated, purebred cow and to butcher all his Siberian stock so they wouldn't chew up his house, and especially so they wouldn't bring along all their friends. It was then that he began to appreciate what a real cow was: it was grave, staid, sensible, with a smooth body and a soft udder, but with no uncowlike habits, no goatlike or even doglike manners. When he saw such a cow, he felt blessed—he couldn't take his eyes off it. So it came as no surprise when Ustinov harnessed up Morkoshka one day and went off to see the German colonists who bred real cows rather than some sort of degenerates. He made a round trip of around 120 versts and brought back a chocolate-colored calf with finely chiseled legs and a little head as pretty as a picture.

In Ustinov's house there was an icon of the innocent newborn Baby Jesus lying naked in a manger with everyone gazing at him—the Holy Mother, the saints with halos around their heads, ordinary people without halos, and even various animals, including a little cow. Ustinov was sorry that the icon painter had not seen his calf—that would have been quite a portrait to add to that icon, quite an artistic success! Even at that age the calf's eyes were huge, kind, and even a little saintly, and its whole face expressed amazement, as if at some miracle. Looking at it, you immediately glanced around to see where this miracle might be—somewhere beside you? But you couldn't see it—only the calf could.

Ustinov found a good name for her, just the right one, Svyatka. In addition to everything else, she had been born during Svyatki, the holy weeks of the Christmas season. When he had gotten her from the German colonists, she was already six months old. Recalling that Christmas night that year had been a very dark one everywhere around, Ustinov had asked the Germans whether the night of Christ's birth had been a bright one in their village. When they said, No, on Christmas it had been "tark," Ustinov was happy. In Lebyazhka the popular belief had long existed that if there were no moon or even stars during Christmas, the coming year would be a fruitful one for the cattle, and the fowl would lay an abundance of eggs. Quickly reinterpreting this omen to suit his own purposes, Ustinov decided that a calf born during Christmastide, and on a dark night to boot, would definitely grow up strong and give plenty of offspring. He also found confirmation for his belief in the icon of Christ's birth. In the picture there was a house with wide-open doors, beyond which there were only two little stars blinking in a very dark sky. From the darkness a cow whose portrait could have best been painted from Svyatka was looking in through the wide doorway at the newborn Christ.

From that summer day, 8 June 1909, life changed radically in Ustinov's house. All the womenfolk of the household—Domna, her daughters, and Nikolai Ustinov's mother, still alive at that time—now lived in constant apprehension. What if they didn't manage to rear this saintly calf, what if they were unable to raise it? If a horse was bought or one of their own colts was reared at home, that was a man's task and his responsibility, but a cow was a woman's affair. A sweet and affectionate little thing, with delicate little legs and horns, the calf demanded more looking after than your own human children.

However, it must also be said that as soon as Svyatka appeared at the Ustinovs', and especially after she had given birth to her first calf, their household became a real home. Before then, it seems, it had not been that, and now it was easy to understand why. How could it have been a real home when it was just a stopping-place for the cattle, when they could come and go as they pleased? Horses stand outside a town house, but they stand next to a nomad's tent the same way—the master of the house can saddle up and ride away whenever he wants, day or night. Can you expect any order from the Siberian cattle when they chew your house to the ground? As for the other livestock, they wander around and spend the night wherever they please. They don't have a penny's worth of domesticity. Svyatka was another thing entirely. She had to be fed and watered and milked and cared for at the right time every day. If the mistress drove her out with the herd, she would go; if not, she wouldn't take a single step anywhere. It is true that the farmer feeds the whole world, but first the cow feeds the farmer and his children, his grandchildren, and all his future descendants. Svyatka already knew all this about herself when she was a calf, before she had ever given milk, and she behaved like someone special among all the other farm animals in the yard. Her whole appearance and behavior said, "Look after me, take care of me, and when the time comes, I'll show you all my gratitude!" There was never any question about it—a warm home had to be made in the farmyard for Svyatka right away, a special shed with a little stove in it. At that time this was such a new thing in Lebyazhka that even Ustinov was ashamed of it. Then he got used to it, and in so doing he came to understand how and when a real household begins.

He even noted—to himself, of course, not out loud—that there weren't any real farmers yet anywhere in Lebyazhka, that the Lebyazhka peasants were only in the process of becoming such but had in no way achieved the reality, and that Lebyazhka itself resembled a Tatar village. There were no fences in these villages, for they had no conception of such a thing, and a house would stand there with various livestock wandering around it, dropping manure on the ground day and night. When a house had sunk into the manure all the way up to its windows, it would be moved to another spot. So as you ride up to the aul, you see it filled with thickets of goosefoot, wormwood, and wild hemp, with little houses standing all by themselves, without fences or outbuildings or bathhouses, scattered here and there among the rampant vegetation growing out of the abandoned dungheaps.

Whenever an agronomist, veterinary, or agricultural official from the uyezd or even the gubernia came to Lebyazhka, Ivan Ivanovich Samorukov would make it his very first duty to report, "We have one peasant here who got a calf from the Germans and raised up a cow that beats anything they have themselves!" It was all the same to Svyatka who came to admire her, an agronomist or the Tsar-Emperor. Giving the visitor a passing glance, she would continue to mind her own business, chewing her feed and pouring milk into her udder, as much as from five Siberian cows. She filled her yard with the scent of milk, the essence of the farmstead.

When Ustinov came to see Svyatka this time, she was seriously occupied with her business, lying on the straw with one chocolate-colored side leaning against the shed and the other turned toward the sun. It wasn't very warm, but Svyatka probably figured that as long as there was still some sun she should make use of it. Maybe tomorrow the real winter might come. Ustinov looked at Svyatka attentively, and she at him. "Don't even think about disturbing me!" Svyatka was saying. Ever so gently, however, but insistently, he tapped her on the thigh, and Svyatka got up, turning her head away, not wanting to look at him. Ustinov slapped Svyatka on the back and made her walk around the yard, moving off a little to one side to watch her. "All right, you silly peasant," she consented. "If you just have to look at me, then go ahead!"

Her fur was like copper or some other, unknown metal, but soft, and just by looking you could tell that it was warm. In each strand of her fur, there were two kinds of warmth—one radiated toward her from the sun; the other emanated from her body toward the sun. She had a heavy but careful step, one devoid of anything unnecessary. She walked and listened to hear if the earth were falling under her weight. She took care of the earth and didn't trample it without reason. Ustinov could hear the sound of her breathing, the rustling of her udder and of the folds of skin on her neck, the light slapping of her tail against her legs, the sound of her chewing even while she walked to avoid wasting time, the sound of something gurgling quietly deep inside her, and of her hooves crunching on the frozen soil.

Svyatka walked back and forth through the yard and then returned to her straw bed, but she didn't lie down. Her master had spoiled her appetite for her bed. She closed her eyes while chewing her cud and stood motionless, as if asleep and lost in some dream. "There's life here . . . ," thought Ustinov, "life!" Sitting down on the porch, he began to think about all the threads that stretched from Svyatka to the different ends of the earth.

There had been a time back in '17 when the soldiers were already walking around freely from trench to trench. The Germans had almost stopped shooting at the Russians, and the Russians, at the Germans. Instead they called out to one another from trench to trench as best they knew how, exchanging words of peace, and sometimes even a bit of tobacco. Ustinov had gone out into no-man's-land for some reason or other, and suddenly he saw a German rifle in front of him and felt the sights of the rifle trained on him. Instead of falling to the ground or running away, he suddenly knew what he should do.

He shouted at the top of his voice, "*He, Kameraden, wie hoch ist jetzt der Preis für ein einjähriges Kälbchen bei euch?*"

He had asked, "Hey, boys, what is the current price of a yearling calf back home?" He had learned these words long ago when he had been doing business with the German colonists.

The rifle wavered, and then lowered.

"*Was ist das?*"

"*Wie hoch ist jetzt der Preis für ein einjähriges Kälbchen bei euch?*" Ustinov repeated.

"*Keine Ahnung!*" answered the German in bewilderment. He had no idea.

"*Danke, Meister, gut!*" Ustinov thanked him, turned around, and returned to his own trench, where he said, "Watch out, Comrades, the Germans will be shooting at us today. It's only thanks to my cow Svyatka that I stayed alive just now!" "How do you know?" they asked him. "They didn't shoot at you, did they? And what has your cow got to do with it? Are you nuts?" They didn't believe Ustinov, and one of the soldiers went right on out of the trench to that same part of no-man's-land. A "pow!" rang out from the other side, and the soldier went flying head over heels, shot right through the chest. It turned out that though the Russian lads had not fired a shot for some time and the Germans had also been quiet for a while, as if a truce had been made, the Provisional Government had advanced the army into Galicia,* and the war had flared up again. Later, when it fully hit Ustinov that he had survived, he regretted that the German he had come across had not been too bright. He hadn't known how much yearling calves were going for in Germany. It would have been useful to compare the going price there with what he had paid the colonists for Svyatka.

There was another time that every Lebyazhkan, and even every Siberian, remembered. When the railroad had been built all the way to Vladivostok, the Siberian peasant had taken heart. Now he believed that he would be able to sow his wheat and sell it to Russia and to other countries across the sea. Till then he couldn't do that, for, as they say, it cost "a kopeck for the cart, and a ruble for the hauling." But it didn't happen, and the peasant's hopes came to nothing. The Russian grain merchants made the government institute a tariff. As soon as a railroad car of grain passed through Chelyabinsk, half the value of the grain had to be paid for shipment to Europe. The merchants and landowners suffocated the Siberian plowman. He had gone off to faraway Siberia to get away from them, but their long, cruel arm still found him. The peasants' Siberia was shaken—how could this be? What good, then, were their wide-open lands and spacious fields? Could they really go on living the same way as they had before, without factory-made goods that they couldn't afford, especially because the same long line of supply made it expensive to bring these goods to Siberia? And maybe this was only the beginning. What else would they think up to get back at the Siberian for his abundance of land and his freedom from the landowners? One by one the new immigrants who had not managed to establish themselves began to leave the villages on the steppe to return to Russia. Others gave up farming altogether and went into industry and construction and to the Far East, where, they said, you could make a living one way or another—if not by farming, then by hunting; if not by hunting, then by fishing; if not by fishing, then by prospecting.

But that didn't happen with the Lebyazhkans. The old Siberians could not imagine returning to a crowded Russia crisscrossed by all sort of boundaries. For a Lebyazhkan, remaining a Lebyazhkan was an important thing, a necessity of life. All he had to do was go out into the fields and look at the expanse of the land, the slice of the great Siberian pie that had been cut for the people of his village. The work before him, his plowing or sowing, would make his mouth water with anticipation. But something was shaken even in these old Siberians. Life seemed unsteady to them, too. They had to use their brains and think about life more and note the changes going on in

---

*Area of east central Europe controlled by Austria before World War I, now divided between the Ukraine and Poland.

it. Who could have imagined that a peasant with such fine grain could turn out to be a poor man?

And who came to the rescue, who turned calamity aside? Svyatka! She became the tsarina of life and began to do not only her own work but Morkoshka's, Solovko's, Grunya's, and that of all the other livestock, turning out her fragrant milk and a new calf every year. She wasn't much disposed to have male calves. Much more often than not, she gave birth to females, and these little ones were bought with great pleasure not only by the Lebyazhkans but by folks from other villages as well. Ustinov consequently began to wonder who was more important to the household, Svyatka or his workhorses; he, the man, the plower and sower, or the women who looked after Svyatka. A few years later Ustinov read in the newspaper that only one country, Denmark, exported more butter than Siberia; no one else could compete with the Siberians in this. More than four million poods a year—it wasn't just any old country that could butter a slice of bread that thickly!

Because Lebyazhka and the surrounding area now ceased to be the Promised Land, immigrants were no longer drawn there as they had been before. They no longer begged in the name of Christ for the local villages to register them as residents, and the caravans of immigrants began to go ever farther to the north, to the very edge of the taiga where they had their choice of meadows and hayfields. But Lebyazhka didn't suffer much from this. There was less glory, but less bother, too. And what good was glory to them anyway, after Samsony Krivoi's ancient settlement on the green hill above the lake had almost come tumbling down? Besides, Lebyazhka still had its own mother lode, though not one of gold—the forest was still there just beyond its kitchen gardens. Though the Lebyazhka forest had been the property of the Tsar, it had always served the peasants. And in these years many Lebyazhkans began to make their living from wood. Some took up carpentry; others distilled tar or traded in pine resin.

Even those farmers who never took a step away from their fields also contrived to live differently than they had before. They pooled their resources and bought hay balers, threshing machines, and seed drills. They sent one of the younger and sharper lads off to take courses in machinery so that later he would work not only on his own land but also on the allotments of the other artel members for payment in kind. Once this step had been taken, the next became clear. All the artel members needed to have their portions of land in the same place, next to one another, so they wouldn't have to drive the machinery dozens of versts from one end of the Lebyazhka farmland to the other. After some arguments and doubts, the community humored the artel. At the next reapportionment of land, it assigned the artel a large corner section, far from the village, but with soil that wasn't half bad. The artel divided it among its members according to its own wishes. From then on they began to call the artel "the corner," and its members "the corner folk." But it was also called a production co-op, and if it was a co-op, then it goes without saying that Pyotr Kalashnikov became its leader. There's nothing much to say about the dairy and consumer co-ops. A consumer-society store and a dairy run by manpower or horsepower had appeared in almost every village. But a mechanized factory had also been set up in Lebyazhka. A steam engine fired with scrap wood from the timber industry powered the butter churn and even a sawmill when needed.

This new artel would have continued to progress and would have developed into a new, perhaps happier, way of life if it had not been for the war. The war summoned the machinists along with the other men. "The corner" fell to pieces. Not far from where the new school was now located, the cornerposts of the general machine shed were still standing like lonely gravemarkers where they had been set when construction had begun in the summer of '14. When the Lebyazhkans, not just the "corner folk," but the others as well, walked near them, they all felt the same strange curiosity—would the posts suddenly come to life? Instructors—limping men unfit for the army or young women with bundles of various booklets—were still coming to the villages and making speeches urging the people to "instill life" into the co-op and to exercise "new, unprecedented powers." But except for the booklets they came empty-handed, without textiles or hardware, without kerosene or glass for lamps or windows. What unprecedented powers could there be here?

Remembering all this, Ustinov was now convinced that he had a blood bond with Svyatka, and therefore with every other living creature, and that there was some sort of common law, whether high up in the heavens or down below on earth, for everything living in the world, and even, perhaps, a common prayer. How could it be otherwise if a Svyatka could turn human life around? Not long before the war, Ustinov had begun to ask himself just what he had been born to be. His field and his plowing were dear to him, but still, perhaps he was not so much a plowman as a cattle-breeder. He liked Saint Gleb, the patron saint of domestic livestock, whose little icons the cattle-dealers and farriers wore around their necks. In this picture you could see right off that the saint was one of their own, a peasant, with a peasant's beard, his hair not so neatly combed, and a peasant shirt, most likely homespun, not buttoned all the way up. And this saint knew something that no one else knew about that prayer common to every living creature.

Ustinov repaired and cleaned the manger in Svyatka's stall and chopped some kindling. Since it was still warm, there was no fire in the little stove, but as soon as the real winter began in earnest, he wouldn't be able to do anything else but chop kindling for the fire. He would have to stoke the stove not only in the day, in the evening, and in the morning, but he'd also have to get up at night to do the same thing.

He was embarrassed that he had not gone to Solovko and Morkoshka for a long time. He felt guilty that he still hadn't found out a thing about Sevka Kuprianov's gelding. But neither Solovko nor Morkoshka, nor even the unjustly beaten Grunya, held any grudge against him. On the contrary—when he went to the stable, Morkoshka began to neigh, Grunya snorted a friendly greeting, and Solovko screwed up his eyes and stretched his neck out toward his master. "Hurry up and put my collar on me!" As Ustinov stood awhile without moving, Morkoshka reached out over the fence and touched him on the shoulder with the light-colored spot on his upper lip. The color of Morkoshka's coat was somewhere between a dark chestnut and a light bay, but the right side of his upper lip had stayed as pink as it had been when he was born, almost white. So he looked as if he had been painted chestnut and bay, but as if the painter had not had enough paint for that last little daub and had therefore botched the job because that little unpainted spot on Morkoshka's coat gave away his true color. "Are you afraid of something, Ustinov?" asked Morkoshka. "The end of the world, perhaps?" To tell the truth, Ustinov really was afraid of the end of the world. "No sense in it, master!" winked Morkoshka. "Life isn't a fool either, it won't give in!"

Morkoshka was right! It wasn't the first day that Ustinov figured out that if there is a God, then He surely must be of peasant stock, and so even at the very end of the world, at least one peasant would be left alive! You can't forget your own people no matter what the circumstances may be. And there could never be such a flood or a fire that it wouldn't leave behind some little bug or beetle; and where there was a little bug or beetle, there a little hen or grouse would find a place for itself; and where there was a little hen or a grouse, there would also be a little cow or a horse; and wherever there was a horse, there a peasant would find shelter. And not a peasant who was merely alive, but one with a farm, with a piebald horse or a bay. Or just take Morkoshka—he was so full of life it was incredible! If all that was left of him was a single rib, that would be all that he would need. From that one rib he would regenerate his whole body down to his mane and tail! "Well then, Morkoshka, would there be just the two of us left in the whole world?" When Morkoshka looked at the world, it was reflected in his eyes, as if from inside rather than outside: the porch of the Ustinov house with a curl of smoke coming from the chimney, the well-sweep, Svyatka's warm little shed and her hindquarters, her head being hidden by the shed, and above all this a suitable little piece of sky. Perhaps it was from the sky that the final answer appeared in Morkoshka's eyes. "Don't grieve, Kolya Ustinov, you're safe with me!"

Well, if that's the way it is, the two of them would have to begin with something. For how many days now had that dead branch been lying around in the yard? Such a thing might go unnoticed even after the end of the world. Then Ustinov would take it, shorten one end of it with a sharp rock, fasten two sticks to it on the side, and what would it be? A hoe, that's what! Then he'd fashion the two halves of a horse-collar from a couple of other branches and pad them with soft reeds, and he'd come up with some sort of harness for Morkoshka. And with a hoe and a horse-collar the plow-man and sower would cross himself, and go out into nature to find himself some sort of grain seed, and begin to work his land with his horse! After the first harvest, certainly no earlier, it would make sense to go beating the bushes in the forest for some sort of woman—women were a hardier breed than men. You might even just wait and try baking a loaf of bread of some sort yourself, and its aroma would flush a woman from the forest. Ustinov knew from his reading that there had once been a Stone Age and that people had still managed to live then. Was he then any worse than a Stone-Age man? That just couldn't be! If Stone-Age man had managed to get along, Ustinov would do so all the better! If it was true that humankind would have to start over again from the beginning, then Ustinov held all the cards in his hand!

Ustinov knew that life came from himself; if it ended, it would also do so in him; and if it began again, it would begin with him! Many people in the world had begun to forget this fact. Beginning to think that it didn't matter if the peasant existed or not, they despised the peasant for having his face in the dirt six months of the year, for being the most ignorant of the ignorant. And the peasant, too, had forgotten how to respect himself. He had lost sight of the fact that he is the source of everything, that this source illuminates him, and that he shouldn't run away from this light. But Ustinov had not forgotten this truth and never would. Surely this was why he had been so offended when Rodion Gavrilovich Smirnovsky suggested that he was no longer merely a peasant and would soon cease to be one entirely! He had been so insulted and upset that he in turn had insulted Smirnovsky. Of course, he would have much preferred to insult Grishka Sukhikh, but Grishka was so impudent that insults had no effect on him, while it was simple to insult his brave and beloved commander. You always insult only those you are able to.

But no one should suggest that Ustinov was capable of betraying his peasant calling, no one! Come to think of it, it was Granddad Yegory who had first raised this suspicion. "Oh, you'll leave the land, Nikolka! I feel it in my heart, you'll leave!" he would sigh tearfully. "I won't leave, Grand-dad!" Ustinov would defend himself as best he could. "Why do you think I take on these different jobs with the surveyors and the forest inspectors? I don't do it to leave the land, but to get closer to it, to understand what educated people can do for it! I'm looking for ways to benefit us peasants!"

Yegory didn't believe it. And he wasn't alone—Domna had her doubts somewhere in her heart, and his mother, and even his children had doubts about their father in their still immature little minds. These suspicions seemed strange to him. Why, if you reached out and touched him, you would realize in a flash that he was a peasant, a farmer! His very skin would tell you that. If some meticulous person felt him over carefully, he'd discover many other details as well. He'd find out that Ustinov was a native Siberian, of Poluvyatsky-Kerzhak stock, born in the village of Lebyazhka, on the hill between the lake and the forest. What else could he be? His skin was saturated with none other than the black soil of Lebyazhka, the dust of the surrounding steppe, the scent of the pine forest, the fresh and salt waters of the lakes on the steppe and of the underground springs that surface on the shores of these lakes. Just as the owner of a horse puts his brand on its right or left thigh and in so doing puts his mark not only on its skin and fur but on the horse's whole life, so the land always marks the creatures that live on her, a bug or a man, everything that is there! "You are mine!" declares this mark. "You are born mine. I am your true mistress and mother!" And there is only one thing wrong with this mark—because it is invisible, anyone who wants to can conceal it from others and create confusion and disorder.

Ustinov disliked disorder and didn't want anyone to create it, least of all himself. But as time passed, his own kin and the rest of Lebyazhka abandoned their suspicions. That was in 1911, when construction had begun on a branch line to the south from the Trans-Siberian Railroad. This business had nothing to do with Lebyazhka. They figured that it was closer and more convenient to travel to the mainline station at Ozyorki, and so it continued to be—the branch line passed to the west and barely touched Krushikha Volost and the uyezd. But even though the Lebyazhkans were far from the construction site, various people—engineers, foremen, contractors, feed suppliers—still came to visit, to recruit construction workers, ditchdiggers, and laborers, and to buy up feed and foodstuffs for the workers' rations. Although they gathered a great many workers from among the recent immigrants, there was not much feed or food because the harvest that year had been a poor one. Two engineers appeared at the Ustinov house.

"We heard from someone outside your village that there's a local farmer here, a Nikolai Levontyevich Ustinov, who knows how to work with tools. Is this true?"

"Well, I can work a little with tools and figures," Ustinov said modestly, blushing. "But please, come in and have a seat . . . "

The guests came in and sat down. It was summertime, and Ustinov told Domna to serve some kvass.* They drank a little and complimented the

---

*A slightly fermented traditional Russian drink made from rye bread.

kvass, the cleanliness of the house, the relative absence of flies, and the presence of books.

"Tell us, Ustinov, do you know what a theodolite is?" the senior engineer asked.

"A theodolite—it's the same as an astrolabe in the old sense—is an instrument for measuring the angle to a location that is lower than where the theodolite itself is sitting!" answered Ustinov.

"Well now, Brother!" the engineer exclaimed in surprise and even ran his fingers over the little hammer-insignia on his cap. "Well, Brother Ustinov, you know a lot more than you need to know to carry a theodolite for an engineer! You have carried one, haven't you?"

"Lots of times! I know definitions like that, and I love them. I like to know everything about a thing. Especially the kind of thing you have to hold in your hands."

"Yes . . . So have you ever worked on a surveying crew?"

"From time to time . . . "

"Could you range out a baseline yourself?"

"On even or broken terrain?"

"Even . . . "

"I could . . . "

"And on broken terrain?"

"It would go a lot slower, but I could still do it."

"And where would you record your stationing?"

"Where?" Ustinov was surprised by the question. "In the surveyor's log, of course, on graph paper, and to scale!"

"Stop, stop, Ustinov! Perhaps you've not only carried a theodolite on your shoulder but also know how to handle one?"

"Well, of course, I didn't just carry it around!" Ustinov agreed.

"So what do you know how to do with it?"

"I know how to center on a point."

"And take a reading of the angle?"

"Just barely. In a have-to situation, if there's no one else to do it. Then what else can you do? You have to do it yourself. But marking out the working angle to the given line—that I can do. The engineers trusted me with that, though just with the laying out of the forest boundary lines."

"And just how do you do that, Ustinov?"

"Like everyone does it: I align the zero of the limb and the zero of the alidade, aim the scope at the landmark along the baseline, and then I loosen the alidade and with the screw adjust its zero to the required degree on the limb! And then, of course, I take a good look at the vernier."

"You're priceless, Ustinov!" The engineer slapped himself on the knees, and his colleague just stared with his eyes bugging out and his mouth, minus two upper teeth, hanging open. "That's what you are, Ustinov! But can you calculate the volume of an excavation from a drawing?"

"Reserve or spoil bank?"

"Spoil bank!"

"Well, it depends on its shape. If it's complicated and takes breaking up into simpler shapes, then it takes me too long to figure it out. With my education, anyway."

The engineer pulled a surveyor's notebook with graph paper out of his knapsack, sketched a spoil bank in plane and profile, wrote "scale 1:100" on it, and put a sharpened pencil in front of Ustinov. "Figure it out!"

Ustinov went into the kitchen, washed his hands, splashed cold water on his face, wiped himself dry so that no drops would fall on the page, and started his calculations. While the engineers chatted, looked out the window, and examined the cabinet of books, he worked for a long time and didn't rush himself. "Let them wait! They're the ones who want me to do this, not me." Finally he told them that he had calculated the spoil bank and hoped he had gotten it right.

"Well, let's just have a look!" said the engineer. He took a slide rule out of his pack and began to move the hairline quickly back and forth and to pull on the slide. Finishing his calculations, he fixed his gaze on Ustinov again. "Well then, Ustinov, I'll take you on as a surveying technician. Salary: fifty-five rubles a month, including expenses, plus overtime!"

"Would it be for long?"

"Well, full time, of course! For about three years! As long as the surveying and construction are going on! And when the railroad is finished here, you'll most likely come along with us to some other construction project. You're practically a technician already. You won't be coming back to your cattle now, will you? I'll even take you on as my permanent assistant, not for just three years!"

"But why would I have to come back to my cattle," asked Ustinov, "when I'm not going to leave them to begin with? Especially if it's for three whole years or forever! If it was for three months, then maybe I would go!"

"Do you drink?" asked the engineer.

"Why wouldn't I have a drink on a holiday?"

"And could you treat me to some right now? Do you have any?"

"Why wouldn't I?" Ustinov called out to Domna to serve them something.

"Well then, if you have some on hand, it means you're not a drinker," the engineer said. He knocked back his drink and asked once more, "Did you understand me? Fifty-five rubles a month and overtime?"

Later, after the engineers had gone to spend the night in the hayloft, Granddad Yegory came out of his little room and, spreading his hands in amazement, exclaimed, "Now ain't that somethin'? Yessir! Fifty-five! And extree work besides! Did ya really turn it down, Nikolka? Are ya a fool, Nikolka? I don't understand it! I ain't seen you behavin' like no fool till now!"

So Granddad Yegory, who had plowed his field buck naked and who had been the first to accuse his grandson of abandoning his peasant calling, now fell to his knees before such a salary. But his grandson didn't. He didn't even consider it. If anyone understood Ustinov then, it was Ivan Ivanovich Samorukov. It was just after the engineers' visit that Samorukov had insulted the old men of Lebyazhka by declaring for all to hear that there wasn't a fitting candidate for Finest Man among them, but as for Nikola Ustinov, who was still a youngster, now there was a real candidate for you! For Ivan Ivanovich there had never been anything of greater merit than loyalty to Lebyazhka, and those who deserted the community he hated very fiercely indeed. He even blamed the departed for dying before their time. When Lebyazhka needed to fence in the new grazing pasture, someone or other was put in charge of the thing, and then he up and died! A disgrace! Ustinov's example of loyalty to the community and to the peasantry was a cause for great celebration for Ivan Ivanovich.

To tell the truth, Ustinov would have liked to get something from the land and the peasantry, and from life itself, some sort of good luck and happiness, in return for his loyalty. Sometimes he had demanded, "I have the right, I've worked for it, I've earned it!" Of course, he never made threats. He never said, "So that's the way it is! I haven't had any luck here, so I'll just give up on Lebyazhka, the land, and all my movable and immovable property, and go off to be a surveying technician or maybe something else!" He knew that life was not afraid of threats. If you don't want to live it, fine, don't. But to want something and ask for it—now that you could do!

Only lately had Ustinov become confused. He didn't know what he could ask for and wish for and what he couldn't. When he had tended Svyatka, hadn't he wanted to raise a champion, make a lot of money, and have his picture taken with her so he could hang it on the wall in his house? Well, he had achieved that. If you added up Svyatka's milk yield and kept a close account of it, she would set records for the uyezd and maybe for the whole gubernia! But what good was this to anyone now? No one was keeping records of milk yields or buying up milk these days. What could you get for milk now except paper notes, who knows whose, money good for who knows what? Somewhere in Russia people were starving, but here Svyatka carried her huge udder with useless pride, not knowing that her butter was no longer traveling by rail to the different countries of the world and that no one had the slightest desire to publish her photograph.

And so the most reliable asset in Ustinov's life had now turned out to be good for nothing, a liability. He kept feeding Svyatka and milking her, but what could he do with all the milk his own family couldn't drink? Instead of real success, look what a mess he had, what a fool the wise man had become! Ustinov was not used to playing the fool, he couldn't do it! Maybe he should just bash Svyatka in the head with the butt-end of an axe, as hard as he could right between her slender horns! Would he be a wise man again? If she fell to the ground and the earth in Ustinov's yard trembled under her motionless weight? If the rest of his livestock froze in terror? But Ustinov wasn't capable of that frame of mind either. And he remembered those goatlike cows he had once fought and chased away from his house. They were still getting along just fine. They didn't have to give milk to their masters since their masters had told them, "Go off and find your own food wherever you can! If we need you we'll call you back to the yard, and not before then!" The war had passed these cows by without noticing them, and God only knows if they noticed the war. This half-wild creature's tenacious grip on life was exactly what Ustinov had miscalculated.

A scientist named Liskun had come from Moscow or St. Petersburg to see those very cows. He knew everything there was to know about every kind of cattle, and although he worked constantly with thoroughbreds, his greatest interest had always been these black-and-white, shaggy-haired Siberians. He said that they were good cattle, with one misfortune—poor masters! He said that if these cows were fed a bit better, if their masters warmed even just a little water for them in the winter rather than letting them drink from a hole in the ice, if any sort of roof at all were built over their heads, if they were milked patiently and thoroughly to accustom their udders to the work, then their milk yield could be doubled, and then some. And since the fat content of their milk was almost twice as high as that of purebred cows, who could say which was better—to have one domesticated Svyatka, or two or three of those capricious little cows? Cows that were so mistrustful and unaffectionate toward humans perhaps because they had guessed that sooner or later people would create chaos and savagery among themselves and that then they, wild beasts themselves, would have to rise above the proud Svyatka!

Ustinov would have liked to know what sort of man this Liskun was. Was he clean-shaven, or did he wear a beard like Saint Gleb, the patron of domestic livestock? And how come no one else had thought this way about these beasts, but he had figured it out? My God—how simple it was! Liskun's name and patronymic were Yefim Fedotovich. A peasant name, a name you could trust. It was a shame they had never met. Ustinov would have repented of his sins before Yefim Fedotovich alone. He would have told him how he had beaten these seemingly ignoble cattle with a club, how he had taken action against them with military strategy, hammering horseshoe nails into the log walls of his house. He would have confessed his sins and talked with Yefim Fedotovich about life.

Everything alive knows who was born why, who is to live where, who can and cannot eat whom, who is supposed to hop around on the earth, and who is to fly in the air—all of this is firmly fixed for everyone. Except for humans. Humans—just you wait and see—will find a way to leap off the earth altogether, to leave their fields and their livestock, and what can they expect then? What if you fly off somewhere? Into damnation, into the unknown? Into some final war among yourselves? Into a war between people and all other living creatures? Wouldn't that also be a civil war, brother against brother, cruel and senseless?!

"Yefim Fedotovich! Yefimushka! You're the one I'd like to discuss this subject with, not Grishka Sukhikh, or even Father-Commander Smirnovsky—the subject of life on earth! Can you tell me what it is all about?"

Kudeyar

That night Barin began to howl in the yard in desperate alarm. Ustinov woke up and listened. It was not just Barin who was howling—other dogs were crying out in the Glazkovs' yard, and even the Kruglovs' watchdog, old as the hills and completely gray, was trying his best to join in, but coughing hoarsely as if someone were choking him.

"Could it be war?!" was Ustinov's first reaction. Frozen by its suddenness, he felt confused and too weak to jump out of bed. No unexpected occurrence is worse than one that you have been waiting for endlessly, one that you think will surely come tomorrow, but then it comes today . . . Forcing himself to take some deep breaths, Ustinov remembered that he had been a soldier not so very long ago, that war was not a thing that you got used to, and his weakness passed. "Well," he thought when he had awakened completely and recovered from his initial fright, "it can hardly be that, anyway! If it really was war, we would have heard something or other lately about White units, or Red units, or partisans!" There had not been a word about any uprisings, punitive battalions, or partisans—all of that had passed by Krushikha Volost and those adjacent to it. There had not even been any word about the government itself. It hadn't come sniffing around, and if the Provisional Government men had the brains not to go sticking their noses into other peoples' business, then praise God for that!

Listening some more, Ustinov was sure that any minute now someone would come knocking on his shutters. He was used to the fact that no matter what sort of event took place, whether by day or night, his neighbors would always come running to tell him about it. Someone hurried by on the street without stopping at the Ustinov house. "Is it the woodcutters again?" he wondered. It had been the same the first time they had come—it had been night and the dogs had barked, though not very loudly and not all at once. His guessing eased his mind, and he continued to wait for Ignashka Ignatov to come and get him. Ignashka had come knocking the last time.

Domna woke up, and as if Ustinov, who was still lying beside her, was supposed to know everything in the world without leaving the house, asked, "Well, what is it, Kolya? Again?"

Ustinov did not answer.

Domna rose up on one elbow to ask, "Is it something bad?"

"Where would something good come from these days?"

Domna also began to listen, but calmly. That was the way she was—as long as her man was beside her, everything in the world was fine. As he got dressed, Ustinov asked himself, "What am I for Domna, a stone wall behind which nothing can touch her?" He wanted Domna to be frightened.

"Kolya!" She had put her head back on the pillow. "Go out and see what's going on and then come back and tell me!"

Another thing that amazed Ustinov was that whenever he was gone from home for a long time, as when he had worked with the forest inspectors, or the surveyors, or when he had been off fighting for three years, Domna had never been at a loss. Her spirits never sank. She ran the household as she should have, worked day and night, and knew how to make her daughters work. During the war she had remodeled the bathhouse into living space, in which she quartered two Austrian prisoners of war who certainly did not sit around with nothing to do. The household didn't fail or go downhill. But as soon as her man was beside her, it was as if a hand had lifted her cares from her, and she became slow-moving and impressively handsome, walking around the house quietly singing songs. She still kept house, of course, cooked, took care of her grandchildren, spun with speed and skill, but she didn't go out to tend the livestock anymore. That wasn't any of her business now, although she had undertaken to nurse Grunya with a poultice of medicinal herbs for horses, and even of those meant for people. But she did this only because of the special friendship that had long existed between her and Grunya. She didn't even look after Svyatka or milk her anymore—that was her daughter's job.

On Sundays Domna would dress up in her good clothes and sit down to embroider or to knit mittens, scarves, stockings, all sorts of things, and after dinner she would put on her Orenburg shawl to visit the neighbors, where she would shell sunflower seeds or knit some pretty thing, this time in the company of other women. And God forbid that anyone should interfere with this routine of hers—she would really take offense then! In all Lebyazhka there were only two such women who always had to be women and to follow their own particular personal habits, no matter what might happen. Domna was such a proud woman, and so was Zinaida Pankratova. All the other women knew nothing of this—they lived in a state of continual labor and woe. There were those who were never free of bruises and those who took on all the household work, except the plowing and sowing and reaping, even though they had living husbands. Nothing can be said about the widows—they had so many troubles that they couldn't see the sky above them, and maybe not even the earth beneath them, either.

"Get up, Domna!" said Ustinov as he dressed. "Hurry up!"

All right then, she'd hurry! She wouldn't protest. She, too, began to move quickly, but even in her haste she felt bewildered. "This is a fine thing! Sunday isn't over yet, is it? This is my day!"

As soon as Ustinov had rushed out onto the porch in his hat and sheepskin coat and Barin had come running up to his feet howling, the same reluctance swept over him. "It's war!" It couldn't be anything else! When he heard someone walking on the street, he shouted, "Hey! Who's there?"

"Wha'?" across a fence, an old man answered and began to cough.

"Is it war?"

The man finished coughing and answered, "I don't know myself, goddammit!"

"Wait up there! I'm coming!" Running from the porch into the street, Ustinov caught up with Prokopy Kruglov, who lived two houses down.

"Is it war?" Prokopy asked him the same question.

"I don't know!" Ustinov answered.

"But who is fighting? The Whites? The Reds? Someone else?" Prokopy asked again.

"I just don't know!"

"Then let's go to the square. Maybe we'll find someone there who does!"

They walked quickly to the square, running the last bit of the way, and at that moment the alarm began to sound there, the small but clear-voiced bell that had hung since time immemorial between two posts next to the village assembly building.

"It's a bit late to be ringing that, the bastards!" Prokopy Kruglov said angrily as he ran. "All the people were already awake and in the streets, but they didn't ring the bell, as if it were none of their business! It's disgusting, goddammit!"

"But who are 'they'? Who didn't ring the bell?" asked Ustinov.

"Does it matter who? Someone should have sounded the alarm!"

"But who's supposed to do it now?" Ustinov still tried to ask as they ran. "No one's responsible for that nowadays—there's no watchman on duty, not even a guard at the assembly house! No one! There aren't any real authorities!"

"What do you mean? There's still a policeman there! He eats our bread, but he's too lazy to ring the bell? Or at the least it should have been one of you from the Forest Commission! You're around when there's woodcutters to catch, your own men to tie up hand and foot, goddam you, but there's no one who can yank on the bell rope when they should, goddam you all to hell!"

"All right Prokopy!" Ustinov answered. "Run faster now, or I'll leave you behind!" And he thought, "Lebyazhka has a forest guard of twenty-four armed men, but no one thought to put a night watchman on duty! Look how many papers and minutes the Commission has written, how many investigations it has carried out, but here it's like the wind has blown them all away somewhere! Maybe Prokopy is right?!"

On the square there were already more than a dozen men bunched together not far from the peaked roof of the assembly building, with others running in from the side streets. There was a pale, transparent, almost full moon in the dark sky. In the faint light the outlines of the houses on all four sides of the Lebyazhka town square melted away and resembled rounded haystacks instead of houses. Only the peaked roof of the assembly hall pointed sharply upward. The square was on high ground, on the very top of the hill, and from there the forest could be seen, a dark wall against the white of the night, and above it, a pink, an almost red glow. There was a fire out there. Beyond the edge of the forest, something was burning steadily, with a fierce glow that flickered upward and outward. Sometimes the black forest seemed to be split by fiery cracks, but then they would close up again, and the flames would be locked up behind the jagged fortress wall once more, bursting upward only from time to time and melting in their own glow.

As soon as Ustinov had reached the square and had looked at the glow of the fire, he shouted to the others, "Men! Grishka Sukhikh's place is on fire!"

Instantly he pictured to himself how the flames were devouring the good-sized buildings of Grishka's homestead and how the shaggy, disheveled Grishka, limping on one leg, was urging his taciturn farmhands into the flames to save his property and leading the way into the furnace himself. But no one was surprised by Ustinov's words. Everyone knew without his saying it that it was Grishka Sukhikh's homestead that was burning.

"Of course! There's no one else living out in that direction!"

The men went on standing and staring at the glowing cloud, shining red above the forest, swaying from side to side, rising and falling, dying down and flaring up again. People kept coming to the square, but, strangely enough, the more of them there were, the quieter they became, and now no one even bothered to ask any questions.

"And who is that ringing that bell?" Someone, perhaps Prokopy Kruglov, suddenly asked. "And what for? Goddam him!"

The bell rang out twice more and then also fell silent.

"Men!" Ustinov shouted. "How can you do this? A man's place is on fire! A Lebyazhka man! Even if he's a freeholder and off on his own, he's still a Lebyazhka man! How can we just stand around with our hands in our pockets?"

Prokopy, who was standing in the same place not far from Ustinov, turned and said, "Quit it, Nikolai Levontyevich! Stop it!"

"Stop what?"

"Disturbing people. Hollering at them!"

"I'm calling them to help! What kind of disturbance is that?"

"Don't you see that everyone is standing around calmly and that you're the only one who feels the need to shout?!"

"It's arson!" Ustinov suddenly guessed.

And immediately some of the men came up to him and began to discuss the question of whose handiwork it might be.

"The partisans could have done it. Even though there's been no word about them, they still could have shown up and done it. They have to start with someone, and they couldn't have picked a better one than Grishka—he lives off on his own, and he's a rich man. Richer than everyone else!"

The men agreed with this interpretation, but other suggestions followed.

"Grishka's hired hands did it. They put up with him and put up with him, and then they got tired of being like dumb animals, and they did it. No one can get away with exploitation!"

"Grishka gave the Commission a map that marked off six desyatinas of forest, seven, even! He threatened to shoot anyone who set foot on that land! I hear tell he's already shot at someone. And so the Commission . . . "

Again everyone agreed, and they even seemed to support the Commission—that's what needed to be done with Grishka! After each had come up with a theory better than the last, there was another suggestion.

"Sukhikh set fire to his own place! Day after tomorrow about this time, he'll have an excuse to set fire to all Lebyazhka! Pretending to get even!"

"And you?" Ustinov tugged on Prokopy Kruglov's sleeve. "You really aren't going to go help Grishka?"

"Me?" Prokopy answered in surprise. "Like I'm supposed to more than anyone else? Like maybe I need Grishka's gratitude that much?" He thought a moment, cleared his throat, and added, "Grishka is too rich, goddam him! For these times, he's way too rich. He's managed to cut himself off from the world, to leave the village, so let him get out of trouble by himself! Goddam him!"

Ustinov wouldn't leave him alone. "Prokopy! Aren't you a rich man yourself? Haven't you dreamed about a freehold yourself? Haven't you envied Grigory? Haven't you wanted to follow his example? How many working horses do you have in your yard? Six already? And that still isn't enough for you, is it?"

"It used to be like that, Nikola. But these days I don't care much for Grishka's example!" Coughing again, Prokopy Kruglov walked away from Ustinov.

Just at that moment someone standing up in a sledge drove quickly out into the square and shouted, "Whoever's going to the fire, get in! Quickly!" It was Rodion Gavrilovich Smirnovsky. He held back his horses and waited, but no one got in with him, no one even answered him. "Who's coming?" he asked again.

Ustinov jumped into the sledge. Whipping the shaft-horse, Smirnovsky sped off toward the red light of the fire. The horses' stride was short but fast, and as the frozen ground, lightly covered with snow, rang out beneath their hooves, it sounded as if a whole herd of horses were rushing off somewhere into the whitish night. Smirnovsky followed the almost indiscernible road, keeping to the side to avoid the deep autumn ruts. Trees and their large, shapeless shadows, blurring into one another in the snow, rushed at the sledge from the right; from the left the edge of the earth seemed to be visible out on the fog-shrouded steppe, a precipice from which the ghostly fog was slowly rising as the moonlight flowed down into the depths of the abyss. Smirnovsky, in a sheepskin coat and a Caucasian fur cap, continued to stand as he drove. He kept his eyes on the road in front of him; only when they were halfway to their destination did he glance in the back.

"Who's back there? Is it you, Levontyevich?"

"It's me, Rodion Gavrilovich!" Ustinov answered.

When they had almost reached that sharp salient of the forest beyond which the red flames were now brightly blazing, Smirnovsky reined in the horses and shouted, "Jump in!" and someone unexpectedly bumped his head on Ustinov's knees and shouted hoarsely, "Fire! Fire! Flames! Flames!"

It was Kudeyar, almost a holy fool, the man who had spent his whole life proclaiming the coming of the end of the world. He had been running to the fire when Smirnovsky picked him up. After falling onto the sledge and catching his breath, Kudeyar stared at Ustinov's face until he recognized him. Then he threw his mittens into the sledge and picked them up again to stick them in the belt of his short peasant coat, hardly fit for winter weather. Digging both hands into his beard, he repeated, on his knees, now as if it were a prayer or an exorcism: "Fire! Fire! Flames! Flames!" while one earflap of his hat dangled in the wind and slapped him in the forehead.

Now the forest was more and more brightly illuminated. The pine trees were lit up as if it were daylight, a bright dawn, or the beginning of sunset. The branches of some trees, their needles, and the snow on the needles had grown transparent, as if turned to glass. Crack! Crack! Crack! The dry beams of Grishka's homestead could already be heard snapping in the fire. The crackling rose and fell like the sound of a rifle range.

Amid this sound of gunfire, Ustinov thought, "We run, run, run—to the fire! We have to—none of the rich men are coming, not the Kruglov brothers, not even Grishka's own rich brothers, Fyodor and Dementy. The ones who are rushing to help are those who never had anything to do with Grishka and never will—Lieutenant Smirnovsky, the holy fool, Kudeyar, and me, Nikolai Ustinov!" And he, too, repeated to himself, "Fire! Fire! Flames! Flames!"

Now the horses had passed through the salient of the forest and had brought the sledge out to that fire and those flames. The fire had already done its work and was dying down, but this was the time of the most intense heat. Grishka's buildings—the big house, a barn almost as large, if not larger, the long, squat cattle shed, and even the frame of the well—blazed hot, red and bright inside as well as out. The fire had spread from one end to the other of every beam, melting deep inside where the flames found it cramped and stuffy. On the outside, above the beams, there was an altogether different kind of fire, and the two flames, the internal and the aerial, hastened to wrest from one another everything that could burn, crackle, sparkle, and turn into coals. The first thing that Ustinov saw in the bright light, not in the fire, but next to it, was a wagon with two horses hitched to it and piled high with large and small boxes. The horses, both dark-gray carriage horses, were tethered to a tree. The skin on their backs was continually twitching. Because their reins were tied to the very bottom of the tree trunk, their faces were pulled down to the ground.

At the edge of the huge red circle of light stood a small shed, spared by some miracle, with pine trees on the other side, also lit up red from top to bottom. Sparse shrubbery hugged the ground, and beyond the shrubbery you could see the steppe with its light snow, dark knolls, the tracks of roads, and the barely visible ridges of plowed fields here and there. Other than the horses hitched to the wagon, there was not a single living soul to be seen anywhere, neither people nor livestock nor fowl. Then a huge black dog, its iron chain gleaming in the fire, emerged briefly from the darkness of the pine forest, and then another, standing on three legs, peeked out from behind it, and then both of them disappeared again.

Jumping out of the sledge and tossing the reins around a tree, Smirnovsky asked, "Has everybody died?"

As Kudeyar began to recite his incantation again, loudly and rapidly—"Fire! Fire! Flames! Flames!"—Ustinov silently imagined what had happened. Everyone, both the people and the livestock, had perished in the flames. Grishka alone had survived. He had brought out the horses and the wagon and had loaded the boxes on the wagon, but, not content with that, had rushed back to fetch more of his property and had died, too. Even though Ustinov didn't say a word to Smirnovsky, he knew that Smirnovsky believed the same thing, and even Kudeyar understood what had happened. But Grishka Sukhikh was still alive, and they soon caught sight of him.

Sitting on a footstool on the other side of the fire, looking into the flames, and smoking a cigarette, he was wearing a woman's plush jacket, cinched up with a soldier's belt, with yellowish patches of wadding visible through holes burned on the shoulders and back. Into the bosom of this jacket he had stuffed some kind of small bundle with two dangling ends of motley-colored cloth. His head was bare, and from his shaggy hair, it seemed to Ustinov, a light wisp of smoke was rising. Holding his cigarette in one hand, Grishka was pulling with the other at his beard, the left side of which was singed and gray, to shake the ashes out of it. Smirnovsky, Ustinov, and Kudeyar walked up to him, but Grishka did not stir. He just sat and smoked and pulled at his beard. He stared at the fire with interest and even sympathy, the same way people stare thoughtfully at a campfire.

"Grigory? Did you lose your animals in the fire?" Smirnovsky asked.

Without answering, Grishka shrugged.

"Did your livestock burn up?!" Rodion Gavrilovich asked again.

Grishka shrugged again and replied, "Does that make any difference now?" He thought a moment. "That don't matter now . . . "

"And your people? Did your people die, Grigory?"

"Does that make any difference now?" Grishka answered again. "What's burned is burned. Once and for all."

"Fire? Fire? Flames? Flames?" It was a question now. Kudeyar was no longer trying to convince them. "Flames?!"

"Did someone do this to you, Grigory? Do you suspect anyone?" asked Ustinov.

Spitting out his cigarette butt, Grishka turned toward Ustinov and laughed. "Interesting that you should ask, Ustinov! Very interesting!" He rolled another cigarette, got up from the stool, approached the fire, and stretched his hand out toward the flames. Grishka waited until a small ember fell into his upturned palm—the flames were throwing out sparks and embers by the thousands—then quickly lighted his cigarette and returned to his place on the stool.

The fire seemed to take offense at this casual treatment and got furious. It began to crackle and roar once more. There was no place left for it to go, nothing left for it to eat. The time of the greatest and most reckless feasting had already passed, the time when the fire had tossed itself from side to side, from one delicacy to another, finding dry, yielding wood everywhere.

Now it licked every beam a second time, searching for anything it had over-looked and not gobbled up right away. It wasn't so much a fire now as a source of heat that scorched the air around itself, but it still wanted to spread to the pine trees, and from them to the whole forest, and from the whole forest to the whole world. But the trees, though they crackled and turned glassy and dropped their singed needles, did not catch fire, and so the flames began to stretch out toward the little shed that, though com-pletely lit up by the fire, had not burned. The fire reached for it; its light penetrated it from all sides and fell on it from above. Steam rose from its wet roof, on which the snow had long since melted.

"Come on, boys!" said Smirnovsky. "At least let's save this little shed! Why don't we try? We can take these beams and move the burning beams farther away from it! All right? What do you have in there, Grigory? Grain? Something else?"

"I have different kinds of stuff in there, Rodion," Grishka answered hes-itatingly. "Seed grain. Pressed wool. Tar. Window glass. There's different things in there."

"That shed is already safe, Rodion Gavrilovich! The fire can't get at it now!" said Ustinov.

"It can't reach it?" Grishka was suddenly animated. "That's no good! We'll fix that!" Getting up from his stool, he wrapped the hem of his jack-et around his hand, grabbed a burning brand out of the fire, and, limping on his lame leg, ran quickly to the shed, stuck the brand into a crack be-tween two planks in the front steps, broke it off, and tossed the other half up on the roof. The fire caught immediately in both places, on the porch and on the roof, less above, but more fiercely on the steps. The fire licked the door, blackened it, and then seemed to back away from it, but only for a moment. Then it clung to the planks of the door and jumped higher still, to the cornice, and from there to the walls, and then, believing once more that nothing could ever stop it, that it would never be extin-guished, that it would have something to devour without end, it leapt joy-fully into the sky.

"What the hell are you doing, Grigory?" asked Smirnovsky, his Kalmyk eyes blazing with anger.

Grishka returned his cigarette to his mouth and answered, "I'm only sorry that I can't set fire to the earth itself! It won't burn! If I can't live on this land anymore, then I'll damn well burn the earth itself! I'll goddam well do it! I'll goddam well burn myself and set fire to the whole uyezd! You can goddam bet on it!"

"What?" Ustinov was bewildered. "What's the land got to do with it? What's the earth got to do with it? Is it to blame for anything?"

"Isn't it? If I burn or drown, then everything around me is to blame!"

"But didn't you pull these boxes out of the fire, Grigory? You were getting burned yourself, but didn't you still pull them out of the fire? Doesn't that mean you need your possessions?"

"I dragged them out!" Grishka agreed. "Whatever I could. And whatever I can't carry away, even if it's my own property, even this land here, even the pine forest all around it, even you, Ustinov—let it all burn! Every goddam thing! Every last bit! Especially you, Nikola!"

"Your own brothers are here in Lebyazhka!" Ustinov protested. "If you are going away, you could leave your things with them!"

"What kind of brothers are they?" Grishka asked. "They're a joke!" Sukhikh laughed, walked up to his footstool, grabbed it by one leg, and threw it into the fire. "They're a joke, by God! What have they come up with? Brothers!" He spat out his cigarette and stomped on it out of habit. He turned around and walked over to his wagon. A minute later, swearing at the horses and everything else with every word he knew, Grishka Sukhikh was driving out of the fire-lit circle into the dark, silent steppe, driving away without a backward glance.

Kudeyar shouted to him, "Grigory, why are you doing this? Did you set fire to your own place, Grigory?"

Holding back his horses, Sukhikh turned in his seat, and shook his fist. "It's a good thing it's you, Kudeyar! I'd burn any other man on the goddam spot for those words! I would have shoved any other man into the goddam fire, and it would have been a good thing!" And once more, not having a whip, he urged his horses on with a stick, and then he turned around again. "I don't have time to wait, or else I goddam would! I'd sit for a while and see who else besides you shows up at my little campfire! A firebug always comes out to take a look at his handiwork, just like a murderer comes out to see his victim! But I don't have the time, and maybe no one else will show up besides you three! So, see you later! Good luck, Comrade Brothers! We'll meet again! You can count on it!"

Beating his horses even harder, Grishka receded even more quickly out of the fire-lit circle and disappeared into the dark steppe. And then from the darkness they heard him sing a strange song, not even a man's song, but a woman's: "Fly-y Cossack, fly-y like an arro-ow . . . " A black dog ran out of the forest after Grishka, its iron chain clattering along the frozen ground, and behind it another, badly burned, running on three legs.

Smirnovsky, Ustinov, and Kudeyar stared silently at the dying fire. Having reduced the little shed to a heap of coals, once again it was unable to continue its violent life.

"Well?" asked Smirnovsky. "Let's go!" He went to the sledge, with Ustinov following.

Mumbling some more about fire and flames, Kudeyar remained where he was and then shouted, "Nikolai Levontyevich! We can't leave here! We just can't! You know it—we just can't do it!"

"Why?" Ustinov asked in surprise.

"What do you mean?" Smirnovsky turned around as well.

"We just can't!" repeated Kudeyar, waving both arms. "It will be just like Sukhikh said: they will come! The very ones!"

"Who?"

"The arsonists! And if we don't wait for them, don't see them, don't find out who they are, then we'll be the same as them! Arsonists! Sukhikh was right! We can't leave!"

"Let's go!" Smirnovsky insisted angrily.

"But I'm not asking you, Rodion Gavrilovich! I know it's no use. You stay, Nikola! I'm asking you, I'm begging you. Stay! Listen to me!" He rushed up to Ustinov.

"Nikolai!" Smirnovsky said, looking at Kudeyar. "You get behind him, and I'll get in front, and we'll get him onto the sled and take him away! We can't leave the man here by himself, can we? Let's grab him!"

"And where will we take him, Rodion Gavrilovich?" Ustinov asked. "He'll come running back anyway. And he'll put up a struggle while we're on the road. It won't work!"

"Yes, I'll come running back anyway!" Kudeyar repeated. "And I'll put up a struggle in the sled! I will! And I'll call on you to stay here, Levontyevich. I'll beg you and weep! Why don't you want to stay with me?"

"I just don't want to."

"Should I tell you why, Ustinov? You're afraid of the truth! You're afraid of it and of me! And you've been running, running, running away from me for almost your whole life! But I won't give up, I'll catch up with you, if not today, then tomorrow. I won't let you run away from the truth to lies! I won't! I won't let you! Don't run away anymore, Nikola Ustinov, stay with me!"

"All right!" Ustinov nodded. "Go on, Rodion Gavrilovich, we'll sit here where it's warm, by the ashes."

Dismissing them with a wave of his hand, Smirnovsky jumped into his sledge.

▲▲▲

This man called Kudeyar had an ordinary name, Dmitry. Dmitry Panteleymonovich Yankovsky. His ancestors came from Minsk Gubernia and had also been Old Believers. At first the generations of Yankovskys had lived in Lebyazhka the same as everyone else. They plowed, sowed, and harvested. But then they began to die out: the children, when they were still babies; the adults, without leaving children or grandchildren. And in the end there remained only Dmitry Yankovsky, also childless. He lived a long time, but he didn't continue his own clan. He was the last to bear his unlucky family name. True, for a long time now, no one had known his last name or his first name. Everyone had forgotten them, and having forgotten them himself, he lived by the name of Kudeyar. For many years in ancient Russia there had been an outlaw named Kudeyar, even more than one such outlaw, and all of them buried great stores of treasure that no one has ever discovered. Just why such a name stuck to the powerless peasant Dmitry Yankovsky is anyone's guess. It stuck, and that's all there is to it.

With his half-blind old woman, Kudeyar lived in seclusion in a little house not far from where the new school had been built. He would go out into the fields and work until dinnertime, and then he would throw his tattered coat in a furrow, lie down on it with his hands behind his head, and stare and stare into the sky without moving a muscle. The horses would wander nearby in their harness, nibbling at a bit of grass or simply looking around, but their master would pay no attention to them. No one would hear a single word from Kudeyar for weeks on end, but he was always ready to listen to other people. Whenever the men got together to sit on a log by the lake, he would sit at the edge of the group and listen, but he stayed as quiet as a mouse. Kudeyar seldom left Lebyazhka, even to go to the market at Krushikha. Even then no one had to talk much to persuade him to give up a third, or even a half, of his produce in return for selling it for him instead of his having to bother with it himself. But once in a great while he would hitch up his horses and go somewhere far away, to the railroad or to the uyezd center. Then after listening to various fellow travelers and conversing with folks as he lolled empty-handed about the marketplaces and roadside inns, Kudeyar came home and opened his mouth.

"Men! Christian peasants!" he would shout as he ran up and down the streets of Lebyazhka. "The railroad will soon crush us all! It will smash everyone, women and children, old men and women! It will devour the gray hairs of the old and the blue eyes of children and babes still wet from the womb! Men! People! Christians! Listen to me, to Kudeyar! Listen, everyone, don't turn away from the sacred truth. The peasantry is facing its end, and amen! We don't have much time left to plow and sow under this sky! We've already fed the cities, and the people there are possessed, making things they don't need—useless hats, useless jackets, and useless boots, each one the price of a workhorse. They're making evil machines of iron and writing blasphemous books, and they're flooding the whole world with this obscenity. For their pleasures and inventions they blacken the entire sky, suck the juices out of the earth, and destroy the one that feeds them, the peasant plowman! They drive him out of the fields, out from under the blue sky, into their smoke and fumes and their hideous, inhuman life! They will exterminate us as if we were a plague, they who are themselves the greatest plague, obscene and sinful, a horrible leprosy! And so it was foretold in Holy Scripture, for you will have no enemy or destroyer unless you raise one yourself. Peasant brothers! Do not go into the cities anymore. Do not set foot on their unclean earth. Do not breathe their stench and leprosy. Do not take them the slightest crust of bread. Let them understand, there amid those noxious fumes and smoke and unbelief, just who among the people lives in righteousness and who in sin and obscenity, for only a great famine and pestilence can return the people to reason, and truth, and belief in the one true God!"

Kudeyar had gone running around Lebyazhka, and according to rumor, even around Krushikha the last time. The people had already begun to suffer plenty, but he still went running around and shouting, "They've killed the Tsar! They've killed the Tsar, his children, and many others with him! They've killed the Tsar, and the peasantry will be killed the same way! It will! It will!"

Listening to Kudeyar's howling then, Ustinov had thought, "The hell with you—what a lot of fuss about nothing! Look how many people have been killed already in Russia, and who is more to blame than anyone? The Tsar is to blame—who else? So why should he escape killing? He was killed by the life he made—he could have made another and survived! It's enough to remember the shooting in 1905—why should the Tsar get out of it scot-free?" It made Ustinov angry. He wouldn't have shot the Tsar himself, it was none of his business, but he could well imagine that someone might consider it his business. If a person caused shootings and senseless wars, should he always come out of it unscathed? No, it should be just the opposite—whoever had the power to execute someone should also risk his own neck. If he executed someone for no reason, let him answer for it with his own head. Otherwise, there would be no control over the executioners. If that doesn't suit you, then don't become a tsar or a ruler, become a peasant.

Kudeyar was right in that: there was no more holy, no more human calling than that of the peasant, no, there wasn't. So go work, feel the grit of the earth between your teeth, sleep on the hay in your field hut, feel your arms and legs and back ache after every spell of heavy work. Does it hurt? Is it hard? But then your head isn't on the block, and you'll never do any harm to anyone, but will always help people. But could you really get anything through Kudeyar's thick skull when he went running around the streets like a lunatic? When you ran into him, he would stare into your eyes with his own wild eyes, push his beard into your face, and wave his arms, showing you the end of the world.

Two or three of the Lebyazhka men would start to drink whenever they listened to Kudeyar, despite the fact that it wasn't a holiday and that they were up to their necks in work in their fields and at home. Because of their men's reaction, the women took a strong dislike to Kudeyar, and as soon as he appeared in the street, they would chase their men into their houses and lock their doors.

"Now just why do you think everything is so bad?" Ustinov would ask Kudeyar. "What's bad about it?"

"Everything!" he would answer. "Everything there is!"

"Look at the sun shining up there! Is that bad?"

"It too will be extinguished . . . It will grow dim and shine no more."

"Why would it go out? It shines; it gives life! It gave me life! Here I am, alive, and my wife and kids at home are alive, too. So why are you urging me to shout that it's all bad?! That's what's bad! It's not fair to run life down and insult it!"

"Will it last such a long time? Will everyone at your house live for such a long time?"

"Don't go asking for trouble, Kudeyar!"

"I'm not asking for trouble—I'm calling for the truth! I'm opening people's eyes. We are all doomed, all of us peasants!"

Ustinov's meetings with Kudeyar didn't drive him to drink, but he did say that it was Kudeyar himself, with his crazy warnings about the end of the world and the peasantry, who would bring that end down on their heads by depriving people of health and strength. He was contagious and could easily infect others with his disease. Not Ustinov, but he couldn't vouch for everyone else. And what's more, Ustinov repeated again and again, idleness was the cause of Kudeyar's disease, and his idleness was caused by his not having any kids. Childless people simply turn into oddballs—one amuses himself with birds, another races pigeons, someone else raises cats. Those aren't real peasants but eccentrics! Whoever has kids, especially if he has a houseful of them, will never indulge in such hobbies or worry about all these different ends of the world. He has to concern himself with the life of his children, not his own death. Ustinov said this to Kudeyar's face, but behind his back and only to himself he said things a little differently, because Kudeyar's fear, incoherent, almost sheeplike, was also a part of life. It was in life, it was in the air, it existed, and Kudeyar sensed its existence. Not even the sheep could sense it the way he could.

It really was true that people walked the earth, lived off it, and were fed by it, but didn't know how to take care of it and didn't even want to. They could only insult it! When they get some soil on them, they say, "Look how filthy I am!" Ustinov was a man of clean habits. He loved to steam himself in the bathhouse and to rinse himself under the water tank, but to speak of the soil as if it were filth—how could people do that? A person is born from his mother's body in blood and in the afterbirth's residue that is thrown on the rubbish heap—but would anyone call his mother filthy? All people are born of the earth—children and fathers and mothers and ancestors and descendants—but do they recognize her as their mother? Do they love her? Or do they only pretend to love her, when all they really want is to take and take from her, even though love itself means knowing how to give? A person who truly loves cannot help but give. The earth is always ready to perish for the sake of people, to be eaten away for them, to turn into ashes, but just try to find the sort of person who will say, "I am ready to perish for the sake of the earth! For the sake of her forests and steppes, for the sake of her fields and the sky above her!" At such a moment you can't help remembering Kudeyar.

Do people perhaps really need soothsayers like him? To remind them of their unpaid debt to the earth, to life, and to God? To make them beware the end of the world and to keep them constantly aware that it could really happen? Such soothsayers are called holy fools. They are despised, yet no one becomes a holy fool by force or by order. People become holy fools, incur scorn and shame and torment, of their own free will, by the command of God alone, because they understood when they were born that this cross had been given to them and they had to carry it! And a person lays this heavy cross, many times greater than the strength of any one man, on his own feeble shoulders and carries it to the end of his life. It was not completely without reason that nature had created Kudeyar. She had created him, and everyone had to decide for himself whether this Kudeyar was a plague or a panacea.

▲▲▲

Smirnovsky rode off, and Ustinov and Kudeyar remained. They sat down on a huge tree stump. All around them it was still as light as day. The flames of the fire had died down, but the coals, some small, some quite large, glowed brightly from within.

Kudeyar whispered calmly, "Fire! Fire! Flames! Flames!" Then he asked, "Nikola? Could all life begin all over again?"

Ustinov had thought about this more than once, but he had never shared his thoughts. Now he replied, "Why do you ask?"

Repeating Ustinov's thoughts as if he had heard them from Ustinov himself, Kudeyar asked, "Couldn't the first plowman lay down the first furrow all over again? To give life a new beginning and to rewrite the Holy Book? And to let man set out on a new, truly human path? A fresh path! One soiled by no one and unbroken by any ruts?"

"No!" said Ustinov, surprising himself, because earlier he himself had dreamed about this, and now he had to deny that dream out loud. "No! It can't happen! There is only one earth, and one human race. It wants everything for itself, demands everything, but no matter how much a person has wanted and demanded a second life for himself, no one has managed to get it. And no one will! If millions have not managed it yet, no one will ever manage it!"

"And if there's a fiery revolution? And people kill each other? Is this perhaps that fire in which everything will burn, and from the ashes of which everything will begin all over again? What did you soldiers proclaim in the front-line trenches when the revolt and the uprising were going on?"

"All sorts of things . . . Mostly about how to end the war and how to take the land for the peasants, the factories for the workers, and power for all the people."

"And is that all?"

"That's about everything. I don't remember anything else."

"Then it's clear!" Kudeyar sighed deeply. "There's not much time left till the end. The only end that can still be far off is one with some kind of beginning before it!"

"Our lives must also have an end, Kudeyar!"

"What do I care about my life? The hell with it! A real man can't just live in the present!"

"But you believe in God, Kudeyar! How do you believe in Him?"

"I don't believe in the same God as everyone else . . . Not a one of them knows Him, the real God! They only think they know."

"And do you know? Have you figured it all out, Kudeyar?"

"I have learned one thing—no one can understand the real God! He did not give man that capacity."

"Are there two Gods? The real God, and the other—who?"

"The other one is temporary. He lasts only for a day. You live with Him for a day, and that's it! Is that one life really the point of it all? Can the real truth be found in that? That temporary God doesn't even know Himself what will happen tomorrow; He cannot decree how the children will live after their fathers. And without a decree from God, how can God Himself be? How does He exist, and where is He? If there is no decree from God, then that is the end of everything!"

"Well, I'm partial to the present God, to our God, Kudeyar! He is for the earth, and I am for the earth, so everything is just fine, and we will go on living as long as we are meant to! And we will die together, He and humankind! He established the order of life for everything on the earth, for every living creature, and from the kindness of His own soul he gave humans reason and said, 'You be the boss, establish your own order!' And when you and I can't make proper use of this kindness, it's not right to blame Him and to push Him aside! That's neither holy nor human. So, as long as we are alive, we should get on with life together. But that other God is too distant. Ignashka Ignatov says that He can't even see our candles burning!"

"That's the difference between us right there!" Kudeyar said, pointing. "There it is! Now I understand how much you dislike me, Ustinov! You hate me!"

"Am I supposed to like you in return for this kind of good will, Kudeyar?"

"In return for the truth! For the real truth! You are a monster, Ustinov. You should know better than any other why you should love me, but you don't love me, you don't listen to your own conscience! You hide from me! And from yourself! But listen, do what I beg you to do—go and shout the truth to the people! Go! Destroy this difference between us! Gather the assembly in Lebyazhka and cry out:

" 'I confess my lies; I have concealed them from myself and from you, the people; I lived in them day and night! And if I renounce the lies and draw near to the truth, it is the truth that the end of the world and the peasantry cometh, it is drawing nigh! Humankind is destroying its benefactor so that it might perish in turn! Understand this, one and all! Let us all go farther than our ancestor, the Elder Lavrenty, went. Let us go away from this hellish railroad, away from the corrupt and greedy cities. Let us desert our village of Lebyazhka and curse the name of Samsony Krivoi for betraying the sainted Lavrenty and leading our ancestors back to this sinful place, open to corruption and fratricide! Lavrenty knew the real truth: you should not return to a cursed place. Even from a distance he sensed that the Poluvyatsky whore-maidens were already dirtying this place with their feet and that they would also trample the Orthodox faith and any path to the one true God!'

"Shout it, Ustinov!" Kudeyar begged him. "If I shout it, they laugh at me. If you shout it, the words will touch their souls. If they don't listen here, then take a few provisions and go to other villages and call on other people to go off to unknown lands, away from the lies and the slaughter of fratricide that have been prepared for all of us, if not today, then tomorrow! Warn the people that it is better to be killed and burned than to kill and burn! Warn them, I beg you! Warn them to have some human pride, not to ridicule the peasant with savage scorn, not to use him and then discard him like a worn-out shoe, spit on him, and wear him to shreds until there is nothing left!"

"That's nonsense, Kudeyar! Nothing more than grief and fear, helplessness and horror. No sense can come from horror. Nor truth! Nor life! Only death!"

"If death comes from truth, then so be it! Even if that is the only thing that comes from it!"

"The shouting would be for nothing. Senseless! Like the cawing of a crow!"

"They'll understand you, Nikola! Everyone knows it already in his own soul, vaguely, like in a dream, but no one will shout it out loud! So you shout it! Awaken the shouting in everybody's soul!"

"It's none of my business! I'm a worker, not a shouter!"

"Do it just because you're not supposed to! People will understand—the man is not supposed to, yet still he cries out! And they will believe him! And they will understand that we all live in a world of falsehood! In a fake world, a world contrived out of thin air! Everything in it is artificial—all the deeds and words and false truth and false books! Murders! Avarice and destruction! Everything has been contrived as if for the good, but what for, really? For your own ruin and damnation, that's what!"

"And in return will you do the plowing for two men, or even three? And look after my cow, Svyatka? And feed my family? Do you want to swap lives, Kudeyar?"

"I can't do what you do, Ustinov! You know I can't." Kudeyar watched the fire for a bit and adjusted his cap. Its earflap kept slipping down onto his forehead. Then he said, "I wish I'd never been born, Ustinov! That would have been happiness!"

"The real Kudeyars buried treasures for future people. But you not only won't leave any treasure, you don't even want to have been born!"

"I have a treasure, Ustinov. I have the truth! But I'm not burying it. I want to unearth this treasure for everybody, but nobody sees it or wants it or needs it. It would be better for me to burn, Ustinov! I could burn right now, couldn't I?"

"If you burn yourself, what will that prove?"

"It won't prove anything. Can you really prove anything to monkeys with words? In the cities they're now saying that humans are descended from monkeys. They proclaim it loudly, and whoever doesn't want to be the relative of a monkey is called stupid and ignorant! If that's the way it is, then why shouldn't people kill each other? What can you expect from a monkey? What kind of reason or feelings does it have?" Kudeyar got up from the tree stump and walked over to the fire. "If I burn myself the same way our ancestors did, won't I at least prove something to you, Ustinov?"

"No, Kudeyar, you won't prove anything!"

In answer, Kudeyar looked up at Ustinov and began to whisper, not exactly a prayer, but something like it:

"Lord!" whispered Kudeyar, "I considered Nikolai Levontyevich Ustinov a wise man, devoted to the truth! But herein lies deception, Lord! He does not want to know the least bit of truth either! And when he knows it, he hides from it. He is afraid of a word of it for himself or anyone else. A lie is truer than the truth for him, that is what he preaches! He wants lies not only in life but also in death, and even on his deathbed he will be a stranger to the touch of Your truth!

"Where are You, the real God? Why do You allow evil and obscenity in death, let alone in human life? Why, Lord? And why do You punish those who have seen into Your truth? You give them a voice, but this voice cries in the wilderness. Why do You give them hands when there is no one to reach out to, and no time to do it, and nothing for them to take hold of but evil and lies? Am I to use my hands to reach only for my own eyes, to tear them out and see the world no more; only for my own ears, to press against them with terrible pain and deafen them with desperation; and only for my own breath, to stifle it? Why have You given the lonely righteous feet to walk for truth and human friendship, from childhood to old age, from one end of the earth to the other, but never to get anything except bloody calluses? Lord! When You inspired the truth in my soul, why did You give it eyes, hands, feet, and ears—why? I beg You, Lord, not for myself, but for those yet to be born with the truth in their souls. Don't give them eyes, ears, hands, or feet—let them be blind and deaf and immobile! You would be blessing them and freeing Your faithful servants, servants of the one true God, from great sorrow and suffering!"

When he had finished, Kudeyar stared at Ustinov. "Well? Do you understand me now? Why I wish I hadn't been born?" He paused a moment. "Listen, Ustinov, why don't we burn our hands and feet in the fire? Let's do it this way: you push me into the fire, and I'll pull you in after me! We'll push each other! All right? It's so simple, Ustinov: humans were separated from the animals by their ability to make fire, and they must return to the circle of the earth through fire! Let them end the way they began! This circle is the truth! When life lost its meaning for our ancestors, they did not drown themselves but burned themselves. Doesn't that fact make it the truth? Well?! Shall we do it, Nikola?"

For an instant the coals in the fire flashed hot and piercing, right in Ustinov's face. But the fire needed more ashes. Human ashes.

"We will never be the way we were when God created us!" Kudeyar whispered again. "So then why should we exist? If the time for which we were created will never come? Why should we live blindly in a stranger's dwelling? In the diabolical iron dwelling of the hunters?"

"I don't want to take my own life, Kudeyar!" Ustinov retreated a step. "It wasn't given to me for me to destroy it myself! And why do you despise the monkeys and sin against them? They have no part in human misfortunes. If they could speak our language, they'd have lots to say! I trust each and every living creature, and I keep no secrets from them, even in my prayers! And they don't hide anything from me! If you want kindness from life, then look on it with kindness, in a person or any other living creature! Your way of looking at it has murder hidden in it—it's the same thing you are rebelling against! And if truth needs neither hands, nor feet, nor eyes, then who needs truth itself? Who needs idle truth, only words, prayers, and shouting? No, I don't want to rebel against hands, feet, and eyes, and blame them!"

"Let it be so!" Kudeyar repeated stubbornly with closed eyes. "Let them be blind, deaf, and motionless for all time to come!" Then he opened his eyes and shouted, "Away! Far away from here, from this foul liar, Judas Ustinov! Away! He won't shout the truth! He won't burn himself! It's because of him this fire is burning! He set this fire and does not repent! Fire!

Fire! Flames! Flames! Good-bye, Ustinov! Good-bye, my eternal enemy! I am running away from you!"

At last you could smell the fire, the smoke and the odor of burning. That's when you can smell it, when it has finished. Something was bubbling and boiling where the little shed, the one that Grishka Sukhikh had torched himself, had stood not long before, maybe tar or axle grease, and a sheet of window glass that had been baked in the flames reflected a violet-blue light. "Sukhikh must have been preparing to build something with such a supply of glass!" Ustinov thought. He turned and walked back to sit on the stump where he had just been sitting with Kudeyar.

How far had Kudeyar carried him away? Whom had he been urging him to serve, what god, what flames? Ustinov could not imagine himself serving anyone unconditionally, neither a god, nor a commander, nor fire. He had served as a soldier, and no one had asked him if wanted to serve or not. And since that's the way it was, he had served with cunning, never volunteering for anything and always staying in the middle of the pack. That way you're most likely to survive and to finish your hitch sooner, too. Only once had Ustinov been unable to restrain himself, that time when he had dismantled and assembled the Maxim gun in front of some officers, as if he were bucking for a promotion. Later he had cursed himself repeatedly—why would a real peasant need to show off like that to prove he was a soldier? It was stupid! Childish! Of course, it wouldn't do to pretend to be a fool or to play sick either—your conscience and your comrades wouldn't allow it. You have to make it through your hitch the same as everyone else, and maybe even die, and that's a business you can't dump off on someone else. But medals and Orders of St. George had never caught Ustinov's eye either. Medals were for peasants like Smirnovsky who put military service on an equal footing with farming, whereas Ustinov wouldn't compare any other business, let alone the service, with farming, and certainly not the fire to which Kudeyar was calling him.

Watching the dying fire, almost extinguished except for an occasional flaring ember, he felt that it had not been the first time that he had talked with Kudeyar the way he had that day. He was surprised to imagine remembering something that had never happened, but then he understood why he did. It came to him.

He was a small boy when he heard the legend from the adults. Handed down by word of mouth, the legend was also said to have been written down by one of the Old Believers who could read and write. This manuscript, bound as if it were Holy Scripture, was either in the keeping of Ivan Ivanovich Samorukov or in some secret place known only to him and to two or three of the other old men. The curious had asked Ivan Ivanovich more than once to show them this handwritten book, along with the rest of his secret cache of ancient icons and other things. "After I die you'll find out what's there and what isn't!" he had answered. The years passed, but no one ever saw this book, and fewer and fewer people were curious about it. The Lebyazhka folk had too many other things to do—with the cooperatives, the school, trade, the forest, the dairy industry, all sorts of things—and no one had any time to think about the olden days. But now Ustinov remembered the legend.

▲▲▲

When the Elder Lavrenty led his flock beyond the Baikal Sea, he brought them to a deserted place: rocks everywhere around, a transparent stream, a sky as blue as blue can be, the air pure and cold. It was a prayerful place, a godly place, a place like Palestine itself. The Elder Lavrenty also pointed out that the place was close to the border of the country; so, if the German Empress or somebody else in the Germanized city of St. Petersburg stretched out her hand to oppress the people of the Old Faith here, it would be easy for them to cross that border. A ruler would be less liable to oppress her subjects, good ones or bad ones, if she understood that they might be easily and eternally lost. Lavrenty added that since various tribes there professed non-Orthodox beliefs, the schismatics could easily blend in with them, and no one would persecute them.

"It will be good for our faith here!" he said. "We couldn't find a better place for it!"

"But what have you brought us to, Holy Father—to God, or to the work of God's hands?" the Elder Samsony Krivoi asked the saintly Lavrenty.

"It will be good for our faith here!" Lavrenty repeated.

"But what about the people of our faith? Will it be good for them, too? On this cold and stony earth?"

"This land is all God's, and His alone!" the saintly Lavrenty replied. "This is why it is possible to comprehend God's truth in the cold, while in the warmth of paradise and worldly comfort people pass it by!"

"Your words are true, My Holy Father and Brother!" Samsony agreed. "They are true, for we see God all around us in everything. In the desert, in dark caves, and in the heavenly gardens of Jerusalem, He is everywhere. But it is not here, among dead stones, that He labored in the sweat of his brow, for this land is not adorned with tall forests, thick grasses, or fertile soil. And if this place is so fitting for prayer and the hermit's life, for the comprehension of the spirit of God, that it might be called a holy dwelling place, then other places have been created for the sacrament of God's work, that is, for life and the continuation of the human race. We have already passed by those places, those abundant lands where we lived for a summer, cast seed into the soil, and partook of our daily bread from the earth, but we scorned that plenty for the sake of this desert!"

"For the sake of our faith, do not be seduced by the worldly life! Partake of the good, not in fields of grain, but in your soul!" Lavrenty insisted.

But, unwilling to give in, Samsony Krivoi replied, "We have scorned the bounty and the work of God given to humankind! Let us return, then, to what we have lost, to what God has set aside for us. If we will not partake of the fruits of His labors, then who will? Will the wild beasts partake of them, since humankind has refused them with contemptuous haste? If so, then who will add his own mind, his hands, and his diligence to the mind of God? And his own transitory life to His eternal life?"

"Abuse pours from your lips, My Brother Samsony! Come to your senses! What is the purpose of this appeal with which you trouble the souls of our flock? Is not prayer eternal, and is not the flesh only a temporary vessel in which the contained spirit can attain God's truth? If one vessel perishes, another will be found in another piece of flesh . . . "

"You are speaking of the lot of a hermit, My Brother Lavrenty, and that lot is eternally holy! Whoever takes it upon himself has assumed the debts of many hundreds and thousands of people, and these people are then given their own destinies that they are obliged before God to fulfill with the same heartfelt joy and diligence as the hermit does. But if any word for God is valued more highly than deeds for God, on what will the words then stand? On whose labors and efforts? My Brother Lavrenty, let us divide our flock: those who are more concerned with prayer can remain in this holy desert, and those who are inclined to apply their hands and feet and flesh to the earth and the fields of grain can return with me to that green hill where we once plowed and sowed!"

"That is a betrayal of God and the faith!" judged Lavrenty. "A betrayal! Prayer is the preservation of God's world, but human hands will lead it to destruction and ashes! Prayer is abstention from ruin; it resides in eternity, and eternity—in it! The flesh, though it be slight, is a destroyer! Just as it is not eternal in and of itself and is ready to decay at any moment, so it brings decay and ashes to the whole world whenever it touches it! And it hungers for the same decay and destruction in whatever forests and fields and lands there may be! And it creates putrid cities, and temples, and palaces, and fortresses, not out of God's understanding, but out of its own contriving and depraved arrogance; and it compels people to make their homes in this unholy garbage heap, separated from God and the world, to live and give birth and be born in it as garbage themselves! And there is nothing eternal in its presence, for what is eternal is none other than what is untouched by human hands, whether in the depths of the earth, in the heights of the heavens, in the eternal darkness, or in incessant prayer! Any human touch is a moment of filth and corruption! And damnation! Only faith is immortal and eternal—nothing else—and these cold, dead, desert stones are symbols of faith. Perhaps there is less faith in living people who have not attained immortality but work against it than in these heartless stones! Lead your flock to that damnation, Samsony, no longer my brother! Lead them with the mark of damnation on your brow! Go!"

When they arrived in the prayerfully silent land beyond the Baikal Sea, the people of the flock were exhausted, their souls worn out by the long journey. They were oblivious to the Elder Samsony's proposal and to Lavrenty's damnation of him. Praying on the bank of a river as transparent as tears under the cold sky, the people all called out to God for help, hungry for a commandment from Him, believing in Him. But the time had come for them to divide themselves forever into two flocks, and, sobbing and trembling as if in the throes of death, they parted from one another.

"I take your curse upon myself with great sorrow, My Brother, Holy Lavrenty," said Samsony Krivoi as he left, "but I cannot accept the cold and the hunger of our women and children, and I cannot remove from my memory those fields of ours in which we sowed our seed along the way and from which we raised our crops. But one thing I can do: I can take on my own soul the sins and suffering of all those who follow me, and excommunicate my soul from glory forever! May the burdens of my flock be lessened, may my burden be made less, for I lead them, not with deception, but with my own suffering." And in parting, the Elder Samsony Krivoi asked the Elder Lavrenty what words he should now offer up to God.

Lavrenty answered, "Those words should be—damnation for humankind and a prayer for His forgiveness."

With that the two Elders parted company forever.

▲▲▲

And when Ustinov and Kudeyar parted, it was the same. Kudeyar to this day had remained with Lavrenty, while there was no question about Ustinov—he would always have followed Samsony Krivoi!

Well, once you chose to follow Samsony Krivoi, you had to go on living, to try as hard as you could, and even harder. And then suddenly Ustinov remembered about Sevka Kupriyanov's gelding. "You stupid peasant, Ustinov, you'll let the horse slip away! Some buyer will show up, and that will be it. You'll miss your chance! And then you'll kick yourself for it!" But just as Ustinov was about to march on home to Lebyazhka, Deryabin and Ignashka drove up in a small covered wagon. Deryabin tossed the reins to Ignashka and came up to Ustinov. It was winter already, but Deryabin was still wearing his light military overcoat and had not even buttoned it up all the way. Although he wasn't a big man, he seemed to be hot-blooded.

"What's going on here?" he asked.

"Everything has burned up," Ustinov answered, glancing again at the smoldering heap of ashes as if for the first time.

"If someone sets fire to something, it burns! What else could happen?!"

"Who? Who set the fire?" asked Ustinov. "Do you know?"

"Does it make any difference who it was?" asked Deryabin with a surprised shrug. "If someone makes too much trouble for people, does it make any difference who sets fire to him? Whoever was the first to do it should be thanked! It seems, Ustinov, that you've forgotten about Grishka Sukhikh's little drawing of the seven desyatinas of forest that he marked off for himself and defended from our Commission with a gun in his hands!"

"But didn't he just threaten to do that, just threaten to use his gun, and nothing more?"

"And do you have to have him kill somebody? Would you stop making a fuss about this fire if he did?"

"I don't have to have that, Deryabin."

"Your question sounds as if you do!"

Ustinov became even more confused.

"If that's the way you feel, I'll tell you that it did happen," Deryabin said after a pause. "Grishka Sukhikh did shoot at someone. You just don't know about it!"

"Who?"

"At Leonty Yevseyev, the former commander of our forest guard."

"I didn't hear about that," sighed Ustinov. And then a new and alarming thought occurred to him. "You mean that it was our own guard that burned Grishka out?"

"Not necessarily! There have been a lot of theories so far! His hired hands could have done it, or some former buddies that he's fallen out with—there are more than a few people he's insulted, after all! I've always been amazed myself how stubbornly and patiently Grishka's hired hands have put up with his exploitation! Two strong men, but with him they're like puppies! Kittens! I've talked to them and explained their situation to them, but without any results. So they could hardly have done it!"

"So no one knows?"

"I'm trying to explain it to you, Ustinov: no one needs to know! Whoever did it has my thanks! If they don't want to say anything or come forward, then we should respect them and hide them instead of looking for them. Why talk about it? So Grishka Sukhikh can kill them? Why should we give them away if they did the right thing? Just keep in mind, Ustinov, times are such that a lot of things are going on, and just who is doing it all? No one knows! If Grishka has been burned out, that means that the civil war has already begun in Lebyazhka, and does anyone ask who does what when there's a war on? They don't! In war the only thing that matters is getting things done, and who did them and how is of no importance! Since you fought longer than I did, you know that in war you need to know as little as possible and to do as much as you can as fast as you can!"

Ustinov, tired of disagreeing, seemed to agree with Deryabin.

"So did Grishka manage to carry away his belongings?" Deryabin asked.

"He drove away in a loaded wagon and had a bundle stuffed in the front of his coat," Ustinov recalled.

"Just so he doesn't come back to us in Lebyazhka with his spite and revenge! And if he does come back, whose fault will it be?"

"I don't know."

"Yours, Ustinov! It will be your fault!"

"Mine?!"

"Yes, yours!"

"I don't understand."

"You don't understand, and that's the whole point! Someone goes and burns out Grishka, and you start asking questions, 'who, what, why?' But he shouldn't have been burned out—he really should have been killed! Because if we don't deal with him, he'll deal with others. It should have been done, but because of you, it couldn't be—you'd want to find out who did it! You would condemn others! You're the most educated and capable man in Lebyazhka. You only talk like a peasant, but you have ten times more than just about every other peasant in Lebyazhka! Just about every one! So people would listen to you and condemn whoever you do. And the person who wanted to improve things for everyone would become the village outcast. There just wouldn't be any life left for him in Lebyazhka. Now just stop and think about it yourself. Grishka Sukhikh has not been killed. He's alive! And if he comes back and revenges himself on Lebyazhka, who will be to blame? You will, Ustinov! Thanks to you, he is alive and will come back. And when he does, who will be the first he'll lay his hands on? Well, maybe it will be me. But you will surely be the second! And then maybe he'll figure you should have been the first, after all. But you don't understand this, Ustinov. You don't want to understand. That's it . . . So, shall we go home, Ustinov? What else is there to do here? The fire has already burned everything up. Let's go."

Polovinkin Has Left

Ustinov slept till noon the day after the fire. Domna didn't wake him, and he heard her in his sleep as she covered him with a blanket and told someone, "Let him sleep for a while!" He woke with the firm and final intention of going that day to see Sevka Kupriyanov and have a talk with him about his gelding. There was nothing else to do. If he waited for someone else to say something to Sevka on his behalf, it would be too late. By then he might have sold the gelding. But before he could go to Sevka, he had to give his livestock some hay. That was his son-in-law Shurka's job, but you could do a thing ten times over while you were waiting for Shurka.

Ustinov set up a ladder to climb up onto the flat floor of the hayloft and used another, lighter ladder to get up onto the top of the fragrant, almost untouched haymow. Built above the cattle barn, his hayloft was arranged in two tiers. That way the hay kept better, and the meadow hay for Svyatka could be stored separately from the dry field hay for the sheep and horses, though the horses could be given either kind. He had to toss down four pitchforks of hay this time—one for Svyatka, one for the sheep, and two for the horses.

Ustinov had always liked being up in the hayloft. He was at home—there were his garden, and his house, and the hay that he had mowed in the hot month of July—but at the same time it was as if he weren't at home at all. He was up so high that he could see many farmyards all around, as if he were holding them in the palm of his hand. He could see the lake—on the near shore there was a mix of blue and white patches, half snowy smoothness and half ice, and on the far shore, on the Krushikha side, both blended with a yellowish haze, most likely from the sunlight mixing with the snow and ice. In the summer when the weather was nice, you could see the village of Krushikha from there, but in the summer there was nothing to do in the hayloft, so you hardly ever saw Krushikha then either.

Lake Lebyazhka could be so amazing in the summertime! You could not only see its blue-grayness but hear it, too. It rustled and whispered as if a huge pine tree had been transplanted from the White Wood into its watery depths, into the deepest, most bottomless spot. The lake whispered to itself, for itself, and then on market days it was filled with real human voices. The Lebyazhka folk rowed over to Krushikha rather than riding clear around the lake. It was shorter and more convenient that way. The Krushikha town square, the site of a great deal of commerce for several volosts, sloped right down to the shoreline. So, as you sat there, you could invite a customer to come down to you to buy vegetables, fish, hemp, honey, forest products, milk products, and any other goods you had brought with you on your vessel.

While these little boats were going to Krushikha, and especially while they were coming back after a profitable market day, the Lebyazhka women, making the water foam with the swift strength of their oars, would break into song. Their work at the oars did not hinder them at all; on the contrary, it added power to their voices and increased their strength and enthusiasm. There was a twofold competition—to see who could row home to the Lebyazhka side the fastest and to see who could sing the loudest, to see from which boat the first song would be heard in Lebyazhka.

The boats that were used to go to market were large, with three or four oars. You could fit a horse and cart in one, along with goods from ten or more households. A strong-voiced woman sat at each of the oars, and the relief oarswomen in the bow and stern sang, too, ready to take over for any tired rower. Sometimes there would be an accordion player sitting in the slightly elevated bow. The women who had been to market would treat him to a pint of vodka, and then—my Lord!—what music there would be on that ark! Not only the ark but the lake itself would ring out with a medley of sounds, high parts, low parts, and harmonies. The Lebyazhkans who had stayed at home would come out to the lakeshore and serve as honest judges of whose song was the first to reach them. Those who had sung the loudest would be triumphantly tossed into the air upon their return, and if the owner of the boat felt generous and was deeply moved, he would not accept payment for the use of his boat but would simply pat the helmsman on the back, and the excited, hoarse women on a softer and pleasanter spot.

Ustinov also loved to run out to the shore, to listen hard, and if he was able, to shout, "I hear the one about the Cossack, about the Cossack!" or "It's 'From behind the island into the channel,' I can hear it!" The others would scold, "Don't make so much noise, let others hear!" and he would wait excitedly for someone else to confirm his guess. He loved all the fussing and shouting and noise and laughter and the barking of almost every dog in Lebyazhka that, it goes without saying, were all unavoidable in such a business. He loved the neighing of the horses the men had ridden as they came to meet their women with their empty bags and baskets and to collect the unsold goods. He loved to watch as the rowers, who had gathered speed for the homestretch, suddenly raised their wet oars and as the boats, no longer in a hurry, came up on the shore, one after the other, right at your feet, with the waves splashing and the hulls scraping on the sand. But, of course, more than anything else he loved to be the first to hear the distant singing, especially since he often managed to make out one or two words or even a couple of phrases before anyone else. There was a secret to his success—he could clearly hear Zinaida Pankratov's voice at a good distance. He found it strange that those standing next to him didn't recognize her voice right away, a voice that was so strong and unlike any other, a voice that led the others and, sometimes intentionally fading, traveled across the surface of Lake Lebyazhka. But he was always embarrassed when Zinaida, having just gotten out of the boat and having barely caught her breath, would suddenly ask, "Which one of you stay-at-homes was the first to hear us?" And they would answer, "It was Nikolai Ustinov—the others hadn't gotten it yet, but he yelled out that it was the song about Stenka Razin!" Holding her excited breath, Zinaida would tuck the loose hairs under her kerchief and laugh in his face. "Stretch your ears out farther, Levontyevich! And look sharp with your peepers. Maybe you'll hear or see something else, eh?"

Well, that's what happened in the summer. But that was a long time ago, before the war. But if you listened hard, you could hear the noise of the lake even now, coming from somewhere on the ice or from under the ice . . .

In the other direction, a bit more to the left, was the edge of the White Wood, at first growing right up against the Lebyazhka kitchen gardens, marked out in the snow by the slender strips of wattle fence, but then, as it turned ever bluer, veering off to the side and looking like nothing more than a dark ribbon. Between the lake and the edge of the forest, Kudeyar's little house, without a garden and with only a single tiny shed of a barn, used to be visible; but now the view of the house and barn was blocked almost completely by the new school with its honey-colored logs, the four bright little windows that Ustinov had glazed, the wood-shingled awnings over the two entryways, and the two chimney pipes, both streaming brownish smoke.

The chimney in the middle of the roof was smoking heavily; the other, at the edge, only lightly. That was as it should be. The big pipe came from the stove that heated the two adjacent school rooms. At that very moment the children were sitting at their homemade desks, and the bespectacled schoolteacher was going from room to room, teaching some children their letters, while others a little older and more advanced were copying arithmetic problems from the blackboard and solving them. The school custodian lived under the smaller chimney pipe in a tiny little room. She rang the bell to announce the end of each lesson, mopped the floors, and stoked the stove, and if one of the Lebyazhka men missed his turn to fetch water for the school, she herself went with yoke and bucket to the hole cut in the ice of the lake. What else could she do? It had to be done! Another duty of the custodian was to shoo all the children home from school after lessons were done, for the children liked the school so much that otherwise they wouldn't go home until they were fainting from hunger. This custodian earned her daily bread with difficulty, and she managed to live in her little room, not just by herself, but with two little children. However, being a soldier's widow, she was satisfied with things as they were. Of course, only a soldier's widow could be satisfied with such a life. But the community, supporting the woman through charity, insignificant as it was, was also satisfied with this arrangement, especially as her children were good kids, not spoiled at all, and the older of the two, such a bright girl, was already helping her mother with some of her duties as well as going to school without leaving her own home. This difficult arrangement, even though it was a living for the mother and her children, had always touched Ustinov's heart. After throwing down three pitchforks of hay, he paused to take one more look at the school and then at his neighbors' yards to see who was doing chores among his livestock or chopping wood or harnessing his horses to go for hay or somewhere else.

It wasn't until he was hefting the fourth and final forkful of hay that his glance fell upon the yards of his closest neighbors, and then he froze in confusion. There was Sevka Kupriyanov's gelding, pacing in Kruglov's yard, two houses away! The gelding was generally unremarkable. Its coat was the same color as Morkoshka's, only dull, and it was not a large animal. But as soon as Ustinov began to observe it over Sevka's fence, he immediately noticed one particular quality—its very forceful gait. When it walked to the left, it moved its head downward to the left, as if thus adding power to its stride; when it walked to the right, its head made the same movement to the right. Many horses move that way, but Sevka Kupriyanov's gelding strode with particular conscientiousness, serious and preoccupied, not forgetting for a moment that what it was doing was the most important thing on earth. In this respect it looked a lot like Solovko, only more independent. Solovko slept as he walked, though you wouldn't notice his drowsiness in the least. Sevka's gelding was walking with this gait between the Kruglovs' two barns, from one end of their yard to the other. Its new master must have given it freedom: "Let it walk around a bit, get used to things, take a look at where everything is in the yard!" Without pitching that fourth forkful of hay, Ustinov rushed back down to the ground.

In the Kruglovs' yard he came face to face with the gelding. For a moment they both stood stock-still. They looked at each other and found that they could not tell their own souls apart. Brightly but shyly, the not quite light-bay, not quite dark-chestnut gelding seemed to say, "There he is—it's me! He is me, and in all the time I have lived on this earth, I have never found a man who could understand me completely, could understand all my charming qualities, my angelic soul! There has never been one, and I had stopped believing that there ever would be! But then you turn up, Nikolai Levontyevich Ustinov! Don't mind my size. Even though I'm not so big, I can do a lot! Yes, I can!" And the gelding turned and began walking again with its tireless, diligent, sensitive gait—it knew the best way to show itself to Nikolai Ustinov. Feeling as if his heart would burst, Ustinov rushed into Prokopy Kruglov's house.

Rarely did someone drop by Prokopy's house like that, especially on a weekday, because work went on in that house day and night without a moment's pause. Not counting Grishka Sukhikh, the Kruglov brothers were the wealthiest farmers in Lebyazhka, and the wealthier of them was the older one, Prokopy. He had a proper peasant house, with an iron roof and a full-sized annex, outbuilding after outbuilding built right up against one another in the yard, and six working horses. Sevka Kupriyanov's gelding made the seventh. It was an enviable home, but life in it was not at all enviable. Its residents wore patched and threadbare clothing and were gloomy folk with never a moment to spare. Prokopy was too busy to chat with his neighbor across the fence, and his wife was too busy to join a gathering of the village womenfolk even once a year. The girls had no time to dance and sing. The lads had no time to go courting properly. From time to time in the autumn, Prokopy would harness a team of horses and seat a son, dressed in a red shirt and a new cap, in the back of the wagon, and they would go from village to village looking for a bride. In a week they would return with their business accomplished, having found a bride, performed a wedding, and collected the dowry. It would be a while before anyone remembered the young bride's name in that house. For the first year she would be called "Hey, you!" and "Hey, come here!" For this reason the Kruglovs were nicknamed the "hey-yous" in Lebyazhka. After all that, who would want to visit that house? But Ustinov went. He went at a run.

When he opened the door, he got an incredible surprise: there were already guests at the kitchen table, and instead of just sitting there they were having a bit to drink. The guests were Forest Commission Member Polovinkin and Sevka Kupriyanov with his son Matveyka. But Ustinov was even more amazed when he heard that Prokopy Kruglov was talking politics.

"There is no reason!" Prokopy was saying, squeezing his long, thin beard like a mop. "No reason! What good would it be fer us to have put out the fire at Grishka Sukhikh's?! It wouldn't have done no good fer us to put it out. In a week or so some real authority will show up and they'll take care of it. They'll hang all the arsonists from the first tree they come to! Enough of all this disorder—it's long since time for some new and powerful governmental authority to take matters in hand!"

But, really, Prokopy had never known anything beyond his own yard and fields, and no one had ever heard him use words like "authority" and "governmental" in his whole life. His only concern was to increase his homestead and to exhaust himself with work more desperately each year than he had the year before, and nothing else. And that still wasn't all: Prokopy was downright happy to see his new and uninvited guest.

"A-ah!" he shouted. "Who's up and come to see us?! Sit down, Levontyevich! Let's have a drink to your health—down the hatch!"

"Well, why not?" Ustinov thought as he threw off his hat and coat. "Everyone will be a little drunk, and I'll be able to make a deal for Sevka Kupriyanov's gelding! Lucky for me, everyone I need for that is right here!" Having taken a look at the snacks laid out on the table—pickled mushrooms, cabbage, cranberries, and cold mutton—Ustinov heaved a deep sigh and shouted, "Here's to the very best of company!"

He glanced at the Kupriyanovs. Father Kupriyanov raised his glass above the table, though wearily and not very high, but Matveyka, gloomier than gloom itself, didn't move a muscle. He wasn't even drinking—he was still not allowed to celebrate on an equal footing with the adults. After all, a sixteen-year-old isn't a man yet, even if his shoulders are broad as an ox's.

"Here's to your new worker, Prokopy!" Ustinov, a little while later, raised his glass again. "What is it, your seventh? Or your eighth already? Anyway, to the new one!"

"Yes," Prokopy readily agreed. "We were just sealing the bargain with a drink with the Kupriyanovs here, father and son, goddammit! And with Vasilyevich Polovinkin. And now with you, too, Levontyevich Ustinov!"

"But why do you need more new workers in your yard, Prokopy? Even the old ones don't have anything to do since there's no one to sell grain to and money is worthless."

"That's just what I'm saying: when a strong government returns to power, it will give both grain and money a real place in life! No-o, I'm not doing it for nothing! I took Savely's horse here on the eve of the revival of that new government!"

"And what if it fools you and doesn't come? What if a strong government, one with money, isn't restored?"

"Then I'll fool it, the bastard! I'll use all my grain for moonshine! I'll start drinking and kicking up my heels enough to make any government sick! And, all of you here, don't be looking at me like I don't know how to do anything but bust my guts working! I'm already on such a spree that I'll drink my way through whatever kind of power or government there might be! If the authorities deceive without end, then I don't owe them anything either . . . Goddam them! I'll give it to them. I'll send them a-running!" Prokopy first threatened someone or other with a finger, then grabbing his long beard, all scraggly black, red, and gray, he threatened once again with his beard in his fist. "That's what! I'll remind them of everything. Even if they got no bread and are left with no company but drunkards! They'll miss me, the tough peasant worker, but it will be too late! I'll send them a-running . . ."

"You're really an odd one, Prokopy! Who will get the worst of it? You will!"

"All right! Let it be me! But if a real power doesn't appear, if it plays tricks, there'll be such moonshining throughout all Russia that no force will be able to stop it. So let it come now in time for my new acquisition, the bay gelding. Did you see what a gait the gelding has? What a stride it has? Did you notice? Goddam it!"

"I noticed . . . ," Ustinov replied with a heavy heart. "How could I not notice? He has a plower's gait. A peasant's horse, not some carthorse . . ."

"Exactly! I know you're a man with a sharp eye, Ustinov," Prokopy chuckled and suddenly gave him a wink.

At the same moment Sevka Kupriyanov's former gelding also seemed to be winking and asking, "Can you just imagine to yourself, Nikolai Levon-tyevich Ustinov, how I could pull a plow teamed up with your Solovko? Or even with Morkoshka?! I could cheer Solovko up and tame Morkoshka's character, and what a job we'd make of it! What a job!" Ustinov looked aside in an anguish close to despair.

The Kupriyanovs had sold Prokopy a worker and were having a drink over the deal, but why had Polovinkin showed up here? True, he was almost the only man in all Lebyazhka who had for a long time envied the Kruglov brothers and their endless labor. "Yessir!" Polovinkin would say from time to time. "Yessir! You know what the Kruglovs have? They really have some-thing, ye-es! That's really something, yessir!" But that "yessir!" could hardly be the reason that Polovinkin was with Kruglov now. There had to be another reason. He was a member of the Forest Commission, and Kru-glov needed him for something. That is what Ustinov guessed, and again he took heart.

"But we, the Forest Commission, will smash your stills, Prokopy! We smashed them once, and if we need to, we'll smash them again. We won't let you use grain for drink! We'll keep you from sinning! It's not just us—

any authority in Russia, even the weakest one, will always take the moonshine business into its own hands and have a monopoly. No one can evade such a monopoly, not for any price, because no business in Russia is more profitable or ever will be! And so you won't be able to sell your grain or use it for moonshine, and your new worker, Sevka Kupriyanov's former gelding, will go to waste! You'll feed it, but its work won't be worth a spit to you! It makes no sense at all! How much did you give Savely for the horse? How much did you get from Prokopy, Savely?"

So far, only Ustinov and Kruglov had participated in the conversation, but Ustinov now thought of bringing Sevka Kupriyanov into it. What if Sevka hadn't yet sold the horse and it still wasn't too late to get in on the bargaining?

But Sevka, who did not want to answer Ustinov politely, was quiet for a moment, then muttered into his glass, "Whatever I got, it's mine . . ."

Also entering the conversation, Polovinkin said quietly, "Savely, there's no reason to hold a grudge against Nikola. He wasn't the one who tied you up that time in the forest! It wasn't him at all! You remember—he didn't even dismount the whole time. It was Deryabin and Ignashka, and Petro Kalashnikov, the "Co-op Man," and, to tell the truth, me as well, without meaning to, who tied you up. Remember? Well?" And addressing his host separately, Polovinkin added, "What a business that was!"

Still staring into his glass, Kupriyanov replied just as gloomily as before, "It wasn't Ustinov who tied us up. No. But then later he laughed at us!"

Ustinov spread his arms in surprise. "I didn't laugh at all! Just the opposite, I—"

"You laughed, you laughed, Uncle Nikola!" Matveyka suddenly burst out. Plunging his fork into a pickled mushroom and raising it above his head, he shouted again, "You laughed! I thought before that you were a good man, but you done something low, Uncle Nikola! You have, by God!" There was such a tone of despair in Matveyka's voice that the adults, too, fell silent, and Ustinov found himself with nothing to say.

"If you weren't laughing at us, Ustinov, you would have done the same as everyone who tied us up did." Sevka Kupriyanov was now even gloomier than before.

"And what was that?"

"It's simple! Polovinkin here was the first to come to see us at home and to express his sympathy for everything that had happened. And Kalashnikov, too. And even Comrade Deryabin—he met us on the street and asked us not to think badly of him . . . It was only two of you, bosom buddies, you and Ignashka Ignatov, who never even said a word to us. Bosom buddies!"

That's how it had happened! Ustinov had been so embarrassed that he kept putting off going to see Sevka about the gelding. That was exactly why he hadn't gone to see him. But he should have! Silently Ustinov cussed himself out for being stupid and slow.

Prokopy Kruglov, not wanting any arguments in his home, said, "So, what did I give Savely for his horse, goddam him? It wasn't money or even a trade that we agreed to, but to scratch each other's backs. You don't understand? This is how it is: I'll set Matveyka up in the city with room and board and even with some kind of job. I'll set him up through my in-law, and Matveyka will go off on my skinny old bowlegged nag and leave me this fine-stepping gelding! You sure noticed, Ustinov, it's got one hell of a stride! You wouldn't have the strength to ruin a horse like that, by God!"

"So you got the horse for practically nothing more than a thank-you, Prokopy? And one with such a stride?"

"No, I don't want to take or give anything for a thank-you, Uncle Nikola!" Matveyka burst out again, even more venomously than before. "I want to take and give honestly! Pa and I ain't beggars to be making do with thank-you-kindlies!"

"But why do you need to get a city job so suddenly, Matveyka?" Ustinov wanted to know.

"So, Uncle Nikola, so I can come back to Lebyazhka as some sort of official, maybe even a soldier, and exterminate Ignashka Ignatov! And the whole Commission, too! Well, I'd have mercy on Uncle Polovinkin, he's a good man even if he did tie us up. But as for the others . . ."

Turning his back to the table, Matveyka looked out the window in stubborn silence, and Ustinov understood that it would be useless to try to convince Matveyka or explain anything to him. He had been able to convince eighty-eight woodcutters from the steppe when he had to, but he couldn't for the life of him convince one boy!

"Just look at what's become of my son." Kupriyanov Senior heaved a deep and drawn-out sigh. "He's stuck on this one point, and that's all there is to it! That's all he has to say to me, or his mother, or his Uncle Rodion Gavrilovich Smirnovsky, or anyone else in Lebyazhka! It's terrible! 'I want to go to the city, come back as an official, and destroy Ignashka Ignatov!' As for me now, I've just about forgotten and forgiven that time when the Commission tied us up in the forest. But Matveyka here fans the flames in his own heart every day. It's terrible for his parents!"

"I'll go see Sukhikh, Grigory Dormidontovich!" Matveyka, with his back turned on his own father and his stubborn face reddening, spoke again. "I'll work as his hired hand or anything else he wants! I'll find him, wherever he is, if only he'll take me. He shouldn't be too far away. I know the villages where he has drinking buddies. Grigory Dormidontovich invited me to his place a long time ago. I'm a healthy lad—I can hold a prize bull in place by the horns! Grigory Dormidontovich really likes that! The Commission was afraid to tie him up in the forest that time. He would have flattened them on the spot, so later the Commission secretly set him on fire! That's what happened!"

"But why would you go to him, really?" Ustinov asked, though without hope of dissuading Matveyka.

"Because we're two of a kind. The Commission tied me up with rope and burned him out, and now we'll be against you!"

"The Commission didn't set fire to Sukhikh. That's not true, Matveyka!"

"Who else would have done it, if not them?"

"You should listen to your own uncle instead of Grigory Sukhikh, Matveyka! You should listen to Rodion Gavrilovich Smirnovsky and hear what he has to say! He's an intelligent and educated man. He's a brave man!"

"I did listen—when I was little. Until you, the Commission, tied me up with ropes. But you did tie me up, and so now I know who my friends are and who's my enemy!"

"You came here for nothing, Nikola!" Ustinov told himself. "For nothing! It's turned out shamefully! It's useless. And a peasant should be ashamed if anything goes to waste!" He silently began to cuss himself for getting carried away by his hopes. Instead of hoping and dreaming all this time, he should have been looking for another horse for sale in Lebyazhka and the other villages. He had forgotten that a deed left undone is worse than one not begun!

But then Prokopy suddenly put his hand on Ustinov's shoulder and asked, "So I got the horse for a thank-you, did I, Nikolai Levontyevich?"

"That's what it seems like . . ."

"If that's the case, Nikolai Levontyevich, then why don't you just take it from me, for the same price—for a thank-you? Well?! What are your eyes bugging out for? It's simple—take it for that same 'you scratch my back, I'll scratch yours!' I know you need a horse. He'll pull a load with your old man Solovko, and he'll be a good match for that restive Morkoshka of yours! And you, Ustinov, you help me out with the Forest Commission. Be a good neighbor and tell me what you are all doing and planning there! If the Commission votes to smash my stills, you and Polovinkin here just raise your hands in my favor! That's all! And the horse is yours! However things may be, you're an influential man in Lebyazhka these days, goddam you! And when the government returns, you won't want for something to drink! I'll fix things with the authorities, and you'll fix things for me, and everything will be back in order! And then Matveyka will come back and destroy Ignashka Ignatov, and he'll see his old horse in your yard, and he'll forgive you and won't lift a hand against you! You'll forgive him, won't you, Matveyka?"

"No! I won't forgive him, Uncle Prokopy! Not me! Just the opposite!" Still blocking the window with his broad, man-sized shoulders and his round, childishly sullen face, the younger Kupriyanov gave his answer and then didn't move a muscle.

This whole time Polovinkin had sat silently with open mouth, but now he began to shout, "Take the horse, Nikola! Take it while you have the chance! Goddam you, Nikola, you're a lucky man! He's giving you a horse for practically nothing! Take it, don't be shy!" Dropping his head onto Ustinov's shoulder, Polovinkin covered his face with his hands and sobbed loudly. He was envious. Someone, but not him, could get a horse for free, a hard-working horse, a most excellent horse! He sobbed again, dropped his hands, threw his head back, and said in a voice now full of suffering, "Take the gelding today, I tell you! Tomorrow you and Prokopy might start shooting at each other across the fence—one will become a White, the other a Red, and you'll start shooting! Take it right now! Don't wait another minute!"

Polovinkin's venomous envy, unexpressed until now, was making Ustinov sick. His ears roared, and something gave a start inside him, then subsided. But Sevka Kupriyanov's former gelding, exhaling a hay-scented warmth right from its belly, asked, "Well, Nikolai Levontyevich? Well?" It was all Ustinov could do to repeat feebly, "Just like that? Just like that, Prokopy? Just take it, and that's it?!"

"You can lead it into your yard this very minute, and in harness and collar!" Kruglov answered and rose from the table.

A minute later they were all outside, all the guests and all the members of the Kruglov household who had not been heard or seen till that moment, and Prokopy's younger brother, Fedot, as well. There was an unimaginable uproar. Prokopy Kruglov, with his gray-flecked brown beard, was bubbling over with glee, thoroughly drunk, shouting and waving his arms. Matveyka was the only one who didn't go out into the yard, but remained seated where he was. Such a state of confusion in the eternally quiet and gloomy Kruglov yard—from which it had never been possible to borrow even a single nail but from which a working horse was now simply being led away for nothing more than a thank-you—attracted a great crowd of people. There were men there from almost that entire section of Lebyazhka, some in hat and coat, some in only a hat, and some without any winter clothing at all. The women, gathering up their skirts, came running. There were also countless children, one of them hopping along in one boot and holding his other, bare foot in his palm so it wouldn't freeze stiff. Then Barin came galloping up, too, overjoyed, believing his master to be a hero. Jumping up on his hind legs, he licked Ustinov in the face. But the hero's hearty toasts were already making little multicolored circles float before his eyes and turning the ground weak and shaky under his feet. With every passing minute he felt more and more ashamed and uncomfortable. But then, like a Gypsy, Prokopy was already shoving the reins into Ustinov's right hand, and Sevka Kupriyanov's former gelding, its eyes flickering, was staring its new master in the face. There was no time to decide if they flickered with happiness or with something else entirely.

Going completely limp, Ustinov asked Prokopy once more, "For nothing?"

"Take it! Lead it away!" Prokopy pushed Ustinov's shoulder with one hand and the gelding's head with the other. His motley, scraggly beard, dangling between his long arms, almost slapped Ustinov across the eyes.

At the gates, which someone had suddenly opened wide, Ustinov shouted, "I'll give you thirty-two poods of grain! I won't take it for nothing!"

A number of people shouted something after him, Prokopy more loudly than the rest. "You see what we Kruglovs can do, Nikola! Goddam you! You see how grand we Kruglovs are!" And Fedot Kruglov, already completely gray even though he was the younger of the brothers, stuck two fingers in his slobbering mouth and gave a piercing whistle.

Ustinov led Sevka Kupriyanov's former gelding into his own yard. The gelding, in breeching and collar, stamped its hind feet and breathed loudly onto his back. As if he had eyes in the back of his head, Ustinov saw the gelding's gait and the diligence with which it followed its new, longed-for master. Ustinov was flushed and sweating from shame, but happy all the same. As he walked he thought, "It's all right. A man can do anything when he's drunk, it's no disgrace!" He led the gelding home and placed it side by side with Morkoshka, who, like a true friend, already understood everything, was overjoyed by his new companion, and neighed loudly. Ustinov ran into his house and ordered Shurka more sternly than usual to load thirty-two poods of grain onto the sledge immediately and to take it to Prokopy Kruglov's yard. Then he dropped onto his bed and, half-drunk, half-sober, half from joy and half from shame, fell into a dead sleep.

▲▲▲

However, Ustinov was not allowed to sleep it off properly. An hour or so later he dreamed that Ignashka Ignatov had come to wake him and take him off somewhere. Domna, showing Ignashka the door, was explaining that after the fire and a sleepless night her man was out of sorts and needed to rest. In his dream, Ustinov himself was shouting, "Really now! Is there a war going on or something? Am I in some sort of campaign, that I have no time to sleep? I'm at home in my own bed, that's where I am!" Gasping for breath from anger, from a pressure in his chest, Ustinov couldn't get enough air, and when he awoke, he heard that it was true—Ignashka wouldn't give up even here.

"Right now, Domna Alexeyevna," he was insisting in a hoarse and serious voice, "right now. You're a smart woman, but this is not something you can understand! Get Levontyevich out of bed!"

When Ustinov came out into the kitchen in an exceedingly foul mood, Ignashka didn't even give him time to come to his senses. "Get dressed quick, Nikolai Levontyevich," he said. "The whole Commission has been waiting for you to show up!"

"What for, Ignaty?"

"It's a big secret! Comrade Deryabin will explain it to you himself when we get there! But I can't—I don't have the authority!"

While they were walking along the street, Ustinov thought, "They're calling me because of the gelding! 'How can a member of the Commission take a gelding from a kulak for nothing?' That's what they'll ask me. For promising friendship? For telling him what the Commission is doing and sticking up for him in front of Deryabin? They'd have to call me down for that! And even throw me out of the Commission!" After they had gone a few streets farther, Ustinov continued his silent debate: "All right, then! Let them disgrace me, but Sevka Kupriyanov's gelding is mine now—I won't give it back! It's decided once and for all. I can't give it back, and I don't intend to! 'And if you talk about duty and honor, then a peasant's first obligation is to make sure his children are well fed and well dressed and only secondly to serve on any sort of Commission!' That's what I'll tell them. 'So, my fellow citizens, you can strip me of my authority as a Commission member, and I'll take my gelding! I will fulfill my first and holy duty, not with you, but with my new worker, ally, and friend! Otherwise, my heart will burst, and my hands will go limp and be good for nothing!' " Ustinov checked his thinking to be sure: was his answer the correct one? It was.

Though he usually did not devote very much thought to his daughters, his grandchildren, or Domna, but thought about his horses and Svyatka instead, he was sure that if he were not the family provider he wouldn't have a house or a yard, or Svyatka, or even think of her. He would be living by himself, and maybe even preaching the end of the world every day, ready to throw himself into the fire like Kudeyar, or he would have invented some other bachelor's pastime. Ustinov repeatedly recalled one loner in Krushikha who had run around the village shooting cats and another total oddball in Barsukova who had ridden around on a ram as if it were a horse, sometimes letting it have its way, sometimes butting heads with it. Such people were contemptible. Their knees had never felt the warmth of their own kids and grandkids, and the idea of being a breadwinner was worth as much to them as sunflower seeds. But now these loners came too often to Ustinov's mind. Perhaps the hour of the loner had struck, the time to smash everything, to burn and kill . . . But no one cared a whit about what people would think about all this killing in the future, years from now. Everyone was full of pride in their conviction that they were bringing happiness to people yet to come, but were they, really? Workers can bring happiness with good horses, and fathers and grandfathers can bring happiness to their children, but loners? Never!

They arrived at the Commission. Just as he was, Ignashka sat down on his stool in the corner and stayed there, quiet and serious. Kalashnikov stood silently by the window with one hand buried in his shaggy hair. Polovinkin and Deryabin were sitting at the table, Polovinkin with a confused expression, Deryabin angry and tense, as if ready to shout, "Charge!" and run to the attack.

"Well?" Deryabin asked. "Is the news good? What do you think? Just how will you go about your life after this news?"

"I don't know what you're asking about, Comrade Deryabin," replied Ustinov, as if confessing to something. "How am I supposed to know what you're asking about?"

"What am I asking about? They've declared a new government in the city of Omsk! The dictatorship of Admiral Kolchak, the former Minister of War of the Siberian Government! What the generals didn't manage to do in Petersburg, what didn't work out in Moscow, has happened in Siberia! There never were many generals in Siberia, but now generals of every stripe and nationality have come running to us from all over the world, and they've made a counterrevolution! Read!" Without looking at him, as if Ustinov were to blame for that dictatorship, Deryabin held out a gray, crumpled page from a government newspaper called *The People's Freedom*.

Ustinov began to read.

Events have come to pass with breakneck speed, and one cannot help but ask, "What will the future bring us?" With the transformation of the Siberian Provisional Government into the All-Russian Government, everyone expected government life to flow normally, and the question of the final overthrow of the Bolsheviks after the capitulation of Germany, which had supported them, was close to a solution. But now, "as a result of extraordinary events that have interrupted the activities of the All-Russian Provisional Government, and in view of the difficult position of the state," the Council of Ministers has entrusted power to a single person, Admiral A. V. Kolchak, giving him the title of Supreme Ruler. In other words, political circumstances have forced us to seek refuge in dictatorship . . . For the moment we may all the same be relatively calm, because the Council of Ministers created a few days ago still remains in power . . . On the other hand, the personality of Supreme Ruler Admiral Kolchak inspires confidence that there will be a certain amount of calm in the coming year . . . It is the obligation of all citizens who love their country to submit without complaint to the situation that has taken shape, the result of exceptional circumstances and efforts to save the Motherland.

As soon as Ustinov had finished reading, Deryabin, still not looking at him and even angrier than before, said, "And that's not all, that's not everything! Take another look, there!"

There followed the proclamation of the Council of Ministers: "Army and Navy Vice Admiral Alexander Vasilyevich Kolchak is promoted to the rank of Admiral," and a little farther down was another proclamation:

> On this date, by the decree of the Council of Ministers of the All-Russian Government, I have been designated Supreme Ruler.
>
> Also on this date, I assumed the office of Supreme Commander of all Russian land and naval forces.
>
> —Admiral Kolchak, Supreme Commander of All Russian Armed Forces on Land and Sea.

"That's how it is done, Citizen Ustinov!" Deryabin again reproached not only Ustinov but also everyone else present. "So what do you have to say?!"

"But we ain't saying nothing, Comrade Deryabin! We ain't said a thing!" protested Ignashka, blinking.

Ustinov felt uncomfortable for himself and everyone else, but at the same time his shame was mixed with relief. "Such colossal thievery goes on in the whole world," he thought, "and for everyone to see! And I'm ashamed that I took a horse dishonestly from Prokopy Kruglov! It's ridiculous to feel embarrassed!" Not knowing exactly what to say, he waved a dismissive hand on behalf of everyone.

"So he's an Admiral. The affairs of the forest don't have anything at all to do with with him, do they?"

"Everything in the world is Admiral Kolchak's business now that he's taken power into his own hands. A pretender is always concerned with everything!"

"Comrade Commission Members," said Kalashnikov, jerking away from the window. "It is essential for us to publish an appeal to the people to say that no matter what power might arrive here, it must understand us, our popular activities, our peaceful intentions, our desire to establish order, and our most ordinary human desire to live like people, in harmony with reason, without bloodshed and fratricide!"

"Wouldn't that be foolish?" Deryabin asked. "When the Admiral's soldiers show up in Lebyazhka with those Czech animals, do you imagine, Kalashnikov, that the first thing they do will be to read our appeal? They won't even take it into the outhouse with them! The very first thing they will do is hang you and me, that's what! No, we must do something entirely different: greet those soldiers with heavy fire! Because if we don't beat them to it, they will do it to us! And it would take us a long time to pay them back for that first loss! And now you have the floor, Ustinov! I've had my fill of listening to Kalashnikov!"

But once again Kalashnikov did not give Ustinov a chance to say a word. "We can't be the first to start it!" he protested. "It's the imperialists and capitalists who are in a hurry to start making war and killing, and whoever is first even boasts about it: 'We weren't caught napping! We got the jump on our neighbors!' But the people should never do a thing like that! Until someone touches them, until someone does them an unbearable injury, the people will not take up arms against anyone. They know that attitude is the source of their righteousness, and they need that more than any first victory, more than the first simple military success. So now, Ustinov, what is the truth? Tell us your opinion."

"Oh, this nobility of yours is so stupid—'the first, the first!' " Deryabin exclaimed. "How many times do I have to repeat the facts to you? That we, the working people, have been whipped, beaten, oppressed, deceived, and murdered for a thousand years counts for nothing, and now that we have risen up against a thousand years of violence, we are told: 'You can't begin first!' And who says this? One of our own, a workingman! I don't know how you can be so dense! You just wait, Kalashnikov, until the Admiral has hanged all the workers on the railroad and in the workshops and all the politically conscious peasants out in the villages. He will do it. It doesn't frighten him to be the first. So speak, Ustinov! Why won't you say anything?"

But Kalashnikov, sighing heavily, once again checked Ustinov with a gesture. "It wasn't just the working people who were beaten and killed for a thousand years! Weren't tsars killed, too? Weren't princes and nobles suppressed, too? There isn't one completely rational class in all mankind. But as soon as a man begins to understand that life is arranged the wrong way, all he gets for his understanding is a whack on the noggin! 'Don't think. Don't try to understand!' Well, understand things just for yourself, but if you try to understand for the sake of others, life will never forgive you. In that case, there is no place in life for you, and you will lose everything! But all the same—words should come before weapons! And if we won't live to see the result, then our children will. Words will prevail, believe me, Deryabin! They will! Even if it's at the expense of our labor and our deaths, they will prevail!"

"How many times I've envied the beasts!" sighed Ignashka from his stool by the door. "They got a real understanding about who is supposed to eat who, and who ain't to be touched. But with us, everyone does as he pleases! Today your neighbor's your friend and brother, and tomorrow he up and shoots at you! And there ain't even no need to say that I'd be happy to trip up a few folks myself!"

At last it was time for Ustinov to speak, and he began, "We mustn't be the first to start! No! Why has this war stayed away from Lebyazhka so far, and even from all of Krushikha Volost? Because no one was the first to start something! If someone were to be first, then in the blink of an eye there would be not only a second and a third but a tenth and a hundredth! Even though we curse each other sometimes and don't respect ourselves or our neighbors as human beings should, still, you see, we've kept our wits about us. No one has given in to the provocations of these times and taken some property or other from a neighbor or taken revenge on someone who did him wrong in the past. No one has yielded to that damnable, inhuman, murderous spite that tempts a man like the devil: 'Kill, destroy—it'll make you feel good!' We Lebyazhkans haven't tossed the kind of spark that could start a fire, and no! we won't . . ." But here Ustinov stumbled. "Grishka Sukhikh was burned out . . . ," he said quietly.

"Burned out! Yes!" Deryabin repeated and stared hard at Ustinov.

"When we're sitting here in the Commission, we speak our minds," Ustinov said, his ardor now quite gone, "but when we have to explain our convictions to the people, will we know how?"

"That's a point . . . ," Deryabin said, shaking his finger angrily at someone or other. "Everyone really loves all this democracy, but just ask one of these democracy-lovers if he wants to hear the sound of shooting."

"I know it, too, Ustinov," Kalashnikov began again. "Our words are weak, even powerless. But we don't have anything else, and we have to live with what we have! We will keep calling for rational thought and human understanding! We will appeal to the people always to be members of society, and if society cannot live by rational principles, or at least by cooperative ones, then it means certain death for one and all. It is true that a person in power and a person under his power have never understood one another, nowhere and never. But shouldn't that moment of understanding still come someday? Really, if it doesn't come, then how will either one of these people live?" Sadly and quietly, Kalashnikov shuffled the papers on the table. "Everything I've had in my own thoughts is written on these pages and in the cooperative manifestos I keep behind an icon. Let us continue together. Let us put together whatever each of us has in his mind and heart right now. Let's sit down and write our appeal together, even if it takes all night."

As Kalashnikov reached for the ink bottle to pass it to Ustinov, Polovinkin stood up from his stool and began to speak loudly, abruptly, and angrily, as if to an enemy, as if to someone who had offended him terribly:

"But this here ain't got nothing to do with me! Nothing at all! Whatever you decide, it's no business of mine, and never can be! As long as the Commission was only concerned with the forest, I kept my mouth shut and put up with it. As long as the whole government in Siberia was temporary and everything around us was temporary, even our Commission, I put up with it. But if a strong government has showed up, be it full of generals or the proletariat, then I got no business left in any kind of Commission, none at all! All this here Commission wheeling and dealing and loose ways is making me sick! I been afraid to look people in the eyes for a long time now! I can't look them in the eyes when healthy men is sitting in someone else's house, just like today, when our host, Kirill, is away from home, and, instead of farming, they're busy with a bunch of papers! And they chatter and tell each other's fortunes like they was girls at a party with nothing better to do! Whoever can outtalk the others is the one who's right—he's a fine one! It makes me sick!

"And I'll tell you what, it's long since time you had a real government to knock all these loose ways out of you for once and for all, knock them out before it's too late, before this damned pox, this plague of blabber, infects the whole of Lebyazhka and everywhere around it! This here civil war is from just this kind of loose blabbering, and nothing else! It's the cause of all of it! It's to blame for everything! How they blabbered and blabbered at the front! They ruined Russia there with all their chatter. They wore themselves to a dead faint, till they were gasping for breath, but that wasn't enough for them. They ran home from the war to the land, but they brought their God-cursed infection with them, and here it is! Plague after plague and pox after pox—you'll be sorry about the Tsar and the Tsar's sergeant major who punched you in the face and ordered you: 'Attention! Silence!' You'll truly regret it! Your hearts will bleed!

"So, I've said my piece . . . I've kept quiet so many times, all twisted up inside—this here's my first and last speech. This is it! All of it, thank the Lord and the Holy Mother of God! You're not saying anything, you're not speaking a word against me, but I wouldn't believe a thing you said anyway, I'd only curse you! You ain't got nothing to say! Everyone else around here is just people, just plain folks, but all the smart ones have turned up here, the most educated of all. It looks like their pants is full of fleas—day and night they rub their behinds against their chairs and can't calm down for a minute! They think that's a man's most important business! You think there'd be the same kind of clever little lawmakers in the other villages, too, such educated ass-scratchers, but there ain't any anywhere else, they've only showed up here with us! It's a disgrace and a shame! They claim they'll make gentlemen out of peasants, grow sunflowers in the outhouse! In-tell-idiots out of in-tell-lec-chuls! Idiots!"

Crossing himself, Polovinkin turned about-face like a soldier, and added without turning around, "Phooey! On the lot of you! And phooey on myself! I'm leaving here once and for all! I'm going to the bathhouse to wash myself off! I felt this coming, I told the women to heat it for me right away!" And in the kitchen he spat loudly on the floor.

As soon as the kitchen door to the back porch had slammed shut, Ustinov thought, "My God, how good Polovinkin must feel right now! How spirited and lively, without a bit of dreary lethargy! Polovinkin's freed himself of his obligations to the Forest Commission forever! And what's more, only today Polovinkin had most likely promised to stick up for the interests of Prokopy Kruglov in the Commission. But he slammed the door and—bang!—that was all that was left of his promise! If only I could slam the door like that and settle accounts with Prokopy over Sevka Kupriyanov's gelding the same way!" But what was possible for Polovinkin was impossible for Ustinov or Kalashnikov, impossible! And when Ustinov thought about it, Polovinkin's leaving the Commission was really not so unexpected. Ustinov probably understood his reaction better than anyone else, for he had known Polovinkin for a long time.

They lived in different parts of the village—Polovinkin on the hill, Ustinov on the lakeshore—and had never been in one another's houses, but their fields had shared a common boundary for many years. Neighbors in the fields before the war, they also saw each other in the same place after the war. That spring, Ustinov had just returned from the front. After spending three days at home, he made haste to harness Morkoshka and set out for the fields before sunup. Except for the crunch of frost under his wagon wheels, it was quiet. Then dawn broke on his solitude, and as the sun tinted the forest blue and illuminated the fields, the birds began to sing.

Ustinov loved bird song. It was genuine, not something contrived. A dog will fawn on a man and express its love, but at the same time it will always be thinking about scrounging some tidbit. The birds sing, but they don't expect anything in return. They need nothing but the song itself. Even when a bird is dying of hunger, it will be silent for a while, but then it will begin to sing. It doesn't look to see who is listening to it. It has no ulterior motives, and perhaps that is why its song has so much harmony. Listening to all these nameless singers, Ustinov still couldn't believe that he was alive, back from the war and riding out to his own field, but he felt that he was the most incredibly happy man on earth.

And then suddenly—what was that? There seemed to be an icy echo from the direction of the White Wood! His wagon wheels clattered and crunched through the frozen puddles, and the same ringing sounds echoed from the woods. He didn't guess right away that someone else, also in an iron-framed wagon, crunching the ice in last year's ruts just as he was, was riding toward him. It was Polovinkin who was coming, also for the first time since the end of the war. They met at the former boundary of their fields and exchanged a few words, but without asking each other for any details or mentioning the war. They had no desire to do so. Perhaps each was displeased with the other for disturbing his fairy-tale solitude, and half an hour later, as soon as the ground had thawed from the night's frost, each was already plowing his own field.

How Ustinov's bones had ached and throbbed those spring days! How the particles of earth had gritted between his teeth! He got up before dawn, not because he wanted to, but because the aching in his bones wouldn't let him sleep and he had to knock the unbearable fatigue out of them with still more work. Fight fire with fire! But to tell the truth, knowing that Polovinkin's bones were throbbing even more unbearably made it easier for Ustinov.

On the fourth day of this arduous plowing, Polovinkin came to him, asked for a smoke, and hemming and hawing, said, "You know, Nikola, the least you could do is wake me at dawn every day. Give a good whack on a piece of iron or something! No matter when I wake up, no matter how early it may be, I hear you already driving your horses down the furrows. I get a move on, sometimes even without a bite of breakfast, harness up, and then all day I envy you and cuss myself. 'How did Nikola Ustinov get to work before me?' I can't forgive myself, something gnaws at me inside, maybe my conscience or something . . ."

"But then you always finish later than me, Polovinkin!" said Ustinov, attempting to calm him. "I'm already unhitching my horses for the night, and I can still hear you alone in the dark, plowing one more furrow! I'm envious, too!"

"But I was just making up for the sleepy morning time, for being a sinful and lazy good-for-nothing! It doesn't matter there, in the dark, what you're making up for!"

"All right!" agreed Ustinov. "I'll beat on the plowshare with a piece of iron in the morning, but then you quit before nightfall! It's also hard for me to fall asleep when you're still working!"

And so they agreed, but all the same, Ustinov still plowed more land than Polovinkin and, most important, his field was more handsome and even. His rows were lined up tidily, furrow against furrow. The two workers were not alike. Ustinov compared himself to Morkoshka, and Polovinkin to Solovko, who could only pull and pull. He had strength but little talent.

In homes like Polovinkin's, not even the little kids are allowed to watch the work from the sidelines to understand how things are done. At the age of five, a boy is set on a horse and told, "Get used to harrowing, kid!" And he does. But he gets used to drudgery, not to work. All he knows is how to pull, but without thinking, without understanding, let alone any pleasant talk. When that's how it is done, a peasant's homestead won't run right even if he works himself to death! The sowing won't get done on time, even if he goes into the fields earlier than anyone else. Things won't go right at the market—he'll sell cheaper and buy dearer than the others. His plow won't be the right kind, his separator will have the wrong milling sieves, and his improperly padded harness will rub his horses' backs raw. Exhausted by all this unimaginable drudgery, such a peasant's old woman will always be sickly, too.

Polovinkin finished his army service and came home alive, but the war and the endless sitting in the trenches hadn't helped him to figure things out, not even with hindsight. All his life he had done things the wrong way, not worked the way he should have, and he came home without learning anything. He was just as much like Solovko as he always had been. And, really, you can't just tell a man that he's doing things wrong. Many people see that it's the wrong way, and they sympathize and sigh, but they don't say anything. Explanations and advice won't put new arms or legs or a new head on a man! Although Polovinkin maintained a noble silence, there were others who blamed life for their own faults and inabilities, and their homes were dungeons to them; their yards, prisons; their wives, witches; their children, little demons; and the whole peasantry and the labor of the peasant, a cruel joke and nothing more. Chuck it all and run off! But such a peasant will not run off because there is no haven for him anywhere.

When the Lebyazhkans began to elect the Commission, they chose with care. Whatever the Commission might be, they were setting up the only authority in the village. They elected Ustinov unanimously right away. He was different from other men. He was educated and had his wits about him. Although a first-class peasant, he was not quite a peasant through and through. But men of the soil to their fingertips were rarely elected. Such men weren't involved in the cooperative movement, in forest inspection, or the rural committee. They weren't in charge of anything and didn't want to be. Only one such man is ever elected to any commission, to any kind of community service, where his permanent function is to fail to understand something or fail to do something or other and thus to prevent the clever ones from thinking too much of themselves and becoming too distant from the masses. Looking this man in the face every day and confronting an example of the most backward of the masses, the clever ones can never forget what it means to have to work with them! Polovinkin had been elected to the Forest Commission to fulfill just such a function.

And once again Ustinov and the others found themselves feeling uncomfortable, separated by the Pankratovs' table, at which they sat facing one another, like two fields sharing a common boundary. Seated at this table, Ustinov had done everything quickly and sensibly. Polovinkin, watching him from his seat at the edge, had kept his silence, angrily stewing without even being able to define the cause of his anger. When he finally did speak, it was as if he had said, "You keep showing how smart you are! You showed it to the Tsar and gave him a good kick in the pants. And now the simple folk are busy doing the same thing. But it don't make no difference to me who's got more power over me and can show he's more smarter than anyone else! Be it the Tsar or my own neighbor, I hate and despise them just the same! They're all special, in a class by themselves, and there's too many of the rest of us to pay any attention to. But I know this about myself—I'll always be one of the others, one of those left behind! And so will my children! And my grandchildren! And since that's the way it is, I've spit on the lot of them, the clever ones, of whatever kind or class! No matter what power they have over me! I spit on them, and then some—they're no kinsmen of mine! They're strangers!"

Polovinkin really was a good peasant, honest and hard-working. Although both honesty and a love of labor were heavier burdens for him, an untalented man, than for an able and successful man, he adhered to these values and never betrayed them. If he envied someone, it was always an inward envy, almost silent, as if from a distance. Only rarely was his envy vocal. His family name, Polovinkin, like the names Glazkov and Pupkov, was also derived from a fairy tale, the story about the maiden Anyutka, one of the six Poluvyatsky maidens.

▲▲▲

It had been a fierce winter—so went the tale—and the Kerzhak schismatics, who were not used to it and found it absolutely unbearable, sat in their sod huts without sticking their noses out-of-doors. But the Poluvyatsky maiden-brides, to whom the freezing cold was nothing, wore a path across the hill, running to and fro day and night.

An Old Believer family, simple people, would be sitting without a care in their sod hut, drinking currant tea and warming themselves by the stove, when suddenly their little windowpane would ring with the sound of rapping. It was a Poluvyatsky maiden come to lure some lad outside. It was Anyutka luring Vlas, that's who! She would start with the window, then soon she would be knocking at the door.

So Vlas's aged parents locked the door from the inside. When the family members needed to go out into the yard, they would ask their father for the key, which he carried around his neck on a cord with his cross. Only when he gave them the key could they unlock the door and let themselves out.

But Anyutka, standing outside the window or the door, would not give up. She would coax, "My little Vlasik, Vlasenochek, run out to me, and I promise to treat you to a nice meat pie! I baked it myself, and I've brought it to you, nice and warm!"

Inside the locked hut, Vlas, the Kerzhak lad, endured this for some time, and then he donned his hat. He didn't run for the door, but crashed right through the window with his hat on and disappeared from his parents' sight in the wink of an eye, as if he hadn't even been sitting there by the stove with them drinking currant tea!

Well, Vlas's parents and sisters and brothers dragged their feet. They didn't use the key to unlock the door right away and didn't go rushing off to the Poluvyatsky side. So when they finally did come running, burning with anger, to Anyutka's house, Vlas was already there, drinking tea with his sweetheart. Real tea this time, Chinese tea.

"But how can you do this, Vlasushka?" His parents, his brothers and sisters, and whoever else was there at the time, all beseeched him. "How can you drink tea in a stranger's house? How can you touch your lips to a stranger's cup, a heathen's cup? Oy, it's the end of us, oy, the end! Don't you have any use for your own home, your own cups and spoons, anymore? And for your faith? And for the two-fingered sign of the cross?"

"Don't be angry, don't fret, Father and Mother, brothers and sisters!" answered Vlas. "Take a closer look and see how I've worked everything out! I brought my own cup with me from home! Here it is! I take a sip from Anyutka's cup, then one from my own! I'm forsaking our customs only halfway! Is that really such a bad thing, this one half? Just one? One tiny little half?"

"Such a smart aleck! And when you cross yourself, where will your 'half' be then?"

"I'll do it the same way! I'll make the sign of the cross with three fingers, but I'll hide half of one finger in my palm! Just enough so it won't stick out too much, enough so people won't stare! Like that! My little wife, Anyutushka, and I will always do it only like that, half-and-half!"

And that's how the name Polovinkin came to Lebyazhka, from *polovina*, the Russian word for "half."

▲▲▲

Those very first Polovinkins knew how to be clever and crafty, but now they were completely lacking in this quality. In those distant times that's the kind of stories that were told, but now there was nothing to cheer a body up. Polovinkin had gone, and the Commission was left to mull things over.

"It's the masses who've left us, by God!" said Pyotr Kalashnikov. "And just how could we have avoided becoming separated from the masses, Comrades? Can this be really happening?"

"It can!" confirmed Ustinov. "And not only we, but the government, too, can wind up without the masses, without the people!"

"How can it be without the people, Nikola?" Kalashnikov asked. "I can't understand it! Where will the people go?"

"That's just it: people have nowhere to go. There will be people, but it won't be the people! Not when they don't have a common language! Until they find one for themselves, what kind of a people could they be?"

"Polovinkin has left . . . ," Kalashnikov searched for an explanation. "He has more of a sense of public duty than that, but he's afraid that nothing will come of it! What's more, he's afraid that Admiral Kolchak will come and crush any social activity, including our Commission. And including Polovinkin himself!"

But Deryabin disagreed. "Polovinkin left because Kolchak is a lot more to his liking! He's for Kolchak! He's for a military dictatorship!"

"Polovinkin left because he doesn't know himself what is better or worse! So he just left! To avoid getting confused!" Ustinov thought out loud.

"Aha, aha!" Ignashka Ignatov said, raising a finger and waving it high above his blue-gray head. "So even Polovinkin don't know what is best and what is the very worst! And we don't know neither. Which means we ain't out of touch with the masses at all! What does being out of touch mean? That's when someone knows something about themselves, but the masses are left in the dark and don't know nothing. Well, that's not what we have here—we don't know nothing neither, and that means that we, the Commission, ain't out of touch! And I'll tell you for sure, if that's the way it is, then let's get to writing our appeal to the people! Or else we'll have gotten started on it only to forget all about it! But if we're in step with the masses, then we can't just forget about it!"

"Kolchak has come, and Polovinkin has gone . . . ," said Ustinov. "That's really the way it is! But what does it mean?"

Circles and Lines

Was it now up to Deryabin whether or not there would be a Commission? Suppose he were to say, "So Polovinkin has had enough of our talk and meetings! And there's no reason to write an appeal!" If he said that, the Commission would be split up, and that would be the end of it. Ignashka would immediately support Deryabin, and Ustinov would back Kalashnikov, and the Commission would be completely divided. A lot of things had happened in the Commission, but there had never been such a moment, no . . . The Commission members regarded each other thoughtfully. Would they be able to part company the way Polovinkin had just done? Would they still be together, or would each one of them be on his own, starting right now? Did they still share common interests? Was there even more difficult work to be done that they would not face together? Or was there some other way of looking at it, some another answer?

Three of them—Deryabin, Kalashnikov, and Ustinov—sat looking at each other, trying to guess each other's thoughts, and the fourth, Ignashka Ignatov, squirmed on his chair with impatience, only partly understanding what was going on.

"It sure is the truth—we don't do anything here but talk!" Kalashnikov was the first to break the silence. "We're working people, peasant farmers, the feeders of mankind, and soldiers who defended their country. We've founded a co-op and sung 'Labor Will Rule the Earth,' but still the time comes when all we have is words! They may be strong words or weak words, but that's all there is. We're just like little babies who can babble words but can't do anything. It's a crying shame, but what else can we do? We will write our appeal!"

"And just who will we address?" Deryabin asked with grudging anger, but at the same time he moved his stool up to the table and took a short, saliva-smeared pencil out of his shirt pocket.

"Citizens and Comrades . . . ," Kalashnikov began in explanation. "All men and women who want to be human beings . . . "

Late that night they finished writing.

The population has learned of the arrival of a new power in the city of Omsk. It is clear that other changes will follow this one, and there will not be an organization or association or a single person in Siberia who is not affected by this.

And so, in realization of that which is to come, the Lebyazhka Forest Commission has put before itself the question of whether or not it is still needed. Will it be in conflict with the new system of government in Siberia?

We are informing those citizens who have the desire to hear us out, most of all our electors, that the Commission intends to continue its existence.

Here is the train of thought that led to our decision.

Although man calls himself a thinking creature, his mistakes, delusions, and cruelty to his own kind remain beyond comprehension. Thought becomes powerless to understand all of this. But, nevertheless, this is still not the end of mankind, and there is still a glimmer of hope for reason and sincere repentance for its past errors.

But when man transfers this unthinkable trampling of mind and heart to nature, then people can have no future, and their shameful and horrible end is inescapable because it would be the end of all consciousness—human, divine, or of whatever other power there may be. And if so, man already has no reason to live. Is that really life, if it seeks to hasten its own demise and turns everything living, or even dead, into ashes? No, that is really nothing but a disgrace!

The Lebyazhka Forest Commission is convinced that no government will see a single drop of opposition in the Commission's activities. The true purpose of power is rational law and order, but there can be no law and order unless people protect all of nature and the earth on which they exist, and it is precisely this protection for which the Commission strives. Who if not the peasant, who feeds all of mankind, including rulers and leaders, should be involved in such protection?

We are convinced, and deeply so, that in the rational future mankind will accept one or another law of nature as a foundation and only then adapt its own human law to it. For example, under the laws of nature, not one beast, even the most predatory, destroys another, no matter how weak it might be, but only feeds upon it according to its true needs, only for the sake of preserving its own life. From now on, man, too, will have to recognize the law of the impossibility of one tribe or people destroying another, that is, the impossibility of civil wars.

But that time will not be coming soon. We, of course, will not live to see that. However, as long as we are still alive, we must strive for this wisdom. Why else would we possess it?!

And so, fellow citizens, we will continue our work, modest as it may be, for the benefit of ourselves, the benefit of our children (which is the same thing), for the benefit of the government and the state, which will be there in our time and for a long time after us.

Fellow citizens! We will not boast, but a fact is still a fact: even though we have made certain mistakes, we have achieved such an allocation of the forest reserves that nearly an absolute majority of the citizens have accepted it as being just and fair. When has that ever happened in the past? This has never happened before, and that means that we have taken a look into a just future. For the people we have established a price list for construction timber, firewood, and poles; and even though everywhere around us we see economic ruin and decay, no prices at all, and not the least bit of order, our prices are in full effect.

We have taken the first measures toward the restoration of the forest undergrowth, the establishment of forest industries, and the like. Our Commission turns toward nature, to the most rational order on earth, and it is precisely this that has allowed us to have an effect, small as it may be, on the disorder in the everyday life of our village community. Our fight against the moonshiners, for which, again, the overwhelming majority of citizens, the women in particular, cannot help but express their sincere gratitude, serves as an important example by itself.

We will make no secret of it—it is difficult for us to cultivate in ourselves a conscious relationship to public property and self-discipline, but all the same, the cooperative experience that has been gained and the current work of the Commission give us hope for ourselves.

We appeal to you, the citizens of Lebyazhka, to support in every way the community organization that you yourselves have elected, the only such in the village for the present, and therefore all the more essential for the affirmation in all of you of the citizenship and understanding that cannot be created through anything else but just and equal social cooperation.

War rages all around, and in the glow of its sinister light, already so close by, the activity of our Commission might seem to be a useless and even foolish pursuit. But in reality this is not so, for any work for the benefit of society should be performed now with all the responsibility that people have toward one another. It is precisely now, as never before, that this is man's holy duty and obligation.

Our ancestors did not lead us into Siberia so that we would destroy its lands and forests and ourselves in feuding and fratricide. Our great-grandfathers had faith in their own wisdom and in our wisdom, and we are only continuing this faith!

In the course of its late-night sessions, the Forest Commission had long since burned up the reserve of kerosene in the Pankratov house, and now the light came from a little fat-burning lamp that spat and sputtered, its hemp-fiber wick crackling and smoking, now flaring up, now almost going out. Its thick yellow light cast coal-black shadows on the table, the floor, and the walls, shadows of Pyotr Kalashnikov's curly head, motionlessly propped on one hand, Deryabin's sharp nose, Ignashka's profile, his head nodding lower and lower, then sharply jerking upright. Ustinov's shadow, which fell on both table and floor, was in constant motion because he was serving as scribe. When they had finished their work and everyone had heaved a sigh of relief, they looked at one another tenderly, and not without pride. Just look at what they had managed to do, look at what they had written! Deryabin pulled the sheaf of pages toward himself.

"Now here's what we'll do, Ustinov! You make a clean copy of everything just as it is here. No one else can understand your handwriting as well as you can. The rest of us will come here in the morning, and each of us will make another clean copy of our appeal, maybe even more than one, so it can be distributed as widely as possible." He sighed and thought a moment. "But who knows? It's also completely possible that we have worked in vain. These days we should concern ourselves with arms, and nothing else, as many villages and uyezds have understood already."

"No, I don't agree!" Kalashnikov protested hotly as if they hadn't argued about it before. "If there is no other way out, we will fight! But you have to fight silently, with your lips pressed tightly together! That is, I have to know that I have said all there is to say, that I didn't forget a single word of persuasion and common sense. Not a single word! If no one wants to hear and understand me after that, then there really will be nothing left for me but arms! Even though I'm getting old and am not a military man, I'll still go off to fight in the first wave! If Admiral Kolchak starts acting like a criminal and a beast, treating us like the ataman Annenkov is treating the people in Siberia, like Semyonov in the Baikal, like Denikin in Russia,* I'll go without a second thought, and if I am killed, I won't regret giving up my own life, because living under arbitrary rule, a mockery of government, is much worse than dying! There is just one thing I can't do—fight while believing that I did not clarify everything to my enemy, did not explain myself, and that he therefore fights against me because of his own lack of understanding!"

"Well, that's just fine for your enemy," Deryabin smirked. "He's a smart one. He's happy that words like 'democracy,' 'freedom and equality,' and 'duty and social consciousness' are being uttered even among the simple people. And while you're saying all these words to him, he'll shoot you first! 'Bang! Have a taste of democracy!' "

---

*Grigory Semyonov, Cossack captain who organized a White army in the Far East, was eventually named Supreme Commander of all armed forces in Eastern Siberia and the Far East by Kolchak. Anton Denikin, one of the organizers of the White Volunteer Army in the Don region, took personal command of the army in April 1918.

"Let him! I'm not doing it for him but for myself!"

Ustinov sat silently, thinking how hard it would be to copy the appeal. His handwriting had never been neat; he didn't have the knack for it. And now he was also dying to take a peek, if only with one eye, at Sevka Kupriyanov's former gelding, now his very own. Besides that, while the appeal was being written, he had already thought so much about every word of it that he didn't have the strength to sit at the table for many hours more. But he just had to do it. Deryabin and Kalashnikov continued to argue till they were exhausted. Then the other members of the Commission went home, and Ustinov adjusted the wick in the saucer-shaped lamp and set to work.

In the quiet house a cricket chirped, the clock pendulum knocked, the lamp wick crackled, and the pen in Ustinov's hand scratched on the paper. Ustinov also heard the sound of his own breathing, and he made each breath fit the movement of his hand across the paper. Even though he very much wanted to run off to his yard and have a look at the gelding, still his work seemed to be going smoothly. He mulled over every word of the appeal as if he were taking each one into the palm of his right hand and then using the slender schoolboy's pen to put the word back onto the large white page. The Commission had appropriated this marvelous paper from the office of the previous forest authority and now used it sparingly only for special occasions. "Although man calls himself a thinking creature. . . ." "Is that really life, if it seeks to hasten its own demise . . . ?" "We are convinced, and deeply so, that in the rational future. . . ." As Ustinov wrote carefully, letter by letter, word by word, phrase by phrase, the meaning and hope of these letters, words, and phrases rose up before him more and more clearly. And when Ustinov had written "and that means that we have taken a look into a just future," and he was really feeling that glance, that future wisdom, someone disturbed him. Zinaida appeared beside him. He lifted his head from the paper and asked, "What are you doing?"

Zinaida smiled, almost laughed, but across her face, darkly lit by the oil lamp, there flashed something like fear or cruelty. Putting her hand over the sheet of paper, she covered the words before Ustinov and said in a serious tone, "I also keep feeling that I'll find what I'm looking for! I'll stretch out my hand a little farther and reach it. Just like you are right now . . . "

Ustinov looked at Zinaida silently for a moment before he asked, "So you can tell?! You can tell that I'm searching for something?"

"I can tell everything about you, Nikola! Don't you know that? Are you pretending that you don't know?"

"You're imagining it! You're imagining something that doesn't exist!"

"Don't hide your eyes from me. Look at me! I follow your every step, Nikola, yes, I do, every day! I was in the forest that night. I was listening when you made that speech to the woodcutters from the steppe. When Grigory Sukhikh went to your cabin in the fields, I knew about that, too, why he had gone and what he had to say! You went to see Rodion Gavrilovich Smirnovsky, but I had run there before you did and talked with the officer about the same things you did. And I also know that Grishka Sukhikh got burned out last night and that Kudeyar tried to talk you into jumping into the fire with him!"

"How do you know?" Ustinov shuddered.

"Even when I'm not nearby, I know everything about you from wherever I am!"

Ustinov said nothing, then asked with a smile, "Maybe I should have listened to Kudeyar? Maybe I should have jumped into the fire with him?"

"Maybe so. You would have burned up once and for all! Both for yourself and for me. But you won't jump into the fire, Nikola. No, you won't . . . "

"And what if I suddenly do?"

"There is too much life in you to let you jump into the flames, so much life, but it is blind somehow. It doesn't see that a woman is following it and won't fall behind, not even by a single step!"

"That must not be! A man can't live with someone else's shadow!"

" 'Must not!' The only way I live is the way I'm not supposed to! I think and hope the way I must not! I dream the dreams that I must not! During the war I wished that you would come back alive and Kirill wouldn't! Can a person really wish that? Kirill, that angelic soul, and you, perhaps damned to hell?! It's because of you that he's out carving on his little porch day and night, distilling moonshine on the sly, but he hasn't harmed a single hair of your head. Why did I invite the Commission into my house? I wanted to repay Lebyazhka with the same kindness that the village showed me so long ago. I wanted some sort of justice to be created in my own home, some kind of human peace at a time when war is burning all around us—that's what I wanted! But how has it turned out? I've reduced everything in the world to myself alone—I want to see and hear you in my own house every day—and that's all! That's everything! Can a person really deceive and betray people just because of you? If that's the way it is, if I'm living in the middle of nothing but 'must nots,' then let's just run away! Anywhere, it doesn't matter where! An Austrian prisoner of war in Krushikha ran away with one of the married women. An Austrian, a foreigner! And God has commanded you and me to do it, too!"

"Are you out of your mind, Zinaida?!"

"Well, then what if we drown ourselves together? You didn't want to burn with Kudeyar, but how about drowning with me? In a hole in the ice?"

"A hole in the ice and cold water—how are those better than the fire of the holy fool Kudeyar?

"Aren't you ashamed again, Nikola?" Zinaida asked, bringing her dark, hot face with its wide-open eyes up close to him. "Aren't you ashamed? Not even the least bit?"

"I am ashamed!" Ustinov admitted, turning away from her. "You bring me to it, and who knows to what else!

"Well, thank you for that at least! At least I can bring you to something. And don't hide your eyes again, Nikola! You won't be able to get through life with your eyes closed! Open your eyes and look straight at me! Well, what do you see?"

"You. Zinka Pankratov. What else is there to say?"

"What do you see? Do you see that I'm not fit for love?"

"I didn't say that. I don't see that."

"I'm too old, right?"

"I didn't say that!"

"Am I cross-eyed or one-eyed? Pockmarked?"

"What are you saying? Good Lord!"

"Only fit for the Lord, is that it?"

"Why just for Him?"

"So I am fit for love, for human love! So why don't you love me? Don't blink your eyes, answer me. What am I to do with my fitness? What?"

"You need to calm down, Zinaida."

"Never in my life!"

"You have no shame at all, by God! You're ready to ruin my family, my wife, my children, and my grandchildren! So you're a woman! There's more woman in you than you know what to do with—all right. But you are also a mother! You raised your own sons, but now you want to destroy my own flesh and blood, my little grandchildren? How can these two things fit together inside you? You wish me happiness? It's nothing more than an illusion! What happiness will I find if I betray little children, just like Cain did? There's not much difference between you and Kudeyar, Zinaida. He summons all mankind to follow him, but he's never raised or fed a single person himself! But you're even worse! Kudeyar has never known fatherhood, and no one's asking him to, but you are a mother and are betraying motherhood! And you're trying to talk me into becoming a traitor as well. Lebyazhka took you in and fed you, and now you're spitting on it! It doesn't mean a thing to you! The community has entrusted me with a task, but you're trying to tempt me. What good would I be as a community worker then? I'd be everyone's laughingstock, every whining sniveler's. Everyone would point their finger at me and ask, 'What kind of man is he if he gives in to a woman?' We can't do anything of the sort. But you think that we can! How many people would we make unhappy if I agreed to do what you want? How many truly human and important plans would we ruin? I would be afraid to look people in the eye afterwards, and myself, too!"

"You're wrong, Nikola, I do have a conscience. It's suffocating me. It has me by the throat. But I can't live my whole life in a state of suffocation! And I can't live my whole life without any understanding or sense—and without you, Nikola. I just exist, waiting and waiting for you to explain it to me . . . ''

"Explain what?"

"Everything! Everything on earth! I borrow newspapers from my neighbors and read them at night, but I can't understand them."

"And I can?"

"You can! You know everything. You know about every subject there is. That's what offends me more than anything else. You are stupid about only one thing—you're stupid and ignorant about me. Don't you understand that I didn't become a speechless slave to the village of Lebyazhka in return for the food it gave me? That I wasn't fated to experience human kindness only to be reproached with it for the rest of my life? So I'd blame myself and deny myself? And I am not a slave to Kirill Pankratov just because I liked him once. That's how it was—I liked him. He spoke beautifully and looked at me like an angel. So what? Haven't I repaid everything and won my freedom by now? Haven't I plowed and sowed for him? Didn't I give birth to his children and raise them? Didn't I keep silent when carving his little porch became his whole life, the dearest thing to him on earth? I have not betrayed my conscience, no, I haven't! I have honor! And if my conscience is stronger than I am, let it kill me, let it dry me up, let it turn me into a scarecrow instead of a woman—I won't be offended. And even if I am offended, I won't complain to a living soul! But just look at me, Nikola, and see—I'm not pockmarked; I'm not withered up; it isn't just God who has a use for me but people, too! So why do you, a man, refuse me? And deceive me and yourself, as if that's the way it should be? I will never accept that. I will never, ever, accept that!"

"We can't!" Ustinov whispered. "We can't!"

"There's so much spite in you, Nikola! Can't you really see what is happening to me right now? Don't you really understand that my maidenhood, my married life, my whole life, has not been like the other women's, that I've broken away from those women and am not the same as they are, that their woman's law means nothing to me? I'm all alone now, and in my loneliness I've lost all fear. I'm not afraid of anything, and I can do anything! I'm fed up with being afraid—I've had enough of it! I hid my fear, my shyness, my shame about not being like all the others. The women say, 'Zinka's a brave one, she's not afraid of anything, just like a man!' They didn't even want to know how frightening it was for me to separate myself from the women but not to be able to approach the men, not to know how to pick out a husband and give him a wink—'come over here to me!' After the man's work that I had to do, I was scared to death, not knowing if I would be able to give birth to sons properly! And now that I have overcome my fear and done everything a woman is supposed to do, what else have I got to be afraid of? What other fear could I imagine for myself? And what for?!"

"We can't!" Ustinov shouted again and pushed Zinaida away.

Her head tilted backward, and her eyes closed. But then she slowly straightened up on her chair, licked her lips, and demanded, "What kind of man are you?! Where have you come from, and why? Grigory Sukhikh has the strength of three or four men, and he'll do anything I tell him to, anything I say! If I order him to kill you, tomorrow there won't be a trace of you left on earth! If I tell him not to kill you, he won't lay a finger on you, even if you insult him and make fun of him as much as you want! Grishka Sukhikh has always had the greatest respect for you, and you are his enemy for one reason only—because of me! But if I tell him to, he'll forget that reason, too. And you? Where did you come from, to dry up my soul and torment and crucify my body? From where? You are the most evil of men! You are my murderer!"

Such a curse! Looking around the room as if afraid someone would hear her, Ustinov asked, "Why are you saying this to me? I've never done anything to you!"

"That's why you are a horrible beast, for doing nothing to me! Well, you told the story of Alexei the Man of God—you did do that. But what else? Nothing else! You're like a stranger! Like some foreigner. I'm following a shadow. A ghost! And the only thing this ghost wants is for me to become a shadow, too, like him!" Zinaida held her head in her hands and caught her breath. "You're a clever man, Nikola! And I was happy for your cleverness, I trembled with joy! But when I came to you and got close to you, I knocked my face and my whole body against that cleverness. It hurts so much!"

"Isn't it enough that Kudeyar calls me to his side? If I go rushing from one side to another, where will I be? For you, I am a man, but who will I be for myself? Who am I if I'm brought down and bewitched by a woman? Who will I be before God?"

"God will forgive and understand . . . "

"Never!"

"Always! God forgives people for murder and senseless war, but not for love? What kind of God wouldn't forgive love? Didn't He forgive the Poluvyatsky maidens when they enchanted the Kerzhaks? And He didn't simply forgive. All the people of Lebyazhka were born because of that sin!"

"Those were maidens and young lads, not married women!"

"Don't tell me that—a maiden's sin is worse than a woman's! I know from my own experience: how many years did I carry a sharp knife in my boot to defend myself against sin, to protect my future! But since fate deceived me, now I'm ready to turn the knife on it!"

"You should have gone after Grishka Sukhikh, Zinaida, not me."

"So now which of us is the shameless one, the one without a conscience?"

Ustinov began to feel uncomfortable again, but this time he hid it and repeated stubbornly, "You should have gone after Grishka Sukhikh! Hasn't he always courted you? For how long now?"

"And still would . . . If I let him."

"So let him! Call him back from wherever he's run off to!"

"He won't go far away. He'll show up, if not today, then tomorrow, to take a look at me across the fence. To see if I need anything. Maybe I need a share of his riches? Or maybe I've got a mind to hide from my husband? Or maybe I need to give up on you? Just one look is enough for him to understand that people are saying that he's a wild animal! But there's praise about you. You're kind and intelligent! And so that's how it is. The wild animal understands me, but the kind man—not the least little bit! Even if I say it over and over, all the livelong day, even if I howl and holler at the top of my lungs! Why is that?"

Ustinov didn't want to answer, so he asked, "Did anyone die in the fire at his house, on his freehold? At Grishka's place?"

"The people got away safely. He knew it was going to happen and took them away to a village on the steppe beforehand.

"Who set fire to Grishka?"

"I know it wasn't you."

"But does Grishka know?"

"He knows all right . . . But what do I care about Grishka? It's not him I dream of being with and running away with! Let's run away, Nikola! Let's hide away!" Zinaida whispered feverishly, remembering something else. "Grigory will hide us from the whole world. He will! And he'd die without saying a word to anyone about where we were and what we were doing!"

"Aren't you behaving like a serpent, Zinaida?"

"Everything is possible for me right now! Everything! But if anyone can save me from it, it's you and no one else! Save me, Nikola, once and for all! Aren't I trying to save you? What wouldn't I do to try and save you!"

"You're trying to save me? From whom?"

"From everyone! Someone will be sure to kill you now! If not Grishka, then Matveyka Kupriyanov. If not Matveyka, then those woodcutters that you turned away from the forest! If not them, then it'll be our Lebyazhka policeman. Up to now he's been a nobody, a cipher, but now that a strong government has sprung up, he'll do his duty for all he's worth to show his loyalty. It will happen!"

"What wrong have I ever done him? I don't wish anyone ill, and I don't have anything at all to do with him, that drunken loafer!"

"It will happen! You'll post your appeal on the wall of the village assembly hall, and it will happen!"

"There's nothing in the appeal but the truth."

"Oh, Nikola, Nikola!" Swaying her handsomely large head, Zinaida smiled sadly and tenderly. "What kind of government, what leader, would let you, a peasant, turn out to be smarter than him? Don't you see, the Commission has taken a mind to learn about power, how it should behave and how it should understand things! It talks about the forest, but at the same time about nearly everything else on the face of the earth! Someone really needs to save you while you're still alive! And I know that without a woman's care, without a woman's sense of caution, you'll perish! You'll die! Understand that no matter how much I want you for myself, for my never-ending love, it's all necessary for your salvation! If it wasn't necessary, I would back away! You can't be left alone in life without Zinaida Pankratov! If I leave you, you won't go on living! I know that everyone needs you right now. Smirnovsky needs you, and Kudeyar needs you, and your family, and the Commission. Everyone wants you, everyone comes to see you, almost falling on their knees before you, but when it comes to saving you, there's no one but me! Understand me!" Gently stroking Ustinov's head as if he were a small child, Zinaida touched him with an intensity of caring and tenderness that he had never experienced before. Never in his whole life.

His head spinning in this brief moment of new, totally unfamiliar life, Ustinov started to sink into its dark, trembling depths . . . What she said was true. He knew himself when everyone around him was expecting his concentrated attention. His old parents had expected it, and his wife, Domna, and his children and grandchildren expected it, and all his movable and immovable property, and his fields—the whole wide world expected it from him . . . All through his military service, everyone from the sergeant major to the Tsar had expected and demanded it, constantly threatening to destroy him if he failed to be attentive. But Ustinov had never been lovingly and anxiously caressed; he had never had such an experience until that moment. And now both caresses and loving concern were being offered to him as a gift. If only he wouldn't be shy! Zinaida's other hand was already resting on Ustinov's shoulder. Was that touch happiness? Or was a terrible sorrow touching him like this?

"People always take the least care of the one they need the most!" whispered Zinaida. "That's why you and I and the whole world must see that what I'm doing is justified: because no one else but me is taking care of you! And you do me wrong if the passion of life is so strong in you that you have enough for everyone, even for strangers, enough for even Kudeyar the holy fool, but you have none for me! Can you really be so unfair?"

"You've said too much, Zinaida . . . "

"At long last! I've been talking to you like this for more than a year now, but always in silence, half the time in tears! And always all by myself!"

As she pulled his head against her shoulder, he resisted her, but weakly, imperceptibly. He no longer found it possible to be silent, but he didn't know just what he should say.

"During the war my first feeling was that I'd be killed. It was sure to happen!" Ustinov said softly into Zinaida's ear, then paused. Had his premonition come true? Then he smiled. "But it didn't happen. And then in the second or third year in the trenches, I dreamt that I would live! I don't remember what sort of dream it was or what it was about, but the dream came true!"

"It was just at that time that I began thinking about you, here in Lebyazhka!" Zinaida sighed. "Without closing my eyes! I started thinking about you and never stopped!"

"It was a long time ago. But just recently I had the same dream again. I still don't know what it was about, but I know one thing—I will live! I must, and I will! There is war all around and it's coming toward Lebyazhka, but I will live, nevertheless!"

"When did you have this second dream of yours? Was the Commission already meeting here at this table?"

"Yes . . . "

"That's why I brought the Commission to my house! To make you have this second dream!"

"That's nonsense . . . "

"Dear God, when will you ever realize how many different kinds of things I know about you? But don't be afraid—I won't try to teach you to think about yourself. You don't know how to do it, so don't, that's fine. Surely a real man doesn't need to! And if others are constantly drawing on your strength while you don't even notice it or don't ever criticize anyone for it, then all right! I won't try to interfere. But I won't let them tear you to pieces and scatter your bones! Whether it's one person, or all of them together, or everyone on earth—I won't let them!" At that moment, Zinaida's large, hot hands would not have surrendered Ustinov to anyone, and Ustinov himself did not want to leave their grasp. As they held his head first against one of her shoulders and then against the other, she laughed in wonder. "It feels so good to hold a strong man in my arms! Dear God, it feels good!"

"I'm not a strong man . . . I'm giving in to you. What kind of strength is that?!"

"Don't you dare contradict me!"

"Are there many others who would never have given in to you?"

"Not many! Not many at all! All of you on the Commission were elected as the most special men in the whole village of Lebyazhka! Ignashka

Ignatov, our special messenger, and Polovinkin, too, the peasant's peasant. That's why Polovinkin left—he couldn't take the likes of the rest of you, he wasn't up to it. But of the three of you—you're still not like the others! You're not like anyone else!"

"But why do you need to sort us into categories?"

"Because you're the smartest of all of them! And the best looking! Even your wife is the queen bee of all Lebyazhka! Because she's married to you!"

"Don't bring Domna into this! Don't!"

"I won't!" Zinaida agreed. "But I'll still talk about how handsome you are, you can't forbid me that. You're fair-skinned and blue-eyed, and you simply shine with light. When you laugh, I can't understand why everyone around you isn't laughing, and when you're thinking about something, everyone should think and think along with you. Your shoulders are broad, and they've never been fatigued by anything. Your forehead is smooth and unwrinkled. Your hands—"

But at that moment they both clearly heard footsteps outside in the yard, under the unshuttered window through which the moonlight, as yellow as the glow of the oil lamp, fell into the room. Then someone tapped lightly at the window. Ustinov stood up and looked at Zinaida.

She let out a moan touched with fear, but then she said, "It's not Kirill . . . It's not him. Kirill went to Krushikha for some carpentry supplies, on horseback . . ."

The footsteps in the yard had ceased. The flame of the oil lamp crackled dully, and there was nothing more to be heard.

"Zinka?! Is the door latched from the inside?"

"Yes . . ."

"Open it! Quickly!"

As if she were blind and moving in total darkness, with her hands extended in front of her and her head thrown back, she passed through the room. Then footsteps and the metallic sound of the doorlatch were heard in the kitchen. Ustinov bent over the paper and with sloppy haste copied a few more words from the appeal: " . . . mankind will accept one or another law of nature as a foundation, and only then . . . " The kitchen door slammed shut, there was the sound of cautious footsteps, and a strange man, wearing a knee-length sheepskin coat and carrying his hat, entered the room with Zinaida behind him. The two of them sat down on stools on either side of the door and were silent for a long time.

"Well?! Well, hello, mistress of the house!" the stranger finally said and quickly added, "Pavlovna!" Then, spreading his fingers, he tidied his long shock of hair. He had not taken his hat off for some time, so his blond or reddish hair—you couldn't tell which in the dim light—was flattened down like felt.

"Hello . . . ," Zinaida answered. But she didn't call the man by name, and Ustinov still didn't recognize him.

"Don't you know me?" the stranger asked uncertainly.

"I know you, Cousin . . . ," Zinaida sighed.

"Well, fine!" As the stranger grinned with his large, thin-lipped mouth, Ustinov recognized him—it was Venya Pankratov, Kirill's first cousin!

In one hand Ustinov could still feel Zinaida's warmth, and the other hand had not yet moved from the appeal: "one or another law of nature, and only then . . . " He had not managed to finish the line with some much-needed word.

Thin-faced, beardless but unshaven, with a long chin and narrow, deep-set eyes, Venya stared intently at Ustinov, trying to remember everything he knew about him. It was Venya's habit to look people over like this, probably ever since the time when he been a village leader. From last winter until the present autumn, he had been the Chairman of the Soviet of Deputies.* He had always been defending somebody. Whoever took offense at Ivan Ivanovich Samorukov, or even at the whole village, would go and complain to Venya. He would hear out the complaint, sometimes making a few notes, and afterward he would go from house to house to explain what injustice had been done to the man. He didn't see any misfortune in the fact that they could barely make ends meet in his own household, but if someone else was falling into poverty and ruin, Venya would be the first to defend him. When the Provisional Government and the Czechs overthrew Soviet power, Venya Pankratov had been arrested almost the same day, taken to the city, and thrown in prison, and if anyone in Lebyazhka should have suffered such a fate, it was he.

"Have you escaped, Venya?" Ustinov asked.

"Yes, I have."

"Where are you hiding?"

"Wherever it's most comfortable."

Embarrassed, Ustinov fell silent and turned away.

Zinaida got up from her stool, suddenly weak, her head drooping, and asked Venya, "Are you hungry?"

"I'm not hungry, Zinaida. But I have some business with you, with both of you."

"With both of us?" Ustinov repeated.

Coming up to the table and lowering the wick of the lamp a bit more, Venya said, "You will hide me in the cellar, Zinaida! When the Commission meets in the morning, you, the both of you, see to it that they don't work very long and they all go home quickly. Except for Comrade

---

*The Soviets, or councils, of elected representatives of striking workers appeared in 1905.

Deryabin. After I have met with him, you will hide me again till nighttime. I'll leave at night, just like I came, quietly and calmly. Do you understand? When will Kirill be coming home?"

"No sooner than the day after tomorrow . . . "

"That's fine for me, too!" Venya turned to Ustinov. Ustinov couldn't see his eyes, but it was easy to guess that Venya was watching him carefully. "I was looking to meet up with you, too, Ustinov!" he said finally. "How can I say it in a few words? Don't think that Lebyazhka and the area around it can stay out of the war! It can't! Get that through your thick head, and be armed and ready to fight! Get yourself ready, and get others ready! There was still some hope for a peaceful outcome under the Provisional Government of that Vologda priest's son, but now, under Admiral Kolchak, such a hope is nothing but stupidity and insanity! Do you understand? I have some advice for you: go away. Hide—just like me! Do you understand?"

"No, I don't, Venya," Ustinov answered. "And until someone opens fire on Lebyazhka, I won't understand you and won't be able to. So don't try to explain it to me!"

But Venya started to explain anyway, in a hurry and in detail. He began to explain Kolchak's "Position on the Provisional Establishment of Government Authority in Russia" and his emergency powers. He talked about the old tsarist governors returned to power with the title of Gubernia Director and about the English battalion in the city of Omsk. Venya Pankratov lived hidden away from people, but he knew everything, while Ustinov, a free citizen, knew nothing. But Ustinov had his doubts. People knew an awful lot these days, but all the same they didn't know how to live, and every day they forgot even more about it.

Ustinov was suspicious of this endless knowledge. Without knowing exactly what it was, he was suspicious about something. If a man knew one thing or another, Ustinov might envy him a bit, but everything has its limits, and there is nothing on earth that can't be carried to excess. Excess and misunderstanding in matters such as those Venya was discussing could be very bad. What if a man suddenly looks into something inhuman, something that will make him inhuman? A man has to guard himself against such disaster! It was said that Ustinov was a knowledgeable and intelligent man, but Ustinov knew that he had a special knack. From his mother or father or maybe from nature itself, he had learned to pay heed to the most important wisdom, none other than nature itself.

When spring comes, you have no choice but to harness your team and plow, whether you are smart or stupid, kind or mean, whether you are satisfied with life or curse it! When fall comes, life is again determined for you, what you must do and what you must be concerned about. That is the wisdom of all wisdom, and your own is no match for it! And so it is

in all things! Children are born to you and then grandchildren, and again
everything is determined, just what you have to do for them all to be alive
and well!

He had reared Svyatka, but was it the work of his own hands, his own
enterprise and wisdom? It was not his wisdom. He could not treat Svyatka
however he pleased, and who knows who was master over whom—he or
Svyatka? It was not she who had to look after him, but the other way
around. He had to give her feed and water and keep the stove heated.
He couldn't just order her to stand out in the cold. He couldn't impose
penalties on her according to her service; he couldn't even rise above her
in rank. An intelligence greater than his was in command. Were they not
all living souls, human or animal? Even an inanimate object like grain
determines the course of life for you. It tells you loudly when to plant
and when to sow, when to sell, and when to buy! Even your wagons and
sledges give you orders and tell you what you need to do with them and
when to do it.

Ustinov's own wisdom and laws somehow fit into this universal
natural wisdom and law. They fit in because he didn't get too carried
away and listened sympathetically and attentively to orders from above.
But Ustinov reacted with suspicion toward human decrees about how
he should live. He listened to them, but far from always. If one man
taught another mastery of some skill—well digging, land surveying, or
plowing—that was another matter. Then the capable man was not much
different from the intelligent man. However, if your teacher is intelligent
but unskilled, then just where does he get the right to teach, especially
if he is teaching you how to live? Where did Venya Pankratov get the
right?

Till now, Ustinov had gotten by without Venya and had not lived badly
with his own understanding of things. He had been able to fend off poverty,
but he had not been tempted by riches. He had not pawned his hands or his
body or his soul for the sake of wealth. He could keep on living his life
without Venya's teaching. Why shouldn't he? He had lived his life and had
even been an example to many without being anyone's teacher. He had
never dared to say to Domna, or his daughter Ksenia, or even his son-in-law
Shurka, "You shouldn't live that way, but this way, like this . . . " He had
shown them the example of his own life day after day, but had never called
on others to emulate it. He had never been an agitator, not at home, nor at
the front, nor anywhere else!

It was very difficult for Ustinov to believe people who seemed to know
about everything around themselves, about what was being done
incorrectly or correctly in Lebyazhka, or the city of Omsk, or in Moscow,
St. Petersburg, or Berlin. It was not a human thing for someone to know
more than the world and nature knew, whether he was the neighbor across

the fence, a general, an emperor, the village priest, or the patriarch of all Russia! Nature had no reason to create a man who was smarter than herself. She had no reason and, most likely, no power to do so. She knew how to do everything, but not that. It was long since time for people to understand nature's reasoning, especially now. Such understanding was desperately needed, but just now everyone had gone crazy with his own pride, and everyone was trying to teach everyone else, not with books, but with weapons. Ustinov didn't believe Venya Pankratov, the intelligent peasant, persecuted and righteous, eternal defender of the downtrodden, no, he didn't! Venya Pankratov, a peasant descended from the Old Believers, had been terribly afraid of war for several years, but now he himself was calling people to it, trying to convince them that they couldn't get by without it. There were probably many he would convince of it, but not Ustinov, no!

In the back of Ustinov's skull there was an aching and itching irritation, and in his soul there was nothing at all of what Venya would have wanted. He moved the fingers of his left hand ever so slightly, trying to cool them off, but the warmth of Zinaida's shoulders, hands, and face would not leave them.

All the time that Venya was talking about life today, Zinaida sat in stiff silence on her stool by the door, her hands now and then trembling slightly on her knees, as if searching for something without finding it. When Venya suddenly stopped talking, she shuddered sharply and swayed on her stool.

"Why don't you give me a little something to eat after all, Zinaida? Something cold will do!" said Venya, rising from his seat. When she had left, he shut the door behind her, came close to Ustinov, and swiftly whispered, "And you just mind, Ustinov, that you don't tell anyone that you saw me or talked to me! God forbid! Maybe I could forgive you myself, but it's not up to me alone. Be sure you understand that!" he hissed. "Others might not forgive you."

"You think you have to explain everything, Venya! Why?"

"So I'm explaining it: God forbid!"

"But do you even believe in God, Venya?"

"I don't. Not a bit. I lost my faith a long time ago. I'm not telling you for my sake, but for yours. Not really even for yours. I know that you're a man who can figure things out. You know when to talk and when not to. But what about the others? How about Shurka, for example, your son-in-law?! What if you let something slip in front of him?"

"Why mention Shurka?"

"Just for example."

"There's no need for an example! Is Shurka really such a threat? He hasn't a care in the world!"

"He might even be useful sometime later. But for now, he can't be relied on. He chatters too much! Just watch out, Ustinov! I'm giving you fair warning!"

▲▲▲

In the morning everything went as Venya Pankratov had ordered. When the Commission met, Zinaida whispered a few words to Deryabin, who then said that he didn't feel well and was going home, but actually went down into the cellar. Soon Ustinov suggested to Kalashnikov and Ignashka that they put off copying the appeal till the next day and that in the meantime they show it to Smirnovsky and Samorukov. Let wise people give their advice and tell them whether they should make any additions or changes. Perhaps they, too, would sign the appeal? The three of them left the Pankratov house. Now Venya and Deryabin could come out of the cellar and conduct their conversation in the main room . . . But most likely they wouldn't because they would still feel better and safer in the darkness.

Walking slowly down the long street on the lakefront, Ustinov continued thinking about Venya. Venya was not staying at home, of course, not even with his relatives, because the minute someone picked up his trail the Krushikha police would search at his brother's and in-laws' first of all and might even burn them out, arrest them, or lay hands on them. Venya was hiding with someone whom no one would suspect, but who knew everything that was going on in Lebyazhka, when the Commission was in session and when Kirill was leaving for Krushikha to fetch his woodworking supplies. That meant that there were already more than one like him in Lebyazhka, maybe even ten of them, and while the Forest Commission was working at the Pankratovs' house, their circle or cell was gathering in some other house or cellar and having an entirely different conversation. They wanted to structure life in an entirely different way. They wanted to prepare the Lebyazhka forest guard for war and already knew which neighbors would soon be shooting at each other. They knew who needed to be arrested first of all and who would give them away to the authorities if they made the slightest blunder. And in Kruglov's house, still other people were gathering, the wealthy ones. They had plans and a reckoning of life entirely their own!

Wasn't it amazing how people loved to do what they least of all understood and knew how to do?! Everyone was continually remaking life, but if only he could get just one look at a man who was life's true master. Was he tall or short? Bald or curly-headed? If only such a master would just once show off his creation and say, "Look at what I've made, just look what I've done! Isn't it a marvel?! Where is there even one flaw, even one scratch?" But Ustinov had never met such a master, not once in his life.

Of course, people change, and children cannot live as their grandfathers did, but why go crazy with every new turn in life? Why were Prokopy

Kruglov and Venya Pankratov involved in this business? Were they smarter than Nikolai Ustinov? No matter what one might say, at that moment Polovinkin, not very bright and God only knows how capable, was more to his liking than anyone else. When Polovinkin understood that he didn't know the business at hand, he spit and got out like an honest man, even a wise man. Ustinov had always thirsted for simplicity and clarity, but now, more than ever before in his life, he wanted these qualities, because he was powerless without them, as if without air or without life itself. At one time, he remembered, he had almost managed to seize that simplicity with both hands. It had been in 1911, at the time when the railroad engineers had come to hire him, promising to pay fifty-five rubles plus overtime.

Ustinov had purposely invited the engineers to spend the night in the haybarn, and in the morning he went to see them to expound upon a theory he had. They were educated and intelligent people who treated Ustinov well and had a high opinion of him. Just awakened, the engineers were lying on the fresh hay and drinking fresh morning milk from cool clay mugs.

"May I know your Christian name and patronymic?" Ustinov asked the senior engineer. "Last night we discussed the theodolite and other subjects, but I never learned your name. That's not proper!"

"You and I have the same name!" the engineer answered, stretching out on the hay. "My name is Nikolai. And my patronymic is Sigismundovich. Do you understand?"

Ustinov didn't understand at all, but he nodded in agreement.

"What topic would you like me to discuss?" the senior man wanted to know.

"Well, you see," Ustinov said happily, "I do have some ideas about things! It's like this: there is a figure called a circle . . . "

"There is indeed!" agreed Nikolai Sigismundovich.

"And in nature there are also little sticks, some quite long."

"Straight lines . . . ," the senior engineer suggested.

"But sometimes they are too short to be straight lines. You can't even see them."

"Then they are points . . . "

"They're not points, and they're not straight lines, but more like tiny little sticks."

"Well now. And so?"

"So this, Mr. Senior Engineer: besides these little circles and sticks—let's say they really are straight lines—besides them, there's nothing else in the world!"

"That's quite a story!" the senior man said in surprise, setting his mug down on a dented plank of the hayloft floor. His toothless partner gaped at Ustinov.

"It only seems like a story at first! But if you look closely, it's the genuine truth and the way things are," Ustinov assured him. "It is, by God! Just take any old object, like this piece of straw here, or my finger. The whole thing is drawn with nothing but straight lines and curves. And what is a curve? It has to be a part of some circle! It might be huge, as big as the earth, or too small to see with your eye, but it's still a circle! Take the petal of a flower. It has not one, but many curves on it. That is, a part of one circle turns into part of another one, but still there's nothing else there but circles and lines, lines and circles! And that's how it is with everything in the whole world, dead and alive! Yes!"

"Yes?!"

"Yes!" Ustinov insisted.

"But what about steam? And smoke? They don't have any of your little circles and sticks, do they? Then how can they exist, Nikolai Levontyevich?"

"Steam and smoke and water, too, true enough, are made up only of points. But even they strive to become a figure, to become a cloud. But then I'll have something to say about them, about completely formless objects, a little later, if you will permit me, Nikolai Sikis . . . " Ustinov stumbled badly on the senior engineer's patronymic.

But the engineer smiled and said, "Well then! Go on!"

"Well, have you ever taken a good look at a barrel with hoops?"

"Yes, I've had the occasion."

"A barrel doesn't move within its hoop. Why? Because the barrel is a circle, and the hoop is a circle of almost the same size, of the same diameter, to speak correctly. But if the hoop becomes even the slightest bit larger than its barrel, then the barrel will start to roll around inside it. Then the barrel sees the hoop almost like a straight line, and a circle and a line always produce motion! You know, Mr. Senior Engineer, I wasn't the least bit surprised when I understood that the earth is round and endlessly circles the sun! That's the only way it can be: it's the same law and order of the movement of a circle along a straight line! Or even along a curved line, if its curve is too slight in relation to the object that is moving along it! In the same way, you could say that no straight line on earth can be too long and that every line bends and, little by little, becomes a curve. Every line tries to become a circle and to turn back on itself, that is, to close. This is the source of any movement on land, on water, or through the air, and of all other kinds of movement, even the movement of man from fetus to child, from child to adult. That is also a kind of circle."

"A model of the universe?"

"That's it, Nikolai Sikis . . . That's how learning shows in a man: the learned man sees the same thing as the uneducated man, but he can find just the right word for what he has seen, 'universe!' "

"Well, let's suppose it's so . . . But what about God? Where do you put God in your model of the universe, Nikolai Levontyevich?"

"Here's where: in the largest circle of all! The one that everything else fits into. The one that is so big, so huge, that it seems like a straight line to everything else on earth, so that everything else moves and repeats itself endlessly within that greatest of circles, in the birth of children from their parents, summer from spring, winter from fall, in the winds and waters and all manner of things . . . That's why there is no icon that shows the face of God, because He is the hugest and most boundless circle of all. There are icons for all the saints, but not for Him!"

Nikolai Sigismundovich, who till then had been dressed only in his snow-white undershirt and the white sheet that Domna had laid down for her guests, got up, took his uniform jacket from where it was hanging on a nail, slowly put it on, then turned to Ustinov.

"Fine! I give in! I'll pay you not fifty-five, but sixty rubles a month, plus overtime! Room and board included! I will, God bless you, since you're such a brainy and clever man! Are you satisfied now? Finally?"

Ustinov climbed down from the hayloft without saying a word, quickly and silently harnessed Morkoshka, and rode out of the yard to the fields. Squinting as he peered up at the round sun in the sky, in which roundness could also be seen, he rode along the country road and felt the truth of what he had said.

Well, of course, he had gotten pretty worked up back then in the now-so-distant year of 1911 when he had explained to Senior Railway Engineer Nikolai Sigismundovich how to use a theodolite to mark out a given angle to a location or to calculate the volume of a spoil bank. He had stuck his neck out even more in explaining the underlying principles of the whole wide world! Well, of course, the whole world was not made up only of little circles and sticks, and he had not really taken offense back then over the engineer's reaction to his theory. But all the same, the little circles and sticks did exist in some shape or form, no matter what the Sigismundoviches of the world thought about them! Ustinov had most likely been offended by his own frustrating limitations. Could he really be so far away from the truth, from the true arrangement of the world, from the most vital simplicity that held everything together, that he couldn't even stretch out his hand for it? Was he to get up earlier than everyone every day and see the sun come up, but never wonder how and why it rises?! He had reached out toward these questions, and in answer a five-ruble note had plopped into his palm—sixty rubles minus fifty-five leaves a fiver! But now things were entirely different: stretch out your hand for that same simple truth and the answer might not be a fiver in the palm, but a rifle butt in the head! Why?

If you could look into the order on which the whole world was founded, Ustinov believed that you could also live decently in that world according to that order . . . Now as he walked along Lake Street and looked at the familiar log houses, in which he knew every inhabitant, he had strong doubts for the first time. Was it really possible? Did people have the capacity, even a limited capacity, to live decently ordered lives? And over and over again, Ustinov longed for his circles and lines.

The Teeth of the Harrow

Winter brought its own law and order. Lake Lebyazhka was first hidden by a thin coating of ice, then frozen solid. The village of Lebyazhka was powdered with snow, and in a few days the branches of the trees in the forest were also covered with white. The whole forest, which until yesterday had been a dark blue, now truly became the White Wood. From one edge of the sky to the other, heavy white clouds thickened and spread over the forest and the neighboring area. The frost came. A chill breeze rustled and hummed across the frozen expanse of the lake. Sometimes it managed to reach the shore and the streets of Lebyazhka to pinch the children's ears, etch patterns on the windows, and wander about the yards, ruffling the feathers of the chickens, ducks, and geese. It would threaten a blizzard, but it lacked the strength to become a real storm and would flee back to the misty gray lake, leaving the village streets and yards in peace. Now the poultry that had been about to take cover would look around, crawl out into the light again, and soon begin to crow, quack, and honk as loudly as if it were spring. The young children, still growing and carefree, would burst outdoors with piercing shrieks, and forgetting the ear-pinching frost, pursue the retreating breeze on sleds and ice-chutes, racing down the bank and onto the lake.

Smoke hovered above the patchwork of houses, still bare of winter's smooth covering of snow, then straightened out and carried the aroma of freshly baked bread and hot cabbage soup up from the stoves into the clouds. The adult residents of Lebyazhka—many of them, anyway—waited anxiously for fierce frosts and and wild blizzards. They hoped that bad weather might block the path of Kolchak's forces. There was good reason for their anxiety and hope. A few of Kolchak's units, some only a handful of men, some with up to a hundred bayonets, would now and then break away from the cities and railroad stations and wander about the villages and settlements. In one village they had flogged and hanged people, in another they hanged and flogged people and confiscated property, and in a third they also mobilized all the young men. But the Lebyazhkans' hopes were not realized. Instead of bringing a real freeze, the weather took an unexpected and unpredictable turn. A thaw set in, it began to drizzle, and the fog spread from the lake to the shore. There was nothing left for people to do but console themselves: "Well, fine, if that's the way it is! Fine—it won't be so easy for Kolchak's men to move through the two hundred versts to the village of Lebyazhka in all this damp and wet and fog . . . And why would they want this faraway village anyway? It's completely useless to them, by God!" Consolation doesn't care what crutch it leans on. It just wants to lean on something, even if only briefly.

At this gloomy and stifling time, when there weren't even any pedestrians on the streets, Zinaida ran into Domna Ustinov in a little lane between two wattle fences. It was like a bad dream! To Zinaida it always seemed like that. She just could not accept the fact that Domna was an Ustinov, Nikola's wife, the mother of his children, the grandmother of his grandchildren. Because Zinaida didn't want any of this to be true, many times in her dreams it seemed that none of it was true and that the reality in which it was true was only a dream.

"No, no, may God strike me dead!" Zinaida thought every time she saw Domna, even at a distance. "This woman just can't live by the same laws as everyone else! She lives by some false foreign law! If she lived by the same laws as everyone else, she could never have become Nikola's wife! The mother of his children! The grandmother of his grandchildren!" But what really frustrated Zinaida was the impossibility of proving this fraud to anyone. She couldn't prove it to a single soul! Even if she were to shout, drown herself in Lake Lebyazhka, or set fire to the whole village, no one would begin to see, no one would believe it, no one would understand her! No one but she would ever notice this terrible mistake. People were born without arms and legs, born blind, deaf, dumb, insane, or disfigured; people were stillborn or doomed to a premature death in childhood; but such occurrences were always plain to see. Here, however, a mystery had been born that was unknown to everyone in the whole wide world except Zinaida Pankratov!

Domna stood on the narrow, partially snow-covered path, and Zinaida's bad dream went spinning off to some unknown place.

"How are you getting along, Zinaida Pa'lna?" she asked with interest.

"Fine . . . "

"Me, too!" She turned her face first to the right, then to the left. "See?"

Her complexion was very fair. Everyone in Lebyazhka gossiped about how Domna would never go to bed without first creaming her face with yogurt. Large, round, slightly protuberant eyes were set in that fair face. She was dressed in a black velvet jacket with white trim, a downy shawl, and brand-new felt boots. After one glance at her, Zinaida remembered that it was Sunday. She had forgotten what day it was, but Domna was Sunday from head to foot.

"And what brings you to our lakeside, Zinaida Pa'lna? Where are you off to?"

Zinaida had come to the lakeside for a very simple reason. Since that night when Venya Pankratov had appeared like a ghost, she had not seen Ustinov, and she needed to peek through the curtains in the windows of his house to assure herself that Nikolai Ustinov was still alive. The Ustinovs' house had two windows overlooking their yard, and these were visible through the wattle fence to the right. Although Zinaida did not look in that direction, Domna threw a quick glance at her own fence.

"Where are you off to?" she asked again.

"I'm just . . . out walking . . . "

Domna smiled and asked, "How is your husband, Kirill, getting along? I haven't heard anything about him for some time now."

"He's all right," Zinaida sighed heavily, "the same as always. He works on his porch and makes things out of wood. That's how Kirill is. It's true, there's not much to be heard about him . . . " Then suddenly she walked right up to Domna and demanded loudly, "And how is Ustinov? Our well-known Nikolai Levontyevich? Is he busy with all his toils and troubles?"

Another woman would have gotten angry, would not have been able to control herself, and would already be shouting, "You bitch! So you're fooling around with someone else's husband at night, are you?! Luring him into your house! Turning up under his windows to peek at him! For your own living husband and everyone else to see?!" Any other woman would have reacted like that. If an unfortunate widow would never be forgiven such fooling around in Lebyazhka, why should a married woman like Zinaida? But Domna didn't shout. Recoiling for just an instant, she looked angry, but just then a wet snowflake landed on each of her cheeks and melted, dripping down like tears, washing away any anger or any impulse to insult Zinaida, and the same Domna stood there as before, beautiful, nicely dressed, and still kind to all.

"But isn't Nikolai Levontyevich at your house almost every day with the Forest Commission?" she asked. "Can't you ask him how he is?"

"I can, but he hasn't been there with the Commission for three days . . . " Zinaida realized that there really was something in Domna that made her worthy of being the wife of Nikolai Ustinov. But this realization frightened Zinaida even more, and she regretted with all her heart that Domna was not shouting desperate insults.

"Nikolai Levontyevich always has toils and troubles," Domna explained, "in the Commission or at home. He's never lived a day of his life without toils and troubles, even when he was young, let alone as a grown man, a father, and a grandfather."

"Isn't living with such a man perhaps a little dull for you? With such a busy and serious man?"

Domna only smiled again and paused. Then she recalled, "Sometimes it was dull, sometimes it was! I didn't get to enjoy much of my youth with him. All our grandparents were living with us and took care of the kids and did a good job taking care of the livestock. So the two of us could have spent all our time enjoying holiday parties and games. But did that ever occur to Nikolai Levontyevich? Not in the least! If he wasn't out in the fields, he was sitting with a book in his hands or writing in a schoolboy's notebook. And that's all. Even on every holiday."

"So why did you marry such a dull man?"

Just how and why they were having this conversation was a mystery, but they were, and as quietly and calmly as before, as if she were talking to a close and much trusted friend, Domna answered, "My father, my late Papa, told me to, and so I married him . . . "

"You obeyed?"

"I obeyed. I understood what Papa told me. It would be pretty dull while I was young, but later things would make up for it."

"Have they?"

"Well, of course! After a year or two had passed, I took a liking to his habits. And I'm astonished now when I hear noise and swearing and drunkenness in someone's house, when I see the women's bruises or even witness a scandal! And when a man sends his wife out into the fields or out to the cattle while he crawls up above the stove and sleeps, I think it's a terrible shame! I'm used to having things different, to having things go well, and I know that Nikolai Levontyevich will never do anything to make them go bad!"

"An easy life—not a woman's life at all!"

"It's the most feminine life of all! And I tell you—I've earned it! All that came after Nikola settled down to be a peasant, one with status and respect, but what was he to begin with? There's nothing to remember about his youth—that's the sort of young man he was! You never saw or heard him among the other lads and eligible bachelors; all he ever had anything to do with was books! The girls didn't notice him, he was such a poor specimen then, and he didn't understand a thing about them either, which girls were nice and which weren't! A nice girl would be insulted by the idea of marrying such a fool. But I married him, thanks to my father! After that there were a few women who tried for the impossible, but it was like trying to bite your own elbow! It was too late! Berry-picking time was over!"

Suddenly Domna smiled and then even began to laugh, the way a wise woman would smile and laugh at a silly, good-for-nothing little girl. This was Domna in real life, not in a dream! Touching Zinaida's sleeve, she imperceptibly drew her along from the lane into the street, as she continued to reminisce about that "berry-picking time" when she had truly been the best catch in Lebyazhka and had never gone to a party without her high-heeled yellow lace-up shoes. This was at the same time that for a bottle of vodka and a pair of used boots Zinaida's father would have given her away to anyone who wanted her and that she had carried a sharp little knife in her boot top to fend off unwanted men.

So that was the opinion of Lebyazhka's most marriageable maiden, of Domna with her high heels. For her, Nikola Ustinov had been a poor specimen of a bridegroom. She had accepted him unwillingly, sacrificing herself, almost out of pity! She hadn't even noticed how many maidens had eyes only for him and how much the other lads respected him. Zinaida hadn't had the courage to think of him as a bridegroom. She hadn't dared! So when Ivan Ivanovich had asked her which of the lads she liked, she had told herself that her tongue would shrivel up the very moment she said, "Nikola Ustinov . . . " And so she hadn't said it.

And now they were walking quietly side by side, the two most beautiful women in Lebyazhka. Just like dear friends—you couldn't pry them apart! It was as if one of them still stood in her yellow high-heeled shoes just as she had as a maiden, having never once stumbled in her life, having never suffered any misfortune. The other knew about those high heels only from a distance and from rumor. Nevertheless, the two of them were now walking side by side as equals, causing wonder on the Sunday street that, though quiet and almost empty, was all eyes. But Zinaida did not continue to behave like a barefoot, silent, silly little girl. She clasped her friend's arm and looked cheerfully into her face.

"Why don't you take me to your house, Domna! I've never been a guest in the Ustinov home!"

Domna stumbled. They silently passed a few more streets, and there it was—the Ustinovs' fence and gate. Domna tugged on the clean, knotted, tanned leather strap attached to the gate-latch, and there it was—the yard, the porch, the house of Nikolai Ustinov! The man lived the same as everyone else. In the kitchen Zinaida saw a large table in the corner under the icons, a tile stove with deep-blue trim on the top, and a bright yellow sleeping bench above it. She glanced into the main room, which was clean but, of course, not like that room at her own house where the Commission was meeting. At her house there were potted ficus plants, a chest of drawers, a table, and that's all, but here the room was strewn with all sorts of clutter. A pile of children's clothing was lying right on the floor, and a cradle hung from the ceiling. She caught a glimpse of babies with bare tummies, Ustinov's grandkids, and between them their mother, Ustinov's daughter Ksenia, barefoot, freckled, and pregnant, waving her arm as she hastily sewed a torn collar on a tattered fur jacket. When she saw Zinaida, she nodded but said nothing, expressing her surprise only to herself. What was Zinaida Pankratov doing in their home? Ksenia was not a bad-tempered woman at all, but she was a bit too simple, and she swallowed parts of her words when she talked. A little farther on in a tiny little room was something you wouldn't see in Lebyazhka homes, except at Ustinov's and Samorukov's and the homes of two or three others. There was a glass-doored cabinet filled with books.

When she was a girl back in Russia, Zinaida had seen more books than this, not in a peasant's house, but in a gentleman's home, a manor house, where she had been a housemaid. She fetched firewood and water, washed the floors, and also caught the eye of the young gentleman of the house. Just returned to his parents' house from boarding school, the young man immediately began to teach her to read and write. At first he read out loud to her, and then he made her read the same books. The almost endless number of books had amazed her. They completely covered two walls, book against book, without even a fingerbreadth of space between them. Zinaida had been a willing and capable pupil. She remembered the day when she realized that a person might have enough free time to read all those books along the two walls from corner to corner and from floor to ceiling. But just at that moment the young gentleman teacher laid hands on his pupil. He didn't touch her gently, but right away grabbed her breasts. Flushed and sweating, he shoved her down on a mahogany divan with two open-eyed lions carved on its high back. But the pupil wasn't at a loss for long. The next moment the teacher was lying on the floor, his nose wet and red, and his feet up in the air under the perplexed gaze of the lions.

That had been the end of Zinaida's schooling, and her life in Russia was also soon over. That autumn she and her older brother convinced their parents to move on. Hitching up their little mare, they set out from Tambov Gubernia for Tomsk Gubernia, for Siberia. The parents rode on the cart with brother and sister walking alongside. If her brother had not fallen sick and died, emaciated by dysentery, their journey would most likely have brought them to someplace entirely different, some fairy-tale settlement full of kind people. Zinaida had never taken offense at Lebyazhka or complained about it, but she felt grateful to those other people, the ones they had not reached because of her brother's death, the ones she had never seen. She dreamed about them for a long time. They called her to come to their own, unknown land, and she regretted that while she was still in her native Tambov Gubernia, working in that gentleman's house, she had not managed to read something, in one of those beautiful books with gold titles, about these little-known people. She should have read something and learned a bit about them for the life yet to come.

Now, in the Ustinov house, close to the rows of books behind the glass doors of the cabinet, Zinaida felt this unfulfilled desire and her still greater sense of loss pressing on her heart. Greatly offended, she sighed in envy of Ustinov. In his books he had found and understood everything that she had been unable to! "Why does he hide what he knows?" Zinaida wondered. "Couldn't he make at least this one sacrifice? Couldn't he tell me what he has read in his books? Would he be any worse off for that? He must talk to Domna about it. To her it's of no interest, but he must tell her all the same! He's the one I should have learned from! And if this teacher had given free rein to his hands, I would not have pushed him away."

Meanwhile Domna had taken off her shawl and jacket, removed her black felt boots, wet from the unseasonable damp, and tossed them onto the stove to dry. "Take your things off," she said to her guest, but as her guest stood with her coat on, still looking at the cabinet of books, Domna looked at them, too. "Let him read, God bless him!" she said. "Another woman would have burned all these books long ago so her man would stop playing like a child, but I don't care. It's a waste of money, but it saves arguments. I have enough on my hands scolding my son-in-law Shurka! Because of him alone, there are more angry words than you can count. No, let the books be! He can't get into much trouble from them! Take off your coat, Zinaida!"

Domna's guest sat on the bench by the stove and took off her boots. Just as she opened the door to toss them out into the entryway, Barin jumped through the door into the kitchen.

"Shoo! Where are you going, beast?" Domna shouted angrily at Barin. "Don't you know better than to come into the house? Shoo! Get out of here!" She grabbed an oven fork from under the stove, but Barin didn't retreat one step. He lay on the floor and began to tremble. Shaking his long body, all covered with dead pine needles from the forest, he raised his head and let out a plaintive, fearful howl.

"Where is the master of the house?" Zinaida immediately asked. "Is Nikolai Levontyevich at home?" When she had entered the Ustinov house, she had been terribly afraid of running into him. She didn't know what to say to him or how to greet him. But now she was afraid of something else entirely. Her fear was something she still did not understand, but it was powerful and chilling. "Where is he? Where is your man?"

Domna was not apprehensive of any misfortune at all. She blushed with embarrassment for her guest who, though uninvited, was a guest all the same. She turned away and again began to threaten Barin with the oven fork.

"The man of the house, Levontyevich, is in the forest!" Her answer was annoyed. "If you really need to know, he's been in the forest since early morning. He left on horseback." Barin howled without pause, and Domna shouted at him again. "Get the hell out of here, you good-for-nothing! Really! I'll smack you in the mouth with this fork, by God! You don't believe me?"

Whether he believed it or not, all Barin did was bare his teeth and shake his head. Wet all over, he had ice on his tail and ears; Zinaida bent over Barin and grabbed a handful of his fur where it was the most conspicuously stained. Her fingers came away wet with something brown and smelly.

"Blood! It's blood!"

"Well, so what? Aren't there enough places where the damn mutt could get himself scratched? He's a meek one, but once he up and tore the ear clean off another dog even though it was a full head taller than him! Just tore it right off!"

"It's not Barin's blood! He's not wounded!"

"And whose is it? Do you know? Tell me, whose blood is it?"

"It might be Nikolai Levontyevich's . . . ," Zinaida answered, sobbing and covering her face with her hand.

Then Domna lost her temper completely. "That's just what you'd like, isn't it, my oh-so-welcome guest, my proud beauty?!" Domna threw the oven fork in the corner, kicked Barin, turned, and went into the main room. "Nothing bad will happen to Nikolai Levontyevich! He fought through the whole war and came back to me alive and in one piece! He heard my prayers and came back, and now nothing more will happen to him! So I don't believe you! I don't believe wicked and envious people! I won't believe anyone!"

One after another the wet snowflakes tapped against the windowpane as if some invisible person wanted to come into the house and was cautiously and timidly fingering the glass. But Zinaida had a feeling that somewhere out in the dense forest, where there was none of this caution, something bad had happened. There ruled a hand that was cruel to all, blind and deaf to any blood and pain. Still holding her needle, Ksenia came running in from the main room. Frightened and pale, she believed Zinaida.

"Something te'ble has happened! The dog is telling us something—something has happened to Papa!"

Zinaida grabbed her shoulders and asked, "Who was Nikolai Levontyevich riding, and when did he leave?"

"He was on Mo'koshka He's a good ho'se, but a lot of things could have happened. It's the t'uth!" Ksenia couldn't pronounce the sound *r,* but she spoke quickly, trembling all over, her eyes fixed on Barin, who was already standing up on his hind legs, beating on the door with his front paws, calling them to follow him.

"I'm coming!" Zinaida promised him. "I'm coming! Ksenia!" she shouted sternly, as if she were the mistress of the house. "Run out into the yard, harness a horse, and we'll go! Barin will lead us!"

"But we don't have a ho'se now, Zinaida Pal'na! We don't have one! Papa left on Mo'koshka, and my husband Sh-u-u'ka went to the ma'ket with Solovko and the new one, Sh-u-u'ka went to the ma-a'ket, and G'unya's lame . . . We don't have none, what'll we do? For the life of us, what'll we do?!"

And with these words Ksenia grabbed her huge belly and began to wail at the top of her voice. She kept trying to explain something to Zinaida through her wailing and tears, but Zinaida was no longer listening. She had gone running out of the Ustinov house.

When Kirill went out onto the back porch a half hour or so later, he saw that his wife was frantically harnessing their piebald mare as a dog jumped and howled impatiently beside her. He took a closer look and saw that it was Ustinov's dog, Barin.

"And where are you going?" Kirill asked his wife timidly. "It'll be getting dark soon!"

"It can't be helped!" she answered. "It has to be done! Open the gate for me!"

▲▲▲

Before daylight that Sunday morning, Ustinov had saddled Morkoshka, strapped on a day's provisions, grabbed his rifle, called to Barin, who was rushing around whining impatiently like a puppy and didn't need to be called, and set out for the forest. Ustinov just had to get away from all the confusion of the past few days. How good it would have been to plow for a while, to exhaust himself in his furrows till he lost consciousness! How insistently his arms and legs were begging for it, out in the fields how joyfully his head would have emptied of all this endless bother, how confidently the blood would have pounded in his temples, how secure in the purpose of its life-giving labor! All over his body his skin would have itched and ached, echoing the busy, tired buzzing of all his organs and glands! Life was sweet, even if sometimes you stupidly called it something else. But the time of plowing was now walled off by winter, a winter with some sort of strange, surprisingly late thaw.

He went to look at the birch grove to see if it was fit for the tar industry about which the Commission had spoken so long ago but done nothing. The stand of birches was large and impressive, their bark glistening wet from the recent weather. The birch trees did not suspect that if the right calculations took place in Ustinov's head at that moment, their bark would be stripped off in the spring and used to distill tar. Then from the ground up to their first branches, they would stand reddish and naked, and instead of turning green with thick, impenetrable foliage as they should, they would greet the lushness of May and June and then the summer with only tiny, grayish little leaves. But to the birches' good fortune, Ustinov decided that the grove was a bit on the small side and the total reserve of bark not large enough. The tar would be of low quality, good only for gluing pots. There would barely be enough bark to manufacture tar soap in case the current situation continued into the spring and still no one had any needles, factory goods, or soap for sale. It looked as if that's how it would be, and no change for the better could be expected from anywhere or anyone. Admiral Kolchak would hardly be able to see that needles, matches, and soap were available and a man didn't have to rack his brains for them.

How had he come to power? And why? Whenever the peasants discussed how one government was being overthrown and another taking its place, Ustinov had tried to keep his mouth shut. He felt that the peasants were all making judgments in ignorance because they believed that power could be divided up like money. A thousand is counted out to one person, ten thousand to another, and a million to the liveliest. It was as simple as that. But there should be something else in power, the desire to improve things for people, to serve them, not oneself, with faith and truth. Peter I not only deposed his sister Sofia but stuck her in a dungeon as well. That was true, but when he later served in battle as a common gunner and worked as a shipbuilder, was he doing that for his own monetary gain? Ustinov, in contrast to the others, believed with all his heart that a people chooses a government for practical reasons, for gunnery and carpentry, for moving forward to meet the people's expectations. Each time a new government was declared, he would think, wearily, but almost with full confidence, "This one will do it! At long last! The people have lived to see the day, after all!"

But Kolchak, who had come to power very much like a pig, gave him no cause for hope at all. "Oh, you bastards, you're eating without me, are you?! Well, then give me the biggest piece! Everything is mine, and the others can have what's left!" You couldn't put it any other way since the man had arrested half of the ministers himself, and killed some of them to boot, and forced the rest of them to promote him to Supreme Commander—from Vice Admiral to Admiral, from Commander in Chief to Supreme Commander. Then on the spot he had issued a decree that all the people were to subordinate themselves to him, the Admiral, Commander, and Ruler, and these two things were placed in the newspaper side by side on the same quarter page, and his henchmen had added that everyone who loves his homeland should submit to the situation without making a fuss! Couldn't he at least have taken his time a bit and stretched the business out to two newspapers?! Couldn't he at least have specified his own punishments if he failed to carry out all the promises and oaths he had made when he took power into his own hands? No, he didn't have a word to say about that, just about submitting to him without a fuss: love your homeland, that is, Kolchak, and that's all. That the homeland had endured for thousands of years and might be foolish for only a moment meant nothing to him!

When you are riding all alone in the forest, surrounded by hoarfrost and mist, and there isn't a single living soul anywhere around, it is very simple to call anyone you want to account. So Ustinov called on Kolchak and asked him, "Aren't you ashamed of yourself? Can't you do anything like a human being?"

"It's beyond your comprehension!" answered Kolchak. "It's clear to me what needed to be done! Such are the circumstances!"

"Fine! If it's beyond my comprehension, then that's that!" Ustinov agreed, although silently he decided not to abandon the question completely. "And true enough, there are, of course, circumstances. There can be no life without circumstances! Personally, I've never been in a position of power, I don't know anything about it, but I do have a question: why did you need to take power at this particular moment?"

"Because it was necessary!"

"That doesn't mean a thing! To this day the Siberian Government and you, the Minister of War, have insisted to the people that it was necessary to continue the war with Germany, that for the good of Russia the alliance with the Entente must not be betrayed when so much blood had been spilled already! To this day you, Kolchak, have accused me, Ustinov: 'Ustinov deserted from the front, and I, Kolchak, have had to settle everything, to show my own nobility and honor!' Isn't that right?"

"Precisely!" Kolchak nodded.

"But look what's happened now—Germany capitulated just a week and a half or so ago! All over the world soldiers and their wives, parents and little children sighed with tears of joy and embraced each other. The Lebyazhka veterans sighed, too, even though they had left the war long ago. There is no joy for anyone in war. There are only tears, shame, and misfortune for victor and vanquished alike. This was especially true because the mustachioed Kaiser Wilhelm, who loved to be photographed with helmet and saber, didn't want to abdicate and so continued the war for a few more months, sending hundreds of thousands more of his own soldiers and the enemy's into the fraternal fellowship of the grave . . . But one way or another, the shameful war is over. The question is—why do you need power after that? Why do you need to be an Admiral, or a Commander in Chief, or a Supreme Ruler?"

"To save the Motherland! From the Bolsheviks. To save her for your sake, Ustinov. But you lack the social consciousness to understand that, Ustinov! That's the whole point!"

"So you have all the social consciousness, do you, since you are thrusting it upon one and all in such great quantity?"

"Yes, I do!" answered Kolchak.

"But then why did you come to power so irresponsibly, in such an unseemly and ignoble way? Where was your sense of social responsibility when you took power? No, I don't believe you! What sort of noble savior of the Motherland can you be after that? When Germany capitulated and the war ended, a stone fell from my soul, but you replaced it with another one almost heavier than the first!"

"Time will tell, Ustinov! You will thank me yet! Just wait!"

"Nothing is as simple as making promises, not just to some Pyotr or Ivan, but to all the people at once! And then there are always circumstances! Maybe today, right this minute, you'll summon the landowners back to Russia?! And draft the Siberian peasants into your army so they can fight with the Russian peasants for those landowners?! Is that social consciousness? Is it? No one except the Supreme Commander himself could dream up social consciousness like that! Everyone else would be ashamed!"

Kolchak, riding alongside Ustinov on a gray dappled horse, puffed out his chest and replied, "But I am a hero! I'm all covered with medals for service to the Motherland!" His elegant nose was thrust forward, and his hand rested on his gold dagger. "Can't you see?! Or do you doubt me?! Don't you believe your own eyes?"

"I don't doubt it at all! And I always believe my own eyes! A hero—that's just fine and dandy! But why spoil such splendor with supreme authority? I know you've commanded sailors, but what about peasants? You understand the landowners, but what about the peasants? We could have turned one of our own heroes, Lieutenant R. G. Smirnovsky, into a Kolchak, maybe not a great one, but one of our own, a Lebyazhkan one. But he had the wisdom and the nobility not to accept such a role! He knows what a peasant is and didn't let medals make him deny his peasant blood!"

No, the two of them could not come to an understanding, and Kolchak on his dappled horse angrily disappeared into the bushes by the road. At that very moment Barin leapt out from the same spot with his tongue hanging out, his eyes fixed on Ustinov, his bark cross and scolding.

"Really, Ustinov, have you lost your wits completely? There are quail and grouse with wet feathers everywhere, heavy on the takeoff—you can shoot them on the ground or on the wing. You do have your rifle with you, don't you? Or have you gone crazy already? Phooey! I'll run away wherever I please! I'm fed up with you, you neglectful and good-for-nothing master!"

Clumsy under his stiff rain gear, Ustinov waved his arm angrily at both Kolchak and Barin, then turned Morkoshka toward none other than Syoma Prutovskikh's place. He rode two and a quarter versts—he knew distances there down to the sazhen—along the narrow clear-cut that had not been trimmed for some time and was overgrown with pines and birch saplings. At benchmark No. 37 he turned left, almost due north, along another clear-cut, passed the beautiful, dense Brusnichny water meadow with its many-boughed, moss-covered pines, and was soon at the little cabin of Syoma Prutovskikh.

Prutovskikh's forestry service as a warden and later as a guard had begun not only before the birth of Nikolai Ustinov, but maybe even before the time of his father, Levonty Yegoryevich Ustinov, and continued some seventy years. No one knew for certain because when Syoma Prutovskikh passed the age of fifty he not only stopped showing his age but didn't seem to change in appearance at all. He never had any trouble with his teeth, his hearing, or his vision, and when people asked him how old he was, he would answer, "However many years I've lived, that's how old I am!"

Syoma followed his own way of life. He neither plowed nor sowed, but fed himself from the forest on mushrooms, berries, tubers, fish from the small forest lakes, and, once in a great while, wild fowl and rabbit. He got married from time to time, but his spouses didn't last long. At these times of family life he had a house in Lebyazhka, at the very edge of the village, at the edge of the forest. He would show up there for a day, or perhaps a week, repair his outbuildings, trade wild honey for bread, and return to his cabin beyond the Brusnichny water meadow to lead a life of solitude. However, you could catch sight of Syoma Prutovskikh at any time of the day or night. All you had to do was go into whatever corner of the forest you cared to, to the most distant section, and knock your axe against a tree a dozen times or so, and there would be Syoma, asking, "Well? What might we be doing with you now, eh?"

The Lebyazhkans had tried chopping in three or four different sections at the same time, but even that didn't help. Syoma would catch one person in the act and track down another. As soon as a man hid the freshly cut timber beneath a fence and scattered straw or garden waste over it, the next day Syoma would be sitting on that very timber, squinting at the sky and calling to the woodcutter, "Well? What might we be doing with you now, eh?" And then you just had to wait to see what else Syoma would say. If he squinted, sighed, and said, "You're a good person . . . A fine man . . . ," no misfortune would follow. But if Syoma said, "A bad man! I know what kind you are!" and looked down, the affair could wind up not only with a fine but even with prison. And there were times when it did just that. With his cockaded cap on his head and his badge on his chest, Syoma would appear in court in a frock coat and the riding britches of a uniform. Even the officials would be surprised at how sternly and strictly he gave testimony, accusing the woodcutter under the strictest paragraph of the Statutes Concerning Forest Holdings of His Imperial Majesty's Treasury.

Once Syoma had sent one of the Lebyazhka peasants off to prison, and for a long time, two years. Lebyazhka could not recall such a thing happening in all its history and decided to hurt Syoma, maybe even break his neck. Syoma showed up at Ivan Ivanovich Samorukov's house.

"It's not the Tsar that I'm protecting," he told him. "The Tsar's far away. I protect the forest, which is close by. If the people want to do me in, let them! But just think first: I've gotten along with these people and their fathers before them, but when they put some young and nimble forest guard in my place, how will he run things when he doesn't know anyone, doesn't know who among you is good and who is bad?"

Ivan Ivanovich gathered the old men to discuss the situation, and they decided that whoever touched Syoma was Lebyazhka's enemy. And then it happened that a village constable came to arrest the same man that Syoma had sent to prison. The man had bought a stolen horse and rebranded it. Although he had known full well that it was stolen, he had been seduced by the low price. The Lebyazhkans had never suffered such a shame before. That peasant had turned out to be a bad man after all, and Syoma had seen it as if in a crystal ball!

Syoma lived all alone in the forest and would sleep wherever night found him, just as long as there were pine branches above his head. He avoided people, didn't accept the order of their lives, didn't pray to God, and didn't comb his beard. Rabbits and squirrels, elk and bears were his family and friends, but man was almost an alien creature to him. But even so, he could accurately judge people's character. If he thought someone was a good person, then that's what he was, and if he thought someone was a bad person, then he was bad in every way! Ustinov was amazed more than once. Could it be true that you didn't have to live among people to know them, that you could live like a hermit in a cave or a bear's den and judge from your lair what was bad, what was unnatural in a man? Syoma did not reveal his secret. He liked Ustinov and was always ready to talk with him about bugs and beetles and forest inspection, but when the conversation turned to people, he would fall silent. There was a great mystery in human existence, and Syoma knew something about this mystery, but he didn't want to confide in anyone.

"Do you ever think about dying, Syoma?" Ustinov had once asked him.

"That has nothing to do with me . . . ," he answered.

"What do you mean?"

"This world or the next—it makes no difference to me. They're both the same to me."

"And what do you know about heaven or hell? Are they the same, too?"

"Exactly the same! Either here or there, I'm always the same no matter where I be! And if that's the way it is, it don't matter to me where I am and what's around me."

"God might judge things differently."

"Why would He? If He's made me this way for all my life and kept me alive all this time, why would He be changing His mind?"

More than once Ustinov had wanted to return to that conversation and had waited for a chance to do so, but then things took a different turn. Syoma caught some woodcutter who said to him, "It's easy for you to fine a peasant, Prutovskikh. You know in advance that there's neither heaven nor hell waiting for you! You'll have the same job in the afterlife—you'll collect the stiffest fines you can from the dead souls!" Ustinov was to blame for this misinterpretation. He had told his wife about his conversation with Syoma Prutovskikh, she had told the other women, and Syoma's words had come back to him, only not with the meaning he had intended. Domna might not have done it accidentally. She despised both Syoma and Kudeyar and said that they were frightening people. After this incident Syoma not only wouldn't talk with Ustinov but often wouldn't even say hello to him. When they ran into one another, he would lower his shaggy head, hide his eyes, move a shoulder slightly, and that was all. You could take it any way you wished, as hello or good-bye. Because Ustinov and Syoma had not finished their conversation, had not touched upon what was most important, Ustinov very much regretted the way things had turned out. A few more years went by and, just before the war, Syoma, who had seemed immortal, died nevertheless.

He died under a pine tree where he had happened to stop for the night. When his horse appeared in the village with its saddle still on, everyone understood that some misfortune had befallen Syoma Prutovskikh. But because it was during harvest time, a time of heavy, hot labor, no one was ready to go off looking for him right away. When they did find him, his corpse was already old and putrid. A police inspector came with a doctor, looked from a safe distance at what had once been Syoma, and said, "He died a natural death. Have a funeral and bury him!" And so they did. But many things could have happened—maybe his death was a natural one, and maybe not.

Syoma was no more, and a new forest guard came, one to whom you could slip a few rubles and then cut wood all night with two axes and a saw. After the Stolypin Reforms, rich peasants began to settle out on their freeholds and needed Lord only knows how much timber for construction, what the state allotted to them and much more besides. Grishka Sukhikh was one of these freeholders, and where there are the likes of Grishka Sukhikh, there can be no work or life for a Syoma Prutovskikh. Syoma would not have called a single one of that lot a good person. For him, every last one of them would have been bad.

And there it stood—Syoma's broken-down little cabin. It was tiny, but then it was built from logs only an arshin in length, with one little window and no entryway, but with a tin stovepipe. The door was held shut by a huge log that must have weighed twenty poods. Syoma didn't use locks; when he went out he would just prop the door shut with a log.

When they found Syoma dead, the police inspector ordered them to enter the cabin and take a look to see what was there. But they didn't want to mess with the door prop and crawled into the cabin through the little window. Ustinov didn't even go inside. The police inspector had chosen him as an official witness, and even though it was the harvest, the time of the heaviest labor, Ustinov had agreed. He wanted to have one more look at everything that touched upon Syoma's life and death. In the cabin there turned out to be dried berries, an icon with a map of the forest preserve and various notes under it, a whole pile of medals for long and exemplary service, some hunting supplies, and a chest with some clothes. Ustinov watched through the window and reported all the objects to the inspector, who wrote them down in the report. But Syoma's death was just as silent as his life had been, and Ustinov discovered nothing, not a word, not a sound. The man had been himself. When he lived, he existed, and when he died, he was no more. He had taken all trace of himself with him. There is much that people carry away with themselves into the unknown.

Now, many years later, Ustinov felt that of all the strange qualities of human beings, Syoma Prutovskikh's strangeness was closer to him than anyone else's. It suited him and pleased him. Perhaps it was only because Syoma never forced it on anyone. On the contrary, it had to be drawn out of him, one word, one glance, one sigh at a time. There was nothing left for Ustinov to do but to try to remember everything they had said to each other.

"Just look, Nikola," Syoma would whisper with round, wide-open eyes, "just look—a pine seed so small that you could fit two dozen of them into a newborn's nostril just falls to the ground, and a tree twenty sazhens tall grows from it! How does that happen? How many months does an animal live inside its mother, feeding off her? But what happens here? What kind of motherhood does the earth have? What kind of fertility?"

"There must be something written about that in some book, Syoma!" Ustinov would answer. "It must be written down somewhere!"

"No, it isn't!" Syoma would say, waving his hand and his beard. "If it was, the whole world would know about it, but no one knows this mystery! No one! I might know more about it than anyone else. I know about life firsthand, so let whatever the others dream up secondhand—and thirdhand and tenthhand, all their other clever ideas—let them put those in their books!"

Now, riding along the clear-cut and remembering Syoma, Ustinov looked at those twenty-sazhen-tall pines and was amazed by how they had not only grown out of tiny little seeds, but had also brought themselves to completion. That is, they had everything—a trunk, branches, and as many pine needles as necessary. Once it gets started, nature, unlike man, knows how to bring its business to a successful conclusion, and so on the very crown of the pine tree it puts out one more little green shoot. A tree may be ancient, but its treetop is like a nursing baby. The tree lives its life, not in itself, but in this infancy, is pulled upward by it, begins with it, and dies with it. That new growth will die, and the dry-topped pine will already be beyond saving. It cannot evade death, no matter how powerful, beautiful, or tall it may be, no matter how widely it has flung out its lower branches, no matter what bright foliage it may be wearing. It dies, not from its ancient roots, forever hidden in darkness, where death would not be seen, but from its youth, raised high above everything else. It should have persuaded its lower branches not to keep the earth's juices for themselves but to let them up to the top, to that bright bit of green that lives almost in the sky itself and draws the whole life of the pine—needles, branches, trunk, roots—toward itself. But the beautiful lower branches with their many boughs, like tree trunks themselves except for growing horizontally instead of perpendicularly, must have been slow-witted and careless, and so the top of the pine was already dry, which meant that its death had begun. That's just how simple it was to push your life in the wrong direction, to mistake death for life . . .

Night and day, all his life, Syoma Prutovskikh had served this kingdom of pines, the kingdom of the White Wood, and had taught others to serve. If the wood had truly become a thing of the people, a forest for everyone, couldn't Syoma have immersed himself in his work and perhaps never died? But transferring the White Wood from the Tsar's ownership into the hands of the people was now turning out to be a slow, clumsy, even stupid process. When all the soldiers in the regiments, divisions, and armies threw their caps into the air and proclaimed the power and property of the people instead of the Tsar's, the thing seemed done once and for all. But now, two years later, no one knew which way everything had gone, forward or backward. Backward, it seemed . . .

But Ustinov didn't visit Syoma's little cabin. He would have had to crawl in through the window; he'd have busted a gut trying to get that log away from the door, a motionless sentry put on duty by Syoma Prutovskikh. Let it just stay there and stand guard over the empty dwelling. But even though Ustinov didn't visit the cabin, he had set out for the forest because of Syoma. It was always that way—if you remembered Syoma, you wanted to go into the forest, and if you went into the forest, you'd remember Syoma. Just as he had been a man of the forest, the forest, the White Wood, was human, but you wouldn't notice this human world of wood and pine needles while sitting at the table with the Commission. You could see it and understand it only in the forest itself. Would Ustinov ever discover whether Syoma had died a natural death? It had happened so long ago that time had faded the event to a colorless gray, like that great block of rotting wood propped against the door.

The Lebyazhkans were full of mysteries, beliefs, and legends about the White Wood. One of these legends was a tale that was like Ustinov's relative, already part of his family, for it told the story of the Poluvyatsky maiden Domna.

▲▲▲

If you count carefully, there were six unmarried women among the Poluvyatsky settlers, but only five maidens: Domna had been betrothed and given in marriage not long before the Kerzhaks returned from beyond the Baikal Sea to settle on the green hill between the lake and the forest. She had married one of the Poluvyatsky lads, but he had disappeared. He went away on a long journey hauling freight and never returned. No one knew where his life had led, what wind had carried it away. What was Domna to do now? Was she married or free? Was she still a wife or a prospective bride? Was she to love someone or to wear the black of mourning? Her spouse had disappeared without a trace, but what if he were to reappear, full of love for her? Has that kind of thing ever happened?

And then, as if to make things worse, everything was turned topsy-turvy. The Poluvyatsky maidens began to wear paths over to the Kerzhak side, charming the lads there, tempting and attracting them; but, without even being asked, a Kerzhak lad came to stand under Domna's window. The only husbandly chore Domna's lost husband had managed to complete was building a little cabin with a single little window. The Kerzhak lad came and stood under this window from morning till night, and sometimes all night, too, trembling with embarrassment as he stood and stared at the unadorned little window. What was Filipp, the young Kerzhak, silently waiting for? Not knowing whether Domna was a wife or a widow, was he too shy to utter a single word? Or was he waiting for her husband, to be sure that he was really gone?

The whole Kerzhak side was in a mad uproar over Filipp's behavior. How could he behave like this?! It was a bad business! Either the Kerzhak lads were being seduced, or one of them refused to walk away from a widow's house and stood in front of it as if bewitched! At least the other lads were choosing maidens who were chaste, even if they adhered to an evil faith, but Filipp was choosing a widow who had been married in a demonic ceremony and possessed by a stranger! There was a difference! Besides that, the widow was a few years older than Filipp. And was she really a widow, after all? What if her lawfully wedded husband were to return? The Kerzhaks had reason to hesitate, and the Poluvyatsky side also kept their distance. "What will be will be," they said, "but we won't have anything to do with it!"

And then someone decided to play a trick on Domna and started the rumor that someone had seen her spouse somewhere, at the Demidov factory, or maybe in the army. He was alive and well, they said, and had asked them to give his regards to his countrymen and tell his wife to behave herself and wait for him. He was sure to come home, though it might not be any time soon. When the rumor reached the lad Filipp, the expression on his face changed, and he deserted his post. He was no longer seen under Domna's window. When the rumor reached Domnushka as well, she did not open her door or shutters for many days. She sat locked inside, and no one knew if she was alive or dead. Finally she opened her door and went running in tears to Filipp to beg him to come stand under her window.

"What for?" Filipp asked. "You're a married woman! Go wait for your own husband!"

"But I can't wait all by myself!" replied Domna, bursting into tears again. "If you await my fate with me, then I will wait; but if I am all alone, I have no fate, sweet or bitter, married or widowed, none at all! I won't live a week without you standing there! Save me! Stand beside me just a year longer! Wait for me, and I will wait, I'll be able to do it then!"

How she begged!

Time passed. The former Poluvyatsky maidens forgot how they had once trampled paths over to the Kerzhak side and how they had enticed their bridegrooms. They had one baby after another, some two, some three, and Lizaveta, who had married Ilyukha with the stone eye, managed to bring even four babies into the world. There was no longer a Kerzhak side or a Poluvyatsky side, for they had come together on the green hill. But Filipp still stood at his post every day. Well, since that's the way it was, since there was no longer this side or that side, someone thought of telling the truth to Filipp and Domna.

"It was only a rumor! It was made up on purpose! Go ahead and get married now! Look how many years have passed! Now we wish you only peace and love!"

"What?" Domna and Filipp asked. "If it wasn't true, who started that rumor? Who made it up?"

"Everyone's forgotten who it was! It was a long time ago!"

"Then why did everyone believe this rumor, if it wasn't true?!"

"But no one believed it! No one! Only the two of you! Everyone else knew that it was just a rumor! Now you forget about it, too! When will the wedding be? Will you invite guests and your kinfolk?"

"We won't be inviting any guests or kinfolk! We don't have any friends or kinfolk, only betrayers!"

"But then what will you do?"

"We will leave you! We'll go far away, and forever! We'll run away from the whole world!"

"But where will you go? Isn't the world the same all over?"

"We'll go where everything is different, where the water is green even without the grass, where the grass and the white pine forest stand without water, and where people and deception do not live together!"

And so, with their few belongings tied up in bundles, they left, and you couldn't tell whether they were husband and wife, lovers, or a monk and a nun.

They went away and were forgotten, but many years later a Lebyazhka man happened to go into the forest and found a sod hut in which there were human bones and some clothing. People wondered whose dwelling it might have been, and then they figured it out—it was Filipp and Domnushka's bones, their clothing, and the crucifixes they had worn under their clothes! Then they remembered that Filipp and Domna had said they were going to the White Wood, as bright and transparent as the water in the lake. That's where the White Wood was, it turned out, no more than thirty versts from Lebyazhka. And so it is always—you think that you live far away from miracles when one is sitting right beside you, unnoticed!

At the time of that sad discovery, the White Wood got its name.

▲▲▲

Ustinov searched in the tale for some part of his own fate but could find nothing. There was definitely something in it that touched Domna and him, and Zinaida, too. But because it didn't touch them clearly and sharply, only from somewhere far away, it was impossible to understand just what it was. One thing, however, was clear in both the past and the present, in both fairy tale and reality, the White Wood. Imaginary or real, it was as clear and sharp as crystal.

The trees all around were powdered with snow. A very late thaw had turned the air so thick with fog that it seemed almost unearthly, but it was still fragrant forest air, saturated with the scent of trees and, here and there, the smell of grass. As a loudly cawing raven flew in a half circle in the sky, Ustinov could hear the air humming and whistling under its wings. A minute passed, and another raven soared in the same distant semicircle, following a path only it could see, repeating the prophetic cry, and moving with the same surging rush of swift flight. Ustinov stopped and listened. What were they prophesying? What if he guessed? Ravens don't fly that way over the steppe, but he had seen them do it many times in the forest.

Ustinov waited a while longer and then prodded Morkoshka, who was only too happy to obey and couldn't wait to go home. Barin, too, was restless. He had been leaving his mark for a verst all around, barking at the grouse, begging his master to shoot. He had definitely noticed the rifle behind Ustinov's back and couldn't imagine that he had brought it with him without knowing what he was going to do with it. But Ustinov already knew that he wouldn't be shooting; he wasn't in the mood for it. The forest was quiet. He noted that there were no freshly cut trees. Might there be some sense in the labors of the Forest Commission after all? Because Ustinov had guessed that it would be wet that day, he was wearing a raincoat over his sheepskin coat. The raincoat, which had been his father's, had never worn out and never would. Even if you splashed a whole river on it, it wouldn't let a drop through. Ustinov was comfortable inside it, but because the unbleached material had gotten wet and hardened, he sat inside it as if enclosed in a hollow tree trunk, unable to turn left or right, let alone shoot game as Barin was so eager to have him do.

It began to snow harder, with heavy, sticky flakes. Understanding that there would be no hunting that day, Barin began to stay closer to his master. Morkoshka also quickly figured out that there was no longer any reason for him to be driven to and fro about the forest. Their path now lay straight home, and he began to step livelier. Swaying, dozing off, Ustinov inhaled the warm, moist air inside the raincoat, and finally he realized that it wasn't so much because of business that he had gone to the forest but simply because he wanted to go. To go to Syoma Prutovskikh, to that clarity in which Syoma had lived his whole, long life, to Syoma's little sticks and circles. Ustinov's own wouldn't yield their meaning to him, so he would have to make do with someone else's, from the past.

And just at that moment when Ustinov clearly understood why he had come to the White Wood, Morkoshka jumped over a fallen birch, and Ustinov was thrown forward. A skillful and experienced rider, he stayed in the saddle, but Morkoshka fell to the ground. With his right leg pinned under the horse, Ustinov felt something like a nail stabbing him in the fleshy part of his thigh, then nausea and pain. But it was much more painful for Morkoshka. He sobbed and neighed so much that Ustinov immediately understood him: "I'm dying, master!" What had happened? How could he be dying without knowing how or why?!

By looking and poking around and feeling the stabbing pain in his leg, Ustinov slowly realized that a harrow had been placed teeth upward on the road and covered with snow and twigs—a heavy wooden harrow with two rows of iron teeth. Oh, Morkoshka, Morkoshka! Once he had saved the plow from the iron tooth of a harrow. He hadn't wanted to damage the plowshare, and now he himself was dying impaled on the teeth of a harrow! What kind of fate was this? What seer had foreseen it? Steaming blood poured out of Morkoshka, and as it dripped under him, Ustinov could hear it gurgle and feel its warmth. Believing that his horse would obey him even as he was dying, he tried to raise Morkoshka, to prod him in the withers and the neck. And Morkoshka did try to obey—he lurched upward, raised his head, and flailed his legs, but fell back again. Barin, madly rushing about, baring his teeth, crying, frantically licking first Morkoshka, then Ustinov in the face, was suffering great shame, for he felt he should have given warning of the harrow, he should have sensed it. But he had been running around in the rear and had noticed nothing.

"Go home, Barin! Go home quick!" Ustinov commanded, rubbing his ears and patting him on the back with his free hand. "Run! Get help! Go home!"

Barin ran swiftly away. "Someone will come for me," thought Ustinov, but then Barin quietly returned, his fur standing on end and his teeth bared. He sat down beside his master and began to growl.

"Go home!" Ustinov shouted again. "Listen to me, goddam it! Go ho-ome!"

But Barin still would not leave. Trembling, his ears quivering and his teeth bared, he stared into the forest to the right of the road.

"Barinushka! Little brother!" Ustinov began to coax. "Run home now, for God's sake! Come on now, run home, there's a good boy! We don't have any other choice. There's no other way out, you understand! Go on, boy! Well?!"

Curling up his wet tail, Barin started forward again along the road. He moved carefully, as if there were traps and snares laid all around, and looked around, bristling, trembling, and sniffing, as if someone were lying in wait for him behind every tree. Then Ustinov understood why Barin did not want to go and leave his master: there was someone in the forest. It was the person who had laid the harrow, teeth up, on the road. The one who had covered it with snow and branches. Him! Coming back again, Barin asked with a wild look, "Well? Do you understand now? Yes? What will we do now?"

A decision had to be made. Slowly, quietly, and clumsily, Ustinov began to reach for the rifle behind his back. Pinned to the ground by Morkoshka and encumbered by the coarse, stiff raincoat that held his trunk and leg like a pair of pliers, he couldn't turn his body at all. But he exerted himself, freed his right shoulder, and finally got the rifle into his hands. Putting the stock to his shoulder, he pointed the barrel at Barin.

"I'll kill you!"

Barin muffled his growls even more and, moving as if the ground were burning his paws, started off down the road. But he stopped again, looking back at Ustinov and his rifle. Ustinov began to shout again and, unable to see if Barin had really left, kept shouting for some time.

"I'll kill you!"

Before he died, Morkoshka flailed around on the iron teeth of the harrow, and when he raised himself slightly one last time, Ustinov managed to pull his leg partly out from beneath the horse, but it still remained pinned under Morkoshka's body up to the knee. Morkoshka dropped down again and moaned. Ustinov heard the horse's ribs scraping against iron, his breath whistling in his throat, and a muffled gurgling in his chest and stomach. He quivered once more, jerking in a long and intense spasm, and stopped moving.

"Morkoshka! Morkoshechka! Don't die, for God's sake! Don't you dare!" Moaning, Ustinov pressed himself against the lifeless, suddenly bony body as if he were trying to warm himself with Morkoshka's body or to warm Morkoshka with his own. His wound burned with a lacerating, searing pain, but Ustinov could not distinguish whose pain it was, his or Morkoshka's. As the raincoat shrank more and more, squeezing his waist, shoulders, and head, the warm, moist hollow inside it became the sole focus of his life. An hour earlier the White Wood with its meadows and clear-cuts and the steppe beyond it had been open to him in whatever direction he might wish to go, but now the only space left to him was that under the old raincoat. From there, from within this tiny shelter, he aimed his old rifle at the rest of the world and lay motionless and silent in his own and Morkoskoshka's blood. He wondered if someone in the forest was waiting impatiently for his death.

"Kudeyar was right to try to push me into the fire," he thought. "I should have burned myself then, not waited for someone else to kill me . . ." And who could they be, these strange people who needed his death? And why did they need it?

The Woman Question

That Sunday when Ustinov had ridden Morkoshka into the White Wood, at that very hour when he was suffering on the harrow's teeth, the members of the Commission were signing their appeal at the Pankratovs' house. Kalashnikov, who had some time ago entrusted the Commission's business almost entirely to Deryabin, now insisted after a long argument on having things his own way and had invited Ivan Ivanovich Samorukov and Smirnovsky to sign the appeal. Ivan Ivanovich signed with his now infirm and indecipherable hand, Smirnovsky with a whole row of almost straight little lines crowned with a semicircular flourish. After he had signed, Smirnovsky thought for a moment, raised the pen with the nib pointing upward, inspected it attentively, and asked that two more sentences be added to the appeal: "We are threatened not only by a civil war over all of Siberia but also by one between ourselves, the residents of a single village that has long been known for its cohesion, unity, and mutual assistance. Therefore, if we have not completely lost our honor and good conscience, we should take any steps we can to move away from this terrible discord!"

"There!" Kalashnikov said after Smirnovsky's addition to the appeal had been accepted. "This will be our straightforward answer in the light of day to that base nighttime note!"

"What note?" asked Smirnovsky.

They showed him a scrap of paper that someone had thrust between the shutters of the Pankratov house during the night, a tiny scrap on which was written in a sloppy and slanted hand: "You Forest Commission bastards you Soviet hooligans we will twist your heads off in a week."

"There's a step away from terrible discord for you!" said Smirnovsky, tugging at his mustache.

"They's smart ones, Rodion Gavrilovich!" said Ignashka, who had signed last, blinking his eyes. "Look what words they come up with straight off! They take care of honor and conscience and everything else all in one swipe!"

Smirnovsky turned away, and Kalashnikov and Deryabin were also embarrassed on behalf of their fellow Commission member. Ignashka, who must have noticed the general unease without understanding its cause, sighed and tried to change the subject.

"Just hope them Kolchak men don't sniff out our own military maneuver!" he said in a tone of secrecy. "The one we Lebyazhkans made on the Zhigulikha road! As long as that don't happen!"

This comment created even more confusion. The Lebyazhka men had always known what should be discussed out loud and what should never be mentioned. The "military maneuver" that Ignashka had recalled for no apparent reason was just the sort of incident that every resident of Lebyazhka had taken a silent oath to forget forever.

In August, when the Siberian government was mobilizing the young men for the war against Soviet power in Russia, many affected villages resisted. They freed the young draftees from the militia, and instead of the young lads, the veterans appeared at the enlistment stations saying, "Take us! Arm us!" But the government would not take the veterans, for during the October Revolution they had turned their weapons against their commanders and it would be easy for them to do the same again. The Lebyazhkans were the only ones who gave up their lads to the White Army without the slightest resistance, seeing them off with full honors. The young men were to be taken to the uyezd center under guard, as if they were convicts instead of defenders of the Fatherland. A small unit of Lebyazhka veterans, the fathers of the draftees, followed secretly behind them, and somewhere over the border of their own oblast, at night, these men chased off the militia and freed the draftees. Later some officers came to Lebyazhka to make an inquiry.

"Where are your young men?" they asked. "Who released them? Where have they gone?"

Since the lads were well hidden in the forest and field cabins, Ivan Ivanovich Samorukov just blinked, spread his hands, and replied, "We're completely stumped! We haven't had a letter or a word from any of them! What have the commanders done with them? What secret duty have they given them?"

Now that he had come to power, Kolchak was taking cruel revenge on the villages that had resisted the autumn mobilization. This situation made it all the more unpleasant to recall the "maneuver," but Ignashka had let his tongue slip.

After coughing quietly into his fist, Ivan Ivanovich cautioned, "It would be much better for you to forget about that incident, Ignaty, while you're still dragging your own noggin around with you!"

"What d'you mean?!" Ignatov asked uneasily. "What's that about my noggin?! Ivan Ivanovich, it's more than happy to forget things—right away something entirely different will pop into it!"

"You just tell it to forget that one, too, if it still wants to hang onto your shoulders!"

Nodding in agreement, Ignashka rubbed his neck. They all looked at each other with a certain feeling of warmth. A secret always brings people closer together, and that particular secret was sharply etched in everyone's memory. But that wasn't the full story. There had also been the conversation between Ivan Ivanovich and the officers. Going after Ivan Ivanovich was the first order of business for the two officers who had come to find out what had happened.

"Are you the Village Elder?"

"See for yourselves. Could the Elder really be someone as old as me?"

"The policeman pointed to you! And they did the same in the volost! So did the people!"

"I can't say nothing about the volost or the police, Mr. Officers, they might be making an honest mistake! But the people are lying—you can't believe them! What do the people want? They only want to shove things off on anyone they can, so long as they're not held responsible themselves!"

"Well then, is there an Elder in this village? Who is he?"

"You might say that Nikita Kostrikov can still be counted as the Elder."

"Where is he?"

"Our Nikita Petrovich is in the graveyard. He's lying there dead."

"And why wasn't another Elder elected? A live one?"

"But the live ones don't got time for it. They don't got the time to elect one or be elected."

"Convene the village assembly and elect an Elder today! Call the people together!"

"The people won't come, Mr. Officers! I'm trying to explain to you, the people are no good. That's why everything's so hard to get done these days!"

"Well then, we appoint you as Elder! And that's the end of it!"

"How can it end with me, Mr. Officers? Who would believe me, Mr. Officers? Without an election? Without democracy?!"

"You sniveling old coot! 'Democracy!' Would you like a touch of the lash?!"

"I read the Siberian government newspapers, Mr. Officers! I read Mr. Vologodsky's speeches! So I know the word! It comes to mind every day! And not just by accident! I didn't get the word from myself, but from Mr. Vologodsky!"

"Mr. Citizen Comrade Vologodsky could use a good thrashing himself for corrupting the people!" one of the officers said.

"Shhh . . . ," Ivan Ivanovich put his finger to his lips. "The people might overhear and think Lord only knows what about our officers! They've been raising money among themselves for the valiant Siberian army!"

That was another story altogether. When money began to lose its value entirely, Ivan Ivanovich had drawn a sum from the Lebyazhka Mutual Aid Fund and transferred it to the Gubernia Administration for the needs of the Volunteer Army. Later he would show the receipt to anyone who came to town. He showed it to the officers, too, and they quieted down some. After supper at Ivan Ivanovich's house, they rode away.

"No," all the members of the Commission were now thinking warmly, "this little old man, Ivan Ivanovich Samorukov, isn't through yet! Lebyazhka can still use him!"

Even Deryabin, who did not like Ivan Ivanovich and sometimes even hated him, said, "Citizen Samorukov, really, you haven't been the Elder or anyone else in Lebyazhka for a long time, but still you can make things happen! Tell me, what have you got going these days? How are things with you?"

Ivan Ivanovich did not take offense—at least he didn't show any sign of it—and, leaning slightly to one side on his stool, he began a leisurely account of his doings. He had exempted more than ten of the poorest households from taxes that fall. For some he had contrived a certificate of absence of head of the household; to others he had suggested filing a petition for loss due to poor harvest and temporary disability of the head of the household. He was good at coming up with things like that, was Ivan Ivanovich. He also warned the richest of the peasants that they must contribute no less than twice the norm of grain to the community store, and they did so without protest. The most important thing he revealed was that he was the first to look through all mail addressed to the Lebyazhka policemen. He told the policemen how to answer their superiors and how to carry out their orders. The policemen had received instructions from the uyezd and even the volost to keep the Forest Commission under strict observation. Ivan Ivanovich didn't miss a thing and personally dictated the policemen's reply: the Commission was doing nothing more than promoting enthusiasm for the Siberian government.

"Well, and what about Kolchak?" Deryabin continued his meticulous questioning.

"It's a bad business with Kolchak, boys! I'm even afraid that our policemen will slip out of my control and go completely over to the Admiral!" sighed Ivan Ivanovich.

"You've controlled them up till now? How?"

"I pay their salary. Both the healthy one and the one who's sick and worthless."

"Where does their salary come from?"

"From the Community Fund. From the Mutual Aid Fund. And from the community grain store, too."

"Well, keep doing your fatherly duty—pay them!"

"I'm ready to. But I'm telling you, the police might get other ideas now. They might run away from me to the Admiral."

It turned out that the Forest Commission had not valued Ivan Ivanovich in the least, whereas, in fact, maybe it was only thanks to him that it existed. Without Ivan Ivanovich, the policemen might have reported a good many things. That's the sort of old man he was, this former Finest Man.

When in the recent past the volost had begun to repair the roads and to arrange the apportionment of responsibilities for hauling material and for the elections of the volost court and Village Elders, all the surrounding villages had imposed a condition on Lebyazhka—not to let Samorukov anywhere near the business! Ivan Ivanovich had a knack for always turning everything around so that Lebyazhka would receive some benefit. Though a strong believer, he considered the ability to deceive the authorities or the whole volost to be a gift from God. After deceiving someone, he would go to Lebyazhka's simple little church and for some time whisper prayers of thanksgiving before the holy images. But he considered deception of one of his own, a Lebyazhka man, a great sin. If you let him, he would whip the hide off anyone who cheated his neighbor out of a kopeck. Once a Lebyazhka man had carried away another's haystack and then, a year or two later, had died. At the funeral, at the grave itself, Ivan Ivanovich raised the lid of the coffin and spat in the face of the corpse. The other old men were indignant, but Ivan Ivanovich told them he would spit in the face of any man who indulged in thievery, and it made no difference to him if it was while the man was alive or after he was dead.

Almost since the time of Samsony Krivoi, there had been Samorukovs in the ranks of the Finest Men for the third and even fourth generation, but this rascal, habitual foulmouth, and trickster was first among them all. Those previous Finest Men, also named Ivan Ivanovich, had been of an entirely different character and had had another sense of order. They read prayers, talked with the old men like members of the clergy, and kept the young people in line. They rarely interfered in community affairs—that was what the Village Elder was for.

When Ivan Ivanovich was reminded of his predecessors and sometimes even accused of taking too much upon himself by being both Elder and mentor, he would insist, "I'm doing the right thing! Every new year there are more men, women, and children in Lebyazhka! And the temptation to betray the community in some way is also growing. People are learning their letters, and that's a good thing—the holy elders shouldn't be the only ones who can read and write—but it's also a bad thing, because education makes people too different. They get drawn off in too many directions! You can't manage more than one direction at a time—some misunderstanding will always arise. One is more than enough!" But in his old age even Ivan Ivanovich Samorukov, so stern, priestly, and clever, would be at a loss over what to do and would have to agree with Deryabin that any day now the Lebyazhkans would surely begin to shoot at each other.

"We've lived together and fought together against a common enemy, and now we will start killing each other?!" Smirnovsky asked quietly. "How can we do that? I couldn't shoot at anyone, not even you, Deryabin! No, I couldn't! Could you shoot at me?"

"At you?" Deryabin repeated, squinting.

"At me!"

"That is up to you, Lieutenant. It depends on what side you take!" Deryabin rapped his finger on the table. "If you take the wrong side, then what's the point in asking?"

"And just how would you shoot me, Comrade Deryabin?"

"What do you mean 'how?' "

"Well, standing? Prone? From a kneeling position?"

"Isn't it all the same?"

"When it comes down to it, it doesn't make a difference, but it's interesting to imagine."

"If the time comes, we'll imagine it. We'll shoot at each other in whatever way is most comfortable for us without imagining anything except how to hit the bull's-eye."

"Yes," Smirnovsky drawled, "ye-e-s-s ... How much has been said about the unity of Russia? About brotherhood and friendship? But no matter how important and holy these words are, no one has any use for them. They're as worn out as a nag that's lame on all four legs! Am I right or wrong, Ivan Ivanovich? Well?"

"Who knows, Rodion Gavrilovich? How many times have I said it? No one knows how to live, and that's the greatest misfortune of all. So much life is given to people, but no one knows how to use it. All they can do is mess it up. Because of this inability to live, everyone has his knife in everyone else and is full of malice. And it builds up every year until every nook and cranny is filled to overflowing with it, and it will crawl out of the caves and crevices into the daylight. If man knew how to make use of life and all of nature, where would all this malice come from?"

"Ivan Ivanovich is right!" Smirnovsky nodded. "What kind of story is this? We Russians brought down Batu Khan, Peter the Great defeated the Swede Carl and permanently reduced Sweden from a great power to a minor one, and we did basically the same thing to the Turks. We made Napoleon take to his heels, and in this war, inglorious as it was, we saved France, and not for the first time either. So then why don't we know how to live with each other? Why don't we take care of ourselves and everything we have—our customs, our family relations, our relations with fellow countrymen, our national unity? I've been in parts of the Caucasus where, if you call a soldier a pig, his whole squadron will be insulted and be your enemies for life. But we cuss a blue streak at each other as if that's what we're supposed to do! Are we rich soil for growing a harvest for other nations, or are we just manure? Will everything going on now finish us? I was in a hospital in Moscow and went straight to officers' school from there, but between the two we were taken around to the Kremlin and to museums and galleries . . . My God, what treasures! What greatness! They made your head spin! But with us some fateful barrier has been erected between greatness and baseness. Each exists by itself, and the greatness is unable to control the baseness and drive it out of our lives!"

"You have the pride of an aristocrat, Smirnovsky!" said Deryabin. "Blind pride! Once upon a time we Russians beat the Turks, and you're still proud of it! We beat the Swedes, and again you're proud of it! But I don't give a damn about any past victories. I remember something else altogether, how much Russia oppressed other nations! Why don't you remember the history of oppression, Lieutenant?"

"I do remember it! How could I not remember it? As long as there are wars in the world, armies will exist for one purpose only—to win! If we had not defeated the Turks or the Swedes, they would have defeated us. But just remember, Deryabin, remember, all of you—when the Russian army invaded other nations, it proclaimed only its power, nothing else! It never considered those it defeated to be second-class humans or enslaved them as England did. Even though the Russian army was an army of serfs, it didn't institute serfdom in the countries it conquered as the Spaniards did and didn't exterminate native tribes as the French did. It didn't force them into the army to fight for it, but protected them from the invasions of others. And we didn't go into other nations with the cross and the sword and impose our own faith on them. Russia didn't wage any religious wars. The only thing close to it was the oppression of our ancestors, the schismatics, and then there was enough of the wisdom and spirit of Christ in people to keep them from waging war! And what's more, no nation but Russia has had so many other nations unite with it voluntarily—the Armenians, the Georgians, the Ukrainians, and others, too! They joined us with equal rights. An Armenian was the second-most important man in the government after Alexander II; the officer corps of our army was full of Georgians; and the Ukrainians were never seen as any different from Russians and have settled from one end of Russia to the other in any place they wanted to, much more than Russians have settled in the Ukraine. They've even come to us here in Siberia. No one anywhere has treated a Little Russian as a foreigner."

"Is that what Russia is, a heaven on earth?" Kalashnikov asked doubtfully. "Of course, wouldn't it be heaven if everyone in Russia tried hard?"

"What kind of heaven do you mean?" Smirnovsky smiled. "If that could only be the case! But there is no heaven on earth anywhere, for either conqueror or conquered. Often there is no choice. And when there is, nations choose the lesser of two evils. Who should rule over them? The Turks? The Poles and the Austrians? The English? Many have chosen Russia because they hoped that, instead of ruling over them, we would rule together with them. Even if it's not, Lord knows, such a progressive country, it's still more trustworthy. But look what we're doing—we've begun to fight each other!" Pausing to wait for some thought that never came, Smirnovsky sighed and said, "To be either a man or a government is never simple and clear-cut. A Russian man or government, especially . . . "

"What are you complaining about, Lieutenant?" Deryabin replied. "What ideas your superiors have drummed into your head! You'll never outlive them!"

"I've drummed them into my own head, Deryabin. I sought them out in books and in life. I needed them when I, a peasant, went into the army. I wouldn't have gone without them."

"You need to plow more, Lieutenant, you need to plow!" Deryabin smiled again. "Make your speeches out in the fields! Maybe then you'd develop a decent working-class consciousness, and you wouldn't have time for all these patriotic pursuits. How many desyatinas did you sow when you came home from the front?"

"Six."

"You might have sowed ten, and maybe then your brains would be working right!"

"If I had sowed ten, you'd shout at me even louder, 'Kulak! Enemy!' You'd want to take aim at me even more! Even though God only knows how you fought and how you plowed! You didn't sow ten desyatinas either!"

Waiting a moment, Deryabin asked with a sympathetic sigh, "Isn't it true that your nephew, Matveyka Kupriyanov, has run away from Lebyazhka? To a place you don't know about or, perhaps, do know about?"

"It's true. He's hiding. I don't know where."

"What? You couldn't restrain your nephew, Lieutenant?"

"I couldn't. He's not my son."

This bit of news stopped the conversation momentarily. Everyone thought about Matveyka Kupriyanov—a sixteen-year-old man, a sazhen wide at the shoulders, such a young bullock, strong, evil-tempered, and stupid. Where had he gone off to now? What was he up to?

"What's going on in the wide world?" Smirnovsky asked. "Has someone, perhaps, got his hands on a newspaper?"

"What newspapers can you find now?" Kalashnikov dismissed the possibility. "There aren't any papers, and there's no news. We sit here in Lebyazhka like gophers in their holes. You open one eye and look up, and if the sky is up there in its usual place, you're satisfied with that much. But your own fate is also up there in the sky, and don't you need to know a bit more about it?! I just looked at a scrap of *The People's Freedom*. It said: 'It has been learned from reliable sources that the Bolsheviks have shot Shalyapin.' "*

"You read it yourself?"

"With my own eyes! I'm quoting it word for word!"

"Well then, that was his fate!" said Ignashka, making the sign of the cross. "Look how many people of all different callings have got killed. One more or less, what difference does it make?"

"It does make a difference, Ignaty!" Kalashnikov objected. "And in the case of Shalyapin, it makes an enormous difference. Do you know who he was? Shalyapin? God only knows how great a singer he was! Perhaps there has never been anyone like him, and there won't be ever again. Nature won't give people another singer like that!"

"Well, if they shot him, someone had to do it! Someone's interests were served by it. He was a singer, sure, but maybe an enemy of the people, too?"

"With his songs? What kind of enemy?"

"He didn't sing what he should have!"

"And what should he have sung?"

"I don't know much about singing, mind you. I can carry a tune on the accordion, but not that good. But if a body really needs to, he can figure things out!"

"You can't believe anything these days!" Smirnovsky was skeptical. "You have to see who benefits from it. The Whites would benefit if the Reds shot Shalyapin. They wouldn't waste a minute, they'd just write, 'They shot him!' "

The harmony that had arisen among the members of the Commission when Ignashka, seemingly out of place, had recalled the "military maneu-

---

*Fyodor Shalyapin (Chaliapin, 1873–1938), the famous Russian basso, was not shot by the Bolsheviks but emigrated to the West in 1922.

ver" with which the Lebyazhkans had freed their lads from the mobilization, that brief but pleasant and warmhearted moment of harmony, had once again soured. Falling silent, the Commission members looked at each other a while longer.

Then, turning to Smirnovsky with a note of suspicion in his voice, Deryabin said, "Well, all right, Ivan Ivanovich here, good or bad, is a public man. You can't argue with that. He's been the Finest Man—for how many years now?—and it's understandable if he shows up at the Commission of his own free will! But I'd like to know, Lieutenant, why you decided to come and see us. Why you came just now! Who incited you to act? Who was your agitator? It wasn't Nikolai Ustinov, was it?"

"It was you!" Smirnovsky replied. "You!"

"Me?"

"I said, you! You were my agitator."

"You're really stretching it, Lieutenant!"

"Just the opposite: I came so you wouldn't stretch it too much, Deryabin! So you wouldn't lead the Commission away from the little bit of unity that we talked about and that has just been proclaimed in writing, in our appeal to the citizens of Lebyazhka. If you had led the Commission astray, I wouldn't be signing my name to this appeal. And the point is, Deryabin, you've taken the whole forest guard into your own hands. And that's the way you did it—by stretching things!"

"And to think that we offered you the leadership of the guard! And you refused. Do you regret it now? Do you remember how you refused? So curtly. With such nobility. Are you sorry for letting your nobility get out of hand?"

But because Smirnovsky did not want the conversation to shift to him, he merely nodded casually in answer to Deryabin's question. "I haven't explained that to myself yet. Maybe I do regret it! But we're not talking about me. Why don't you explain why from a guard of twenty-odd men you have singled out six who are particularly devoted to you and whom you are training secretly and separately from all the others?"

"You're a well-informed man, Lieutenant!" Deryabin's expression had become a smile. "Have you sent out scouts? Your own sons?

"My own . . . They're hunters and fishermen, observant lads. They noticed your strike force in the forest, your six men, more than once, and you with them!"

"Well, if it's only me, that doesn't mean anything!"

"Only you, so far!"

"And that's fine! Why should you see anything bad in that, Lieutenant? It's very simple: you can't trust the whole guard. Even in the case of the impending military action against Kolchak's punishment brigades. In that case we need to have a small group, a true strike group, ready for anything.

If it needs to, it can call all the others in after it, the whole guard, and even everyone else in Lebyazhka who understands things properly."

"I can understand that! But did the Commission entrust that job to you? And aren't you keeping it a secret from them, even from Chairman Kalashnikov?!"

"I would have told them about it when the time came!"

"When? When you replaced Kalashnikov? And maybe even after you had arrested him? If he had refused to let you do it?"

"The thought never crossed my mind! By talking like that, you're the first to disturb the unity among us in the Commission! I've been honestly preparing to resist our common and vile enemy! And nothing else!"

"Let's suppose—"

"Just why did you come to us, to the Commission?"

"For the time being, to bring your secret plans to light."

"For the time being. And then later?"

"I repeat: I wanted to be here before you got the idea of eliminating the Commission with your six men. You know very well that you could remove Kalashnikov at any moment. There's no need to hide it because Kalashnikov already knows it himself. Only he won't do anything to stop you. That's the kind of man he is—a nonresister. But I am warning you: your six shock troops will not move against me. Keep that in mind. Almost all of them were in my regiment. I trust them, and they trust me! In any case, I can always conclude my own Treaty of Brest-Litovsk with them!"

"They have been reeducated. They won't listen to you, Your Honor!"

"They won't listen to me, true enough. But they won't move against me either. You'll have to wait a while longer for that. Yes, you will!"

"It can't be helped, I'll have to wait . . . ," Deryabin agreed. "Well, what do you have to say, Chairman Kalashnikov?"

Taking several deep breaths and swaying on his stool, Kalashnikov was gathering his distant thoughts, perhaps not of this world. When he needed to answer quickly, he would often sink into almost prayerlike meditation.

"How can this be happening?" he asked. "Without a doubt, we wish the people well, but they feel insulted! Matveyka is insulted. All right, he's a stupid boy. But Polovinkin? Polovinkin is an uneducated peasant, and when he left, we lost touch with the masses. Do you remember, Comrades, how he called us 'intell-idiots'? Idiots! He accused us of being stupid, useless fakes! Maybe it's true that no one needs us at all and that not one sensible person wants to listen to us useless scribblers. All right, I'm ready to hand the whole business over to Comrade Deryabin. Let him do everything the way he wants! He doesn't suffer from doubt the way I do. Maybe for that reason alone he has more right to be the leader of the Commission. I tell myself all this, but a minute later I'm arguing with myself again: 'What's this, Petro?! Think of the great and honorable spirit in which you wrote that "any work for the benefit of society should be performed now with all the responsibility that people have!" ' And how many things I'm thinking about right now! Not long ago I still thought that as I got older I was finally beginning to understand life! With all my heart I believed in human cooperation! But how is it turning out?

"Well, all right—the peasants in Russia take the land away from the landowners, just as they have before. There were Stepan Razin and Yemilyan Pugachov,* who have never been forgotten among the people. And now the worker wants to take his factory away from the capitalist— that's easy to understand, too. But what are we Siberians to divide, and among whom? We have enough land, so we don't have to fight for it, and there are no factories at all. What do we have to divide up? But we will shoot at each other all the same, for the simple reason that one man has eight horses in his yard and another has only two! That's not war, but robbery! Armed horse theft! Well, fine, there's no end of various ministers and of Chairmen Sukhomlinovs, horse-thief Rasputins, Romanov emperors, ministers Kerensky and Miliukov,† Kolchaks, and the like, and no end to all the things they would like to have and share. But what should we, the people, share among ourselves? What property? The main difference between the people and the bourgeoisie is that the people should not wish each other harm! The factory owner always wants his own factory to put his neighbor's factory out of business. That's understandable, but we aren't factory owners, are we? Or have this enmity and envy seeped into everyone's bones, sparing no one, neither tsar nor beggar?

"We've had our fill of being told that truth and justice live in the people, that the voice of the people is the voice of God, that the people are great, that the people's conscience is greater than anybody else's, and so on! Is it possible we are being fooled?! Being seduced? Maybe we really are unfit for anything, maybe we are mercenary and ready for all kinds of murder and crime and baseness! Where is our own consciousness, the consciousness of the people? The Siberian government took the draftees, but we wouldn't give them up. We freed the lot of them, but less than half a year later are these same lads and these same fathers going to aim guns at each other? No, I can't understand it! Are we, the members of the Commission, already

---

*Stepan Razin (d. 1671) and Yemelyan Pugachov (1742–1775), leaders of major peasant revolts in Russia.

†Vladimir Sukhomlinov, much criticized Russian Minister of War, 1911–1916; Grigory Rasputin, infamous charismatic religious figure and personal advisor to the tsarina; Alexander Kerensky, Socialist Revolutionary and president of the Provisional Government in Petrograd in 1917; Pavel Miliukov, historian and leader of the Constitutional Democrats (Kadets).

thinking about training our sights on one another, prone, kneeling, or standing?! It makes no sense to me. What is happening?"

"So, Petro, are you saying there aren't enough good people in the world?" Ivan Ivanovich asked. "Do you think that's the cause of our troubles?"

"There are plenty of good people, Ivan Ivanovich, but they don't know who they should join forces with."

"With God, Petro! Good people are God's people, and their wisdom isn't crippled by their own pride, but comes from faith, from Christ's commandments. They join God, and God joins them!"

"With words!" said Deryabin. "They join with words, Citizen Samorukov! But what about deeds?"

"Every nation should have not only its own God-given wisdom but a wisdom of state," Smirnovsky responded. "If it doesn't have that, there will be a complete breakdown. A government cannot exist without the wisdom of the people or a people without the wisdom of the state."

"That's true, Rodion Gavrilovich!" Kalashnikov agreed. "The people want the authority over them to have wisdom. Their desire for a wisely human government is inexpressibly deep. More than anything else, that desire has exhausted us with suffering, as if it were the deepest longing of all!"

"And that longing reveals a great truth!" Smirnovsky nodded again, swaying on his stool. "What is truth if not a wise arrangement of life, visible and understandable to all?"

"The army went into Galicia three times," Deryabin began, but Ignashka Ignatov interrupted him.

"Men!" he said. "Comrade Members of the Forest Commission! What's going on here? Shouldn't we be writing something? We're just sitting and twiddling our thumbs!! Someone in the street will be sure to peek in the window and think: 'That's a fine thing! We elected a Forest Commission to get the job done, and there they sit, twiddling their thumbs!' Let's at least write some minutes or something, or else we'll turn out to be shameful good-for-nothings!"

"Just wait a bit, Ignaty!" Deryabin rapped on the table. "I've found me somebody to take notes!" Then he screwed up his eyes. "I'll tell you what you might do, Ignaty. Go run after Ustinov! We need to talk to him about this!"

Everyone nodded to confirm this necessity.

"If Nikolai Ustinov were here, there'd be more peace between us, too," Samorukov said.

He was right. Were Ustinov now sitting at the table, looking attentively around the room, looking deep into each person with a sort of endless interest, everyone would have felt more comfortable and calmer because of that look and because of the way he stroked his blond, almost childish hair.

"But what's the good of running after him?" asked Ignashka, rising a little only to sit down again. "He's gone into the forest. He's still there."

"You just go all the same! We just have to have Kolya Ustinov here now!" Samorukov insisted.

"I'll go, Ivan Ivanovich, only not right this second. I'll go later, I swear to God!" Ignashka promised.

"So what was I about to say?" Deryabin began again. "Yes, three times our army went into Galicia—"

"We know, we know!" Kalashnikov interrupted Deryabin this time. "Everyone knows what you're going to say: three times our army went into Galicia and twice into Prussia! They overthrew the Tsar and shot him. Kerensky fled the palace in women's clothes. And all in vain, you'll say. All the same life still has not brought any good or understanding to the people. And since that's the way it is, life needs to be fundamentally changed! That's what you will say! But how it should be changed without causing worldwide insanity again? That you won't say, Deryabin!"

"Someone like you who's unwilling even to hear about change wouldn't understand," replied Deryabin, losing his temper. "Someone who fears it like the devil fears incense! Why has our green forest burst into flames? Because of Polovinkin, because he left?! Let him go. What does he really think? He's tickled pink when smart people turn out to be as stupid as he is. We had to explain everything to him all over again: the time comes when people are ready, despite any sacrifice, to remake themselves and their whole lives! That is their only hope for the future! The only thing that means anything to them! Everything else is insanity, humiliation, and slavery! Slavery to the Tsar, slavery to your neighbor, and even to yourself! Of course, you can live quite nicely even under slavery and oppression, especially if you take care to praise it. 'Oh, how good and noble it all is; there's nothing better and more just in all the world and never will be.' Your masters will hear you and reward you with a tasty morsel and will even let you sit at their own table, but is that any way for a human being to live?!" Deryabin stopped talking, shook a threatening finger at Ignashka for some reason or other, and then suddenly turned toward Samorukov. "I suppose you will take exception, former Finest Man?"

"Former is right, Deryabin!" Samorukov agreed. "But why? Not because of old age, no. It's because so many people have been born on this earth that almost all the old people among them are has-beens! It's like it is in the forest: if too many of one creature, rabbits or squirrels, say, are born, afterwards a great many of them will die. And, of course, it's the oldest rabbits or squirrels that will die first of all. And our Lebyazhka, too, must not outgrow itself. Its own two hundred households are enough for it, but two hundred and fifty would be more than it could take. As long as it doesn't exceed its own strength, a village can have its own leader and its own order, and there will be one God for everyone. Then everyone can see who each man is and what he lives for. Then the life of our forefathers can serve as an example and can make deeds conform to words. But if there are a million people instead of thousands, then no one can govern or see all of those million folks no matter what sort of leader or worker he might be. And what about me? When I knew what to do, I did it. But if I didn't know, I wouldn't act! I'm satisfied with that. And now I don't envy you men, not a bit. I'm the one to envy because I'll be dying before long, and you'll go on living. I lived, but I rarely talked about life. I got by without such talk, while nowadays you can't say three words without talking about life one way or another. But you don't know how to live. Life is nowhere even near you, it's far away somewhere!" Ivan Ivanovich crossed himself and fell silent.

"I was in the war with Japan, in a medical unit." Shaking his head again, Kalashnikov began to reminisce. "I carried enough mortally wounded men to populate two volosts! As I carried them, I kept listening for one of the dying to tell me what is most important, to reveal some great truth. But no one said any such thing. More than anything they'd talk about their kids, about their wives and mothers. They would often die while remembering their women."

"In the war with Germany, it was the same," Deryabin said.

"It's the same in this civil war and will continue to be!" said Smirnovsky. "Maybe the Woman Question is the most important one? Do you think so?"

Everyone was quiet, and then Ignashka unexpectedly began to giggle, "Hee-hee! Hee-hee!"

"What's so funny, Ignaty?" asked Samorukov.

"Well, they'll say that even Rodion Gavrilovich—," Ignatov answered, covering his face with his hand. "Even he has a Woman Question! Hee-hee! That would be an obscene question, or even worse!"

"How stupid can you be, Ignaty?!" Kalashnikov asked in amazement. "That's what they write in all the newspapers and even in books—'the Peasant Question,' 'the Siberian Question,' 'the Woman Question,' 'the War Question.' Here and in other countries, too!"

"Now you're saying it, too, Kalashnikov! Boy, I never expected it from you, Petro! From the Chairman of our Commission! Is there any sense in comparing them? The War Question and then the—hee-hee—Woman Question? You, too! We'll, I'll be!" Ignashka covered his face with his other hand.

"Ignaty!" said Deryabin. "Weren't you told to run and get Ustinov? To find out if he's come back?"

This time Ignashka did not try to get out of it. He took his cap off its hook, put on his sheepskin coat in the kitchen, and ran off, giggling.

The members of the Commission continued their conversation about the

Woman Question: since the men handle power so poorly, would it not be better to entrust all the power of the state to women? But then they remembered that under Elizabeth and Catherine there had also been great wars and a severe lack of order and that Anna Ivanovna and Anna Leopoldovna had been more spiteful than Ivan the Terrible. Ivan Ivanovich pointed out that during the reign of Elizabeth one-fourth of the State Treasury was pilfered every year and that was even accepted as a sort of Russian law.

"Let's get back to business, Comrade Commission Members!" Deryabin rapped on the table. "I'm not very pleased with you, Lieutenant Smirnovsky, for your thoughtless words! And all of us should be displeased with them!"

"What do you mean?"

"So you found out about my six-man strike force, to your credit and honor. It shows you have the eye of a military man! Fine! But why did you announce it in front of everyone, even Ignashka Ignatov?"

"He is also a member of the Commission! You aren't throwing him out, are you? Doesn't he come to meetings and vote? Which means you trust him, doesn't it?"

"There's trust, and then there's trust!" Deryabin wanted to explain something else to the Lieutenant, but Samorukov interrupted him.

"Why don't you tell us the names of your six-man strike force, Guard Commander? We don't know a thing about them, but we should! Everyone remembers the six holy Poluvyatsky maidens, so don't we need to keep these six in mind, too?!"

Deryabin was at a loss for words.

"You don't want to say anything, Deryabin?" Smirnovsky said after a moment. "Well, then don't; that's all right. Anyway, who the six are doesn't really matter. Besides, I almost know already! I might be wrong about one man, but no more than that!"

Ignashka returned shortly thereafter, puffing and pleased with himself. He threw off his sheepskin in the kitchen, brought his cap into the main room, and hung it again on a nail above his seat.

"Nikola Ustinov is still not back from the forest!" he reported. "I told you he wasn't at home! And our hostess, Zinaida, has gone to visit Domna Ustinov! I saw it with my own eyes as I was leaving: the two of them were going into the house! Now there's a woman question for you, to be sure! Hee-hee!"

Ignashka's report truly must have embarrassed the Commission, though no one showed any sign of it.

"Isn't it the truth?" Kalashnikov said. "Should we put all our affairs into the women's hands and our quarrels, too? Should we give them to Zinaida? All my life I've been amazed at how she can hold a home together alone. And in such cleanliness! Just look at this one little flower. Each petal on it shines with constant joy! Shouldn't we men know how to keep order like Zinaida does?"

The members of the Commission looked at the curtains, at the chest of drawers, at the family pictures on the wall between the windows, at the grandfather clock, at everything they had seen so many times, and again they were amazed by the brightness of the whole room and the objects in it. It was a dim brightness because dusk had begun, but it shone nevertheless.

"Look how much we've stomped about here, men. We started in early autumn, and we're still nowhere near done," Kalashnikov continued. "We stick cigarette butts in the flower pots every God-given day, and even at night, but we still couldn't disrupt Zinaida Pavlovna's order! Now there's a pair of hands for you!"

"Ye-es . . . ," Ignashka sighed. "It would be good to fall into those arms! And just a touch higher than the elbow!"

"Ignashka!" Kalashnikov cut him off angrily. "How can you be so shameless? And with Kirill here at home—he'll hear you! It's embarrassing!"

"What's wrong? You're talking about it yourselves, about the Woman Question, but if I say a word, I'm a shameless person! That ain't fair!"

Once again the members of the Commission warmed to one another, and there was no trace of anger in anyone's eyes. Even Ivan Ivanovich looked on with understanding, but, because of his age, without too much sympathy. Even Deryabin smiled with his thin lips and partially closed his eyes.

"It's true!" he said. "Whenever a soldier at the front dreamed that he had spent the night in his wife's arms, that was enough to make him happy! Later, while they spooned their supper out of the same pot, he'd quietly tell his chum about his happiness . . . Wasn't it the same with you officers, Lieutenant?"

Smirnovsky nodded. "It's amazing how it's that way with everyone!"

Just then Samorukov looked into the yard through the fogged-up window and asked with surprise and even a touch of alarm, "Why has Zinaida, our hostess, harnessed a horse? And in such weather?!"

Ignashka immediately pressed himself against the window.

"Why is Ustinov's dog with her? They're both in a hurry!"

Getting up and opening the door to the kitchen, Ivan Ivanovich called, "Kirill? Are you home?"

"I'm home, Ivan Ivanovich," Kirill answered quickly but quietly, somehow unsure of himself. He had just entered the house from the yard, but he didn't seem to know himself whether he was at home or not. "Why do you ask?"

"Where are you sending your woman? With the weather as bad as it can be?"

"She's going on her own, Ivan Ivanovich. She didn't say where or why."

"Maybe it's something serious? If it's serious, couldn't she call on the Commission men to help her?!"

"She's already ridden off, can't you hear?"

Sure enough, the squeaking of stiff, wooden sledge runners and the impatient barking of a dog carried in from the yard. Ivan Ivanovich scratched his fallen shoulder.

"She didn't even close the gate behind herself, did she? And what's that smell on you, Kirill? Is that moonshine you stink of?"

"I just had a tiny little sip, Ivan Ivanovich. It's Sunday, after all . . . ," said Kirill still more quietly, retreating to the farthest corner of the kitchen.

Chewing his lips uncertainly, Ivan Ivanovich went back to his seat in the main room and addressed the Commission. "Men! How long now have you been having your endless meetings in Kirill's house? But somehow we have seen far too little of our host. There's only a shadow here, not the man. That isn't good, I tell you!"

"What of it?" Deryabin shrugged. "Kirill is more interested in his woodworking than in anything else on earth. We confirmed him for the forest guard, but he's so busy with his own pursuits that he hasn't taken a single step in their direction. Let him be, if that's the way it is!"

"No matter what he's busy with, he's still alive, ain't he? So why do we only see the shadow of a living man?"

Smiling, Deryabin called loudly toward the kitchen, "Kirill, can you hear what people are saying about you in here?"

"I can hear . . . ," replied Kirill's quiet voice. "How could I help but hear?"

"Is Citizen Samorukov telling the truth about you being a shadow?"

"I don't know . . . I know Ivan Ivanovich has always told the truth, for as long as I can remember . . . "

The house fell into an embarrassed silence, and Ivan Ivanovich, the most embarrassed of all, insisted, "You have a voice, too, Kirill! And haven't I stretched the truth in my time? And lied! Dear God, how much of that had to be done! Fine, then: we'll talk some more about this later, one-on-one, Kirill!"

The Commission business seemed to be finished, so Kalashnikov twisted his ungainly torso around on his chair and said, "Ustinov himself is still out in the forest, but his dog is here! Isn't there something not right about that?"

"But Ustinov's dog, that Barin, is downright independent!" Ignashka replied. "If he likes you, fine, but if he has a grudge against someone, they won't be able to control him at all. He might leave his master purely on his own business!"

"No, he's a good dog. He's fond of his master . . . "

"Sometimes. Do you remember, men—it was before the war—that time when Ustinov's Barin ruined the looks of that vacationer's dog? You haven't forgotten, have you?" Ignashka asked, and even though it was an insignificant incident that had happened long ago, everyone still recalled it.

The year before the war started, a woman had come to Lebyazhka for the holidays with a servant, a small boy in a little blue suit, a young girl all decked out in white ribbons, and a pitch-black dog named Madrid. Because the Lebyazhkans did not like summer vacationers, they did nothing to make them feel welcome. The vacationers were strangers, talkative and curious, interested in everything—how the peasants rode and drank, how they sent carts of presents to the rural officials, how they beat their women, how they celebrated weddings, how they cured themselves of diseases. These strangers gawked at everything. God had generally spared the distant village of Lebyazhka from the intrusion of outsiders, but that lady had been a stubborn exception. When Ivan Ivanovich had explained to her that it would be better for her health to live out on the steppe, she had answered that Lebyazhka was a very clean and pretty village and that the Kirghiz Suleiman would bring her kumys* every day from the steppe—the fifteen versts meant nothing to him. Ivan Ivanovich explained that there just wasn't anyone in the village who could rent her a place to live, but she presented a note from a high official: "To the Elder Samorukov. Arrange quarters. Money is no object." And so they were settled in Ivan Ivanovich's house—the lady, her servant, the little boy, the little girl, and the black dog. There was nothing left for Ivan Ivanovich to do but warn the men, women, and even children of Lebyazhka to be polite to their guest.

He explained it to the people, but can you really tell a dog anything? All the Lebyazhka mutts down to the last one hated Madrid, and Ustinov's Barin, for some reason, hated him more than any of the others did. Well-mannered and still young at that time, Barin was a good dog, but, contrary to his true nature, he went around with his fur standing on end, his teeth bared, and murder in his eyes. He would be on guard all day, waiting to see if Madrid would run out of his yard. But Madrid was no fool either and understood the situation. He never strayed from home, didn't even raise his voice across the fence, and although he made no friends, quarreled with no one. For a long time he was under siege like that, but then he was seduced and rushed out into the street after a flighty little bitch. Then Barin got at him, even though Madrid was taller by a head. By the time the men came running to break up the unbelievable yelping and snarling and flying fur of the fight, Madrid had only one ear. The other had been bitten clean off.

If anyone got any obvious benefit from all this, it was Ignaty Ignatov. He went to Krushikha for the veterinarian, somewhere else after medicine, and

---

*A drink made from fermented mare's milk and reputed to have great medicinal value.

delivered the lady to the railroad station along with her servant, her children, and, his head bandaged, Madrid. Madrid was not just any old dog. He was a champion that had won a beribboned medal for his breed and appearance. He should have won more, but, of course, now that he was missing an ear, fate no longer smiled upon him with honors, glory, and medals, and he left Lebyazhka as a premature invalid. Having grown thin and miserable, along with her servant and children, his mistress also left in bitter tears. Ignaty Ignatov alone was happy and satisfied—the whole affair had brought him forty-two rubles and forty-two kopecks.

But now Kalashnikov had his doubts about how it had really happened. That seemed like an awful lot of money!

"But why would I lie about it, Comrade Chairman?" Ignashka began to swear to God and beat himself on the chest. "What's peculiar about that amount? I remember the figure now as I did then—42 rubles, 42 kopecks!"

"And it was gold currency back then!" sighed Samorukov. "You could go to the station, turn your paper money in at the bank, come back, and lay it on the table!" Ivan Ivanovich patted his jacket pockets. "That's how it was! Forty-two gold rubles for a dog's ear?! At that rate, how much was the whole dog worth? You didn't turn your paper in for gold and save the gold till now, did you, Ignaty?"

"No, I didn't!" Ignaty confessed in all seriousness. "It's true, Ivan Ivanovich. I was a fool then, by God!"

"When a state has gold, it is strong!" Smirnovsky commented. "And every citizen in it will also feel strong, because he earns a ruble and knows that no sudden shock can take that ruble away. He can always exchange it for the currency of any nation he wants to. If a prospector finds a nugget or if someone wants to sell some gold object, he can just go to the treasury and get rubles in return according to its weight. That's hard currency for you!"

"And the treasury wouldn't take less than a quarter of a pound in exchange for rubles," Samorukov recalled. "They didn't have time to mess with smaller amounts!"

"Really!" Kalashnikov wondered. "It used to be that if they gave you gold at the market, you'd ask for paper. At least then you could put it in your hat, the lining of your clothes, or in a bag so it wouldn't weigh down your pockets. We thought that paper money was more convenient! How many thousands would those forty-two gold rubles be worth now, in the Tsar's rubles, or Kerensky's, or Soviet ones, or even Kolchak's? It's more than the mind can grasp!"

As they mentally counted the sum at various rates of exchange, they were all quiet, and then Smirnovsky smiled suddenly and asked Ivan Ivanovich, "But just why couldn't Madrid and Barin get along with each other?"

"Well, Rodion Gavrilovich, that's their own doggy business!" replied Samorukov, spreading his hands.

"The dogs' anger didn't cost them much—just one ear, even if it was a golden one!" Kalashnikov sighed. "A pittance!"

"It could have cost more if there hadn't been anyone to pull them apart," Deryabin smiled.

"But that city lady wasn't suffering so much for Madrid's sake," Kalashnikov recalled dreamily. "She was suffering for another reason altogether. Seriously. As a human being!"

"What reason?" Deryabin asked with interest.

"Why did she stay with us in Lebyazhka instead of going to some Kirghiz nomad's tent out on the steppe? The other ladies and gentlemen even liked those tents. They would have a nice new clean one set up and enjoy the kumys and the fresh air. But she couldn't do that, it was impossible. Her beloved, also taking the kumys cure, was staying in Suleiman's camp. And so she stayed in Lebyazhka because she couldn't be too far away, but she couldn't show up too close to him either. She couldn't reveal the fact that they knew one another, and not just as simple acquaintances either! She couldn't, no matter what! Suleiman brought her not only bottles of kumys but also love letters. Every day. Her boyfriend was a medical student who abandoned his studies, exhausted himself, and caught a fatal case of consumption. At the same time that Barin was tearing off Madrid's ear, the student was also bleeding. Hemorrhaging from the throat, he was covered with blood from head to foot, and Suleiman—actually Suleiman's brother—was rushing him off to the station. The student didn't make it there alive."

"But if he was so close to death, why did he go to take the kumys cure way out on the steppe?" Deryabin asked.

"But that's the whole point—he didn't go to drink kumys or take a cure. He went off to say farewell to his beloved. Forever. A tall man with a dark beard, he was good-looking enough, till he caught consumption."

"It's enough to make you cry . . . ," Ignashka was half snorting, half sobbing. "Sure enough!"

"Of course!" Kalashnikov nodded. "She told herself that she shouldn't have agreed to such a farewell rendezvous! Did she think, 'I agreed, and now because of it, because of me, he perished before his time!'? She could have been thinking a lot of things."

"And did they ever meet? At her place in Lebyazhka or in his tent?" Deryabin still wanted to know.

"Two or three times. Not in Lebyazhka or in a tent—they found a place in between, in the White Wood, not far from Grishka Sukhikh's freehold. Grishka had just built his place then, and he had a little shed in a part of the wood about a verst from his freehold. They met there."

"So they did find some happiness, in spite of everything?"

"Well, what joy could they have had when both of them knew that it was all for the last time? Every sigh and glance and word were the last, and there was nothing they could do about it!"

"I suppose he kept his distance from her? The consumptive boyfriend? Was he afraid to infect her? Or maybe she kept her distance from him?"

"Who knows . . . ? Only she could hardly have been afraid! If she had been afraid, she wouldn't have followed him secretly from the city with her two children."

"A mother fears for her children most of all. That's for sure."

"But how can this kind of thing happen to a woman? It's beyond any sort of pity . . . "

After thinking for a minute and chewing his lips, Deryabin asked, "How do you know all this, Kalashnikov? In such detail?"

"I heard it from Suleiman. And Ivan Ivanovich knows something or other about it, too? Right?"

Slightly bowing his sparsely covered, gray head and still staring intently through the wet and gloomy window, Ivan Ivanovich said softly, "Yes . . . "

"They've known it for years, but neither of them said a thing! And they kept it a secret from me, too!" Deryabin smiled. "A gentleman's secret to boot! All right then, let's all go home! We've signed the appeal, and Nikola Ustinov will sign it when he gets back from the forest, and then we'll post it in the most conspicuous places. Let's adjourn until then. As it is, we keep getting off serious subjects and straight into the Woman Question!"

▲▲▲

Lashing the little dappled mare with her soaking wet whip, Zinaida urged it on without even noticing that she was soaking wet herself. It was almost completely dark already. The sledge, moving heavily across the wet snow, slid over the bumps in the untraveled, rough, barely visible road. Barin, too, was barely visible, now as a transparent shadow, now as a dense, dark, demonic shape with sparks in his eyes. Sometimes he disappeared altogether except for the yelping, barking, and whining with which he begged Zinaida to hurry on to the life, or death, of Nikolai Ustinov, his master. Barin was lost in his canine prayers, Zinaida in fear and foreboding. Murky clouds concealed the moon rising over the steppe, but at the edge of the forest, under a solitary tree, there seemed to be two men on horseback. Zinaida stood up in the sleigh and shouted loudly, her voice straining, "Grigory?! Sukhikh? Did you do it, you devil?! God damn you!"

But when the shadows disappeared, Zinaida wasn't sure if they had been there or not. Whom had she cursed? Barin ran past that tree without slowing down or barking at anyone, just as he had run all of this terrible road, howling, choking, and moaning prayers for salvation to his canine God. But Zinaida knew that God would not have acted alone. Anything that had happened to Ustinov had been done by people.

She had been right to beg Ustinov, "Let's go away, let's run away, we'll save ourselves from people, the two of us! They'll make trouble for you, if not today, then tomorrow!" And here was that very tomorrow! It had come! Through the dark, tattered sky, it had fallen down on today.

When Zinaida finally found Ustinov, his face seemed like a pale image to her, whiter than snow, and it wasn't until he asked, "Who's here?" that she believed that he was alive.

"How is my horse? Morkoshka? Is he really dead?! Morkoshechka!"

Zinaida put her hand on the horse's dangling, cold lips and answered, "He's dead!" Not knowing whether Ustinov would live—his voice was weak and hollow, as if heard from the other world—she began to cry. "Who tried to kill you, Nikola?! And why?"

"If only I knew . . . " Ustinov groped about, took Zinaida's hand, and put it on a cold, sharp tooth of the harrow.

"What is it? What?" When she understood, she jerked her hand back as if from something hot and passed it over her face. "It's inhuman! Dear God, it's inhuman! They're worse than animals! Worse than animals!" With difficulty she raised Morkoshka's cold body, pulled Ustinov's leg out from underneath, and dragged him away.

"Zinaida?" He seemed to be noticing her for the first time. "How did you get here?" When she did not answer, he repeated, "How did you get here? I can't believe it . . . "

"He can't believe it! I'm not supposed to be here, right? Someone else should be here in my place, right? But she's not here, Nikola! She's not here, and never would have been here. You just remember that, Nikola!"

"And Morkoshka?" asked Ustinov, his voice even weaker. "Are we really leaving him?"

"He's gone cold!"

"I'm cold, too! Through and through!"

"That's not true! Not completely! I wouldn't have moved either of you if you were cold. I would have left you where you are and stayed to grow cold with you! But as long as there's a single drop of warmth in you, I'll take you away! I'll take you myself! And I won't give you up to anyone!" She dropped him onto the sled and shouted at the mare, "Pull, pull, you! Look alive, pull!"

Barin howled—he didn't want to leave Morkoshka alone either. He fell to the ground and licked him in the face. He didn't want to believe that Morkoshka couldn't be brought to his feet, that it was already too late.

"Is your back in one piece, Nikola?" asked Zinaida, whipping up the mare.

"Yes . . . "

"And your belly?"

"It, too . . . "

"So it's your legs?"

"The right one, above the knee ... But where are you taking me, Zinaida?"

"They didn't smash you up enough, Ustinov!" she answered angrily. "Those people didn't do enough to you! They should have torn out your tongue! And stuck it on an iron tooth, too!"

"Have you gone crazy, Zinka? Why should they have done that?"

"So you wouldn't ask where I'm taking you! So you wouldn't say anything, no matter where I took you! So that you could lie quietly in my house, in my bed! I'll take care of you like a nurse! That's what I'll do now, because that's what it's time to do! I didn't do it before, I was late, and so they impaled you on iron teeth!"

"Are you serious, Zinaida?!"

"Yes! We've been playing a false game: I can't do this with you, I can't do that, I can't do anything! Enough of this deception! The time has come—I'm taking you home! I'm taking what's mine and no one else's! If someone asks, I'll say, 'I found what's mine in the forest, I took what's mine from the teeth of the harrow. I warned what's mine to guard himself against people, to stay away from them! I've followed after my own man for so many years, all alone. There was no one else to do it, so whose man is he now?' Everyone will understand me, everyone who has a soul! You're the only one who doesn't understand, so I won't ask you! You're the only one without understanding, without a heart, but this time I won't look to you, I won't listen, no-o! Enough! Now I'm your nurse, that's who I am! I will nurse you as much as I want!"

"Listen to what I have to say, Zinaida—"

"I've listened enough! For all time to come, I've heard enough of your saying, 'We can't'! That's more than enough for me, your nurse!"

And so, bouncing over the bumps in the untraveled road, now in complete darkness, now by the dim light of a timid moon, they drove on until Barin began to bark and rushed ahead.

"Someone's riding on Solovko, Zinaida," Ustinov groaned. "I can tell by Barin's voice—it's Solovko!"

Zinaida reined in the mare and listened quietly, and Barin, somewhere on ahead, also fell silent. "Domna?" Ustinov wondered. But he doubted that she could have come. Zinaida also thought of Domna, of her velvet jacket with its trimmed collar and sleeves, her fluffy Orenburg shawl, her calm face with its protruding blue eyes. She, too, wondered, "Is it her? It can't be!" They waited silently to see who was coming.

Shurka, riding up and reining in Solovko, asked, "Who's there? Is it one of ours?"

Neither Ustinov nor Zinaida replied, but Barin barked as if asking, "What do you mean, Shurka? Don't you recognize the master?"

Shurka shouted more loudly and anxiously, "Who is it?"

"It's me!" Ustinov answered at last.

"Why didn't you answer me, Dad?" When Ustinov was silent again, Shurka asked, "Who are you with?" He urged Solovko forward and came closer until he could see. "Is that you, Zinaida Pal'na? It's you? Where are you bringing Dad from?"

"I'm taking him away from trouble."

"What trouble? And where is Morkoshka, Dad?"

"He met his end . . . He's done for. And I'm hurt bad myself . . . Who sent you for me?"

"Ksenka sent me, Dad. She found me at Mishka Goryachkin's. I went to see Mishka for a second on my way home from the market in Krushikha, and there she was. But me and Mishka Goryachkin weren't drinking at all. And we weren't playing cards. We were having a serious talk."

"Are you sober, Shurka?"

"I swear on my life, Dad! Me and Mishka didn't touch a drop! Maybe it's still on my breath from the market. Which sled will you ride on now, Dad? In that one? Or ours? Well? Why aren't you saying anything? Do you feel sick?"

"In ours . . ."

Hurrying to move his father-in-law, Shurka dragged him awkwardly out of the sled over Zinaida's knees. At first she sat quietly, not saying a word or moving a muscle, but then she began to ask no one in particular, "And what about me? And what about me? What about me?"

Ustinov moaned with the burning pain in his leg.

"Are you bleeding, Dad?" Shurka asked.

"What about me?" Zinaida kept repeating.

Shurka settled his father-in-law in the sled. Ustinov curled up in the hay as Shurka turned Solovko around.

"Why do you keep on about yourself, Zinaida Pal'na?" Shurka asked in amazement. "What's the matter with you? You keep harping on the same thing! A woman's question! That's just like a woman!"

Hotly whipping Solovko, he urged the sluggish horse homeward.

The Tale of the Maiden Natalya and Syoma the Bumblebee

Once upon a time in Lebyazhka
there was told the tale of the maiden Natalya . . .

This Natalya grew up as the runt of the litter, knee-high to a grasshopper and not a bit taller. Not a single boy had ever given her a second look, so all by herself she announced, "I'm going to get married! That's what I'll do! Everyone else is getting married, so I will, too!"

"Now, now," they said, "you just live out your life as a maiden! No one has asked for you, and no one is about to. It's the fate God has given you!"

"No," she replied, "I will get married! If you don't marry me off, I'll hang myself with a rope! I'll cross the path of all our other maidens. I'll ruin their weddings! All the Kerzhak lads will steer clear of our girls if there's a suicide among them!"

That Natalya was a downright curse! So the Poluvyatsky folk thought and thought about what to do with their poorest specimen, and they came up with something—they had to! And so one day, beginning early in the morning, the Kerzhaks heard the Poluvyatsky folk making a racket on the other side of the hill. There was a great and constant din of pipes and fiddles and singing. What could it be? By noon one of the Kerzhaks came back from the forest where he had been cutting trees.

"I know what they're up to!" he told his people. "I heard the news from one of their men. And I caught a peek with my own eyes, too, when I passed by with my timber."

"So what's going on?"

"They're honoring one of their maidens!"

"A maiden?!"

"That's right!"

"Have they all gone crazy, the heathens?! They're raising such a ruckus over a maiden? Are they marrying her off or something?"

"It's not because she's getting married. They're celebrating her name-day. They'll celebrate it for three days. Maybe even longer!"

"Good Lord!" said the Old Believers, making the two-fingered sign of the cross. "Those Poluvyatsky folk are genuine heathens! If they make such a fuss over every maiden's name-day, when do they have time to pray? And when do they do their work?"

"But they don't do it for everyone. It happens only for one of them, a special one! Her name is Natalya!"

The Kerzhaks wanted to take a look for themselves at what all the noise was about, so they went, and they looked, and indeed, there in a circle of people stood a maiden, knee-high to a grasshopper, all decked out in silk ribbons. The men, women, and children, and even their so-called Poluvyatsky priest, were praising the maiden, hugging and kissing her, raising her on their arms and carrying her around in a circle. It was a wonder to behold!

One of the Kerzhak lads—Syoma, who was nicknamed Bumblebee because he could make a buzzing sound through his right nostril—became very interested, indeed. He asked, "Why do you have such a custom, to praise a maiden so, without a wedding, for no good reason?"

"But it's not our custom! We're telling you thick-headed Kerzhaks, it has nothing to do with anyone, it's not done for anyone, except for our dear Natashenka!"

"And why only for her alone?"

"She's our beauty! Our prettiest one, our dear sweet soul, the light of all the maidens!"

Now wasn't that something! Syoma the Bumblebee looked high and low, at first from a distance and then up close. Where was she, this beauty of beauties? He couldn't catch a glimpse of her.

The next day, when there was the same noise on the Poluvyatsky side, the piping even louder, the fiddles more numerous, and the singing more exuberant, Syoma the Bumblebee thought, "I'll go again! I didn't see the beauty of beauties last time. I must not have looked well enough. This time I'll look with both eyes!" So he went, and asked, "Well, what happens when you

Poluvyatskys marry off this maiden? What sort of noise and celebration will there be then?"

"But we won't marry our Natashyushka, our bright little dewdrop, to anyone! We'll just honor her every year like this. We'll enjoy her ourselves, the pretty little darling!"

Now wasn't that something again! Yes, indeed!

"And what if I, Syoma the Bumblebee, a fine lad—I can buzz through my right nostril—asked for this maiden's hand?"

"Don't even think of it! We have six maidens—five of them anyone can take, but the sixth we'll keep for ourselves! We won't let anyone lay a finger on her!"

And so the celebration around the maiden Natalya, knee-high to a grasshopper, went on for a third day. The pipers were running out of breath, the fiddlers were exhausted, and the Poluvyatsky priest could barely stand on his feet.

And then Syoma the Bumblebee saw the little beauty Natalya! What could he do? Well, this is what Syoma did: he grabbed the maiden out of the circle and ran away with her. She was light in his arms, and he ran swiftly. All the Poluvyatsky folk chased after him, but not one caught up to him.

All his life after that, Syoma boasted, buzzing through his right nostril, "Everyone else got married, but I stole my dear one away in broad daylight! I took her and ran! That's the sort of fellow I am!"

That's how it was; that's how it happened.

And from that time on the last name Shmelyovykh—from *shmel,* the Russian word for "bumblebee"—was also to be found in Lebyazhka.

▲▲▲

"Now wouldn't it be fine," thought Ustinov, "to live in a fairy tale for a while!" Having just awakened, he was lying in bed. In the main room Domna had been telling the tale to their oldest granddaughter, Natashka, Ksenia's daughter, and this Natashka had listened with great interest to the story of that other Natashka. She didn't understand everything, but it all made her happy.

"Tell it again, Gramma, won't you? How does the part go where Syoma the Bumblebee runs away, Gramma? Did they chase him very hard?"

"They chased after him hard as they could, but they couldn't catch him at all!" Domna said.

There seemed to be something in her voice that Ustinov had not noticed before, something that he didn't quite know or had perhaps forgotten. It had seemed that way to him before, but long ago, in their youth, when he would suddenly and repeatedly notice something unfamiliar and unknown in his wife, Domna, in her habits, her voice, or her glance. But too much time had passed since the beginning of their married life for that kind of uncertainty to reappear. "Maybe she's insulted?" Ustinov thought. "Maybe she feels hurt that instead of her it was Zinaida Pankratov who pulled me off the harrow and brought me out of the forest?" But there was more tenderness than offense in Domna's tone of voice as she told the story. "Then maybe Domna is happy that her man is still alive?" That wasn't it either . . . It wasn't joy in her voice, but something else. "Then the hell with them, these women!" Ustinov thought angrily. "You just begin to figure them out, and then you lose your own wits. You get completely lost!" Stretching carefully in bed, he turned all his attention to himself.

He extended his wounded leg and felt it all over. As he flexed and straightened it at the knee, he discovered that he had awakened a recovered man. And then he was frightened by the thought that he might become lame. It was stupid! He had come back from the war in one piece, but from the White Wood—with a hole! True, during the war, besides getting a concussion, he had once been stuck by a bayonet. And that had been very stupid, too.

The Austrians had raised a white flag, and Ustinov's platoon quietly approached their trench. Suddenly, in a flash, some grubby-faced little Austrian stuck a bayonet into Ustinov's hand! His face all screwed up, trembling like an aspen leaf, he had attacked Ustinov in fear. Without a second thought, Ustinov had lunged with his own bayonet, but in the last split second he twisted his rifle to one side and let the soldier with the dirty face live. He just spit on him and cursed him with every word that came to mind. Where was he now, that Austrian saved by a miracle? He was probably healthy as can be, while Ustinov had been wounded again for no good reason! If someone had to be wounded again, shouldn't it have been the Austrian, in all fairness, and not Ustinov?! But justice had responded, though it was late in coming—his leg was his own again and obeyed its master.

Domna was knowledgeable in the use of medicinal poultices and herbs, but she wouldn't treat just anyone. When it came to the members of her own household, however, she would immediately go to the barn, where one corner was hung with bundles of various herbs, leaves, and roots. She would sort through these bundles, feeling, smelling, tasting, inspecting them thoroughly in the light, and then take them into the house to boil them and use them on her patient. True, she didn't have much success with internal illnesses, but various bruises, cuts, contusions, boils, and rashes, as well as rheumatism in man or beast—all those were within her power and knowledge. She never got sick herself, and there had never been a blemish on her fair skin in all her life. Perhaps it was for this reason that the light touch of Domna's hand drew any such impurity from others. And now she was tending Grunya's left foreleg and the right leg of her husband.

Her husband turned out to be more cooperative than Grunya. Even though it was still not very easy for Ustinov to turn his leg from right to left or to rotate his heel inward or outward, that wasn't of much consequence. No one walked around with his heels turned out anyway. But in its normal position, with toes forward and heel back, the leg didn't complain, and if it still hurt, it was too shy to show it. Ustinov told himself that that was how it should be: this peasant's and soldier's leg had measured fields and marched many thousands of versts and was used to everything. So it wasn't in its nature to hurt for very long. It would either fail entirely and be exchanged for a wooden leg or be healthy. And it wanted to be healthy. Nor did Ustinov, having so complimented his peasant's leg, forget about himself, the peasant. He took heart, puffed and grunted a bit, and got dressed.

He went out into the main room. He told Domna, who certainly did not expect to see her husband on his own two feet, to bring him a walking stick. He remembered that Grandfather Yegory had left such a stick and that it was patiently waiting in a cupboard somewhere until someone needed it. A good stick, stout and well-worn, it would now come in handy.

Still refusing Natashka, who kept asking her grandmother to tell her once more how Syoma the Bumblebee had carried off his bride and how the people had chased after him but never caught him, Domna said, "Leave me alone, little one," and began turning the handle of her old-fashioned Singer. She had managed to find some thread somewhere. She was always complaining that she had a sewing machine and even some sort of material, but not a single bobbin of suitable thread. The Singer clattered a few more times and then fell silent. As Domna left her sewing machine to go to the pantry to fetch the cane, she half turned toward Ustinov. "It would be better for you, Nikolai Levontyevich, if you stayed in bed for a while longer! Where are you in such a hurry to be off to?"

Again Ustinov noticed that sound in her voice that had not been there before, but he had no time for that now. He rose, stood, and even walked around on his two legs, and immediately his cares and concerns came pressing in on him from all sides. Before anything else, he took a look around. The scene in the main room was the usual one: Natashka was playing with a rag doll, and Shurka, her father, was also at play. Biting the tip of his tongue in the left corner of his mouth, he was painstakingly carving the squares of a checkerboard on a piece of wood. Shurka had no concern for any real work, never had and never would. When he was working, he never bit his tongue, but when it came to any sort of frivolous, playful matter, it was hard to find anyone more diligent. The middle child, Shurka Junior, was sitting under the table crowing like a rooster. Ksenia was bathing the youngest child, Yegorka, in a washtub, and the baby, all rosy and half laughing, half rebelling, was flailing his arms and legs and scattering droplets of water like a spring sparrow wallowing in the season's first puddle. Soaked to the skin and disheveled, his mother was already exhausted by his antics, but Yegorka kept kicking her in the chest as if he wanted to push off from her and float away to some distant land. Everyone huddled around the flame of the tallow candle in a saucer affixed to a vent door on the Dutch stove. They all got by as best they could with this dim illumination.

"Shurka," Ustinov asked, "did you do as I told you? Have you done it?"

"What are you asking about, Dad?" Cutting deeper into the large, square board with a borrowed cobbler's knife, Shurka seemed surprised.

"Don't you know? I'm asking you about Morkoshka!"

As soon as Ustinov had been brought home injured, he had ordered Shurka to hire someone for two or even three poods of grain to help him dig a grave in the animal cemetery and bury Ustinov's faithful friend Morkoshka. But now, looking at Shurka, Ustinov had his doubts. This jolly young fellow could just as easily have sold as much as four poods to some moonshiner and dumped Morkoshka in an open field to be torn apart by the foxes and wolves. Maybe at that very moment the wolves had already finished stripping the last of Morkoshka's bones and were baring their horrible yellow fangs at each other.

"I did just what you said, Dad!" Shurka assured Ustinov. "Only no one would come help for three poods. You know how people are these days, Dad. So I had to promise four. Like it or not, I gave four!"

"Would you swear to it?"

"Good Lord, Dad! You really don't believe me?!"

"There's a lot of things a body can't get you to do. Even if you swear to it."

Looking insulted and continuing his work even more diligently, Shurka said after a moment, "It's always like this with you, Dad. You never ask about the thing you really need to."

"Well then?!" Ustinov asked his son-in-law apprehensively. He remembered that while he had been lying sick in bed he had constantly felt that his wound was definitely not the last misfortune he would suffer, that it was not even his greatest concern, that he would face the most important problem the moment he was back on his feet again. "Well then? What are you getting at?"

Ksenia lowered her voice at the washtub, Natashka hid her rag doll under her dress, and Shurka, squinting his left eye and fixing the right one on his father-in-law, drew his tongue back into his mouth and slowly began to rub his neck. He gave the impression that he was not sure his throat could manage the words about to pass through it.

"What are you getting at?" Ustinov asked again.

"I'm talking about the gelding that used to belong to Kupriyanov and Kruglov, Dad!"

"What about him? Has something happened to him?"

"Well, you see, Dad, Prokopy Kruglov took him away. He took him back to his own yard. It was a couple of days ago!"

"It doesn't make any sense!" Ustinov shouted and went rushing out into the freezing cold just as he was, with Domna running after him from the pantry.

"Just wait a minute, Nikola! I'll bring you your cane! And put your hat on at least!"

In the bitter cold and misty dusk, the first thing that Ustinov saw was a row of his own new burlap bags laid against each other in the middle of the yard. They were the same bags of grain that Shurka had taken to the Kruglovs in exchange for Kupriyanov's former gelding, five fat, full bags still sewn shut and one half-empty one, that Ustinov had given to Prokopy Kupriyanov in a good and honest bargain. But Kruglov had taken back his gelding and returned the grain as if there had been no agreement whatsoever between the two of them, fellow farmers and practically neighbors! As if Ustinov had never led the gelding into his own yard to begin with! As if that gelding, walking with his unbelievable worker's and plowman's stride, had never walked behind him at the end of the reins, had never breathed on the back of his neck! Ustinov felt a sharp pain in his leg and lowered himself onto the porch steps. Domna plopped his hat on his head, stuck Grandpa Yegory's walking stick in his hands, and ran back into the house to bring him his sheepskin coat.

From the porch, across his own and his neighbors' vegetable gardens, down the slope toward the lake, Ustinov could see the barely visible outline of the posts that the artel members of the manufacturing cooperative had set into the ground when they had begun to build the community machine shed. The war had put its mark on the artel's work and put an end to the construction, but the artel had left the poles standing as a memorial. When he looked at them from a distance as he did now, or especially when at other times he saw them up close, Ustinov always sensed something sepulchral in them, something of the graveyard. But now he saw something else in them—they looked like gallows. There were no crossbeams on these posts, nor ropes, no shrouds in which hanged men would gently swing after their execution. They were all as invisible and intangible as these men's hopes and dreams.

So that's how Nikolai Ustinov regained his health! That's how he stood again on his own two feet! He stood as if he had fallen face down on the ground, as if his present and former horses were walking over him one after another. Morkoshka was walking on him, and his iron-shod hooves complained to Ustinov about Ustinov: "You killed me in the forest on an iron harrow for no good reason at all! For no reason at all, you set off for a ride in the White Wood!" Grunya, complaining that her left foreleg had gone lame for good, hopped around on the prone Ustinov on three legs. Sevka Kupriyanov's gelding, the peasant horse, the worker and plowman, the magic horse, also gave Ustinov a good and thorough stomping with his hooves: "You're a good-for-nothing peasant for letting me leave your yard! Wouldn't I have served you truly, faithfully, and diligently? You, your children, and your grandchildren?" And with his old man's work-weary step, his decrepit yellowed bones creaking and groaning, Solovko slowly trampled his master for a long time.

It was best not even to pity this stupid peasant, Nikolai Ustinov, to whom the affairs of the Commission seemed more important than his own, those of a farmer and the head of a household. He had betrayed his own, and now he was paying the full price. He was the same as his son-in-law Shurka. The wind whistled and blew the same way in both their empty heads! The one had nothing better to do than to make a set of checkers and then play with them noisily at all hours of the day and night, or to horse around with his pals, maybe lock someone up in the outhouse, or to play cards, or to get good and drunk with Mishka Goryachkin, Lebyazhka's cobbler, and wander through the village from one end to the other, raising a ruckus and threatening someone for who knows what. And as for the other! For him, God only knows why, there were all these various doings with the Forest Commission, plans and speeches, and appeals, and endless conversations and bedtime stories coming from every direction, and all sorts of books, and what's more, a crazy woman, Zinaida Pankratov, another man's wife, goggling her wild eyes at him, ready at any minute to take him in her arms and run away with him somewhere, it didn't matter where!

It seemed to people that the two of them—Shurka and his father-in-law, Nikolai Ustinov—were completely different from one another, that one was empty-headed and frivolous and the other, the good breadwinner. But that wasn't the case at all. The end result was the same for both him and Shurka, a household in ruins. And what could be worse than that?

Barin came up, sat down on the porch next to Ustinov, and wagged his tail to ask, "Well? What do you have to say, Master? Do you admit that if it weren't for me, that harrow in the forest would have been the end of you?! Do you admit it?"

Ustinov didn't say anything to Barin. He remembered how the night before, when he was already feeling better, in a dream or half in a dream he had felt the final throbbing of his leg and had heard Barin barking outside. It was not a good sound, but one of alarm, the same as when Ustinov and Morkoshka had lain impaled on the harrow and Barin had rushed back and forth on the forest road, not wanting to run back to the village for help, not knowing what to do. "Well," Ustinov thought, "I keep reliving that terrible moment. Still! It's time to just forget about it!" Without looking at Barin, he reached out and tugged his ear. "Why were you barking last night? Or was I just hearing things?"

"I barked because I had to!" Barin thumped his tail on the frozen, snow-dusted porch floor. "That's why I'm a dog—so I can bark!"

"And you're an old dog already!" Ustinov sighed. "An ancient dog! Old as the hills! If you were a human you wouldn't do anything but lie around on the bench above the stove and be bored. Maybe you bark so much at night, moon or no moon, simply out of boredom? True enough, it must be someone's fault that the years go by and get used up, and you can't expect any fresh and unused ones to take their places. Maybe it's the moon's fault?" He wanted to shove the blame off on someone.

Then this stupid peasant, Nikolai Ustinov, felt the bitter cold. Chilled to the bone, he stirred himself, stood up, and went back into his house. But he went in not quite the same man as he had been before. He went in crushed and trampled by his own horses and with a grudge against himself. When he had gone out on his porch, he had been the owner of four horses, but he had come back with one, or none at all. What sort of worker would the decrepit Solovko be now? As he was in his coat and hat, he walked silently through the main room, past Domna and Shurka, past Ksenka, Yegorka, and Natashka and into his little room, where he threw his coat on the bed and flopped down after it. He wanted to get sick all over again, to know nothing, to listen to the story of Syoma the Bumblebee, deceived for life but happy.

He could have gotten hold of himself and, leaning on Granddad Yegory's cane, limped over to Prokopy Kruglov. But what for? To prove his case? He couldn't do that because he had no case! Drunken Prokopy had shown off to him, also drunk, and they had struck a bargain, for laughs, and taken thirty-two poods of wheat in new burlap bags from one yard to the other, from here to there. So what? It was all a joke! All in fun! Leaning on his crutch, should he plead with Prokopy and explain his situation to him? Ustinov couldn't do that. He didn't have the strength to complain about his own weakness! Should he promise Prokopy to do whatever he wanted, to tell secretly what reports were being written in the Forest Commission, to defend him when he got caught in the forest cutting wood and let him go in peace, to stick up for him when Deryabin or Kalashnikov took away his moonshine still? But when he led Sevka Kupriyanov's former gelding from Prokopy's yard, Ustinov had already lowered himself. He had lowered himself as much as possible, and to save his life he had no strength to go any lower!

Domna came in to him with the candle, lighting up the room, and asked, "Are you sleeping, Nikola? That's good!"

"What's good about it?"

"And what's bad about it?" The candle illuminated Domna's handsome face, calm and relaxed. As long as Ustinov was alive, she didn't believe that anything at all bad could happen. "You're so upset, Nikola Levontyevich! There's no need to be!"

"There isn't?!"

"Not in the least! So we'll buy another horse. We'll trade some grain with the moonshiners in one of the villages on the steppe! You'll be able to stand without your cane and walk around by yourself. And that will be that!"

" 'And that will be that'?"

"Yes, it will!"

Propping himself up on one elbow, Ustinov suddenly began to tremble. A sharp shuddering seized him and shook him. "Get away from me, Domna!"

"What do you mean, Nikolai Levontyevich?!"

"Get out of here, I said. Right now!"

The candle in Domna's hand wavered. "Why?" she asked from the darkness that hid her face.

"Get out!"

She stood silently for a moment, then felt Ustinov's forehead. "You're still running a fever, Nikola! Fine, then—lie quiet and don't move!" She covered Ustinov with his sheepskin coat, took the candle, and left.

At the very moment Domna left the room, Ustinov remembered something that had happened long, long ago. He was even frightened by the suddenness of the unexpected memory, but it was too late to push it away.

It happened in the year 1903, when Ustinov's fields had been scattered about in different locations. He had a share of his father's portion, the assembly had also carved some off the village land fund, and his older brother, now deceased, had ceded a desyatina and a half to him. Lebyazhka had arranged for the next reapportionment of land the following winter. Then all the scattered fields of peasants such as Ustinov would be consolidated into one plot, but that would come only a year later. And so for the time being, Ustinov toiled away in three separate fields, unable to build a cabin or dig a well on any of them, and every day he either had to ride home to the village, about seven versts one way, or to spend the night in his field, lying under his sheepskin coat on a pile of hay under his wagon.

Once during plowing time the rain caught him under just such a tentative shelter. It was a May rain, good for the grain, but also cold as ice, and before long his teeth were chattering. As the water splashed down on him from above and soaked him from below, he thought, "This will be the end of me! I'll catch a chill and be sick all through planting time, even longer!" There was nothing else to do but to ask for shelter at his neighbor's cabin in the adjoining field. So he went to Kirill Pankratov's, but Kirill was not in the cabin. There was only Zinaida. Ustinov felt uneasy and uncomfortable, but he couldn't bring himself to go away either, especially since Zinaida quickly put some water on to boil for tea and even found a piece of sugar to offer her unexpected guest.

After some tea, Ustinov lay on a lath cot and listened to the rain, and through it, to Zinaida's intermittent and heavy breathing. He was terrified that Zinaida would begin to speak to him.

Sensing his fear, she said, "You're a timid one, Nikola! You're all a-tremble!" When Ustinov didn't answer, she stretched out her hand to him. "Are you still here? Maybe you've dissolved from fear and trembling? Into mist and smoke?!"

"Can you really be doing this, Zinka?" Ustinov asked quietly. "I would never have believed you could. No one would have believed it."

"I can't . . . But if you do only the things you can, if that's the only way you live—what kind of life is that?!"

Ustinov never thought about what had followed those words. Even in the single life of the soldier during the war, when the men comforted themselves with various memories, he never gave free rein to his own. A lot of things can happen to a man, and not every step that he takes or every experience that he has should stick with him.

And now, lying in bed, raked over the coals by none other than himself, Ustinov clearly remembered that time and was amazed that Zinaida had never mentioned it—not one word, not a single hint. Could she have forgotten it? Could she repress the memory when she took Ustinov from the iron teeth of the harrow? When she reached for him that night in her own house and would have reached him if Venya Pankratov had not shown up! Was her memory silent? But she knew and knew well: she could begin all over again, but she could not remember how it had once been. She couldn't because he couldn't—he didn't want the memory!

Now Zinaida's apparent slowness and lack of understanding pleased Ustinov, and an old, old love song kept coming into his mind:

> Do you remember, do you remember, my dear,
> How we walked along the path in the spring?
> You told me the whole truth then,
> What will happen with you and me . . .

Not at all surprised by this song that had come to him so unexpectedly, he repeated over and over, "What will happen with you and me . . . " But something else surprised him: Grishka Sukhikh seemed to know about what had happened so long ago! And Grishka had not been able to restrain himself. After remaining silent for so many years, he couldn't keep it up. He had come to Ustinov's cabin in the fields, had kicked Barin angrily and poured out his envy. He had written down his claim to a portion of the forest and had been about to leave, but then he had come back to shout at Ustinov, "Don't lie! Even after Zinka had already married her snot-nosed Kirilka, you spent the night in her cabin! Didn't you? You don't know anything about it? Have you forgotten?!" Had Grishka turned into a wet and hungry wolf and wandered around the cabin that stormy night?

Had he known that Kirill was absent, that Zinaida was spending the night there alone? That Nikola Ustinov was there beside her? Perhaps Grishka Sukhikh, gritting his teeth, had leaned against the window or a crack in the door? At the very moment that . . . ? Or had he found out some other way?

Now Ustinov remembered and understood the words that Zinaida had spoken that night before Venya's knock on the window, and even those she had not managed to speak. He knew them through and through, as if they were his own. "Believe me, Nikola," Ustinov could hear her say now, "we need to do just what I say: we need to run away from here, away from all these people! Believe me, and I will believe in the rest of the world! Without your belief, I can't be a believer! I can't believe in life, in anything! Lebyazhka took me in, supported me, and gave me shelter, but I don't believe in the village, I'm ungrateful! I raised my sons, but I have no faith in them either. If my lack of faith is in their blood, I don't know why they exist. Make me a believer, Nikolai Levontyevich! Only you can do it, no one else! Even Jesus Christ couldn't do it every time, but if you want to, you can!"

It felt both sad and sweet to Ustinov. There he was, a thoroughly unhappy peasant, injured, ruined, horseless, but for someone he was no less than Jesus Christ! Let him be ruined even more, let him be poor and naked and powerless—Zinaida did not fear any of it, just so long as Ustinov was alive. Ustinov would live and be a living Christ to her! When his leg began to hurt again and his head slowly grew dizzy with the pain, Ustinov knew the real source of that dizziness. He had remembered that moment in the Pankratov house when he had clung to Zinaida like a tiny baby and she had cradled his head in her strong hands. She had caressed him, promised him an entirely different sort of life, a life not of this world, and had commanded him to take a look at that life. And so, like a fairy-tale hero, he could now choose his own fate, either that of the mighty Christ or that of a speechless and happy baby, and be fair and just at the same time! He knew he had been very unfair. A woman had saved him, had taken him from the teeth of the harrow, but he had turned away from her just as soon as it was possible to do so and had asked to be taken out of her arms, taken out of her sled and put into his son-in-law Shurka's, and had ridden away without thanking her, without saying a single word of farewell to her!

But now it was time to return to thinking about himself, the injured and useless peasant. "Did I chase Domna away? Should I call her back? She'll come in and chase away these strange thoughts of mine in a second!" But he kept on lying there, silent and motionless, surrendering to the strangeness. "Or will someone come looking for me? Knocking at the window? Like Venya Pankratov came knocking that time?" Granddad Yegory's stick leaned against the head of the bed, and Ustinov touched it. "Let even the Forest Commission call for me. I'll come right away, walking with this stick! I'd go, by God!" But no one called for him. Once again someone with a candle came in to look at him. It was Shurka, at the right time for the first time in his life. Ustinov realized that Domna, who had been offended and didn't want to come back, had told Ksenia to go see her father, but Ksenia had dragged her feet. Maybe she was shy, she was like that sometimes. Then Shurka had volunteered to go. "I'll cheer Dad right up!"

"Can I cheer you up, Dad?" He set the candle down on the window ledge.

"Go ahead!"

"Are you thinking and thinking about the same thing, Dad? 'What in the world will happen now?'"

"You don't care at all about what will happen next!"

"That's right!" Shurka agreed happily. "I don't think ahead or try to figure things out! Never!"

"Is that smart?"

"Smarter than the smartest! Smarter—now don't be offended—smarter than smart people like you, Dad!"

"Well, well now . . ."

"That's right! Look here, Dad, you went and bought Svyatka and built her a separate, warm shed. You got yourself some horses, and you decided to play games with Prokopy Kruglov for Sevka Kupriyanov's gelding! You sit in your Commission for weeks arguing about things—and for what? You keep trying to figure out what will happen. What will happen tomorrow or in a year or two. It's a waste of time! Don't you really understand that? Before 1914 you worried about '16, but no one asked you about all your concerns. Instead they shaved your head and sent you to the front, and that was all! And where did you greet the year of '16? Well, true, you were lucky enough to come back alive and in one piece. It was luck, and nothing else! And now the war is just about to catch up with us all again, but you still keep puttering around. You still don't take the war into account. Instead you count on that lucky chance that you'll be left alive and in one piece as if that were the only fate you had. Did you know last year what this year would bring, what would be happening now? No, you didn't know, you didn't have a clue! So why do you keeping thinking and thinking about the future?"

"You've cheered me up, Shurka, cheered me up good."

"Really?"

"Well, how could it be otherwise?! A cheerful character like you brings one baby after another into the world, but you're not around to make a life for them! But when my children and grandchildren need me, I'm there, I'm right there! I'm in serfdom to them. And since that's the way it is, I can't avoid thinking about the future. A year from now, two years from now, and longer still."

"But there ain't no one who knows what turn their children's lives will take, Dad, let alone their grandchildren's." Swinging one foot, Shurka sat on the edge of his stool. "You work for them today, but who knows if they'll be alive tomorrow? Or say you keep the farm going for them, and then they up and spit on it and go off to work in a factory or take some other job! So then what have you worked for? What did you sweat your ass off for? Or what if you leave your property to them, and then the next day someone comes along and takes it all away from them, down to the last stitch of clothing?!"

"It's not that simple to take a man's own away from him, to take away what he's worked for!"

"But there's nothing simpler! Someone comes along—the Whites, the Reds, or some ordinary person—shows you his revolver, orders, 'Hands up!' and that's that! It's a done thing!"

"You're just like Mishka Goryachkin, Shurka! He's always threatening to burn or kill someone, and you're doing the same! He isn't your friend now for nothing!"

"It isn't for nothing, Dad!" Shurka agreed quite willingly.

Not so very long ago, anyone would have been ashamed to be friends with Mishka Goryachkin, but times must really have changed if it was so easy for Shurka to agree with his father-in-law and even to repeat for emphasis, "It isn't for nothing!" Mishka Goryachkin, the bootmaker, a pockmarked, fussy, scrofulous little peasant, had begun some time ago to proclaim himself the enemy of all Lebyazhka. He would get drunk and run around the village making threats: "I'll kill you! I'll burn your house down! You just give me a little time, and I'll wring all your necks, you farmers! You bastards! Earthworms! You dig yourselves into the dirt like serpents and suck the life out of it, but I won't let you, you bloodsuckers! I'll settle accounts with you! I'll bring you to proper justice!" There were times when Mishka got beaten up, and then he would repent and swear to God that he wouldn't do it anymore, but when he got drunk he'd revert to his natural self.

No one could explain the origin of his wild hatred for every resident of Lebyazhka. Maybe he hated the villagers because sometimes when he made his threats, they would just laugh and reply, "Well now, Mishka the warrior! Go ahead! Who will you kill first?" The blood would rush to Mishka's head and the scrofulous spots on his face would darken. "Maybe you!" he would answer, rolling his eyes. "Fine, let it be me!" Mishka's customer would agree. "Fix the sole of this boot here. And put on a new heel! And do a good job, I won't settle for less! And not without reason!" That's how peacefully they spoke to him, especially since Mishka was not a bad bootmaker, and, more important, he was the only one in all Lebyazhka. But for some time now people had begun to take Mishka's threats of murder and arson seriously. When gangs and punishment brigades were going around

randomly killing, hanging, confiscating, and burning, what would stop
Mishka from taking up the same work? Especially if he had been itching to
fulfill his cherished dream for so many years?

When the Forest Commission was organized, Mishka shouted at them,
too, "The bloodsucking farmers have gotten together! I know why they've
gotten together—to suck other people's blood! To grow fat bellies! To take
care of their dear little kiddies, build them houses, guarantee them a supply
of timber! The bastards! I know everything, I can smell them!" And then
when the Forest Commission endeavored to set up a tar-distilling works,
Mishka, the first to answer the call, decided, "I'll give up bootmaking! I'm
fed up with keeping the bloodsuckers shod and measuring their feet! I'll live
in the forest, then later I'll come back and settle accounts with the lot of
them!" But he didn't live in the forest for a single day. And when the tar
distillers quarreled among themselves, sold the artel's old-fashioned caul-
dron somewhere, and dissolved the tar-distilling artel without ever beginning its work, Mishka, even more enraged at the Forest Commission,
announced, "There's who I need to begin with! Now I know exactly just
who and what!"

"But just why is Goryachkin so spiteful?" asked Ustinov. "What a terror
he is now! Inhuman!"

"That's just the way he likes it. That's the spirit that's in him!" Shurka
explained with a certain pride, half in Mishka Goryachkin, half in himself.
"Just that sort of spirit!"

"People drink an awful lot these days! Maybe that's the reason. It
couldn't be from anything else."

"They always drank."

"You don't say! I've seen Nikanor Gulyayev on the street, completely
plastered, barely able to hold himself together, even though it's a workday.
There's no excuse—no holiday, no name-day, wedding, birthday, funeral,
no nothing. He's simply drunk, and that's all! When was it ever like that?
Without any reason?"

"It never was, but it will be! The people are coming to their senses!
They're beginning to understand that all their endless labor and all their
possessions are no good to them at all. They have no masters, not even
themselves! All those different commissions and meetings are just useless
inventions, all show and fraud. That's the sort of thing they're beginning to
understand. And there's no reason for you to be displeased, Dad, that I'm
hanging around with Mishka. No reason at all! You have to understand
which of us is doing more for the little kids, you, with all your work, or me
when I do just the opposite. I don't despise Mishka Goryachkin. Instead I
treat him nice for one day out of every week, at the very least!"

"But what for? Why do you need to be nice to Mishka Goryachkin once
a week?"

"Why? If Mishka starts acting up, he'll go after everyone, but I'll tell him, 'Don't touch Nikolai Ustinov! He's my father-in-law!' And he won't touch you, Dad!"

"And do you know where you can go, Shurka?!" Ustinov answered.

"As if you saw things any different, Dad!" Shurka wasn't the least taken aback. "You see them the same way, only you count on other people. I choose Mishka Goryachkin, and you take the 'Co-op Man,' Pyotr Kalashnikov, Ivan Ivanovich Samorukov, and Lieutenant Smirnovsky! When they came here to visit you when you were sick, didn't you at least make some kind of deal with them, and hasn't the same thing happened between you as between me and Goryachkin? I'll bet you whatever you want that the same thing happened between you all!"

Shurka's eyes were sparkling. Betting on something, arguing for the sake of a jackpot of kopecks, of meaningless excitement, was Shurka's favorite pastime. You couldn't prove to him that there were people of other principles and of a different breed who were not interested in betting and arguing over who beat whom in checkers, he or Mishka Goryachkin. Although Shurka was a kind man, this excitement over trifles made him spiteful, and he could not imagine that Smirnovsky, Kalashnikov, or Samorukov could come to see Ustinov without any ulterior motive, to speak with him about his health and about the health of all humankind. For Shurka, any conversation was the making of a deal, if not over checkers, then over sharing a bottle; if not over a bottle, then over two or three people being against some third or fourth. Shurka's carefree attitude was not laziness. He was always busy with something, working on something, but it would invariably be something trivial, and he suspected everyone else around him of playing the same sort of games and making the same sort of deals.

The sparkle in Shurka's eyes and his whole appearance were all the more unpleasant for Ustinov because this time Shurka was right, just the least bit, but right nonetheless, for Kalashnikov, Smirnovsky, and Ivan Ivanovich Samorukov had come to visit Ustinov not just to see him but also to reach an agreement about what to do next, about how to lead their lives after that unfortunate incident with the harrow. Smirnovsky had insisted that they had to conduct a secret inquiry to find out who had put the harrow there. Samorukov and Kalashnikov had sighed. Like it or not, Deryabin was right when he said that the fire at Grishka Sukhikh's freehold and the harrow trap on the forest road were trifles compared to the events of the times and that it was useless, even ridiculous, to try to discover who was responsible for them. The times were sick, and what can you ask of a sick man? "This time will die once and for all," Deryabin had said, "and another will be born, a fully just one, and then we will search out and severely punish the perpetrators of even the slightest crime." Ustinov reckoned that it wasn't specifically for him that the harrow had been laid down, but for any member of the forest guard, and that it truly made no sense to go looking for the guilty party. The only thing they needed to do—all they could do—was to be cautious.

"Go, go!" Ustinov chased Shurka away, too. "I can't teach you anything good, and I don't need to learn anything from you!"

"No, you don't!" Shurka agreed. "There's no one at all for you to learn anything from, Dad. You're the smart one yourself. Really, you can learn only from Kirill Pankratov's cousin! Only from Venya!"

"From who? From who?" Ustinov asked with a start. "Repeat that—from who?"

"What is there to repeat . . . ?" Shurka sighed. "You just get well, Dad."

As Shurka left he raised his brows and looked at Ustinov once more with particular interest. "Well then, Dad, what sort of man are you these days, huh?" his look asked openly. "And why was it Zinaida, another man's wife, who took you from the harrow? Why her?! So, Dad, your work in the Forest Commission isn't for nothing. Eh?!"

"Blow out the candle!" Ustinov told Shurka.

Shurka blew loudly on the candle and left.

"Shurka must know about Venya Pankratov," Ustinov thought, stupified with surprise. "Did I somehow say something while Shurka was around? In my sleep, or while I was delirious or something? Venya strictly warned me to hold my tongue!" Checking his memory meticulously, he decided he couldn't have let a single word slip to anyone about Venya, but that didn't lighten his mood. Not for the first time but now with great clarity, he pictured to himself how that very minute somewhere beyond the walls of his house a secret, invisible, cruel, underground life was going on in Lebyazhka, a life in which certain people had no other purpose than to wring some other people's necks. The mystery into which Venya Pankratov wanted to initiate him was no concern of Ustinov. He had no role in it. He tried to live a life that was visible to everybody, and he wanted to know no other, but, nevertheless, the mystery was being revealed to him.

What did enmity between people mean? Enmity meant not only that people quarreled but that if they even saw each other it was like the end of the world proclaimed by Kudeyar! The life of each became a secret, hidden away and revealed to no one. Could you even try to invite Grishka Sukhikh, Venya Pankratov, Smirnovsky, Mishka Goryachkin, Polovinkin, Prokopy Kruglov, Deryabin, Kudeyar, and Ivan Ivanovich Samorukov to share the same table? You couldn't! You could do something complicated, but there was no human power strong enough to do this simple thing!

Even though he tried to live a life visible to everyone, Ustinov was being dragged into some sort of mystery. He hated secrets. They interfered with life. They made him accuse himself and dread that other people, especially his own grandchildren, would accuse him, too. When his grandchildren gathered around his knees and bumped their fragrant little heads against his face, he became their serf. And a good serf should be a healthy man with no secrets. As his grandchildren squirmed around on his knees or sat quietly, the warmth of their little bodies would penetrate not his knees but his heart. How much must he still work for their sake—plow, sow, reap, buy, sell, dig, saw, repair all kinds of vitally essential things?! And, he asked himself in fear, when would he have the time to do it all?

Perhaps it was because of his fear for them that Ustinov did not pamper his grandchildren much, far less than Shurka did. Shurka would even let them ride horseback on him and pull his hair. But what was that to Shurka? He would play with them like that, but a minute later, carefree and whistling, he would leave for the entire day. He never thought about what might be going on at home without him. But Ustinov never stopped thinking about his grandchildren, day or night.

When he had still been at the front and, like all soldiers, had thought about life after the war, that life had seemed free and fine. What would it be like? He and Domna had raised their children. If life was just, what cares would they have when the war was over and the government had been taught how to treat the peasants?! After all, it was none other than the peasants who had rescued the officials of every rank and title, of every persuasion and opinion, from the war, from the ruin of Russia, from the St. Petersburg famine! But the war wasn't over. The soldiers had brought it home with them in their own duffel bags. Just as soon as they had loosened the drawstrings, they heard, "Here I am! Take me in, you peasants! And all you citizens of free Russia!" There was no human treatment of the peasants either, and they began to see how naive their dream of a good government had been.

And there was no trace of that fine, free life for him and Domna. Their son Leonty had died, and his wife, Yelena, was left in an inadequate little house with her two aged parents and two little children, whose main breadwinner was their grandfather, Nikola Levontyevich. Shurka, having finished the war early after serving in a forage detachment somewhere in the rear, had come home, not to his own house, but to his father-in-law's. Ustinov had hoped that Shurka would acquire just a little understanding during the war, but he had been disappointed. Grandfather Nikola was now the breadwinner for Shurka's children as well, and even their mentor, since their father could not be counted on for much discipline.

Ustinov was a breadwinner and a pillar of support for many, but what did he have to lean on, what order in life? How much order did a Russian peasant need, anyway? Just a little bit, but there wasn't even that much! This peasant was more capable of surviving disorder than anyone else, but the present disorder was too much even for him.

The Siberian cooperative that Kalashnikov praised had christened itself with a new name, the Purchase & Sales Company, but when it was immediately caught in unprecedented embezzling in both purchasing and sales, it became the "Purchase, Sales & Embezzlement Company." It exported butter and grain to China and imported manufactured goods, matches, needles, separators, even kerosene, but just as it began to give the peasants hope, it went bust. "Show us some sympathy, Citizens!" the company begged. "The convoys were coming from Harbin with great riches, but they were robbed near Chita!" The peasants' current existence, which it was impossible to call a life, was continuing in that same wildly disordered way. "Everything for the people!" the Siberian Government proclaimed and began to do everything to the people—fleece them, draft them into the army, and arrest them. "Public property!" the newspapers printed, and soon, though not right away, it was understood what that meant. Public property was a pie that really belonged to nobody. No matter how many pieces were snatched from this pie, no one would yell, "Look out! I'm being robbed! Me, personally!" A hue and cry that is not personal is no hue and cry at all, but just some sort of muttering!

But you couldn't tell the kids, the grandchildren, anything about the Purchase & Sales Company or the Siberian Government. They knew their own business—growing up! They demanded to be fed and clothed. They wanted to run off to school with notebooks and bottles of ink in their hands. Make an effort, Granddad, work for the needs of the children! Ustinov had nothing against that. He was a grandfather, but he wasn't too old or too weak to work. Something else was lacking: there should be order and effort not only in one's own yard but also in the country, and if they weren't to be found there, the carefree Shurka would be in the right, and no one else!

Thank God, Lebyazhka, as always, had suffered less than other villages. As long as the cooperative was the village's own, the Lebyazhkans had voted for everything—the creamery, the community machine shed, the Mutual Aid Fund—but as soon as the business touched upon joining up with other villages, and especially with the Purchase & Sales Company and Harbin, the citizens listened to Ivan Ivanovich Samorukov. "You can bring a complaint against one of your own to the village assembly, but who will you complain to against Harbin?" he asked. "Especially these days when no one knows what things depend on? When there are many governments, but no authority? A lot of thievery, and not a shred of honesty? In what direction are things going? No one knows! We can't see the future, so at least we could remember the past, what was bad and what was good back then, and try to make some use of our fathers' and grandfathers' wisdom! But we lack even those recollections, they've been knocked right out of our memory, out of all the people's memory!" The times were like the dry-topped pine tree: instead of pumping the earth's juices up to the high young shoots through which it could continue its life, it sent them to the hardened and callused middle branches. The thicker such a branch is, the denser its needles are, the more freely it spreads branches and twigs out to the sides, the more sap it takes for itself, and the more useless it becomes for the life of the whole tree, for the very topmost, genuinely growing shoots.

The worthlessness of the present time had long since offended Ustinov, but he had tried not to let his deeply rooted grievance stir. "Don't move! Not a bit of sense can come of it!" But now this feeling overwhelmed him. To dispel his grief, he would have liked to read a bit, but there were already two candles burning in the house—one in the the main room and one in the kitchen, where the women were clattering dishes and kneading bread dough—and it would be unthinkable to light a third by the book cabinet. Especially in Ustinov's present state of ruin. Nevertheless, Ustinov got up from the bed and sat down by the cabinet, and at the sound of his movement Ksenia stuck her head in from the main room.

"What are you doing here, Dad, in the da'k? Do you need a light?" Ksenia brought in her candle stub and left with a quiet, shy sigh.

Ustinov loved Ksenia very much. Her sincerity and simplicity made her dearer to him than all his other children. She had never tried to get away with anything or make mischief, but would come running herself, crying, "Oh, Mommy! Oh, Daddy! Look what I done—I b'oke a cup! Oh dea'!" Ustinov loved his daughter now, too, but with a completely different sort of love, one unfamiliar to him and especially to her. She was too old to set on his knee or to spank with a switch. He had to speak to her with words and nothing else, but what kind of words could he use, now that she was a woman, not off on her own and the mistress of her own house, but a grown woman nonetheless, with her own, woman's mind and understanding, and not her father's? She was already not so much his daughter as the mother of his grandchildren. As long as they talked about the grandchildren, there was conversation, but if it was not about them, there was none at all!

The glimmering light of the candle stub had to be used, so Ustinov took first one and then another book from the cabinet, leafed through them, and finally read something that made him press his face close to the lines of print.

> And we are silent. And time is dying . . .
> We are not afraid of the shame of chains—
> And our people wear chains,
> And pray for their executioners . . .

"How true it is!" sighed Ustinov. "Tsar Nicholas shot at the people in '05, and I knew about it, but still I prayed for him! He started a senseless war, risked millions of people, and still I prayed and prayed for him! The regimental chaplain gave the order, and I prayed! As if I knew nothing bad about him!"

> Russia is oppressed, Russia is ill:
> The citizen is in mute sorrow—
> The son does not dare to weep
> Over his ailing mother!

The book had been printed in 1906, and the verses were by Ivan Nikitin. He came from the simple folk, and all the lines in the poem were simple and clear. "The citizen is in mute sorrow . . . "

Two words, *God* and *citizen,* had always produced confusion and dismay in Ustinov. Except for these two, he could easily picture to himself all other objects, animate or inanimate, even if he had never even seen them before. The Emperor or the Empress, the fat French Commander in Chief Joffre or a polar bear, a sea serpent, a precious stone of unusual proportion—all those were within his reach. He would close his eyes, think a little, and there they would be! He remembered how at the beginning of the war it was rumored that the Germans, and our men, too, were flying through the air in machines. All the soldiers had wanted to see how such a miraculous thing had been accomplished. But Ustinov figured it out right away: you couldn't fly without wings, a tail, wheels, or a motor; so shouldn't the machine have all these accessories? And sure enough, the flying machine turned out to have all of these. If you throw a stone or use powder to fire a bullet from a gun barrel, both will fly without any of those things, but they can't come back again. A tail and wings are essential for coming back again. And wheels: it's not enough to drop back down to the ground. You had to keep from being driven into it; that is, first you had to run along it for a ways. On nothing else but wheels.

But the words *God* and *citizen* were impervious to the power of Ustinov's imagination. God was alone in all creation. No one resembled Him, nor He anyone else. Once Ustinov had pictured God as a peasant farmer and then again as the greatest of circles, containing all other circles and lines and the whole wide world, he refrained from further conjecture about Him. The citizen, on the other hand, lived on the earth in countless numbers; but, no matter how many times Ustinov met him, in a general's uniform or naked in the regimental bathhouse, not once did he seem to embody that word that Ustinov had read so endlessly in the newspapers and that, starting in the spring of '17, the soldiers and the officers as well began to enjoy using as an honorific, the word that even the residents of Lebyazhka, especially the members of the Forest Commission, loved to use to address each other as if they were bragging about it. But what about Mishka Goryachkin? Everyone knows that he's verminous scum, but if Mishka raises his hand at a meeting, the Chairman announces, "Citizen Goryachkin has the floor," as if nothing had ever happened, and then everyone listens to the "Citizen" as if they didn't know whom they were dealing with! Everyone understands that this polite deference is a sham, but no one will up and say so. Things could be carried even further if Mishka Goryachkin was already a "Citizen," and Ignashka Ignatov, too. So why shouldn't they make the most important citizens out of the lowliest people? Let them run Lebyazhka, shouting, "I'll ki-i-ll you! I'll set your house on fire!" Whoever is ignorant himself of how to live tries as hard as he can to teach it to everybody else and to life itself. But then what is left for the true citizen, if he really exists? Perhaps to live eternally "in mute sorrow"?

Fine, however it may be, but life doesn't go the way it does in books. If everyone invariably lived according to some single book, the Bible, or according to those lines about the mute citizen, or if life followed the call of a single person, even the holiest of all the saints, life would have run dry long ago. It would have gone the way of Kudeyar, or the beetles and ants, or followed some other, unknown and nonhuman path. But as long as people badger life with their helpless appeals, life, letting these appeals in one ear and out the other, is still life. It still means something in and of itself and knows a thing or two. It will still keep on living!

Ustinov heaved a sigh. Thinking for a peasant was like swimming for a cow! Of course, a cow knows how to swim—if there is no other way to go, it will swim across a river, but being in the water is the business of a fish, not a cow. A peasant can think, too, and sometimes he must, but to get lost in thought—absolutely not!

Ustinov turned his attention to his leg. Even though it was like Solovko's leg, hard-working and unassuming, when it hurt it required some care. As it healed, it needed to be unbandaged, bathed, nourished with medicinal herbs, and wrapped up again. If everything was done carefully, it would never fail him. About to tend to his leg, he stopped. Why was he doing it himself? He called for Domna, after all. She had guessed why she was being summoned and brought a basin and a small bundle of medicinal herbs. Nicely healed, the laceration was covered with a thin layer of cheerful pink skin that seemed to wink at Ustinov: "Fine, then live. Live, peasant! Live, don't think!" Domna washed his leg and began to apply a fresh poultice of various leaves, plantain, cudweed, and some almost round leaves with toothed edges. Ustinov wanted to ask her what kind they were, but he didn't, and she quickly finished the job in silence. When she did say a word or two, he once again heard that same inner voice, not quite familiar, but definitely Domna's own. Agitated again, he wondered if this day would ever be over. There were too many riddles in it, and they echoed in Domna's voice. He wanted to be left alone again and to fall asleep right away. Without any thoughts, without any riddles.

But Domna didn't leave. After she had changed the bandage on Ustinov's leg, she stroked his head and lay down beside him. While her husband had been ill, she had slept separately, in the main room, but now she understood that he had regained his health.

"Your wound is doing well, Levontyevich. It's almost healed!" Anyone in her place would have said the same thing and would have been just as happy. "Don't you fret, Nikola!" she continued after lying quietly for a moment. "We'll live on! We'll trade some grain for a horse in a village on the steppe, and we'll live on. I don't like the looks of that horse that Prokopy Kruglov got from Savely Kupriyanov anyway. It sways a lot when it walks!" Anyone could have said the same thing to comfort her husband. Domna pushed her soft, warm arm under him as far as her elbow. "Don't be cross, Nikola. Who have you got to be cross with—me? I haven't done a single bad thing to you. Not a thing!"

Ustinov felt she was right—if there was anyone for him to be cross with, it was himself! Only . . . He knew the frost was beginning to take a firmer hold. The rafters in the roof crackled above them, and a cold and misty spirit seemed to be wandering the streets and alleys of the village. Winter begrudged the village the recent thaw and wanted to make up for it with interest. It also had an account to settle with Ustinov. "I'll come and show you! If you're still around, that is!" the winter howled like Mishka Goryachkin. As Ustinov listened to the bitter cold strolling back and forth outside the walls of his house, he realized what he held against Domna: she didn't understand the settling of accounts that was to come. Nor did she understand all that had just happened to him. One incident, then a second, then, well, a third and last one, and she thought, "All the bad things are behind us!" When she was at her husband's side, she was incapable of understanding it any other way; she wasn't accustomed to anything else. That was why it was not she but another woman who had known when misfortune had befallen him. Why another, not this one, had come to save him, to pull him from the iron teeth. That's what it was . . .

Suddenly Domna sighed and said clearly, "I'll tell you something now, Nikola. I haven't said anything the last few days, but now I'll tell you!"

Ustinov still didn't move and closed his eyes more tightly.

"I'll tell you!" Domna repeated, pulling her soft, almost downy arm out from under his head, propping herself up on her elbow, and bending her face over his.

"Tell me . . . "

"A baby is coming, Nikola . . . "

"Dear God! To a husbandless widow, to Yelena?!" Ustinov guessed. "How?"

Domna's reproachful glance stopped him. "It's our baby that's coming, Nikolai Levontyevich! Yours and mine. Mine and yours . . . "

Bending his good leg at the knee and clasping it in his arms, Ustinov sat up in bed and protested, "We're too old, Domna! We're already too old!"

"It doesn't look that way."

"But our baby, how much younger would it be than our grandchildren?"

"It will be . . . "

"It isn't good! And everybody will see, even our children! It's a sin against our grandchildren. They will really hold it against us! No, it isn't good!"

"It seems to be fine."

"I imagined every possibility, I thought about what might happen, but I never thought about such a thing, no!"

"Aren't you happy about the baby, Nikola? It will be your own flesh and blood. Isn't it all the same to it who it will be older than or younger than? It's life. That's all it knows, and nothing else! And that's the end of all these words! You aren't happy?! Be happy anyway! It's a sin not to be happy about what God has ordained! You aren't happy? Have you become a sinner?"

Ustinov didn't answer.

"Rest, Nikola Levontyevich." With her soft arm, Domna very gently pushed him down on his back and bent over him again in the darkness. "It's only frightening at the very first. After a day or two, you'll get used to it. Get well in time for happiness, sleep." Secure in the feeling of her own righteousness that had never betrayed her before and had not betrayed her that day either, she began to doze lightly.

"So that's what it is!" Ustinov realized. "That's why Domna told the story about the maiden Natashka and Syoma the Bumblebee in such an unusual voice today! That's what it is!"

For a long time he couldn't sleep. He kept waiting for something. Someone was still supposed to tell him about something. And, indeed, sometime after midnight someone knocked on the shutter, not loudly, but confidently, as if he knew what he was doing. Ustinov got up out of bed and limped over to the window.

"Who's there?" he asked through the shutter.

"Come out, Ustinov! Just for a minute!"

"I'm lame! I'm still not walking on my leg!"

"Just for a minute!"

"But who is it? I don't recognize your voice!"

"It's village business! Come out and you'll see!"

The cold street was quiet. Barin hadn't spoken out. He had left the yard and gone off somewhere. Domna woke up.

"All right, Nikola, go on out!" She stretched and sighed, "Go out and tell them that it's for the last time so there won't be any more of this knocking and disturbance at night from now on. Don't forget to tell them!"

"I don't recognize who it is . . . "

"Your stick is right there by the head of the bed."

"Woodcutters at night, the fire at Grishka Sukhikh's at night, everything at night," Ustinov sighed to himself as he slowly got dressed. Again he recalled the sound of Domna's voice as she told the story about the maiden Natashka and Syoma the Bumblebee. He heaved one more deep sigh and, leaning on Grandpa Yegory's cane and stretching his hand out in front of himself to avoid bumping into anything in the dark, he passed through the main room to the door. That fairy tale was still running through his sleepy mind.

The Big Bear

The Forest Commission gathered its papers and moved to the village assembly hall on the advice of Ivan Ivanovich. "You, the Commission, make an appeal to the people, but then you withdraw into the private domain—you hide away in the Pankratovs' house. That isn't good! That isn't right! You should hold your meetings in a real office!" he insisted. "If you want to talk with people every day and try to find common interests with them, you need a place that's open to one and all!"

Besides all that, Ivan Ivanovich most likely did not want Ustinov, once he had recovered, to be in the Pankratovs' house again almost every day. The Commission agreed with Ivan Ivanovich that it was time for them to go, time to free the Pankratovs from the billeting that had dragged on so long, especially since Kirill, though quietly and discreetly and all by himself, had begun to hit the moonshine. Ignashka Ignatov was the only one who objected. He couldn't understand why people would want to exchange a good thing for a bad one. In the office building, who would treat the Commission to fragrant wheat kasha with honey? True enough, the assembly hall wasn't much to look at with its interior blackened by tobacco smoke and smudged with ink spots and who knows what else. It had one large room and two smaller ones behind wooden partitions, a tiny corridor, and a vestibule. The whole thing resembled one huge jail. Various offices had been housed there at different times: the Village Elder and a clerk under the Tsar; the Soviet of Deputies during the Soviet Government; and the Poverty Committee, dissolved just as soon as it was created. And now under Kolchak, there were again a clerk and two policemen. One of them was sick and good only for paperwork and sitting in the office; he never left the smallest room, where he loitered about, sighing and boiling water for tea on the little stove. The healthy policeman, a man named Pilipenkov with a round, red face, represented the powers that be.

This latest meeting of the Forest Commission was unusual not only because it was taking place in the twilight of the village assembly hall but also because Samorukov and Smirnovsky were again present. The two of them, as if playing the role of observers, were sitting on the long bench to the side of the table behind which sat Kalashnikov, Deryabin, and a very pompous Ignashka Ignatov, who kept snorting for some reason. Also present were Pilipenkov; Prokopy Kruglov and his timidly silent brother Fedot, who had been summoned for the third time for making moonshine; two woodcutters; the village schoolteacher, who had brought a complaint about Mishka Goryachkin's vandalism; and Goryachkin. On the back benches, almost in total darkness, sat a few citizens who were there simply out of curiosity.

The Commission members had decided on their current duties. Pyotr Kalashnikov had taken on the job of writing the minutes, Deryabin would serve as the Chairman, and Ignashka Ignatov was to remain present for the whole meeting, not to go running off anywhere, not to interrupt anyone, and not to fuss. They began with the consideration of the question "Concerning the Breaking of Two Windows in the Schoolhouse by Citizen M. A. Goryachkin." In a quiet, halting voice, the teacher informed them that last Saturday evening, when she had been at the school drawing a map of Europe on a sheet of newspaper because she lacked proper teaching materials, a drunken Citizen Goryachkin had begun knocking on the door. Because she had not let him into the school, he had broken two windows, and through both windows had reviled her with unprintable language and had left after threatening to use force and even to burn down the school.

The teachers in the surrounding villages devoted less time to working with their students than Lebyazhka's teacher did and didn't try nearly as hard as she did, but they were more confident and maintained their dignity. Elected to village social organizations and to cooperatives' boards of directors, they often chaired them, but Lebyazhka's teacher had never done anything of the kind. She had come to Lebyazhka's tiny schoolhouse with its three barely transparent little windows almost twenty-five years ago, and in all that time she lived so quietly and discreetly that no one but the children had caught a good look at her. The children adored her, but for some reason she disappeared forever from the lives of the adults, even of those who were her former students. Perhaps it was because she seemed just barely to be living on this earth. She arrived at school at the crack of dawn and left after dark, satisfied that she had explained the four arithmetical functions, simple fractions, the alphabet, and a few rules of grammar to the children and had told them about the continents and countries of the Earth and its revolution around the sun. The Lebyazhka schoolteacher had never bothered a single person anywhere, nor could she have, but now just such a person had turned up, Mishka Goryachkin.

What bothered him was the teacher's demonstration of the revolution of the Earth. In her school she had demonstrated this phenomenon by dressing a little boy up in pieces of yellow paper and a little girl in black paper, and then having the little boy slowly turn in place in the middle of the classroom while the little girl moved in a circle around her "sun." Making her way through the desks and holding the hem of her dress to avoid getting tangled in them, she turned so that she showed now her face, now her back to the little boy. She was the Earth.

Sometimes the grown-ups would come to have a look at an entertaining lesson, but the teacher met these visitors without joy. Shy around every adult on earth, she was afraid of them, didn't understand them, and couldn't accept them as real people. So she was all the more at a loss when a drunken Mishka Goryachkin arrived to have a look at "the turning of the Earth" and told her that she was a complete fool to make the sun yellow and the Earth black. He demanded that the sun be red and the Earth blue, threatened to break the windows in the school, and carried out his threat that very evening.

When Deryabin asked whether that was what had happened, Mishka dismissed his question with a wave of both hands. "So what? That was just for starters! I'll do more than that if this outrage goes on any longer! She's nobody, an old maid and a dried-up frog," said Mishka, pointing his finger as if taking aim at the cracked lens of the teacher's eyeglasses. "That's who she is, her right there! Who gave her the right to stick a female child into the black clothing of a monk? And show the whole Earth in such a shameful way?! Who and when?"

"Just which outrage are you talking about, Citizen Goryachkin?" asked Kalashnikov, riled and red-faced. He stopped taking the minutes. "Which one? You're the worst outrage, the most malicious outrage there is! How dare you bad-mouth the person who taught the alphabet to practically everyone here, who opened their eyes to reading and writing? I can't understand where a man could get so much spite and shamelessness!"

"Well, then," Mishka retorted, "you just come to me with something to fix, with some shoe or other, and then I'll explain where I get it! But meanwhile tell me—are you saying the Earth is black, too?"

"But what else would it be?"

"Very simple—it's blue!"

"And it seems to you that the fields are blue, Goryachkin?" Deryabin laughed. "And you patch up little blue boots on a blue Earth?"

"That's just it, Citizen Chairman Comrade Deryabin! It's them earth-worms, them dirt farmers that make everything out to be black, out of their own greed. The ones who can't see no farther than their own snotty noses, and their eyes is covered over with the same snot! You just look out into the distance, and what color is the Earth? It's blue! And the sun is red, they sing about it in any old song!* Who gave her, that teacher, the right to disgrace the Earth from beginning to end? And the same with the sun?"

The teacher even seemed to agree with Mishka Goryachkin and to accept his reproach. Adjusting her thin-framed, cracked spectacles on the bridge of her nose, she seemed to say with a suffering look, "There it is! You're all adults here, you're not children! So how can I really have anything to do with you? How can I understand you?" Even Deryabin, his eyes blinking and his sharp nose gone red, was at a loss. Ignashka's mouth was hanging open in bewilderment. The teacher herself would never have thought of bringing a complaint, but Deryabin had sent Ignatov to her to say that she should come and tell the Commission about Mishka Goryachkin's hooli-ganism, especially since the Forest Commission was the guardian of the new school. The teacher had come and explained what had gone on, but now her myopic, timid eyes asked, "What has happened? There's no need for any more complaints or investigations. This is how horrible it can be when grown-ups suddenly decide to get to the bottom of something!"

Sitting on the bench with his legs crossed and his arms folded on his chest, Mishka Goryachkin shifted his eyes, red as a perch's, and lectured the teacher in a voice hoarsened by a cold and drink. "You need to gather your wits together, that's what! Or who knows what you'll be teaching!" His breath smelled of raw vodka and some other unidentifiable stench. "And when an honest citizen comes along and tells you what's right, you go com-plaining about him, you miserable intellek'chul!"

At this point Smirnovsky rose from his seat, walked over to Mishka with his hands in his pockets, and said quietly and sharply, "Stand up!" It wasn't even a command or an order; he was simply telling Mishka to stand.

"Huh?" Goryachkin replied. "What d'you mean?!"

"Stand up!" Ever so slowly, Smirnovsky began to pull his hands from the pockets of the military-style coat that he always wore both fall and winter.

Mishka stood up quickly, hiccuped, and straightened himself out to his full, but small, stature.

"Well?!" Smirnovsky turned to the members of the Commission. "Well,

---

*Goryachkin doesn't understand that the Russian adjective *krasnyi*, meaning "red," at one time meant "beautiful," as it does in the songs he knows.

announce your decision! Deryabin?! Kalashnikov?! Go on!"

"We need to think, Rodion Gavrilovich!" Kalashnikov, deeply embarrassed by everything that had taken place, heaved a heavy sigh and blew his nose. "We'll think of something!"

"Then here's what," Smirnovsky said. "Goryachkin should be instructed to replace the windows in the schoolhouse no later than tommorrow. Starting tomorrow, Goryachkin will be assigned the duty of carrying water and chopping firewood for the school for two weeks out of turn. If Goryachkin does not comply, the Commission will immediately remodel the old schoolhouse and invite the bootmaker from Krushikha or some other village to take up permanent residence there. Are there any objections? Does the Commission agree?"

"That's just the thing, Rodion Gavrilovich!" Kalashnikov agreed with relief and delight.

"There's a real lesson for you, Mishka!" Ignashka gloated. "You just understand the revolution of the Earth the way you ought to!"

Deryabin nodded silently, uncomfortable about his own confusion, about the fact that instead of him it was Lieutenant Smirnovsky who had so quickly decided the issue. "I don't think anyone has any objections," he said, nodding again. "Smirnovsky has made his proposal correctly, and, most important, quickly and clearly. So now, Citizen Goryachkin, you just get yourself out of here. We've decided everything we need to about you!"

Stumbling over the benches and muttering something about arbitrary law and impostors, Mishka Goryachkin made his way to the exit.

"Our next question," Deryabin announced, "concerns Citizens Fedot and, mainly, Prokopy Kruglov! Quiet, Citizens, quiet, all of you! Citizen Policeman Pilipenkov has the floor!"

A huge man with narrow little eyes in a red face, Pilipenkov stood up and fixed his gaze on Ivan Ivanovich Samorukov. He was used to listening to him and to having him take charge; he got his daily bread from Ivan Ivanovich as well. Without taking his eyes from him, Pilipenkov reported that for the third time already a still had been confiscated and destroyed at Fedot and Prokopy Kruglovs'. Pilipenkov made his report without much enthusiasm, as if he were taking the blame for someone else.

"The Commission ordered me to find, seize, and destroy these stills at the Kruglovs'." His muffled voice seemed to come from inside an empty barrel. "The Commission proposed that I make this report, so that's what I'm doing . . . "

When Pilipenkov was finished, Smirnovsky, screwing up his eyes and chewing his lip, asked, "How are we to understand this? You mean it's not the job of the police to fight against the moonshiners? Not their job, but only the Forest Commission's?"

Tearing his eyes away from Ivan Ivanovich for a moment, Pilipenkov came smartly to attention and, as if reporting to a superior, answered crisply, "Not in the least! On the contrary, I'm making every effort to perform my duty!"

It became clear that Pilipenkov, who had experience as a sergeant major, a policeman, and something else as well, was an old hand at this, and everyone was very interested in this sudden transformation of the lazy constable. But at that moment Prokopy Kruglov shrieked, grabbed his long, perfectly goatlike beard with both hands, waved it in Pilipenkov's direction, and launched into an attack.

"A-a-ah, well now, look what Lebyazhka has for a policeman! It's my turn to ask a question now! Just who do you serve, Pilipenkov? The Forest Commission, that sends you out to peek into the houses of free citizens? That calls you to the village assembly and orders you to report whatever it needs you to? Or do you serve the rightful and stable government of Supreme Admiral Kolchak? Can you give me an honest answer right now, without hiding anything?! I'll tell you what, this Forest Commission is nothing to me, nothing! God damn them! But what about you? I'm ready to do anything for the Supreme Government, but what about you? I'm asking you now! Let's figure it out, let's make it clear once and for all who's for who. Then we can really get down to judging and laying down the law to each other! Maybe then—or for sure then—I'll be testifying against you, not you against me!"

Prokopy Kruglov looked around the room with wild triumph, punched his brother on the shoulder, and continued loudly, "Just pay close attention, and just remember what kind of men the Kruglov brothers are! Just remember! And don't go calling us to your court, or in due time we might be calling you before the judge's bench, and Officer Pilipenkov along with you, and we'll be backed up by soldiers with guns in their hands! God damn you! You just think about that, Citizen Policeman, you just use your brains! And what sort of crime is a moonshine still? It's ridiculous, God damn you! You shouldn't look at a man's still, but at his devotion to the government, that's what you should look at! That's the main measure of a man! That's the most important thing! Everything else ain't worth spitting on, it don't count a thing! And no one can compare with the Kruglov brothers in the most important thing! No one! Because you and me, Fedotushka, my own blood brother, won't put up with anyone having their way with us or using force against us, that's what! We'll turn you in to our own true government before you can blink an eye!" Punching his silent brother in the shoulder even harder than before, Prokopy Kruglov shouted once more, "That's what!"

Where had this speech come from? The Commission members had always thought that Prokopy was one of the most ignorant peasants, that all he knew how to do was break his back day and night in his fields or in his yard. But how he had learned to talk now! He really felt his moment had come!

And his speech put the Commission in a difficult position once again. Accustomed to working peacefully, quietly, and privately, away from the eyes of bystanders, the Commission would make its decisions amid the bright greenery of the Pankratovs' ficus, and Deryabin and his forest guard would carry them out somehow, discreetly but quickly. But now everything was different, and Deryabin was again at a loss as to whether to make a speech in rebuttal or simply to shout at Prokopy Kruglov the way he wanted to. And once again, Deryabin didn't speak. Instead, Ivan Ivanovich Samorukov took a pinch of snuff and rose lopsidedly from his bench. "What kind of mockery are we letting Citizen Kruglov make of us? Prokopy Kruglov!" With his arms wrapped around his head, he was not speaking but lamenting. "And we're allowing the same mockery of the representative of the Supreme Government, Policeman Pilipenkov, in front of everyone! So you, Prokopy Kruglov, are devoted to the Supreme Commander, and we simply aren't?! You're disgusting to say that! What do you know about our devotion? Or even about my own? Or Ignaty Ignatov's here? Who else do we, the Commission, serve if not the Supreme Commander and his new government? Where do you get your nerve, you impudent fake? Where were you, Citizen Kruglov, when our whole village took up a collection for the magnificent army of the Siberian Government? Back then even Citizen Ignatov here said, 'I don't begrudge giving as many rubles as I can!' And he gave just that many rubles in actual cash! And what about you, Prokopy Kruglov? What did you say? 'The magnificent army can go to hell!' That's what you said back then!"

"Ivan Ivanovich! Have some fear of God!" Prokopy begged in horror.

But Ivan Ivanovich, unafraid of God, repeated loudly and distinctly, "I swear by the cross to all you citizens here—that's what Prokopy Kruglov said: 'The magnificent army can go to hell!' Pilipenkov here will bear me out, he was there when the words were spoken!"

"Of course," Pilipenkov said, smiling not only with his shapeless, thick-lipped mouth but with his whole red face.

"So let's deal with Prokopy Kruglov like this and enter it in the minutes," Ivan Ivanovich proposed, raising a triumphant finger above his head. "Let's exact a fine of seventy-five poods of grain from the Kruglov brothers. As a second fine, let's confiscate Prokopy's working gelding, the one he got for a 'thank you' from Sevka Kupriyanov. Prokopy has speculated with the horse endlessly and used it to carry the still from his house to his brother's. And let all of this—and maybe anything else we might confiscate in the future—be given to the magnificent army of the Supreme Commander!" Samorukov crossed himself and added, "Well, God be with us. Who's in favor?"

Chuckling, as if they were tossing away some unwanted thing, Kalash-nikov and Ignaty Ignatov raised their hands. Deryabin hesitated a few times, half raising his hand, then lowering it. He was aching to confiscate even more of Kruglov's property, but he certainly did not want to hand it over to Kolchak. As he looked at Ivan Ivanovich with angry distrust, Samorukov winked at him as if to say, "I was just saying that! We'll con-fiscate, but would we really be so stupid as to give the goods away to any-one? Especially to Kolchak?"

"Well, God be with us!" Samorukov repeated, and Deryabin raised his hand, too. After everyone had voted, Samorukov added to Kruglov, "Too little God and too much politics, that's what the problem is! The people have become too politicized! Do you really need to break into politics?! That's why God is punishing you, Prokopy! You'll pay seventy-five poods of grain and a gelding for your politics, and that won't be the last you'll pay!"

After this, the Commission's business continued without further obsta-cles. Once more it was decided to confiscate the timber the woodcutters had taken illegally and to hand it over to the Commission's exchange fund, and Ignashka Ignatov was entrusted with the task of trading that timber for school supplies in the steppe villages. In addition, a fine of ten poods of grain was levied for each illegally felled log. Two members of the forest guard who had squabbled bitterly were given three days to make peace with each other. A few other questions were decided as well, but before they ex-amined the organization of forest industries, the Commission took a recess. Everyone needed to have a smoke and go out for a breath of fresh air, and Pilipenkov couldn't wait to look at the minutes to see what had been writ-ten about him.

"And we were saying that the Commission had broken away from the masses!" said Ignashka Ignatov, delighted with how the meeting was pro-ceeding. "That isn't true at all! Just look—everyone is listening to us, and we're getting everything done and putting everything to rights! The people are on our side! Folks are already coming to our meeting just to have a look, listen for a bit, and learn a thing or two!"

As he looked over the minutes, Pilipenkov was also satisfied because none of Prokopy Kruglov's comments about him had been left on paper. Rubbing his short, squat neck, he asked Ignashka Ignatov, "Ignaty, who does a person serve, really? The strongest, and no one else. The thing is to figure out who the strongest is. But what does the weak man do? Right away he declares that he's all mankind, and that's rubbish! Rubbish, and even a crime! I know—I've served for a lo-ong time! Everyone who's been in service knows: if you don't want to do it, don't join up; but once you have, declare your loyalty loud and clear, at the top of your lungs! And serve in secret, too! Loyal service is impossible without both!"

While Ignashka was listening to Pilipenkov with his mouth hanging open, Chairman Pyotr Kalashnikov invited Samorukov to the table, and a minute later, Smirnovsky, and declared that from then on they should be registered as official members of the Commission. Later the decision would be confirmed at a general meeting of the citizenry.

Just as the recess was ending, Domna Ustinov appeared in the doorway. She was wearing her everyday clothes, an old, faded sheepskin coat and a plain kerchief, but with her gracefully dignified figure, her cheeks rosy from the frost, and her habitually calm, kind smile, she was still a beauty. In fact, she was nothing less than a pretty young maiden!

Kalashnikov, the first to notice her, smiled, too, and glancing around the room, asked, "Which one of us are you looking for so hard, Domnushka?"

"I'm looking for my husband. Isn't he here with you?"

"He's not here . . . "

"What? Hasn't he been here?"

"He hasn't! Isn't he still sick in bed?"

As Domna stood lost in thought, her frosty pink face slowly went slack and gray. "I don't understand it!" she said, leaning against the doorjamb. "I don't understand. Someone called Levontyevich away in the night—they knocked on the window. It wasn't you? They called him away on urgent village business. Wasn't it you?"

"The thought never crossed our minds!"

Everyone was silent.

"Look for him! Search everywhere!" Smirnovsky was the first to come to his senses. "Look for him!"

They looked for Nikolai Levontyevich Ustinov throughout the entire village, and about two hours later they found him in a snowbank just a little below that narrow lane where Domna and Zinaida had recently met and a little above that sandy bank where the boats returning from the Krushikha market would come to shore. Along that gentle lakeward slope overgrown with hawthorn, scrub poplar, and willow, the snow formed deep drifts every winter. Ustinov's skull had been broken with some heavy, blunt object, most likely the butt-end of an axe. There was a bag over his head, his hands were tied, and for some reason Grandfather Yegory's walking stick had been thrust between his hands. Buried in a snowbank not far from him, a rope noose around the white collar of his fur coat, was Barin.

▲▲▲

The Lebyazhkans, sensing the approach of war and misfortune for a long time, had languished in terrified apprehension from day to day, but they didn't understand why misfortune had begun with Nikolai Ustinov. Not only Domna but almost all Lebyazhka had believed that if Nikolai Ustinov ever perished, it would be only after everyone else had. Judicious, kind, and calm, he never acted or spoke uselessly, but always behaved with thoughtful deliberation. The Lebyazhkans had believed that no one could be offended by him or have a score to settle with him. So if he had wound up in the forest on the iron teeth of a harrow, then it must have been by accident. The harrow had been set out, they reasoned, not for him, but for one of the forest guard, for the first person who came down the road. If those evildoers who had set out the harrow as a trap had known that Ustinov would fall into it, they would have taken it from the road. But the Lebyazhkans turned out to be mistaken: the harrow wouldn't have been taken away! Then they saw that even though Ustinov had fallen on the harrow, nevertheless, he was still alive, and so they believed that after that he would surely keep on living and nothing else would happen to him. But once again, it turned out that the Lebyazhkans were wrong.

The Lebyazhka men hurried from one house to another over the crunching snow. The women tore themselves away from their stoves and pots and pans and cradles and went running to visit each other. How could they understand what had happened? How could they discover what Ustinov's death meant? Who would be next? And since it had begun not with just anyone but with Nikolai Levontyevich Ustinov, what else would happen?

▲▲▲

Late in the evening of the same day, all the members of the Commission were again sitting on the benches of the village assembly hall. Together, perhaps, they would be able to figure out what had happened and explain it to the more slow-witted. Pilipenkov appeared. Polovinkin came in, shaggy and silent, moved away from the others, and sat down in a dark corner. It was decided to set the funeral for the day after tomorrow, a secular funeral with eulogies, followed by a burial service. The coffin would be carried from the assembly hall to the church and from there to the graveyard.

Proposing that all the members of the Commission deliver eulogies, Deryabin said, "We'll start with you, I think, Kalashnikov. Give us an answer now. What words will you offer the people?"

"What is there to say?" answered Kalashnikov, closing his eyes and swaying. "All but a few of us here are veterans of various wars. So we've survived some death already, praise God! But there is no war that can completely break our spirit, the souls of us Russian peasants. So why don't we listen to this spirit of ours, to its moaning and pain? That's what I feel, but I don't have any words for it."

"You've already spoken them, Kalashnikov!" Smirnovsky said quietly.

"No!" Kalashnikov disagreed. "My head, my heart, all of me down to the last drop of blood, is filled with Comrade Ustinov. I can see him and hear him and feel him. Can that really be expressed? Never! We can't even hope for time enough to meet a man like Comrade Ustinov again. We won't meet another one! They always point at people like him after they are dead and say, 'There was a man for you!' But by then they're pointing at nothing, at empty space!"

Burning his fingers, Deryabin adjusted the wick of the candle so that it gave more light. The grooves between the boards of the unplastered walls and the broken shadows people cast upon them grew more prominent.

"Well, I'll tell you the whole truth now!" he began. "All of it! We've all had enough, me especially, of talking and thinking quietly and keeping to ourselves our opinion of just what people should be doing! I say that our Forest Commission was just a toy, that's all! And we've come to the end of our little game! Instead of following the path of the most important change in humanity, instead of liquidating Grishka Sukhikh and all these Kruglovs, and maybe even you, Ivan Ivanovich, once and for all, and declaring ourselves an active military force against the despots, we wasted our time with speeches and timber and moonshine stills! We've waited for the death of Comrade Ustinov! When I ask how people understand his death, no one answers my question! Because our society has been completely deluded! People like you, Ivan Ivanovich, have led it into this dark dead end. They've betrayed it completely! And I won't hesitate to say it even about myself. Even I have fallen under your harmful influence, Ivan Ivanovich! Even if you take only the last instance, when under pressure I voted not only to confiscate the Kruglov brothers' property but, swearing loyalty to Kolchak, also to give that property to him! It's shameful! There's only one way out—a merciless war between everyone who wants a bright future for the people and everyone who wants no part of it! And so I'll say, 'Rest in peace, dear Comrade Ustinov. We will carry on the struggle for you, for all your humanity, so that people like you will never again be murdered but will die a natural death among their loved ones. We will carry this struggle to a victorious end!' The time has come to say this to all the masses, to all the people."

Listening to Deryabin, Smirnovsky shifted his officer's fur cap, bare of insignia, from the table to his knees and tugged on his small mustache. "And perhaps we should compose a eulogy together?" he asked. "From the whole Commission? Could we do it? In the presence of the departed, Kolya Ustinov?"

"No, we can't!" Deryabin replied.

"Didn't we write the appeal together?"

"That's an entirely different matter!"

"So we're already violating the spirit of our own appeal? We're admitting that we don't share any common social principles?" Smirnovsky asked.

"What kind of social principles can there be now?" Deryabin answered. "The whole wide world is busted into pieces, and collecting them and gluing them back together are much harder and make less sense than just making everything over from scratch."

"What do you mean, 'everything?' " asked Kalashnikov.

"The whole wide world as it is today, I'm telling you. The whole world. The whole of mankind. Everything has to be done over once and for all. Tear it it down to the foundations and then . . . That's what I mean."

"But why is that necessary?" asked Kalashnikov, spreading his hands. "Even the different plants come together to make one meadow, so why can't people do the same kind of thing? Can't they come together to make something?"

"They can!" said Smirnovsky. "They must! Nations and states! It's not a futile task. People can't exist without cooperation!"

"That's speaking in general. But right now they can't and shouldn't!" Deryabin insisted. "Right now it's essential for people to root out the weeds that have grown thick in every nation and state. That's what should be first and foremost! You, Smirnovsky, what eulogy will you give?"

After tapping his fingers on his knee and shifting his hat from his lap to the table again, Smirnovsky replied, "It's a terrible thing for an honest soldier to ambush and murder one of his own! If this doesn't frighten us, if this doesn't make us tremble, I don't know what will happen! I propose to say this—," Smirnovsky seized the thought that had just come to him. "This murder is a disgrace to all of us. Each of us is under suspicion of this vile act, and the only way we can cleanse ourselves of this filth is to find the murderer! Let's all try to remember what we heard last night. Some footsteps or the sound of horses in the street? The squeaking of a neighbor's gate? Someone's dog barking? Let everyone consider that if the guilty party is not found, then each of us is guilty. Even if we aren't murderers, we are accomplices! This was done by our own people! Would strangers have known that Ustinov could walk again and could be called from his house into the street? It was our own people that did it! People who knew!"

"No, Smirnovsky, you won't be able to conduct a real investigation! Now? That's a whimsical notion!" Deryabin scoffed.

"Then I'll keep quiet!" Smirnovsky replied. He stood up, crossed himself with wide strokes, and sat down again.

"That's right, that's right," came Polovinkin's muffled voice from the corner. "Everyone needs to cross themselves that way at the funeral! So others can see, and us, too, that everything comes from God! And there should be solemn words, loud ones, even if they're sobs. To bite into your very soul. Till it hurts!" Since that day that Polovinkin had left the Commission, loudly slamming the Pankratovs' door, he seemed to have gone completely wild. Always unkempt, shaggy, and dressed in rags, he had now become a completely somber figure, speaking with a muffled cough, grabbing his head with both hands, not looking at anyone.

"It's the government and the churchmen, too, who talk too loud!" Kalashnikov responded. "They've taken over everything, the land, the palaces, and loud words! But we, the people, need to express ourselves in our own way, in a normal voice, but truthfully! What would you say about Nikola Levontyevich, Polovinkin?"

"Well, what could I say, if I speak from myself, and not from God? I wouldn't say nothing. Ustinov was a worker, that's who he was! He was an awful good worker. Him and me were field neighbors, you know. When he started to plow with his Morkoshka and Solovko—would you believe it?—the steam would rise up from his furrow like he was beating the ground with a birch switch in the bathhouse instead of working it with a plow. And from dawn to dusk, it didn't make no difference to him, he never got tired! He'd start up in the morning and finish after dark. You couldn't watch him without envy, and I sinned, I was jealous!" Sticking out his arm, not through his sleeve, but through a hole in his coat, Polovinkin waved it around and added, "And what did I do? I quit bothering with you, with the Commission, I got good and fed up with all your talk, but I came back, and here I am again, listening and even talking myself. All because of Ustinov. He won't leave me, alive or dead!" Polovinkin fell silent.

"He was a real smart one, was our Nikolai Levontyevich, and that can hurt a man!" Ignashka Ignatov, stuttering slightly, began to speak. "And he was honest. And that can hurt a man, too! I'll confess something—for years now I've owed him six and a half rubles, but he was too shy to ask about it. I was even afraid to come to the Commission because of it. I thought that I might be sitting at the table next to Ustinov and he might ask me for them six and a half rubles, but he never once asked me about it! And I'll even confess that I never would've paid that debt if this evil murder hadn't happened! But now I'll pay it—I promise here in front of everybody that I'll give it to the widow, Domna Ustinov! And I'll tell her not to grieve—honest men like that are never long for this world anyway, no, they aren't!"

"No!" Ivan Ivanovich repeated quietly. "No, don't listen to anyone, Nikola Levontyevich! Don't listen to them—listen to me! They're all thinking about themselves and their own business. Go ahead and let them. But I've been tramping the earth for almost ninety years now, I've tramped out just about everything, and after such a long stretch of time, I don't have much of my own business left. I kept alive because every time I took a thing into my hands that I didn't know, that I couldn't say nothing about, right away I thought, 'Well fine, so I don't understand, but others will! Nikola Levontyevich will understand for me, that's who!' And now I'm thinking and adding it up. How many years did I live thanks to you, Nikola Levontyevich? But now that you're gone, there's no reason for me to live, is there? That's the whole thing! And since the moment you died, I've been living nothing but a lie! Living is no good without you. And dying? Who is there to count on if not you? Who else is there to look at with my last glance, who else to listen to as my hearing fades away? I can't count on any of them,"

Ivan Ivanovich said, pointing at those present. "I can't count on those in the Commission who are still alive. And isn't it a frightful thing to die without having hope in someone, Nikolai Levontyevich? That's the situation you've put me in! I can't speak out about your death, I don't have the strength, especially since it was caused by our own villagers. How did such a thing ever happen?

"It's impossible to go on living, but I'm afraid to die. I'm afraid to go to Samsony Krivoi, to fall down at his bare feet, under the thirsting gaze of his one eye! To fall to the ground and offer him that terribly poisoned cup from which he cannot take a single sip! Samsony will ask me, 'Why did I accept such great sorrow, torment, and darkness? And wrath, and censure, and the curses of my older brother, the Elder Lavrenty of holy countenance? For what? For what, if you, my grandchildren, instead of redeeming my sins on your behalf, have poisoned this cup even more by letting sin and shame and terrible inhumanity rule over you? Is it for this that I led you back to the place where you now live, where you were born and baptized?' That is what the Elder Samsony will ask me, and how will I answer? Waiting for his judgment is like torture to me, but I ask for only one thing: 'Lord God! Don't let me languish, call me soon to judgment and the torments of hell! Crucify me, not in this world, but in the next. It will be brighter for me before Your sorrowful face than under the ungrateful gaze of the eyes of men, wicked murderers and sinful beasts!' "

And when Ivan Ivanovich stretched out his hand and grabbed hold of some invisible thing, no one doubted that it was his own death that he had grasped and that he would die that very moment. But he did not die. Lopsided, in tears, stiff and wrinkled, he got up, stood motionless for a long time, let out a prolonged sigh, and ever so quietly left. He paused at the doorway to ask, "Well? How can we? There's no way! There's nothing to be done!"

▲▲▲

Winter was claiming its own, and two days later, on the day of the funeral, the frost was very severe. The sharp outline of the White Wood, in which not a twig or a pine needle was moving, pierced the sky. The thin, bluish-white fog, indistinguishable from the sky, was also motionless, illuminated here and there by a glassy and colorless sun. Caught up in some slow and unseen motion, the sun, bright only at its edges, was distancing itself from the heavens. Only the sun was moving. The rest of the heavenly world was sunk in motionlessness. The earthly world could be seen and heard nearby: the black edge of the White Wood, the white, slightly shining surface of Lake Lebyazhka. The gray specks of the houses of Lebyazhka dissolved into the snow and frost, and the deaf silence was broken only by the thin funeral pealing of the Lebyazhka church bell.

▲▲▲

The Forest Commission's "Appeal to the Citizens of the Village of Leb-yazhka," neatly copied by Ustinov on two large, bright, and beautiful sheets of paper taken from the office of the former forest authority, was pasted on the wall of the smaller room of the village assembly hall. On a long table, in a narrow coffin of pine boards intricately patterned with brown pitch and smelling of resin, lay Nikolai Levontyevich Ustinov himself. His eyes were tightly closed, no longer able to look around the room. There was suffering in his gaunt and emaciated face, and terror was hidden under his closed eyelids, but still he wanted to see something. He was waiting. Everything that could happen to him had already happened, but still he wanted to know what would come next—what people would say about him, how they would carry him into the church and read the burial service over him, how they would fill the dirt in over him in the freezing cold of that day.

Having cried herself out, Domna stood at his head with tearless eyes and also waited. The tears yet to come were ripening and gathering within her. They were the only things left. There was nothing else for her, no other fate. Ksenia stood at her father's feet, dissolved in tears, her huge belly hidden by a worn sheepskin coat. The eyes of Natashka and little Shurka peeked out from under the coat's rust-colored folds. Understanding nothing, the two children could only be terrified. Yegorka, whom Ksenia held in her arms, was silent, having forgotten all about his habit of constant shouting and fidgeting. He watched, and he seemed to understand everything. He was the only one in the whole wide world who understood. Shurka, Ustinov's son-in-law, was also standing there uneasily, as if he weren't standing on his own legs. His eyes covered by his hand, he was crying bitterly and ceaselessly.

And Zinaida Pankratov was there, too. Her face was hidden in the shadow of her kerchief, but her hands, which held a rag and pail, were visible. She had come to the assembly building in the morning. "Why?" they had asked her. "To wash the floor, to clean the place up, at least a little," Zinaida had answered. "I was always looking after the Commission at my house! I'm used to it!" The pail shook and rattled in her large hands—it was the only sound to be heard near the coffin. Then Zinaida set the pail down on the dark, unpainted floor, and there was a quiet hush. Only the sound of Deryabin's distorted, halting voice carried through the wooden partition from the adjacent room.

All the Commission members were in that room once more, and Polovinkin had also come. With his deathly authority Nikolai Ustinov had brought them together again, and everyone sat silent and motionless, listening, or perhaps not listening at all, while Deryabin spoke.

"I don't even want to live such a disgusting life!" He was speaking hurriedly, contradicting himself, full of malice. "It's a mockery of what everything should be! It's not life but an obscene word scribbled on a fence! Stinking shit! It's the lie of lies! No sacrifice can be too great to change this obscenity!

"Now, now, Deryabin!" Kalashnikov stopped him. "You still can't hate and condemn life that much! You can't, even though it killed our Levontyevich! He wouldn't have cursed it that way! I'm sure of it!"

"It's just because he didn't curse it that it treated him this way, with such gratitude! No-o, the minute I open my eyes in the morning I start to curse it and show it up for what it is! You have to understand that everything is wrong. There's no reason or order. It's like a cesspool, even worse!"

"Right now you sound just like Kudeyar, Deryabin! Be quiet in memory of our friend and comrade!"

"I won't be quiet! I won't! Compared to me, Kudeyar is a snot-nosed kid! Calling for the end of the world! That's nothing! That's whining like a woman! No-o, first you need to bully everything on earth! Just as everything on earth has mocked and bullied man through the ages, now the time has come for man to treat life and everything in the world the same way! The time has come! Everything must be done all over again from the beginning, not like it was before, and if it fails to turn out right again, then we'll just push the wreckage off the tracks!"

Although Smirnovsky was sitting with his back to Deryabin, as if he weren't there, he said, "I don't understand. If that's how you feel, how can you be a member of the Commission? How can you do your best to perform your duties properly?"

"That was just a tryout, Mr. Lieutenant! Just as children play dolls to prepare for their lives as grown-ups and little boys play war to learn to destroy each other for real as men, that's how I played in the Forest Commission! And I played hard! But I'm waiting for the time when all the people will be ready to understand the damnation, destruction, and rebuilding of the whole wide world! I'm waiting!"

After Deryabin had stopped talking, it was quiet for a long time. Then Ivan Ivanovich Samorukov began to speak, his old man's words creeping into the silence. In the last few days he had outlived his endless life. His face had yellowed, and his body had become so distorted that he seemed to be turning into something other than a man. One shoulder was twisted up and to the left, the other down and to the right, his neck had hardened into bone, his Adam's apple seemed about to come popping out, and one eye was swollen. But still he sat sighing, for some reason still alive, and now, in a voice alternately loud and soft, he told the story of the Big Bear.

There were different kinds of stories in Lebyazhka. The long-ago tales of their forefathers were all mostly humorous or about love, but this tale was of an entirely different sort. People had all but forgotten this one, but now Ivan Ivanovich recalled it in his final remembrance.

▲▲▲

When the Elder Samsony Krivoi was dying, parting from those first settlers of Lebyazhka, he feared that the Kerzhak and Poluvyatsky people who had become each other's kinfolk and had formed a single village might later be split by a new schism and become enemies once again. Samsony exhorted one side and the other, young and old, men and women, not to create such misfortune and despair for themselves. Howling into the sky, the Elder asked the stars in the constellation of the Big Bear to send a sign to the earth if from their great height they noticed the Lebyazhkans maliciously quarreling and scheming against each other. The sign was to be sent to an ancient grove in the White Wood, to a deep lair in which even the sunlight shines only feebly and which starlight can penetrate only for a brief moment each night. At this sign a blind She-Bear with seven heads, large and small and variously colored, would emerge from that lair, follow the scent of human malice and quarreling, and, sparing neither the guilty nor the righteous, destroy all the houses of Lebyazhka save one. So, it seems, had Samsony Krivoi foretold the future.

▲▲▲

Now Ivan Ivanovich, his head bowed onto his hands, repeated his prophecy over and over until Deryabin rose from his chair to insist, "It's time to turn our attention to Comrade Ustinov for one last time! Take a look— there's a huge crowd of people gathered in the street despite the frost. It's time to begin our eulogy meeting. Personally, I'm ready to give my speech, but if anyone still hasn't thought it over well enough, he'd better just keep quiet! Let's go! The people are waiting!"

"The people aren't waiting for us!" Kalashnikov noted. "They're waiting to see Nikola Ustinov for the last time! And in the face of the people's expectation I'll tell you what I have to say—in the memory of Nikolai Levontyevich I'll call on all the villagers to be united at this fearful hour and to support their Forest Commission."

"But it's all the same—if the people are waiting for Ustinov, it means they're waiting for us, too, for the Forest Commission. Let's go!" Deryabin repeated. "And another thing, Comrade Commission Members—while the eulogy meeting is going on, don't put your hats on! Even though it's so cold out, don't put your hats on, no matter what!"

Just as Deryabin stretched out his hand to open the door, it swung open from the outside, and through a thick gust of frozen air someone shouted, "The soldiers are coming! Kolchak's officers!" From another gust of frozen air stepped an officer wearing a dark-green jacket without shoulder insignia and an officer's fur cap under a hood. He pulled off his hunter's mittens, untied his hood, and stamped his feet to stretch his legs after being in the saddle. While he was stretching and unfastening, some more soldiers came in and crowded the Commission members into the corner. Leaning against the table, the officer shifted a leather satchel with his cold-numbed hands from his left side to his stomach, opened the satchel, removed a piece of paper, unfolded it, and asked, "Is this the Commission here? All of them? The whole lot?"

"All of them, Your Excellency!" Policeman Pilipenkov, who had entered the building with the soldiers, answered smartly, but not without a note of fear.

The officer nodded and began to read from his paper, "De . . . Deryabin? Are you here?"

"I'm here!" Deryabin responded from the corner. "But what's going on?"

"Pyotr Kalashnikov?"

Kalashnikov, too, responded, but hesitantly, as if he had forgotten something about himself.

"The former cooperative organizer!" the officer prompted. "Well now! Ignaty Ignatov? Present?"

"Here I am . . . Here he is . . . "

"Polovinkin?"

"Me, too . . . "

"Samorukov?"

Samorukov let out a loud sigh of relief as if he had been given some reason for hope, and, in a voice not nearly as sepulchral as that with which he had told the tale of the Big Bear, said, "Ivan Ivanovich Samorukov is here!"

"Smirnovsky? Rodion? The former lieutenant?"

"Here!"

"Also a member of the Commission?"

"Yes!"

Another officer appeared, sat down at the table, set a Mauser pistol in front of himself and, glancing briefly at the face of each Commission member in turn, began to rub his frost-nipped face.

"Good job! A full complement!" the first officer nodded to the second.

The second repeated with a Czech accent, "Yes, good job . . . A full complement."

"Pilipenkov? Did the members of this Commission give their right names?"

"They gave exactly the right ones, Your Excellency!" Pilipenkov confirmed.

The officer, who did not seem to trust Pilipenkov, inquired further, "And that . . . well, that local resident, the young desperado who came with us— is he here?"

"Kupriyanov! Matvey Kupriyanov!" Pilipenkov finished for him. "Here he is! He's right here beside me!"

"Come here, Matvey Kupriyanov!" the officer ordered.

Wearing a brand-new uniform jacket with his civilian cap, Matveyka Kupriyanov came forward with an almost military step, faced the officer, and gave a clumsy salute. Although taller than most soldiers, he had the face of a ten- or twelve-year-old boy with an evil temper.

"Can you confirm the last names of these people, Kupriyanov?"

"Which ones?"

"The ones I just called out."

"I confirm all of them."

"And the Village Elder—might that be you, old man?" the officer asked Ivan Ivanovich after finishing his roll call. "Are you the headman of Lebyazhka?"

Ivan Ivanovich merely chewed his lips and said nothing. Pilipenkov took two steps forward again and said, "He is, Your Excellency! Only he doesn't always admit to it. But there's no one else in that place! There hasn't been for a long time!"

"But why shouldn't I admit to it?" Samorukov asked. "When I have to, I admit to it. Since there ain't a real headman, I'll do his job!"

"Will you explain to me who elected the Forest Commission? And when?"

"It was early in the fall, Mr. Officer. The village elected them. At a plenary meeting of the village assembly."

"And is there a record of that meeting?"

"It was all done according to form, Mr. Officer! How could there not be a record? That could never happen!"

"Where did you send the proceedings? To whom?" asked the officer, still breathing on his hands. Though he was getting warmer and warmer, his questions were becoming sterner, and he looked more and more harshly at Ivan Ivanovich.

But Ivan Ivanovich answered more and more cheerfully. His shoulders had straightened up, and his little eyes, which only seemed half-blind, had regained their sight and looked brighter as he said, "We did indeed send a record of the proceedings. To Krushikha. To the authorities."

"Which authorities?"

"I can't say anymore! What government did we have back in the early fall? If only I could remember! Well, whichever one there was back then, that's who we sent it to! That's the long and short of it!"

"Was there a response to your proceedings? From Krushikha?"

"No, there wasn't."

"And what does the absence of a reply mean?"

"That means the authorities were pretty busy back then, Mr. Officer.

They were busy with all sorts of things."

"If the authorities left the report about the election of the Commission unanswered, then the Commission did not have the right to exist! And if it did exist, it did so arbitrarily and without authorization! Do you really not understand that, old man?"

"But we still don't even have papers for Policeman Pilipenkov here, Mr. Officer! He's here himself, he got here back before mowing time, but there's no papers for him at all! Maybe he's unauthorized, too? Maybe you'll order him to clear out of here, Mr. Officer?"

"I'll order him to throw you in the lockup, old man! Do you understand?"

"But how could we not understand, Mr. Officer? We know all about that sort of thing!"

"And here is another question for you, old man: don't you know, haven't you heard that back in June the Provisional Government restored the right of private property? For both land and forest? That the forest of His Imperial Majesty has been transferred to the property of the state? And during that time the Commission arbitrarily appropriated rights to the forest and even organized its own armed forest guard! Isn't this a crime?"

At this point Smirnovsky stepped forward, came to attention, and said to the officer, "I cannot see what your rank is. Would you tell me?"

"Brigade Commander."

"Thank you!" Smirnovsky nodded curtly. "It's a misunderstanding, Brigade Commander! No one in the Commission has assumed power for his own gain. Each has unselfishly and voluntarily fulfilled his social obligations. If it weren't for the guard, the government would have lost much more of the forest's resources. The Commission can present all its documents, accounts, and records upon demand, and you will be convinced of how wisely the people have preserved the natural and national wealth!"

Leafing through the documents of the Commission that lay on the table, the Czech officer held up one of the pieces of paper. "These documents? Yes?" he asked in his thick accent.

"These documents!" Smirnovsky said.

"Oh! Oh! Oh!" the Czech shook his head.

The Brigade Commander again shifted his worn satchel from his side to his stomach, searched in it briefly, took out one more piece of paper, and read out loud.

We appeal to you, the citizens of Lebyazhka, to support in every way the community organization that you yourselves have elected, the only such in the village for the present, and therefore all the more essential for the affirmation in all of you of the citizenship and understanding that cannot be created through anything else but just and equal social cooperation.

Looking up at Smirnovsky with his transparently blue eyes, he repeated,
" 'We appeal to you, the citizens of Lebyazhka . . . ' Well? You went so far
as to call on the people!! And who gave you this right to appeal to the people? Where did you get it? From whom did you usurp it? And here is the
signature of a former lieutenant? A lieutenant, and appealing to the
people!"

"An appeal! Oh! Oh!" The Czech officer raised a finger in the air. "Oh!
Oh!"

"A noble appeal! It would be difficult not to sign it! Impossible!"
Smirnovsky retorted.

It was dark in the assembly hall. The frost-covered windows admitted a
pale light, neither sunlight nor the light of day, in which even the sky was
invisible. Nor was it possible to tell what would happen next, what would
happen before the light of this short winter's day was completely extinguished.

The Brigade Commander stepped back to the window, held the paper
up to the gray light, and read on: " ' . . . the true purpose of power is
rational law and order, but there can be no law and order unless people
protect all of nature and the earth. . . .' Would you listen to that? Former
Lieutenant! Just who knows what the essence of government is except
government itself? Well? Perhaps you do? Or maybe that peasant there?"
Stretching out his hand, he pointed at Deryabin or maybe Kalashnikov.
Then he asked Smirnovsky, "Why aren't you still in the service,
Lieutenant?"

"I was given a medical discharge!"

The Brigade Commander paused, then asked Pilipenkov if Smirnovsky
had any discharge papers.

Pilipenkov barked out, "Yes, Your Excellency, he does. I have seen them
myself with my own eyes."

"Well, well. A deserter according to the law!" the officer said.
"Excellent!"

"I ask you . . . ," Smirnovsky began to protest.

The officer shouted, "Silence! Your last duty in service?"

"Infantry Company Commander."

"Why have you participated in this gang, Company Commander?"

"I have participated in an organ of civil self-government!"

"Self-government? Where? In the village of Lebyazhka! And isn't your
Lebyazhka in Russia?"

"It's in Russia. That's exactly why it was absolutely necessary—"

"Silence! Answer the questions! Which one of you killed your accom-
plice Ustinov? Nikolai Ustinov? Did you do this, Former Lieutenant? Why
shouldn't one of you have done it, one of this gang of brigands called the
Commission? Each of you is as much a bandit as the next!" The officer

caught his breath and thought a moment. "Well, the hell with it! You can all kill each other off—it makes less trouble for us."

"I demand—"

"Silence!" And then, speaking at first to no one in particular and then to Smirnovsky, the Brigade Commander said in an unexpectedly quiet, even contemplative tone of voice, "All this is just taking liberties! All of it!" Although noticeably younger than Smirnovsky, he shook his head in lamentation and went on, "Liberties, young man! Just ask me why I am here in this disgusting little village. In this deepest of animal lairs. Because I have been through this. Would I ever have wound up here if I were not working off a debt, paying for liberties? And you will pay, too, young man, Former Lieutenant!" The Brigade Commander's voice changed to an official tone, and, coming to attention, he asked the Czech, "What do you think, Mr. Timoshek?"

"Thirty!" he said. Then he thought for a moment. "Thirty is not quite enough for Lieutenant Smirnovsky, though . . . Lieutenant Smirnovsky, an officer of the Russian army, should have been fighting against the common enemy, against Germany! Freeing the Slavs from the German yoke! But what did he do? He's in his Lebyazhka! And the Czechs? And Galicia? And Serbia? They're in German captivity. Isn't that right? Thirty isn't enough . . . It's not enough for you, is it, Mr. Smirnovsky? I am also a lieutenant. I know that it isn't enough! It's not honorable to desert your allies!"

"And you, Mr. Lieutenant in the Czech army, are you fighting against Germany? Aren't you also in Lebyazhka?"

"The Bolsheviks won't let me fight the Germans. Are you a Bolshevik? Well?"

"Did the Bolsheviks keep you from fighting the Germans for the whole four years of the war? Did anyone keep the Serbs from fighting?"

"Oh! Oh! Then we'll give you a few more strokes of the rod . . . Let it be forty, then! Forty—that's good!" And the Czech smiled with knowing benevolence.

"Well then, Citizens of the Commission," said the Brigade Commander, also grinning, "you got off easy. Everyone gets thirty strokes, and Lieutenant Smirnovsky, for his special service, gets forty! The weather isn't suited to it—it's freezing out, so it won't be pleasant to undress. But then Siberians can never get used to the cold! Kuzmin?!"

"Yes, Your Excellency!" answered the soldier by the door.

"Do you understand everything? Do I have to repeat it?"

"I understand, Your Excellency!"

"Are the people in the square? The Comrade Citizens of Lebyazhka?"

"None of them have been allowed to leave. All the alleys and gates have been blocked off!"

"Then carry out your orders, and be quick about it! Do you have rations for the horses?"

"For the horses, yes, Your Excellency!"

"We will set out for Barsukovo in an hour! Pilipenkov?!"

Pilipenkov responded, and the Brigade Commander ordered him to inform the members of the forest guard that they were to turn in their weapons within twenty-four hours and swear in writing that they would not leave Lebyazhka.

Just as the Brigade Commander was about to say something else to Pilipenkov, Smirnovsky interrupted him to ask, "Would you permit me to show you one of the Forest Commission's papers? It's a very interesting one! It will tell you a great deal!"

The Brigade Commander nodded.

The Czech officer also nodded and said, "Go ahead!"

Coming up to the table and hastily leafing through the stack of papers, Smirnovsky said in a muffled voice unlike his own, "Just a minute, just a minute! I'll find it right away!"

As the members of the Commission stood shoulder to shoulder in the semidarkness of their corner and silently followed the swift movements of Smirnovsky's hands, Deryabin whispered, "The Lieutenant is trying to get himself off the hook! He's betraying us, the scum!"

The Czech officer sat at the table with his hand on his Mauser and hurried Smirnovsky. "Yes! Yes!" he nodded. "Well?" Suddenly, with unexpected speed, Smirnovsky knocked against the officer with his whole body, and the Czech fell sprawling, leaving the Mauser on the table. A shot rang out, and another.

"Run!" Smirnovsky shouted. "Ru—"

There were moans, the sound of breaking glass, shouting, the blows of rifle butts, another shot and more blows, and in a moment the result of Smirnovsky's desperate attempt was clear. The Czech officer was holding his left hand in his right, a spot of blood under his fingers; the Brigade Commander, searching for his satchel, was fumbling around under the upturned table; three soldiers were lifting Smirnovsky, only partially conscious, from the floor; and, breathing loudly and heavily and looking wildly around the room, the members of the Commission were being pressed against each other in the corner by other soldiers. Through the broken window, more light was coming into the room.

The Brigade Commander found his satchel under the table, stood up to his full height, and, bending slightly at the knees, struck Smirnovsky in the face. The Czech officer hit him from the other side. As the officers beat him with measured blows from the right and left, the two soldiers holding Smirnovsky by the arms and the soldier behind him turned him slightly in the direction of first one officer, then the other. And strangely enough, as the beating went on, Smirnovsky began to show signs of life, moving his head to keep the blows away from his Kalmyk eyes and breathing more and more evenly. Then he straightened up, braced himself, and, throwing his foot forward and to the side, kicked the Brigade Commander in the stomach, at the same instant spitting blood, shreds of flesh, and white fragments of teeth into the Czech officer's face. Once again, bodies thudded against each other and against some other hard object.

"Kuzmin!" shouted the Brigade Commander, racked with pain. "Take them out! All of them! Give each of them eighty strokes, hot ones! Flog them all to death!"

The soldiers began to lead the Commission members out of the building.

"Your Excellency! What are your orders about the man that was killed?" asked Pilipenkov.

"About who, now?" Doubled up on a stool, the Brigade Commander moaned in pain.

"About the man who was killed, Nikolai Ustinov. Should his body be left for his relatives? Or what? He's in a coffin in the next room."

"Put him under the rod! Put him in the same place as the others, the bastard!"

"But he's dead! He's been killed!"

"Under the rod!"

"Eighty. Yes!" the Czech said slowly, wiping the blood from his face. "Eighty . . . Eighty . . . "

As the Brigade Commander got up and staggered to the door, Pilipenkov asked another question. "Your Excellency! Couldn't we let the old man, Ivan Ivanovich Samorukov, off a little easier? The whole village stands behind him, and—why should I hide it—he's been feeding me. He fed me when my pay didn't come from Krushikha, when everyone had forgotten about me here! Eighty strokes would surely mean the next world for him, and how will I keep things in order without an Elder?"

The Brigade Commander, rubbing his stomach with both hands, sighed, "As you wish!" He sat back down on a stool. "The hell with the old man—do as you wish!"

But Ivan Ivanovich, the last Commission member being taken outside, just at that moment grabbed the soldier by the coat. "But how am I any different from the others, Mr. Officer?!" he shouted in a thin, desperate voice. "Why are you doing this to me? I can spit in your little face, too! I've been spitting square in the face of every bastard I met since I was a youngster!"

"Well, Pilipenkov," said the Brigade Commander, "you can have this old goat flogged with the rest of them! And I should wring your neck!"

Packed tightly together in the square in front of the assembly hall stood a freezing and silent crowd of Lebyazhka citizens. Everyone was there—the

Kruglov brothers, Mishka Goryachkin, Sevka Kupriyanov, Kirill Pankratov, and Shurka, Ustinov's son-in-law, trembling in the cold like an aspen leaf. The schoolteacher was there, too, blinking her naively innocent eyes as she looked around, shivering, warming her hands as best she could in her thin muff. All blue from the cold but impervious to it, Kudeyar stood by the porch steps of the assembly hall. Without a hat and with his collar unbuttoned, he kept whispering something about the end of the world.

One by one the members of the Commission were brought out into the square. The soldiers carried Smirnovsky. Kalashnikov looked up in confusion, as if he could not believe what was happening; Ignashka Ignatov, sobbing, stretched his arms out to the crowd; Ivan Ivanovich Samorukov, twitching his lopsided shoulders and still promising to spit in the officer's face, marched with a businesslike step.

"These officers are bastards, yes, bastards!" Samorukov shouted loudly, even happily, to the people. "But Kolya Ustinov, now there's a fine lad for you! He got around the bastards—he up and died just in time! Well, isn't he a fine one?! Eh? He was always a smart one!"

Approaching the Czech officer, stroking his beard, and frequently blinking his frost-covered eyelashes, Kirill Pankratov appealed, "Mr. Officer, I wanted to tell you . . . I escorted some Czech prisoners during the war, and I treated them real decent. Do the decent thing, too, I'm asking you—let Ivan Ivanovich Samorukov go, let our old man go! He's an old, old man, and he's done a lot of good for people through the years!"

"Name?" asked the Czech.

"Whose?" asked Kirill, not understanding.

"Yours, man, yours! Your name! Well?"

"Pankratov! Kirill Pankratov . . . "

"The conspirators met in your house? Isn't that right? The Forest Commission? The conspiracy? Yes! It was written in the document, 'in Kirill Pankratov's house!' That's right! Fifty strokes! Fifty!"

Grabbing Kirill, the soldiers dragged him off with them.

"That's just what you need, Commissioners, you bloodsucking farmers!" Mishka Goryachkin smiled with cold blue lips. "There's your justice for you!"

Deryabin, triumphant and full of malevolent reproach, walked beside Polovinkin and said, "That's just what you all need! To have them flail the hide off you till you're dead! It's a fitting punishment for your blindness! For the noble games of the peasant aristocrat, Lieutenant Smirnovsky!"

"And won't they skin you, too?" Polovinkin asked. "Do you really suppose you'll stay alive?"

"I'm not sorry for my own skin! The hell with it! So long as they teach all you fools a lesson, and those in the square, too! So long as my words are borne out—if you want justice, then let this filthy life be made over! Shove it over the side! Send it to the animal graveyard! It's too bad that Ustinov is already dead! It's a pity he can't see things as they are! He could have seen what he was really worth with all his kindness, with his endless desire to do what is just and good! It's too bad he's already dead and you can't prove anything to him . . . He played a fine trick as our Commission came to an end, don't you see? He up and died before all of us instead of with us!"

At this point Deryabin bumped into Kudeyar and embraced him feebly, as if in horror and despair. But while the soldiers were milling about, he managed to whisper, "Do something decent and important for once in your life, Kudeyar! You're the village holy fool, they'll let you go back into the assembly hall. From there you can get into the storage shed and crawl out onto Lake Street. Venya Pankratov is there at my house, in the cellar, with some other people. Tell them to set up an ambush on the road back to Barsukovo and kill these bastards, every one, down to the last man! Do it, and the people will never forget what you've done for them! Will you do it?! They'll never forget you!"

A few minutes later, gasping for breath, Kudeyar was running down Lake Street. He kept falling down and jumping up again, now catching up with two women, now falling behind them. Domna and Zinaida were also running as they dragged Nikolai Ustinov's coffin by a rope along the smooth and crunching snow of the street.

▲▲▲

The sun slowly left the still, frozen sky, and in the darkness of dusk the White Wood came closer and closer to Lebyazhka. The faint, barely discernible shadow of the forest fell on the sloping hillock by the lake, on the side where the schismatics had once dug their sod huts, where the Poluvyatsky maidens—Natalya, Yelena, Anyutka, Ksenia, and Lizaveta—had run back and forth along paths trampled in the snow, where Ksenyushka, the protectress of horses and of all living creatures on the earth, had stared in silence. Smoke rose here and there above the houses, suspending the snow-covered roofs from the sky, gently lifting them above the earth. Winter was listening to itself, heeding its own nature. The stars awoke. At the edge of the dipper of the Big Bear, two stars twinkled, pointing to the East.